A Lovesome Thing

PRUE LEITH

PENGUIN BOOKS

PENGUIN BOOKS

Published by the Penguin Group
Penguin Books Ltd, 80 Strand, London wc2r 0rl, England
Penguin Putnam Inc., 375 Hudson Street, New York, New York 10014, USA
Penguin Books Australia Ltd, 250 Camberwell Road,
Camberwell, Victoria 3124, Australia
Penguin Books Canada Ltd, 10 Alcorn Avenue, Toronto, Ontario, Canada m4v 3b2
Penguin Books India (P) Ltd, 11 Community Centre,
Panchsheel Park, New Delhi – 110 017, India
Penguin Books (NZ) Ltd, Cnr Rosedale and Airborne Roads,
Albany, Auckland, New Zealand
Penguin Books (South Africa) (Pty) Ltd, 24 Sturdee Avenue,
Rosebank 2196, South Africa

Penguin Books Ltd, Registered Offices: 80 Strand, London wc2r 0rl, England

www.penguin.com

First published 2004
3

The Acknowledgements on pp. 397–8 constitute
an extension of this copyright page

The moral right of the author has been asserted

Set in 12.5/14.75 pt Monotype Garamond
Typeset by Rowland Phototypesetting Ltd, Bury St Edmunds, Suffolk
Printed in England by Clays Ltd, St Ives plc

For Jill and Peter Parker

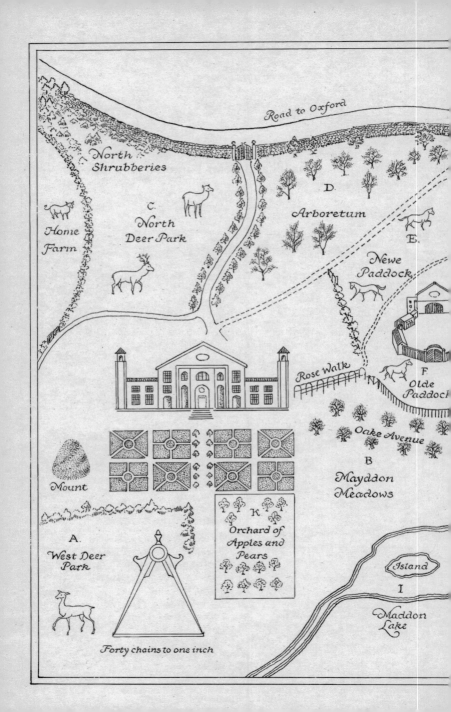

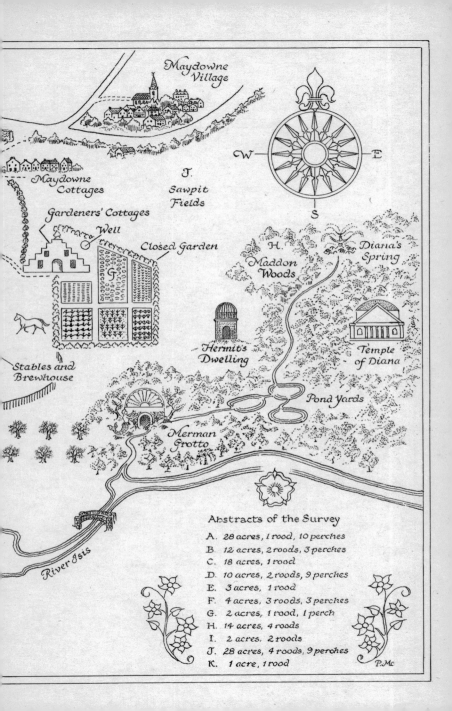

Maydowne
Village

Maydowne
Cottages

Sawpit
Fields

W · E

S

Gardeners' Cottages

Well

Closed Garden

Maddon
Woods

H.

Diana's
Spring

Stables and
Brewhouse

Hermit's
Dwelling

Temple
of Diana

Merman
Grotto

Pond Yards

River Isis

Abstracts of the Survey

A. 28 acres, 1 rood, 10 perches
B. 12 acres, 2 roods, 3 perches
C. 18 acres, 1 rood
D. 10 acres, 2 roods, 9 perches
E. 3 acres, 1 rood
F. 4 acres, 3 roods, 3 perches
G. 2 acres, 1 rood, 1 perch
H. 14 acres, 4 roods
I. 2 acres, 2 roods
J. 28 acres, 4 roods, 9 perches
K. 1 acre, 1 rood

P.Mc

A Garden is a lovesome thing, God wot!
Rose plot,
Fringed pool,
Ferned grot –
The veriest school
Of peace; and yet the fool
Contends that God is not –
Not God! In gardens! When the eve is cool?
Nay, but I have a sign;
'Tis very sure God walks in mine.

Thomas Edward Brown (1830–97),
'My Garden'

Acknowledgements

Writing this book has been a great excuse to do what I like doing best – nosing round other people's gardens. I expect I could have gleaned the facts and figures needed for a novel about an old garden from a single visit to a single garden. But since I found gardeners and garden owners hugely generous with their time, I exploited the opportunity to wander in (and get behind the scenes of) an unnecessary number of wonderful gardens. I am grateful to: Lord and Lady Heseltine of Thenford; Lady Emma Tennant (then Garden Advisor to the National Trust) who took me to Mertoun (Head Gardener Tommy Neillans); Head Gardener Mike Thurloe at Audley End; Peter Stafford, Director at Heligan; Michael and Sarah Galsworthy at Trewithen; Lord Lichfield and Head Gardener Mike Bradbury at Shugborough; and HRH The Prince of Wales and Head Gardener David Howard of Highgrove.

They would all recognize features of Maddon that I have shamelessly lifted from their superb estates. I have also taken slight liberties, for which I hope the owners will forgive me, with Powerscourt in County Wicklow, the wonderful Johnny Fox Inn and the Quinta do Barranca in Portugal.

In addition I have to thank Dr Paula Henderson, Architectural and Garden Historian, for help on the historical detail; Dr Sarah Bendall, Development Director of Emmanuel College, Cambridge for showing me how archives are kept and for checking relevant passages; Nigel James, Head of Maps at the Bodleian Library, Oxford, for allowing a non-reader into the New Bodleian to look at estate maps; Helen Auty, friend and fellow garden enthusiast; Brent Elliot and Chris Wisdom of the RHS Lindley Library for much horticultural help; and sculptor Bill Pye, for permission to invent a work of art by him.

On non-gardening matters, thanks are also due to: Tim Smit, of Heligan and Eden fame, for giving me insights into how a driving entrepreneur might think; PC David Frew of the Thames Valley Police for information on helicopters and light aeroplanes; Dr Pippa Brookes and ex-paramedic Graham White for medical information; and John Hotchkiss, Dr Nick Giles for information on fish in medieval stew-ponds, and Frank McKlintock for his knowledge of Portugal.

And, as always, thanks to Julia Bell of the Literary Consultancy for real help with the first draft, and to Louise Moore and Christie Hickman, my editors at Penguin, for being encouraging rather than tetchy at late delivery and many drafts.

I must thank also Francisca Gervis, my PA, who some-how kept control of the endless rewrites on her computer and saved me from panic when I thought I'd lost whole chapters.

And finally, thanks to Rayne, my husband, who knew nothing about gardens or gardening, but was ever encour-aging about my activities, whether writing or gardening, or indeed anything else.

Prologue

To build, to plant, whatever you intend,
To rear the column, or the arch to bend,
To swell the terrace, or to sink the grot;
In all, let Nature never be forgot.
Consult the genius of the place in all.
That tells the waters or to rise, or fall,
Or helps the ambitious hill the heavens to scale,
Or scoops in circling theatres the vale,
Calls in the Country, catches opening glades,
Joins willing woods, and varies shades from shades,
Now breaks, or now directs, the intending lines;
Paints as you plant, and as you work, Designs.

Alexander Pope (1688–74), 'Of Taste'

Once the garden at Maddon had been all forest and only God chose what should live and who should die. Trees, old and broken, re-rooted where an elbow touched the ground – and tried again, hoping for another life. No one cleared the undergrowth, cut out the dead wood, thinned the saplings, fed or watered. Sprouting acorns took their near-hopeless chances with rot, drought, wild boar, squirrels and a thousand competing seedlings. It was one long story of a million million fights to the death.

For centuries the autumn fall had sweated and mulched into the forest floor so that the leaf-mould gave a cushioned spring to the step. Under the microscope, or even without it, you'd have found the earth alive with creatures as bent on winning as the plants. A humus-rich handful would crumble lightly between the fingers, and you'd breathe in its rich, comfortable, deep smell, as satisfying as mushroom soup.

And hidden somewhere in the underlay were treasures that erupted, unbidden and unseen, and precisely on cue year after year. Drifts of aconites turning their faces to the feeble sun; snowdrops in January cracking the snow crust, to be followed by pale primroses in clumps so artful and perfect it would be hard not to believe in God. Then, one after the other, blue pools of scillas, wood anemones and great lakes of bluebells. As spring gave way to summer, more magic: explosions of campion and frothy seas of meadowsweet or cow-parsley.

A lull then, as though summer had exhausted the wood. But the underground store had richer and stranger secrets. Overnight, giant puffballs would dot the grassy clearings like polystyrene boulders. Blewits and parasol mushrooms tucked up with fallen leaves, while Velvet Shanks, orange and slimy, preyed on fallen elms.

Even the monks from the Priory seldom disturbed the forest. They only approached the river to attend to their stew-ponds, dug near the bottom of the valley where the water runs shallow and slow. They were good at husbandry, hand-feeding the voracious eels on kitchen scraps, herding the largest tench through the underwater tunnel into the catchment, dropping the gate with precision, netting their supper with glee. The younger monks would sometimes caper about and laugh, revelling in brief escape from drudgery and penance. But in the winter those on fish-pond duty had a hard time of it breaking the thick ice, the sleeves of their habits freezing to the skin as they swept their nets after invisible fish.

But everything changed in 1538 when the King's men took the Priory. Then the chant of plain-song and the gentle tolling of bells gave way to sounds of screaming, the crack of fire, the gasping breath of fugitive priests.

The soldiers crashed through the forest, torching the charcoal burners' huts, drowning the monks in their own ponds, skewering others at their prayers, felling those tilling the vegetable garden. They sacked the Priory and left it roofless, silently smouldering.

Less than a year later Sir Francis Maydowne, with a wife and nine-year-old heir, and about to be made the Earl of Axtrim, was the forest's proud possessor. Given to him by a grateful King, the land was 'for plaisaunce and the huntynge of beestes'. The forest was about to become a garden. Or at least a park. It was to be tamed and managed.

Acres of forest were felled to provide a picturesque setting for the hunting lodge, which was built from the stone of the ruined Priory. The remaining forest was invaded by rides and paths. The Pond Yards were enlarged and stocked with fast-growing carp.

The stables, built from Priory stone too, were larger and grander than the size of the house seemed to warrant. But then Sir Francis, now Lord Axtrim, would have to entertain the King. And the King's horses.

The house did not remain more modest than the stables

for long, though. Francis's son John had the good sense to marry a rich seafarer's daughter, Mathilda. In truth, she was a pirate's daughter, but the Queen (for by then Good Queen Bess was on the throne) approved of pirates – provided they plundered for the Crown.

Mathilda built two double-storey Elizabethan wings on to the house, and laid out the terraces and a knot garden, planted flowers and shrubs and added decorative water gardens to the useful Old Pond Yards.

The garden blossomed or suffered along with the fortunes of the Axtrims. In 1700 one of Mathilda's wings burned to the ground and could not be rebuilt. The Axtrim male line fizzled out and with it the earldom.

But in 1730 Maddon struck gold. Lord Augustus Fernley, who had made fortunes in both shipping and banking, inherited the estate. And he was a great gardener.

He splashed out as no one had since Mathilda, whose crumbling Elizabethan wings he demolished to build a new house round the old hunting lodge. He dammed the river to make a lake, garnished the stables with classical pediments and columns, built an ice-house, follies and a great artificial mount, a hermit's cave and a grotto. He enclosed the entire 400-acre park within a high dry-stone wall.

Proud of his achievements, he hired a map-maker. The Maddon Park Map is a beautiful thing. Made of two calf skins sewn together, it measures 5 feet by 5 feet. There is a compass rose in the corner. On the back at one end, visible when the map is rolled up correctly, is a decorative cartouche, within which are a few lines of writing, the title words elaborated with ornamentation and strapwork. The words read:

Mapp and Survey of the Domaine and Landes of Lord Augustus Fernley, Seventh Earl of Axtrim, knowne as Maydon Park, lying in the Parish of Osley in the County of Oxfordshire. Survey'd by my Lord's most humble and Obedient Servant, Thomas Hely of Bladon, in the Seventeen Hundred and Forty Seventh Year of our Lord.

The mediaeval hunting lodge is discernible in the embrace of an elegant, symmetrical Georgian manor house. Three of the old lodge's eight sides form the bay of the central hall, facing the viewer. Presumably three more face the back. In front of the house quaintly drawn deer roam the park. A double avenue of elms and oaks marches each side of the long straight drive to the front door. The main gate has stately pillars each side, with plain balls on top.

Areas of the garden are labelled North Shrubberies, Rose Walk, Arboretum, and have illustrations to match. All the plants and trees are drawn not from above, as a modern artist might, but from the side, as one would see them from the ground.

The mount is to the west of the house, in the park, and the Hermit's dwelling is on high ground to the east, above the woods.

The artist has drawn the paddock fences behind the circular stable building, with a mare and foal inside, and there are tiny rows of cabbages in the vegetable garden. To the west, beyond the meticulously drawn boundary wall, is the beginning of Home Farm, which is so labelled although its buildings are off the parchment. Mayddon Meadows hug the river. The spelling is erratic: Maddon,

Mayddon, Maydon, perhaps indicating later additions to a working document.

There is an avenue of trees, labelled Oake Avenue, leading a mile across the park towards the woods on the east side. The Avenue gives way to a lane in the woods, leading first to the grotto and the Merman's pool (complete with a drawing of a merman seated on a rock), and then on to the Pond Yards. A stream, its source marked with a drawing of a spurting fountain and the words 'Diana's spring', rises on high ground to the north-west and flows through the woods to join the river, feeding the three fish-ponds and the Merman's pool on the way.

The goddess of hunting is further honoured. In a round clearing in the woods is a circular colonnaded building, labelled the temple of Diana.

The garden's glory days did not last long. Augustus's son spent most of his father's fortune at the gaming tables, and what his son did not lose at cards his grandson lost in speculative ventures. The last of the Fernleys died young, unhappy and childless, and left the estate to St Aldwyn's College, Oxford, where the Maddon Archive is still kept. But somewhere along the road Mr Thomas Hely's lovely map was lost.

And subsequent owners did not make maps or keep drawings or plans. Or if they did, they've never been found. The garden's only Victorian archive was the garden log and diary kept by Mr Ferguson, head gardener for forty years from 1840 to 1880.

But the garden's history is there, under the bracken, under the soil, under the forest, under the water. It needs an ardent lover to find it.

1. Spring

When light slants before the sunset, this is
The proper time to watch fritillaries.
They enter creeping: you go on your knees,
The flowers level with your eyes,
And catch the dapple of sunlight through the petals.

Anne Ridler (1912), 'Snake's-head Fritillaries'

Charlotte Warren, one-time architect and would-be horti-
culturalist and plantswoman, glanced at her watch as she
approached the Maddon Park entrance. She was early. She
drove slowly through the great stone pillars and pulled up
at the start of the drive, out of sight of the house. It was
twenty years since she'd presented herself to a prospective
boss and she was as nervous now as she'd been then.
More perhaps. She had to get this job.

She flapped the sun-visor down to check her face in
the mirror. I'll do, she thought. No spinach on the teeth
anyway. She ran her comb through her short brown hair
and took off her sun-glasses. Gardeners, she thought,
don't wear shades.

She looked down the drive, marvelling at its dereliction.
It was almost bare of gravel and badly pot-holed, with
grass and weeds growing in a patchy line down the middle.

Either side of the drive, dead tree stumps three or four feet across testified to a once magnificent avenue of elms. Some stumps were jagged, some sawn off like picnic tables, some were now just weedy hummocks at ground level.

Lotte frowned, shaking her head fractionally. How could three successive owners have just left them there? It must be twenty-five years at least since Dutch Elm Disease took almost every elm in the country. How could anyone live with these ugly reminders? She'd never forget the epidemic because a huge old tree in her parents' Yorkshire garden had been one of the early victims. Every weekend through the summer she'd come home from university to have her father ask her, almost beg her, to agree with him that the tree was getting better, the leaves greener. Or at least not yellower? He had spent £80, a huge sum in 1976, having it injected in a vain attempt to save it.

But the following year the tree was down. He'd sawn the trunk into slices and Lotte and her mother had helped him set them in the grass to make a meandering path. It ran from the back door to the end of the garden, skirting the lush hosta bed on the left, the rockery and pond on the right. It was back-breaking work, but Lotte had enjoyed it.

It was that tree, and its memorial path, that marked the beginning of her interest in gardens. From then on she'd astonished her parents by willingly visiting National Trust houses with them, roaming the grounds while they toured the mansions.

When she met Sam, she'd dragged him round gardens too. He'd proposed to her in Kew, under a double white flowering cherry – he'd pinched a sprig and stuck it in her hair. When Annie was a baby and they were both in their first jobs — she drawing standard windows for cheap-as-possible council housing, Sam a Civil Service trainee — they'd spent Sundays pushing Annie's buggy round Syon Park, Cliveden, Kenwood, the Royal Physic Garden or the Tradescants' in Lambeth. Even when Christo and Jo-Jo had swelled the family to five, they would be more likely to have a day out at Hampton Court than the Zoo.

Lotte smiled suddenly. It's taken twenty-five years, she thought, but at least I'm finally applying for a job I really want.

She restarted the engine and drove slowly up the drive, counting the tree stumps. At least eighty.

Ten or fifteen years ago someone had replanted the avenue with ornamental cherries, placed between the elm stumps. But half the cherries had died and none of them were healthy. Looks like bacterial canker, Lotte thought, peering closely at trunks and branches.

The lawns weren't much better. She noticed how badly the mowing had been done, the grass scraped bare in places and left uncut round the stumps where it fought for space with the buttercups. The grass had not been edged either so it flowed wavy-fringed over the drive.

I hope Mr Keegan is a big spender, thought Lotte. The drive alone will cost a packet.

She was trying to keep cool. All the time she'd been thinking about the elm avenue, she'd been avoiding the thought that this could be a pivotal moment in her life. She'd begun to think architecture might not be right for her while she was still at Oxford Brookes. She had thought it would be about making beautiful places for people to live. Her head was full of elegant buildings in elegant settings. But today's dominant ethic was minimalism, and the dominant demand efficiency. The high priests of architecture were the steel-and-glass masters like Norman Foster, Richard Rogers and Libeskind – men she admired, but did not see herself following.

She'd dismissed her student anxieties as normal – few of her friends were certain they'd stick to their chosen field. But she was a stayer, the kind who finished what she set her hand to. And her parents had invested so much sacrifice and pride in her. How could she quit?

Several things had finally shaken her into action: she'd turned forty and found her first grey hair; her 'baby' daughter Jo-Jo had followed her brother Christo and big sister Annie to school; above all she'd discovered that Sam, her nice, reliable civil servant husband of fifteen years, was an unfaithful bastard. He'd been having a two-year affair with his researcher.

She'd forced a complete split with Sam, left her job and gone back to school, this time to study horticulture and garden history. Three years as a mature student had been really tough, having no money, juggling child-care and study, being on her own. Relations with Sam had been horrible at first – frosty sentences hiding a well of misery as she handed the children over at weekends, acrimony purveyed in lawyers' language. But as she slowly accepted that her preoccupation with the children and work might have had something to do with her broken marriage, she would sometimes catch herself missing Sam, though never her old career.

Lotte parked with care, tucking her little Subaru discreetly into a corner of the great courtyard. She climbed out, took her lace-ups out of the boot and put her handbag into it.

She walked briskly to the front door, carrying the shoes.

Mr Keegan opened the door himself. He wasn't tall, but he was burly and fit, maybe forty years old, with reddish dark hair, a broad, freckled face and confident Irish looks.

'Good morning. Brody Keegan. You must be, er, Miss . . . ?'

'Mrs actually. Warren. Charlotte Warren. I'm usually called Lotte.'

Keegan pulled the heavy door wider and took his time inspecting her short brown hair, wide grey eyes in a pale face, well-cut tweed jacket over a cream polo-neck and fawn trousers, smart shoes on her feet and old but polished lace-ups in her hand.

He smiled at her in friendly fashion, but his next words were not encouraging. 'Yes, well, Mrs Warren, I think we could both be wasting our time.'

She frowned, alarmed. 'Why?' she asked.

'Well, it's obvious, isn't it? I knew you were a woman of course, but not that you were so small . . . Or so posh. This job is not for a delicate product of the public school system.'

He spoke with a soft Irish accent and a broad smile, and Lotte found she was less indignant than she should be. But she didn't smile back. Instead she said, 'I went to the local comprehensive.'

He took the second step down to her level and reached for her hand. Lotte gave it to him, pleased to see him relent enough to observe the civilities. But he didn't shake it. He turned it over and looked at the palm, saying, 'This is not a desk job.' He let her hand go. He was still smiling, but she felt the insult and her chin lifted a fraction.

'Calluses and ingrained grime can be acquired, I'm sure,' she said, 'and, if I understood your agent correctly, you need someone who understands building and restoration, who can do the research and get it right. Or do you just want a labourer?'

As soon as she'd said this she regretted it. She'd spoken quietly but she knew there was an edge of indignation to her voice. Oh God, she thought, I've blown this job already.

But Keegan grinned again. 'Well said. I should at least give you a hearing. But there are four others on the shortlist, all men, and three of them have wives prepared to work in the house. You know we advertised for a couple, don't you?'

No, you didn't, she thought, but this time she had her replies better buttoned down and she answered, 'Well, you said, "Couples Preferred", but I was told . . .'

Keegan interrupted her. 'Anyway, if you are the best, we can find a housekeeper somehow. I wasn't sold on hiring a couple anyway. One is always useless, and if you lose one, you lose them both.'

There was no answer to this and Lotte didn't attempt one.

'C'mon,' said Keegan, turning back into the house.

Lotte followed him through the wide square hall, its marble floor covered in protective polythene, furniture draped in dust-sheets, a decorator's ladder leaning against the wall, surrounded by a huddle of paint-pots. She had just enough time to take in the free-flying double sweep of twin Regency staircases before they had skirted a pile of tea-chests and gone down a passage and into a boot-room.

'Glad you brought some good shoes,' Keegan said. 'Are they waterproof? The ground's still soggy in places.'

While Lotte changed her shoes she watched him take his Wellington boots from the row of posts that held six pairs upside down, ranged in order of size (all grown-up sizes, she noted), and sit down on the wooden bench to put them on. They were 'hunter's' boots, green with those inexplicable little straps on the side. Like all the others, they were very clean, not a single bit of pea-grit stuck in the tread, not a smear of mud on the rubber. Probably has a valet to polish them, she thought.

She observed his clumsiness and impatience as his trouser bottoms rucked up around his calves. She was tempted to bend down and help, to fold the leg of his chinos and tuck it into his sock before pulling on the boot.

He stood up. 'Right, let's go,' he said, reaching up the wall for what looked like a giant machete, the blade about two feet long. 'For the nettles,' he explained. He looked like a boy setting off on an adventure, Lotte thought. He strode ahead of her out of the boot-room, then headed off across the terrace, machete swinging in his hand.

This was Lotte's third interview. Her first had taken half an hour in a London office with Mr Keegan's personal assistant. She hadn't thought she had a hope – she was fresh out of horticultural college, with almost no experience. But Miss Astley, a woman of about Lotte's age, had seemed impressed by her decisive change of direction mid-career and by her academic achievements. Anyway, she'd pushed her through to the next interview.

This had consisted of a short tour round Maddon Park's overgrown orchards and derelict kitchen garden with Mr Keegan's land agent, Terry Simons. Unlike Miss Astley, he was suspicious of Lotte's motives for ditching a solid architectural career for an untried one in gardening. You could tell he thought it was some kind of mid-life crisis.

In both these interviews, Lotte had not told the whole truth. She'd glossed over her subterranean reasons: wanting to get away from a London that held Sam and his mistress, her need to live more closely with her children, her desire for them all to have a country life, her longing for work that was more personal to her, more meaningful than building prize-winning steel-and-glass structures for banks or airports. Instead she'd said that since her twenties she'd loved gardening, landscape and magnificent gardens, but had not thought there was a career in it. She'd become an architect when she should have been a landscape designer. She'd smiled at Simons, saying, 'I was born in the wrong century. Once, grand buildings were part of a natural landscape, part of the same plan. Capability Brown could design and build as well as dig and plant.'

But Mr Simons had not seemed convinced. He'd not shown her the park, or the south side of the house, which she longed to see. She'd gone away sure she was out of the race.

But here she was at the last hurdle and she was still nervous. Ridiculous, a professional woman of forty-five, a mother of three and an independent divorcee being nervous. Lotte squeezed both her thumbs tight in her fists, a childish habit left over from trying to ensure her place in the netball team. She had to persuade Brody Keegan she was right for the job. It was perfect for her, combining her loves and her talents: gardening, garden history, landscape. But most of all it would be a new start. New job, new home, new life.

She followed Keegan down the steps on to a wide terrace from which you could see the sweep of parkland down to the lake, with its ornamental island with a Chinese-looking summer-house on it, the woods to the left, distant farmland to the right. She'd have liked to spend a few minutes taking it all in and asking Brody about the history of the place, but he was marching ahead of her down the shallow flight of stone steps, bordered with ornamental urns, on to a wide lawn.

She followed him, noticing the clover, dandelions and couch-grass in the turf and the unevenness of the surface. It was poor stuff, and it would take a deal of rolling, weeding, feeding, top-dressing with lawn-sand, scarifying and aerating before it was remotely respectable. But she was sure that given the time and money, she could transform it within a year.

In the middle of the lawn there was a newly dug square flower-bed. Beyond this, at the far edge, was a scruffy fence and ditch, and beyond that open parkland sloping down to the lake. Lotte guessed that the ditch had once been a ha-ha, deep enough to keep the livestock off the lawn without a fence, while creating the illusion of uninterrupted greensward right down to the lake.

Keegan strode towards the rose-bed. 'Come and look

9

at my new roses. This is our first serious improvement, and they are going to be spectacular, don't you think? I chose them because orange is my wife's favourite colour. Except Jade calls it tangerine.'

Lotte looked with dismay at the thickly planted hybrid teas, the orange buds about to burst into bloom. What a disaster! The bed was worthy of a Parks Department – it would be strident as hell and would ruin the conceit of the ha-ha.

Keegan said, 'Andrew – that's our current gardener – is proud as punch. Says they are healthy as weeds.' He turned to her, his face alight with pride.

Feeling a shiny leaf between finger and thumb, she stalled with, 'They're certainly healthy. Not a greenfly in sight. What are they?'

'They're called "Tequila Sunrise". I'm having brass labels made for them.'

Worse and worse. 'Tequila Sunrise' is one of the few roses I'd consign to the compost heap, thought Lotte. Red edges to orange petals, stiff stalks and zero fragrance.

Mercifully Keegan did not wait for further comment. He said, 'Come on. You can tell me what we should do with the jungle. And persuade me that you can at least be a leader of sons of toil.'

He didn't give her a chance to do either, but none the less things went better from then on. They walked about two miles round the estate, Keegan keeping up an increasingly enthusiastic commentary as he led the way, hacking double-handed through the overgrown evergreens and grabbing Lotte's arm to negotiate fallen tree trunks or uneven brick paths slimy with lichen.

Lotte warmed to Keegan in spite of herself. He had no manners; he couldn't tell an oak from an ash, and his taste was dire. He had a townsman's eye, seeing big bright things like the forsythia and not noticing the primroses on the banks. Once Lotte stopped to admire a meadow of snake's-head fritillaries. Keegan could not see what she was looking at until she climbed a fence and came back with one white and one purple flower. She held the purple bell to the light so he could see the fine diamond pattern.

'Mmm,' he said, impressed. 'I see what you mean. I was just thinking what an untidy field that is, and that we should mow it.'

Lotte shook her head, adamant. 'You can't do that until July, when the wild flowers have seeded. I should think this meadow is left each year, and only grazed after June – I've never seen so many fritillaries. Aren't they wonderful?'

Keegan took the delicate blooms in his big hand and said, surprised, 'Yeah. I guess they are. But why don't we grow a whole lot of them close to the house, in a flowerbed, so people can see them? What's the point of them in a field?'

Lotte let it go, thinking he was not the type to understand. But his enthusiasm carried her along. He clearly loved the place, and seemed to know every inch of the land, if not its flora.

She thought that it would be good to work for someone so in love with his estate. Then she thought: no, working for him would be a nightmare. All he says is, 'I want to do this . . . I'm going to do that . . . This will become . . . That will have to go . . .' He's not once asked me what I think. Maybe he doesn't want anyone who thinks.

But eventually he charged down a muddy tunnel between tall Nigra bamboos to emerge at the lakeside. He pulled her on to a rickety jetty and said, 'Well, what do you think? Pretty amazing, huh?' His voice was full of triumph, his sweeping arm encompassing lake, park and house.

Lotte said nothing, breath and speech suddenly gone. It *was* amazing. Or not so much amazing as perfect. Utterly perfect. She stared unblinking at the house. The classic Georgian mansion was grand, but it was not a pile. The central section was three floors high, with a shallow pedimented roof. The double-storey wings on either side ended with small octagonal stone towers and identical belfries, their jaunty lead roofs floating in the air on almost invisible supports. The house seemed cosily anchored to the hillside rather than dominating it. Behind it and to the right the land rose gently, covered with deciduous woods. Open parkland continued round the left of the house, rising steeply to a grassy hillock with a knot of bushes on the top.

Lotte shut her eyes for a second, then opened them again, half expecting the vision to have been a dream. But there it was: complete, beautiful and perfect. She had visited hundreds of beautiful houses over the years, but not one had affected her quite like this. Maddon seemed to stroke her soul.

The vista silenced even Keegan and they stood without speaking for a full minute, while the afternoon sun stage-lit the scene, gilding the windows, warming the stone, turning the park an iridescent spring green. It added sparks to the quicksilver ripples in the lake.

Suddenly Lotte laughed. 'It's ridiculous,' she said. 'No one would believe it on a chocolate box.'

Keegan looked pleased at this. Then he said, 'How am I meant to know if you'd fit the bill? You've hardly said a word all afternoon.'

Didn't get a chance, thought Lotte. But she did like Keegan. His impulsiveness and straightforwardness impressed her. He'd bought Maddon Park on a whim, he'd said, because he'd seen a picture of it in *Country Life*. She understood that. If she were mega-rich, she'd have done the same.

He went on, 'How did you get on with my PA? And with Terry Simons?' For once, he paused for an answer.

'Not too good. Miss Astley said I had the right qualifications so she couldn't rule me out in spite of my meagre experience. I thought the agent had crossed me off the list though.'

'They both think I hire people the same way I buy things, because I like them. So to stop me hiring plausible rogues, they weed out the cowboys and con-men in advance.'

Lotte smiled. 'Glad I survived the cull then.'

'Yeah, well, it means they think you could do the job, though I still have my doubts. I'm sure you know the Latin names for plants and have mugged up a heap of garden history, but can you really handle a gang of navvies?'

'Yes,' said Lotte, 'I can.'

Keegan raised an eyebrow.

'I've been an architect for nearly twenty years, been in charge of countless building projects, had a team of draughtsmen, designers and junior architects reporting to me. Sure, I can handle a team.'

'How would you begin? What would you do first?'

This was the question Lotte had hoped he'd ask. She'd thought about it and she answered with confidence. 'Well, obviously I'd find out what your priorities were. But I'd advise getting the lawns weeded and fed, and . . .'

Keegan interrupted. 'Why not just strip the lot and roll out new grass like carpet? Like they do on *Groundforce*.'

'Fine,' said Lotte, smiling. 'I was trying to save you money . . .'

Keegan laughed. 'Saving money is not what I'm good at. Spending, yes.' His arm came briefly round her shoulder, a cross between a hug and a clap on the back. 'So what comes after the returfing?'

'Mostly cosmetic stuff to make the garden round the house look a whole lot more cared for. Remove those stumps in the drive, regravel the drive and courtyard, cut the overgrown shrubberies back, maybe do some replanting, have the terraces relaid where the paving is uneven, stone walls repaired. I'd get all that horrible ivy off the facade . . .'

Keegan had been nodding his agreement, but now he interrupted. 'I like the ivy. Makes the house look romantic and old.'

Lotte shook her head. 'No . . . no. It completely ruins the symmetry of a lovely house. And it's a crime to hide that famous honey colour. The ivy is like some horrible skin disease down one side of a perfect face.'

He followed her gaze. 'Besides,' she went on, 'it will have your gutters and roof tiles off, if it hasn't already. It's a killer.'

'OK, OK,' said Keegan, laughing. 'What then?'

'I'd not do anything dramatic or spend huge sums of money for a year or two while we really do the research. I'd leave the woods and the lake, the park and the orchard for now –'

Again he cut in, his voice a mixture of enthusiasm and authority. 'No. We'll do it all at once. I'm an impatient man, Mrs Warren. And I've got the money. Why not go for it?'

'Because we will make a hash of it if we do. We need to find out about the house, its past owners, what lies under all the tangle.' Lotte's eyes swept the view. 'Take the walled garden, for example. It looks Victorian, but it could be on top of an eighteenth-century garden or even a mediaeval one. It's a question of how much you want to know.'

'But no one knows anything about the house. The agent said it had changed hands six times since 1900.'

'But we can find out.' Lotte undid the front of her jacket to reach into an inner pocket, and extracted a photocopy of a map. Opening and refolding the map neatly so she had the bit she was looking for centre-stage, she pointed to an area designated Maddon Woods. 'Look,' she said.

Keegan read the words 'Old Pond Yards' out loud. 'What the hell's a Pond Yard?'

'Ponds for storing fish. Sort of mini-fish farm. Sometimes called stew-ponds. If you had a river, you could have one.'

He took the map from her and opened it up. It flapped in the breeze and she put out a hand to catch a corner.

'And are these pond things on my land?' His face was

close to hers as they peered at the map together, and she thought she saw a flicker of interest.

'They certainly were. And they might be still. I can't see why anyone would destroy them. But I guess they must be overgrown.' She pointed to the woods on their right, stretching from the lake edge up the hillside to the distant horizon. 'In there somewhere. Modern Ordnance Survey Maps just say Maddon Woods. No mention of Old Pond Yards.' Keegan looked puzzled, and Lotte said, 'This is a 1934 map.'

Still holding the map, Keegan said, 'But how did you find it?'

Lotte explained that when she'd read the advertisement and applied for the job, she'd thought she'd find out what she could about Maddon. She took the map from him, refolding it. 'This is in the County Record Office in Oxford. There's not much else in there though. But I did discover that some of the Maddon papers are in an Oxford college, St Aldwyn's, I think. The College owned Maddon Park before the war. So maybe there'll be a plan to pinpoint where your ponds are. Or were. They'd be near the river somewhere.' Lotte made an effort to keep her voice cool, but she felt her excitement rising.

'Sorry, Mrs Warren. I can see the point in restoring the stable yard or the garden terraces, and I need someone with the knowledge to keep me out of trouble with the planning police. But digging for derelict ponds is not for me. Anyway, I'm going to have a sculpture trail along the river and through the woods, with life-size deer and maybe African elephants and giraffes and so on. Give guests something to look at when they're out walking.'

Lotte put her map back in her pocket, averting her face. She feared it would show disappointment or disapproval.

'I guess you'd better meet the current gardener, Andrew,' said Keegan as they headed back across the park. 'If you get the job you'll have him to contend with. He's worked for three successive owners, all of whom have let him do what he likes – which is not a lot.'

They found Andrew in the stable yard. He was splitting logs and did not look up until Keegan spoke.

'Andrew, this is Mrs Warren. She's one of the head gardener applicants.'

Why is he chopping wood in April, thought Lotte. That's a winter job. There must be a hundred more urgent things to do. She put her hand out, saying, 'You've worked at Maddon for years, I believe?' but Andrew looked her up and down with ill-disguised scorn, spat on his hands and returned to his logs.

Lotte frowned, wondering if this was deliberate rudeness or just a lack of the social niceties. She was about to turn away rather than court another snub, when Keegan's mobile rang and he swung away to talk of software and contracts, leaving her to the taciturn Scot.

She watched in silence as Andrew dispatched several logs. She had to admire his technique. He swung the axe over his head, embedding it dead-centre in the upturned log. Then he reached for the sledge-hammer and swung it with the same rhythmic ease, driving the axe-head deep into the log which obediently fell apart. He used the axe alone to cleave the halves into quarters and the quarters into eighths.

In a pause while he stacked the split wood Lotte said, 'That's oak, isn't it? Did you have a tree down?'

Andrew eyed her blankly and said, 'Aye,' without elaboration.

Determined to be civil, she carried on, 'Do you do your own tree surgery then?'

'Aye,' he said again.

I'll give it one last shot, thought Lotte, and asked whether the ground was still too wet to mow. This got no reply at all. He just gave her his sullen stare and brought the axe down with what Lotte suspected was unnecessary force. The hostility was palpable. Keegan, who had finished his call now, must have felt it too, for he said as they walked away, 'Not much for friendly conversation, is he? Though he's useful at the heavy stuff. Don't suppose you could split logs all day, could you?' He gave her a sideways glance but Lotte felt he was teasing rather than criticizing her now.

'Poor guy. I don't suppose he wants a head gardener over him.'

'He'll come round. He's got to. He's forty-nine, with no qualifications, so he's not going anywhere. And he's on a cushy billet here: nice cottage, decent pay.'

'Did he want the head gardener job?' Lotte asked.

'Sure, but I told him to forget it, that I need someone with more skills and education than he's got. If he gets the hump and quits, which he won't, it's no great loss.'

As she turned off the Westway and headed south towards Fulham and home, Lotte's mind was still a swirl of hopes and doubts.

There was something brutal about Keegan that scared her. His insensitivity was, she suspected, the flipside of his drive and directness. If things had to be said, he said them. But if I get the job, she thought, I'll try to win Andrew over. Poor guy, it must be tough to have an outsider come in on top of you.

Though she was confident — or nearly confident — that she could manage the garden, and even Andrew, Lotte wasn't at all sure she could manage Keegan. How could she work for a man who wasn't interested in what lay beneath his own woods? Who didn't see the point of wild flowers in a field? Who thought a country walk needed livening up with giant giraffes? Who believed lawn genetically modified to stay mown was the way forward? Whose wife was a super-model who liked garish orange roses and was probably going to be a perfect pain?

Suddenly, Lotte laughed aloud. Why pretend? She knew the answer was Yes. Of course she could work for Keegan. She'd work for the devil himself if it meant being head gardener at Maddon Park.

Sure, she cared about garden history, but she could bear it if they ended up with a multi-layered garden: eighteenth-century park, Victorian kitchen garden, twenty-first-century sculpture trail. Why not?

Truth is, she thought, I could even bear the 'Tequila Sunrise' bed. Just so long as it's me that gets the job.

Please God, she very nearly prayed, make him choose me.

2. Late Spring

> . . . think of her
> Wine-dark and heavy-scented of the South,
> Stuck in a cap or dangled from a mouth
> As soft as her own petals. That's the rose!
> No sentimentalist, no maiden sweet,
> Appealing, half-forlorn,
> But deep and old and cunning in deceit,
> Offering promises too near the thorn.

> Vita Sackville-West (1892—1962), 'The Rose'

Brody Keegan looked at the enormous plate in front of him with a feeling of helplessness. He sliced one of the two small dark ovals in half and speared a blood-red piece with his fork.

'What's this?' he asked, waggling the meat at his wife. He knew very well what it was, but these itsy-bitsy dishes annoyed him.

Jade's ash-blonde hair fell forward in a straight shiny sheet, and he could not see her expression. Not that he needed to. She'd be looking all innocent hurt. She didn't look up. 'Wild pigeon breasts with baby leeks and grilled polenta. Don't you like it?'

'I like to be able to tell what I'm eating and I like enough of it. This wouldn't feed a four-year-old.'

Jade swept the hair off her face with a practised move-ment of her head, revealing flawless skin, high cheekbones and curvy lips painted a glossy red. She blinked slowly and settled her green eyes on her husband. 'But you already had the scallop salad, and there's dessert to come. I don't think you'll starve, sweetheart.' She smiled, her eyes hold-ing just enough tenderness and hurt to make Brody back off a bit.

'Maybe not, but I'll end up eating cornflakes later, like last night. The salad thing was bloody invisible, two mouthfuls and it's all over. This is restaurant food, darling, the sort of fancy nonsense I eat the whole time in London. What's the matter with real food? Decent roasts, or chicken pie? I'm a country lad from County Wicklow, sweetheart. I like real food.'

'I could ask.' Jade's voice was cool, reasonable. 'But Jean-Christophe was trained by Gordon Ramsay. He's not likely to stay if he has to make Irish stew all the time.' She took a sip of her mineral water. 'Besides, his food is healthy. Stops us getting fat.'

Brody looked at his stick-thin wife with her square shoulders, long bare arms and high round breasts, and felt himself losing the argument. She was just so beautiful.

Why had she married him? She could have had any number of young pop-star, photographer or media trend-ies for a mate. He was rich, sure, and he indulged her. But he was old enough to be her father. Maybe that was it. Was he a father figure, keeping the demons at bay? The thought pleased him. He wanted to protect her, teach her to relax and trust people, feed her chocolate and ice-cream.

No chance of that. She had hips narrow as a child's and

you could feel her ribs through the thickest of sweaters. But she hated him to press her to eat. Top models had to be thin, she said. Starvation was part of the deal.

Brody imagined her legs under the table, long, elegantly crossed, her narrow feet in four-inch heels. He thought, this is my constant problem with Jade. I never get my way with her, because she just blasts me into submission with a dose of pheromones.

He pulled his mind off her legs and back to the subject of Jean-Christophe's menus. 'Neither of us needs diet food, darling. I've weighed exactly the same since I was an overgrown baker's boy at sixteen.' He patted his solid midriff, his irritation forgotten. 'Muscle, darling, not fat.'

He ate the two pigeon breasts and the leeks in half a dozen mouthfuls, ignoring the polenta. He dropped his knife and fork on top and sat back, saying, 'But I want to talk to you about the garden. There was a woman here today, one of the applicants, and she thinks the garden could be older than the house. She knew a lot . . .'

Jade interrupted. 'A woman gardener? You don't want a woman, do you? I thought we'd agreed on getting a couple?'

'Yeah, well, most of the couples are housekeeper and jobbing gardener types. The gardeners probably know how to dig trenches and grow cabbages, but we need someone with design skills, and with some knowledge of old gardens. Landscape and so on. Charlotte is the business. Posh education, degree in garden history or something. Used to be an architect, loves –'

'But why?' Jade cut in. 'We can hire a garden designer to do what we want. I know exactly what I want.'

'You do?'

'Dead right I do. I don't want some stuck-up cow telling me what we ought to have.'

'And what *do* you want?'

Jade replied at once, 'First off, I want to put a big conservatory on the top terrace and then I want to cover the rest with patterns made of mosaic, or those little glass pebbles, you know, green or blue? With pots and fountains and so on. David Jones showed me the perfect thing in *Exteriors*.' She started to get up. 'I'll get it and show you . . .'

Brody laughed, catching his wife's wrist as she headed for the door. Jade's absolute clarity of demand, the way she always knew what she wanted, no hesitation, no nego-tiation, always amused him. He pulled her on to his lap.

'Not so fast, sweetheart. Let's discuss the principle of the thing first. What kind of restoration we want. What to do first. That sort of thing.'

Jade's bottom lip came out in a mock pout, and her eyes held his. She said, 'Well, what we should really do first is forget the garden and hire David to do the house. The garden can wait, can't it?'

Brody tightened his grip on her waist and shook her a little. 'No, that's just the point, the garden can't wait, because we have to plan everything before the winter, so any excavation can take place . . .'

Jade leant away so she could look into his face. 'But Brody, I've spent weeks in the David Jones Studio, and he's beginning to think I'm wasting his time. You like what he did to the music room, don't you? Why can't we get on and do the rest?'

'Because he wants to bash half the walls and ceilings

down, and I'd like to ask someone like this Charlotte woman what she thinks. Maybe we shouldn't just rip it apart.'

'She must be a fast little mover, your Charlotte.' Jade stood up, pulling out of Brody's arms. 'From gardener to landscape expert to architectural advisor in a day.'

Brody smiled and said, 'Jealous? Is that it?'

Jade tossed her hair off her face and walked back to her seat. 'In your dreams,' she said.

Brody watched her unwind her long body into her chair at the far end of the polished table. He was amused by her hostility to the mousy Charlotte. She wouldn't be if she'd met her of course, but it was gratifying while it lasted.

'Charlotte says we should study the history of the house and garden,' he said, 'before doing anything at all.'

'Oh, stuff that, Brody. We don't want a whole lot of historians and conservation types crawling all over the place. They'd start telling us we can't change anything, can't give the house a proper make-over.'

There was truth in that, thought Brody. In his book, bureaucrats and regulation were twin blights on British enterprise. He took a long pull at his Murphy's and said, 'Look, here's the deal. Why don't you hire your decorator mate to start on the bedrooms and bathrooms upstairs? Do anything you like. Let the famous David have his head.'

Jade's eyes flashed mixed gratitude and triumph, and her mouth broke into her wide trademark smile. Brody felt a little glow of ownership. That smile cost advertisers a fortune.

'Great. Thanks, sweetheart,' she said. 'I'll tell him tomorrow. But what do I tell him about the rest?'

'Tell him I'm thinking what to do, and we'll do these rooms later. And meanwhile I'll sort out the gardener question.'

'Just so long as we get to call the tune. It's our garden and we pay the piper.'

Brody could not help a glancing thought that he paid the piper and she called the tune. But her streetwise toughness was one of the things, along with her drop-dead gorgeousness, that turned him on. He and she were very alike. Both of them had scrambled from the bottom of the heap to the top, with nothing but energy and an eye to the main chance. Only I did it with brains, he thought, and she did it with those eyes, and that smile. The words 'and the rest' jumped into his head, but he dismissed them. He didn't want to think of the route Jade might have taken to the international catwalk.

'So where's this famous pudding? Or do I call for cornflakes now?'

Jade stamped on the bell. A Filipino maid, wearing a white apron and short white gloves, appeared with two big plates on which sliced mangoes, kiwi fruit and Japanese pears were artfully arranged round pools of passion-fruit pulp, spotted with seeds. She put them down on the sideboard, silently cleared the table of the main-course debris, then placed the plates in front of Jade and Brody. She was concentrating hard, and she didn't smile.

Jade's brow furrowed briefly when Brody demanded cream. He grinned at her as he tipped half a jug of it on to his fruit.

'And Brody,' she said, 'the other thing that's really urgent is turning the walled garden into the gym and pool, remember? If we are to spend so much time here, I've got to have a gym.'

'And you will get your gym, I promise. But maybe it shouldn't be in the kitchen garden. Charlotte says . . .'

'Charlotte, Charlotte, Charlotte! One afternoon with a fancy gardener and you want to go back on everything!' Jade flung her body back in her chair, her arms outstretched on the table.

Brody watched her without replying, and she went back into the attack. 'Brody, we agreed! A gym, a pool and a tennis court, maybe a squash court for you, and a summerhouse with a sauna and jacuzzi. And a bar and barbecue! You promised.' She flicked her hair off her face and glared at him. 'And we agreed that it would all go easily into the walled garden. And, anyway, who needs a vegetable garden with Waitrose six miles away?'

Brody thought, not for the first time, how brutally practical Jade was. There was not an ounce of romance in her. He suspected she only liked Maddon Park because it was big and grand, a symbol of riches. Like white-gloved maids and dinner-plates the size of tea-trays. The magic of the place was completely lost on her. He leant forward, trying again.

'Darling, think of the future. Maybe one day we'll have children. Yes, yes,' he held up his hand to forestall her protest, 'I know. You don't want children. But one day you might. You're only twenty-five . . . We may want to live here more than in London . . .' Brody ignored her shaking head. 'We may want to grow our own vegetables . . . Maybe we should at least listen to some advice.'

As the wrangle continued, Brody again felt rising irritation, with himself as well as with Jade. After less than six months of marriage they were bickering like practised old pensioners. How was it that he could sweep everyone else – partners, investors, colleagues – into ventures and adventures, yet could not ignite in his young wife a spark of interest in the garden? She seldom went out of the house, never explored the grounds or walked round the lake.

Brody stomped up to his study. Once there, the familiar business of clearing his briefcase and doing his e-mails worked its magic. Business excited him. He liked the feeling of keeping all the balls in the air, of being in control. And there was satisfaction in quick decision-making, resolving difficulties, arbitrating, considering new opportunities.

He would hire Charlotte Warren. He liked the woman's quiet class. She'd be good. She knew about gardens. And you could see she was hooked on the place. Also, it would be nice having kids around. She had three of them. It would liven the place up.

Brody leant back in his chair and lit a cigar. It was a Davidoff, his favourite. He'd started smoking cigars for the look of the thing, when he made his first pile out of the spicy chicken business. But Jade didn't like the smell of smoke, even cigar smoke. Now he smoked on his own.

He took a slow drag and held the smoke in his mouth, his cheeks rounded to give the flavour room to swirl about. He lifted his feet on to his desk and gazed at the ceiling. Like a tycoon in the movies, he thought. Well, he was a tycoon. That long-ago Irish lad in hand-me-downs now wore Savile Row suits.

And transferring the company to Oxfordshire was proving a good move, though it looked like he'd lose a few wimps not prepared to make the change. Never mind, he'd hire others. And the new great shed of an office on an industrial estate was far better suited to *find-on-line.com* than the expensive old offices in London.

Best of all, he and Jade could live here. Even the fifteen-minute drive to work was a pleasure, particularly crossing the river with the Maybush pub on one side and the Rose Revived on the other, with boats moored under the willows, Oxford students punting up the river and posh customers with braying wives spilling on to the lawns – drinking Pimm's, probably. Every time the Roller sighed over the bridge, he couldn't help a little waft of self-satisfaction. Not bad for a boyo from County Wicklow, eh?

It was bloody perfect, that's what. Except that Jade in London and Jade here were two different people. All fire and fun in London, all sulks and arguments in the country. But she'd come round. She just needed time to fall in love with Maddon, that was all. And to grow up enough to start wanting children.

At 10 p.m. he rejoined Jade in the smallest of the living rooms, one of the few that had already been overhauled.

The estate agent's plan had called it the music room. Brody liked to think of the previous occupants; perhaps Twenties flapper girls dancing to jazz played on a white piano or Victorian daughters singing duets side by side on a double piano stool. And maybe, a couple of hundred years ago, they'd have had a harpsichord or some such. He'd have liked to know something about those predecessors. How they had used the house and grounds. Who had enriched Maddon and who had impoverished it.

Now the music room was bare of instruments but contained thirty grands' worth of Bose and Bang and Olufsen, with all-round sound and a huge wall-mounted plasma screen on which Jade watched countless DVDs. For all its clean minimalism the room was comfy. David Jones had covered the squashy sofa in cream leather, and there was a pale Tabriz carpet under the slate coffee table.

Brody found Jade lying on her back on the sofa, eyes shut, engulfed by and lost in the sound pumping through her headset. She didn't move when he came in and he crossed the room to stand looking down at her. She was wearing a wrap-around skirt, half open now because she'd thrown her right leg over the back of the sofa. One strappy black sandal was on the floor. The other was on her left foot, stretched out along the sofa.

Brody looked at Jade's parted legs and thought to himself, they're mine. I can reach down and run my hand all the way from ankle to knickers. If she's wearing any, that is. She sometimes doesn't. The thought brought a further stab of desire, but he resisted it. For the moment he didn't want her to move. He just wanted to look at her.

Jade's head was flat on the sofa, which was long enough for her to stretch her six-foot body full length with room to spare. Her hair was held back by the headset, like an Alice band, and it made her look young and vulnerable. Her mouth was slightly open, her shiny red lips full and relaxed. One arm was behind her head, flung over the arm-rest with the same abandon as her leg over the sofa back. The perfectly painted fingernails of her other hand rested on her neck, just under the upward thrust of her chin.

Oh Jesus, thought Brody, I came in here to tell her her leisure-centre plans would have to wait, and now I'm going to make love to her. Even as he conceded he'd lost this round, even as he undid his belt and stepped out of his trousers, he recognized that he was being had. Jade's pose of uncontrived and unconscious abandon was both contrived and conscious. Her lips were bright with newly applied lipstick, her skirt was precisely arranged to reveal one leg and keep the other covered. Her knitted top, made of some stretchy stuff, was pulled up slightly to expose her navel, and the top two buttons were undone. And there was an extra cushion under her back, pushing up her tits like an invitation. Well, thought Brody, what did I expect? She's a model, for Christ's sake, she knows how to arrange that body of hers to maximum effect. Her whole pose was an offering, a bribe, and Brody knew it. OK, my darling, he thought, you win.

Afterwards, Jade turned into his shoulder and said, 'Why am I such a bitch?'

He looked into her face and saw her eyes were wet. He kissed them.

'You aren't a bitch. You are the sexiest thing on earth.'

It was rare that Jade was loving and relaxed, un-demanding and soft. But deep and emotional love-making could banish her brittleness. She dropped her defences and became younger, more trusting, less confident.

'The thing is,' she said, talking into his shoulder, 'I hate the idea of some woman with lots of children being here all the time. I hate children. And you love them.'

Brody said, 'Oh, my darling idiot, the gardener's cottage is a mile away. And if we don't like her brats, we'll banish them from the park completely.' He stroked her hair. 'And believe me, you don't need to be jealous of her – she's very ordinary.'

'Really?'

'Believe me.'

Jade sighed, content. Then mused aloud, 'Maybe I can't have children anyway. The dieting has probably fucked me up. And the drugs.'

As always, Brody felt a little shaft of fear. Jade had been clean for nearly a year now. Almost since they met. But she'd been in and out of rehab for years before that. Brody didn't understand the need for drugs. He'd never even smoked a joint. But he knew that Jade had an addictive personality: she worked out like an Olympic athlete; dieted constantly; could not come to bed without going through her full beauty regime; got panicky if she could not see her therapist every week.

'Darling,' he said, 'you wouldn't . . . you're not using again, are you?'

'No. Don't worry.' She lifted her head to look at him. 'No. I'll never go there again.'

Relieved, he stroked the swell of her hip and her smooth bum. 'Then there's nothing to worry about, is there?'

'Except you want children, and I would hate it. Hate it. They would spoil everything. Especially my body. I'm already over the hill for close camera work. I'd be finished.'

Brody didn't pursue the conversation. He just hugged her and stroked her and said they had all the time in the world. He didn't say she could not be a supermodel for ever, or that if she ate a little more and went to the gym and to crackpot therapists a little less, she might be happier. Poor Jade. She wasn't anything like as tough as she made out.

3. Late Spring

Gather ye Rosebuds while ye may,
Old Time is still a-flying:
And this same flower that smiles to-day
To-morrow will be dying.

Robert Herrick (1591–1674),
'To the Virgins, to Make Much of Time'

It rained all morning and the removal men tramped London dirt into the Fulham house, undoing Lotte's efforts to impress the incoming tenants. She was washing up the breakfast things and packing them into the last of the tea-chests when her mobile rang. It was Sam.

'I just rang to say goodbye to the kids.'

She wanted to say, but not to me? Or, I'm not taking them to Australia, you know. But instead she said, 'Sure,' and passed the telephone to Christo who was sitting on the floor, his back to the wall, his straight blond hair completely concealing his eyes as he pressed the buttons of his Game Boy.

Lotte half listened to his subdued monosyllables: 'Yes,' 'I know,' 'It's OK, Dad' and 'I'm fine.' She wanted to snatch the phone out of his hand and snap at her ex-husband, he is fine. He's eleven, not two. Just don't wind him up.

Christo carried the mobile out of the room, presumably for his siblings to speak to Sam. Or maybe so she wouldn't hear.

Lotte, her hands back in the sink, suddenly felt a wave of panic. Would the children be happy? And could she do this job? What if it didn't work? What if they all had to come back to London with their tails between their legs? And wouldn't she be horribly lonely? Even after Sam left, she'd had her London friends and Anita, the cheerful Aussie au pair. And she'd been surrounded by colleagues in the office, then fellow students at college. Now she might be down to the taciturn Andrew for company.

Suppressing her fears, Lotte stowed the last of the cutlery and plates in the tea-chest and stuffed the kettle into the picnic basket with the mugs and things for tea. One of the removal men carried the chest out of the room, and Lotte swung her handbag over her shoulder and picked up the picnic basket. She looked round the kitchen before switching off the light and shutting the door. Goodbye, she thought. No going back now.

The windscreen wipers were losing the fight, and they battled blindly through invisible countryside. Lotte felt bullied by the giant container lorries which flashed her out of their way then drenched her little Subaru as they steamed past, their wheel arches at eye-level. Oh God, she thought, struggling to see through the downpour, why couldn't this day, just this one important day, be sunny?

Beside her, thirteen-year-old Annie was eating a packet of prawn-flavoured crisps she'd bought at the petrol station, and it was all Lotte could do not to snap at her.

Annie's rhythmic crunching and the evil smell of the crisps were maddening. The girl never stopped moaning about her shape, her weight, her spots, but if Lotte said anything, Annie practically threatened her with Childline.

'Nearly there,' Lotte said as they turned off the Oxford ring road and headed towards Botley. She smiled at her daughter, trying to be friends. Annie didn't respond, except to deepen her scowl and slide further down the seat.

'Sit up, sweetheart,' said Lotte. 'If I have to brake suddenly that seat-belt will throttle you.'

Annie shuffled her plump bottom back in the seat and straightened her back fractionally. She was tempted to sigh and raise her eyes to heaven, but she knew she was pushing it.

Lotte craned round to check the back seat. She couldn't see Christo, who was immediately behind her. Nine-year-old Jo-Jo was asleep in a too warm jacket, her Botticelli face pink with heat, blonde curls clinging damply to her cheeks and neck.

'Are you OK, Christo?' Lotte asked.

'I'm fine,' said Christo. 'Did you pack my stamps, Mum?'

Lotte caught the uncertainty in his voice and smiled reassurance. 'Of course I did. And your chess set, and the model aeroplanes.'

Oh God, what if the children wouldn't settle? Christo was such an old-fashioned boy. So quiet and self-contained he'd never admit to being unhappy. He'd join in as told, but what he really liked (apart from books and playing chess on his computer) was doing practical things with his father. Sam came round often and the two of them would assemble complicated 3-D puzzles in Christo and Jo-Jo's bedroom. Poor Christo, thought Lotte, he's probably scared he'll lose Sam. And maybe he will.

The noise of Annie crumpling her crisp packet regained her attention. Annie rolled down the window, but Lotte was too quick for her.

'Don't even think of it,' she said. 'Put it in my basket.'

'What?' asked Annie, innocent and insolent.

Lotte knew Annie was baiting her, but she wasn't going to rise. She shot her a smile. 'I thought for a moment there you were going to toss that packet out the window.'

'Well, I wasn't.' Annie stuffed the packet into the basket at her feet.

Jo-Jo, woken by the blast of wind and rain from the open window, set up a wail of protest. While she and Annie bickered, Lotte switched back to worrying. The transition, she thought, would be hardest for Annie. She seemed so determined to hate the country. In London she'd pleaded and sulked her way to a measure of freedom: she and her best friend Lynette spent hours mooching round GAP and listening to CDs in Tower Records. At weekends, Lotte let her go to the movies or the pizza place with her friends, and occasionally to parties. She'd even been clubbing twice, albeit to an allegedly supervised alcohol- and drug-free teenage club. Oxfordshire, Lotte could see, loomed like a death sentence.

Only Jo-Jo caused her no anxiety. She was spoilt, of course: they all spoiled her. But she was a classic third child; no hang-ups, confident in the adoration of everyone. She'd be happy anywhere.

*

The rain had slowed to a drizzle when they drove through the great stone pillars of Maddon Park and up the half-mile drive with its ruined elms and ragged lawns. Annie stirred herself to wipe the misty windscreen with her sleeve, and Lotte felt the blast of cold air on her neck as Jo-Jo rolled down her window.

When the house came into view, Lotte regained a little of the wonder she'd felt when she first saw it. Even in the rain, and in spite of its size, it contrived not to look awesome or forbidding. She slowed the car and said, 'That's Maddon Park. Don't you think it's the most lovely house?'

'Yeah, it's all right, but we aren't going to live there, are we?' said Annie. Christo thought the house was cool, and Jo-Jo wanted to go inside.

'We can't do that, darling. I don't think we are even supposed to drive in the front gate,' said Lotte. 'There's probably a servants' or tradesmen's entrance somewhere, but I don't know where it is.'

'Are you going to be Mr Keegan's servant, Mum?' Jo-Jo asked.

'Yes, I suppose I am,' said Lotte, 'but he's not very grand, so I don't think we have to touch our forelocks or drop a curtsey.'

'What's a forelock? What's a curtsey?'

Christo had to take on explanations, because Lotte was concentrating on trying to remember whether to take the lane marked 'Stables' or the one marked 'Maddon Cottages'. Maybe she should drive boldly up to the house and ask.

While she hesitated, a figure in a hooded yellow oil-slicker appeared from the side of the house and walked purposefully towards her. She lowered her window, stuck her head out into the rain and said, 'Excuse me, could you tell me where the Gardener's Cottage is?'

As she spoke she realized her mistake. It was Brody Keegan. 'Oh, I'm so sorry, Mr Keegan. I didn't recognize you.'

'Charlotte Warren! Delighted to see you!' He looked it too, his eyes friendly and alight. He poked his head through her window. 'So these are the famous children? Hi, guys. Welcome to Maddon Park!' Then he yanked Jo-Jo's door open and said, 'Shift up, young lady. And I'll show you where you live.' Stalling Lotte's protests with, 'Nonsense, woman, someone has to show you where the cottage is,' he climbed into the car.

'Urrgh! You're all wet,' said Jo-Jo, shrinking from him.

'I am and all. I've been trying to get the ivy off the walls of the house. Your Mum's orders. But it's bloody impossible. We'll have contractors in to do it.'

Lotte opened her mouth to say the trick was to cut the ivy off at the roots and poison it to weaken its hold, then try again in a month. But she closed it again. Plenty of time.

The Gardener's Cottage was an eighteenth-century *jeu d'esprit*. The facade was a one-dimensional step pyramid made from stone blocks, and the arched entrance to the walled kitchen garden ran bang through the middle of it. The house had two entrances, both within the archway and opposite each other. One door led into a good-sized kitchen and a living room, the other into the head gardener's boot-room, office, and a big store. Both sides had winding staircases up to the first floor where two bedrooms overlooked the park and a third, plus a bathroom, looked down into the walled garden. Once a kitchen garden, this was now a muddle of sheds, kennels and fruit cages, with the derelict remains of glasshouses against the walls. Above the bedrooms the attic had been converted into another large bedroom, with views in both directions, and a second bathroom.

The rooms, freshly painted, looked bigger than Lotte remembered, and she was gratified by the children's excitement. Even Annie, who had refused an offer to see the house before they moved ('Mum, I don't want to go. Why should I see some poxy cottage I don't want to live in?') so far forgot herself as to make a bid for the attic bedroom. But Lotte said, 'Sorry, sweetheart. That's mine. But you can have first pick of the others.'

Annie's mouth went down at the corners, and she was about to stomp down the stairs, when Keegan appeared at the top of them. Oh hell, thought Lotte, I'd forgotten all about him.

'You must think I'm so rude. I just got swept up here by the children. It was so kind of you to –'

'Don't be daft, Charlotte. I presume I can call you Charlotte?'

'Lotte. Everyone calls me Lotte.'

'Good. Lotte it is then. I'm Brody, by the way. I just came up to say, when you are sick of unpacking, come up to the house for a drink. Bring the kids. I want you to meet my wife, Jade. OK?'

Lotte felt nonplussed for a second. Did gardeners go for a drink with the boss? Surely he couldn't really want the children?

Brody saw her hesitation and said, 'No nos. You're coming. All of you. That's an order.' His broad grin encompassed both her and Annie. Lotte smiled back, but Annie managed not to. She chose the largest of the first-floor rooms, overlooking the kitchen garden, and disappeared into it, shutting the door behind her.

Lotte fetched the picnic basket with the kettle and the makings for tea from the boot of the car. She filled the kettle in the straight-sided old sink and plugged it into a modern double socket. She was relieved to find the old Aga had been lit and was delivering its comforting country warmth. Also, someone had cleaned every inch of the place. It wasn't just painted, but swept and dusted. The house was spotless.

Lotte stood with her back to the Aga while she waited for the water to boil, and surveyed the kitchen. It was a big room. Plastered ceiling beams suggested it had once been divided into scullery, kitchen and dining room, but now it was one big light space, with a window on to the park at the front and a window and a door out to the walled garden at the back. She liked the warm red of the quarry-tiled floor, the old-fashioned wooden plate-rack, the porcelain sink and the blue-painted plain dresser, with its roomy cupboards below and open shelves above. But she was relieved that the rest of the kitchen had modern fittings, with decent work surfaces and lots of plugs, and space for her full-height fridge-freezer and her big table and chairs.

Lotte poured the water into the teapot, feeling good. This was a great kitchen. All it needed was a decent ceiling light to replace the horrible green plastic one. And some new blinds. Maybe she'd find a fabric in terracotta and blue to pull the dresser and floor together.

She put the cake tin and a packet of biscuits on the dresser, and summoned the children. Jo-Jo and Christo came clattering down, demanding to know, for the umpteenth time, when the removal van would arrive. Annie didn't emerge from her room.

'She's probably got her ear-phones on,' Lotte said. 'Could you sprint up and get her, Christo?'

'No, she hasn't. She's just in a strop,' said Jo-Jo.

But Christo fetched her anyway and they all stood around the Aga, the children wolfing biscuits and cake, until they heard the rumble of a lorry and the view of the park was suddenly blocked by the side of the removal van. The words GREAT MOVE filled the window space.

Agreed, thought Lotte.

By six o'clock the rain had dried to a sparkling evening, as though the air was polished. They walked in their Wellies across the wet grass of the park, carrying their shoes.

Lotte had her arm over Annie's shoulder and was gratified by the affectionate pressure of her daughter's arm round her waist. Annie had given up the sulks, mollified by the size of her bedroom for which she'd been allowed the pick of the furniture. She'd got her dad's old desk, and enough bookshelves for her yards of CDs. And Lotte had said she could decorate the room as she liked, and choose new duvet covers and curtains.

'Well now,' Lotte said, 'do you think the boss's wife is going to look as good as her pictures?' Annie had brought her poster of Jade Allen (in leathers astride a Harley

Davidson) with her from London. But she hadn't put it up yet, Lotte noticed.

'Don't suppose so. She's been around for ages. She must be ancient.'

'Do you think she knows how to ride that motorbike?' Christo asked.

Jo-Jo said she'd enquire. 'And I'm going to ask how much money she gets. I want to be a model when I'm grown up.'

They were changing into their shoes when the front door was opened by a tall man in a dark suit. 'Mrs Warren and family,' he said, smiling. Lotte, leaning against the porch wall with one shoe on and one off, put out her free hand. 'Good evening. I'm Charlotte Warren, and these are Annie, Christo and Jo-Jo.'

It was while the children were politely shaking his hand that Lotte realized he wasn't a Keegan relation or friend but the butler. A butler! She couldn't imagine Brody with a butler. But then she thought, how silly. Of course he has a butler. And a cook and a housekeeper. And now a head gardener.

They followed the butler through the double-height stone-flagged hall to a drawing room on the right. Lotte wanted to stop and look at the staircase, or examine the carving over the lintels, but she was embarrassed by her lack of savoir-faire. I bet you don't shake the butler's hand in polite society, she thought. So she followed obediently, the children trailing behind.

They were ushered into a large octagonal drawing room with a double aspect. French windows gave on to the park and sash windows overlooked the front.

42

'Mr and Mrs Keegan will be down any minute,' the butler said. 'Please make yourself comfortable.' He signalled to the sofa and chairs, and they sat down obediently.

He collected a tray of drinks from the sideboard and offered it to Lotte. It held large flutes of champagne, and three glasses of orange juice.

'Or would you prefer mineral water?' he asked.

He spoke politely, but Lotte felt he didn't care for waiting on the gardener. She smiled at him, trying to win him over.

'No,' she said. 'Champagne is a treat too good to forgo.' She took a glass. 'I'm Lotte, by the way. And you are?'

'I'm Mark.' His face lost its formality and he looked younger as he smiled. 'I expect we'll get to know each other.'

He went out, leaving the tray on the sideboard. A few seconds later, Lotte heard the thud of feet coming rapidly down the stairs and across the hall. She stood up, the children following suit, and Brody Keegan burst into the room.

'Hi,' he said, 'I'm so sorry I'm late. Stuck on a call to the States. Isn't Jade here?' He looked round. 'Ah, she's probably in the shower. She's been doing her work-out. She's religious about it.'

He fetched himself a glass of champagne and turned his whole attention to Lotte and the children, asking them about the cottage. Was it warm enough? Did they need anything? Was there room for their things?

The children relaxed and were soon chattering excitedly as Brody questioned them about their friends, their old schools, their interests. Lotte left them to it and wandered over to the French windows to look at the view.

Once there, the glitter of the sun on the lake and the sheen on the grass drew her out on to the terrace. The wind had dropped and she could smell the late May lushness. There was a magnificent *Cornus kousa* to the right of the main lawn, its bright white bracts a veil of stars. Half a dozen big hawthorns, mixed pink and white, were draped in blossom.

Lotte lifted her gaze to the lake and narrowed her eyes, searching for the rickety jetty on the far side from where she and Brody had looked back at the house, and where, she thought, she'd convinced him she knew what she was about. She looked beyond the lake to where the trees climbed up the valley, and then to the left to Maddon Woods, wondering what lay buried there. She longed to investigate those ancient ponds.

'What are you doing out there?' The voice was young and female with an underlay of South London.

Lotte turned to see Jade standing on the top step. It could only be Jade. Her yellow hair was gathered at the crown, from where it sprouted like a shining fountain or a guardsman's plume. She was wearing narrow dark glasses and some designer creation, made from peach silky stuff that covered one shoulder and her front, but not her arms or back. The hem dipped to the ground on one side, rising to her thigh on the other. Her tanned legs ended in orange sandals with very high heels. What with them and the plume of hair, and the fact that Jade was tall to start with, she pretty well filled the door. If she wasn't so beautiful, and if she didn't have such style and confidence, she'd be a joke, Lotte thought. This is the middle of the country in late spring, not a St-Tropez celebrity party.

'You must be Mrs Keegan,' she said. 'I'm Charlotte Warren. I should introduce my –.'

But Jade wasn't interested in the children. She came down the steps, saying, 'Brody says you are the business. I hope he's right. This place needs someone to give it a kick up the jacksy.'

Lotte laughed. 'Well, I'm looking forward to hearing your ideas. We need to decide what happens when. What's important to you and so on . . . What we should do this year and what we should leave until . . .'

Taking off her glasses and looking blandly at Lotte, Jade said, 'I think you'll discover that though Brody and I disagree on plenty of stuff, neither of us like waiting for what we want. And we both expect to get our way. So I guess you are going to be busy.'

Lotte felt the challenge in what the young woman was saying. But she didn't understand it. Did Jade mean she was to satisfy her rather than Brody? Or that she wouldn't brook delays? Both, probably. She replied, 'I'm itching to start right now. But I've got a week off first to get the children into schools, find a child-minder for Jo-Jo . . .'

'What a bore,' said Jade.

Lotte was tempted to ask, 'For you or for me?' but instead she said, 'Tell me, just by way of a start, what you like best in the garden.'

'To tell you the truth, I don't care about the garden much at all. But I like this terrace. It could really be something if we got a good designer in, turned some of it into a conservatory, had lots of pots and a decent water feature. I've shown Brody some pictures . . .'

This was dangerous territory, and Lotte said quickly, 'It

45

certainly needs a bit of work, doesn't it? The flagstones are positively dangerous. You're probably risking your neck in those heels.'

Jade stood on one leg and bent the other, peering over to inspect her heel. 'Yeah. They are a bit high.' She shrugged. 'Brody says I should wear jeans and lace-ups in the country.'

Jade's speech was mesmerizing. She spoke slowly, almost in a drawl, her face impassive, her slanted green eyes unanimated. But she had a doll-like directness that Lotte felt she could deal with. She's got no taste, she thought, but no guile either.

Lotte asked, 'And what do you dislike most about the garden?'

'Oh, that's easy. I hate those horrible black stumps along the drive. If they were all the same height we could put statues on them or something. That might look OK. But as they are . . .'

Lotte smiled in relief. 'I agree. Absolutely. They'll be the first thing to go. Some might need a stick of dynamite, but go they must.'

4. Early Summer

You'll be in that deckchair in August,
Lungs full of lush green peace,
Just you, your life, and the shed. Heaven.

Steve Ellis, *Gardeners' Question Time* (1997)

On her first day of work Lotte had the table laid for breakfast by seven-thirty, then went up to check on the children's progress. To her relief they were all dressed. Annie, she noted, was already taking liberties with her school uniform: tie half undone, skirt rolled round her middle to shorten it. And non-regulation footwear. But Lotte turned a blind eye. If Annie was brave enough to test her teachers, she must be settling in OK. She'd give it another week before she got heavy.

Jo-Jo was stuffing cuddly animals into her school backpack. To show Melanie, she said. Jo-Jo was to walk to the village primary with her new-found friend who lived with her parents and gran in Maddon Cottages. Lotte chivvied her downstairs.

Christo, brushing his hair, had that closed look of controlled anxiety. Lotte sat on his bed and pulled him on to her lap. He was tall now, beginning to be gangly. His bum felt bony on her thighs and his head was slightly

47

higher than hers. 'Are you OK, sweetheart?' she said, trying to look into his face.

Christo nodded. Lotte wrapped both arms right round him and went on, 'It's tough having another new school so soon. You'd only just got used to Fulham High, hadn't you?' She leant her cheek against his.

'I suppose,' he said.

'At least this time Annie's with you.'

'No, she isn't. She's always with the big girls.'

'But at least she goes with you on the bus, darling.'

'She doesn't sit with me.'

'Who do you sit with?'

'Nobody. I sit on my own.' His eyes met hers. They were brave and bleak. 'It's OK, Mum.'

Lotte felt her throat tighten. She brought her hand up to his head, pressing his face into hers. He returned the hug, turning to kiss her cheek. He looked so solemn she could have wept. Then he stood up and ran down the stairs to breakfast.

By ten to eight she'd seen them off to school. She whirled about clearing the table and stacking the dishwasher. Then, dead on 8 a.m., she crossed the cobbles under the arch to the office entrance, ready for day one as head gardener at Maddon Park.

She walked through the cobwebbed boot-room, cluttered with old Wellingtons, anoraks and jerseys, to the office. The window was filthy and the desk was invisible beneath stacks of mildewed seed packets, gardening magazines and yellowed copies of the *Sun*. Thick with dust, an ancient plant-labelling machine lay on its side on the floor. Both chairs had stoved-in seats.

The store-room told the same story of neglect. Bales of rusted wire nestled up against stacks of glass panes, presumably for repairing the greenhouse and making cloches. Heaps of sacking, electric fencing and stakes lay in a corner, and all around the walls were shelves bowed under the weight of long-forgotten paint cans, tools, pesticides and insecticides. Legislation about lockable poisons cupboards and chemicals stores had evidently passed her predecessors by.

Deciding to leave a detailed examination of the potting and tool sheds until later – she already knew they were in much the same state – she went in search of Andrew.

She found him trying to start the tractor mower. 'Good morning, Andrew,' she said. 'Problem?'

'Aye,' he said without looking up. He turned the key. Nothing happened. He climbed off the machine and, without a word, set off towards the office.

Lotte caught up with him. 'Andrew, where are you going?'

He looked at her with no attempt to conceal his contempt. 'To phone the maintenance chappie.'

'Hang on a sec, Andrew,' said Lotte. 'Do you know what the trouble is?'

'Nay, but I know a mon who does.'

'Let's have a look first. Maybe it's just a flat battery. Or dirty spark-plugs.'

Andrew made no attempt to help her find the catch to lift the hood. He just stood there, hands in pockets, as though it was nothing to do with him.

'When was this last serviced?' Lotte asked.

'Last season sometime. Back end maybe.'

Lotte could feel her anger rising as she checked the connections. But she tried to keep her voice neutral as she said, 'You don't keep a maintenance log?'

'Nay, lass. You'll find there's more to do in this job than bookwork and bureaucracy.'

'I'm sure you are right,' replied Lotte, her voice brisk, 'but some systems actually promote efficiency. And regular servicing is one of them.'

She took a cloth from her pocket and carefully cleaned the plugs. 'Right,' she said, 'let's try again.' She turned the key and the engine growled smoothly into action. She let it run a few seconds, then turned it off.

'Andrew,' she said, her voice polite but cool, 'I don't believe for a minute you were going to ring the mower maintenance people. No one who's been a gardener as long as you have would not check the plugs first. You were just trying to wind me up, weren't you?'

Andrew stared stolidly over her shoulder without replying. Lotte went on, 'Anyway, I hope you were. Because calling out servicemen for something as basic as spark-plugs is criminal. And if it was a wind-up, then all I've got to say is, we've got to work together, and it can be tough or it can be pleasant. You choose.'

Suddenly she felt she'd overdone it. Trying to soften the humiliation for the Scotsman, she said, 'Where were you planning to mow?'

'Yon main lawns.' Andrew jerked his chin towards the house.

Lotte shook her head. 'Could you start on the drive instead? If we mow the house lawns this early in the week, Mr Keegan won't have newly mown stripes for his weekend guests to admire.' She smiled at the stony-faced Andrew, trying to melt his frost.

He didn't thaw. He took a packet of tobacco out of his pocket and rolled a cigarette. 'And if you leave it till Friday,' he said, 'and it rains, he'll have lawns not mown at all.'

'True,' said Lotte, 'but the drive and outer lawns can't take more than two days, which gives us three days to play with. If the weather forecast is good, we'll risk leaving it till Thursday.'

Andrew pocketed his cigarette papers and tobacco, and climbed on to the tractor without meeting Lotte's eye.

She had come looking for him with the idea of getting him on her side. She thought they might walk round the garden together, or sit down over a cup of coffee. But she could see that now was not the moment. So instead she said, 'Andrew, we need to have a discussion, but perhaps it would be better to get the bulk of the mowing done first. Let's meet when you've done the outer grass.'

Andrew put his hand on the ignition key and looked past her. Lotte crouched to peer under the machine. She added, 'And could you please take the blades up a notch? The cut is too short. It's scraping the ground in places.'

Andrew did not immediately do so, instead he drove off without a word, his face immobile, his mouth clamped round his fag. Lotte made a mental note to check his mowing later. She understood his resentment. But she was determined to be obeyed.

Lotte had agreed that she'd spend the week finding her feet and thinking, then present her conclusions to Brody at the weekend. She pushed all long-term restoration thoughts out of her head. She was keen to make an immediate impact on the garden, and the way to do that was to haul it into shape, not start hacking it about immediately. She'd present Brody with a short-term report on what needed doing, and an estimate of the labour and machinery she'd need.

But first she unearthed the filthy telephone in the office and rang Terry Simons, Brody's land agent, the man who had originally shown her round the estate. He was a lot more friendly now.

'I heard you'd got the job. Congratulations. And what can I do for you?'

'Mr Keegan said you could authorize expenditure if he wasn't around?'

'So I can. Within limits.'

'Good. Because I need to sort out the office and stores, etcetera. We need at least two skips, maybe three, for all the accumulated junk, some paint to slap on the walls, then I need a computer and printer, a couple of chairs with seats to them . . .'

Simons made her slow down and itemize everything. She got his agreement to the skips, paint and chairs. He queried the computer, but she insisted that running a garden was like any other business: you needed to keep records of money spent, keep track of planting schemes, record staff holidays, sickness, etc. and log all activity, especially once you started excavation or restoration.

'OK, OK,' he said, 'But nothing fancy. Just a standard pc. Not two thousand pounds' worth of fancy lap-top.'

'I promise,' Lotte said. 'Five hundred pounds, top whack.'

On that first Monday Andrew mowed and Lotte humped junk. She wore jeans and a tee-shirt, lace-up walking boots and an old-fashioned thick linen apron with pockets for tools (now empty) round her middle. Her hands were protected by heavy work-gloves, and she was glad of them: hefting corrugated iron, panes of glass and nail-infested planks of wood went a lot faster if you didn't have to choose your grip with care.

She worked steadily, stopping only for a cup of coffee and a sandwich at lunchtime. She offered Andrew some, but he said, 'Nay, I'll not be needing that,' and sat in his car to eat his packed lunch and drink his Thermos coffee.

At three forty-five Lotte was washing the outside of the office windows when she heard the children coming up the lane. She stopped in mid-swipe, listening intently until she'd heard all three voices, then smiled in relief. Last week she had fetched Annie and Christo from school, but this week they were taking the school bus to the Maddon Park stop, then collecting Jo-Jo from Melanie's and walking home together.

She hurried round the side of the walled garden, suddenly desperate to see them. At the sight of her mother, Jo-Jo broke into a run and barrelled into her. Christo smiled and consented to being kissed. Annie said, 'Mum, what on earth have you been doing? You've got guck in your hair and you are seriously filthy.' Then, without waiting for an answer, she announced. 'I'm starving. Is there anything to eat?'

Lotte laughed. 'There's a raisin loaf. Don't eat it all. And when you've done your homework, you could give me a hand. You too, Christo. I might even pay you.'

'How much?' Annie asked.

Jo-Jo jumped up and down. 'And me! And me! I don't have any homework. I can help you now.'

When Lotte heard Andrew returning on the mower the following afternoon, she dropped the evil-smelling sacking she was hauling out of the store and walked across the lane to intercept him.

She stood in his path. For a moment she thought he'd just swerve and drive past her, but at the last minute he stopped, though he left the engine running. She knew he wouldn't be able to hear her over the noise, and she signalled for him to turn it off. He did so with reluctance, then pulled out his cigarette papers and tobacco.

'Have you finished the outer lawns?' Lotte asked.

With his head down to roll his fag and lick the paper's edge he replied, 'Aye.'

'That's good, because tomorrow first thing you need to walk me through the machine-room and tell me what works and what doesn't. Some of those machines should be in a museum, I think.'

'Better than newfangled rubbish, mostly.'

It's like dealing with Annie, Lotte thought. Pussyfooting around their sulks. In a brisker voice she went on, 'And I'd like to sit down with you in the office so you can tell me how things run round here. We need to plan what extra help we need to start making a difference.'

She didn't wait for his silence, or for him to drive off. Instead said, determinedly cheerful, 'OK? See you in the office tomorrow, first thing.' She gave him a wave and swung on her heel to return to clearing the store.

*

By Wednesday evening the job was pretty well done and both skips were full. One contained metal (leaking buckets, rusted bath-tub, old boiler, defunct tools, wire, railings, sheet iron and a wire cage full of old horseshoes), the other, plastic (compost bags, broken containers of every size from aspirin bottle to water-barrels and dustbins, cracked cloches, filthy sheeting, split flower-pots). On the ground, awaiting a third skip, was a pile of glass and a heap of rotting sacking, carpet, fleece and netting. Finally there was a bonfire pile of broken furniture, painted and split planks, old boxes.

There was some salvage too. Lotte had decided to keep the four wooden scythes and half a dozen sickles. Maybe Andrew had a point: modern strimmers made a horrible noise, required you to sweat behind a mask, and they stank of petrol. Maybe she could master the rhythm of a scythe? She tried one but found it heavy and unwieldy. Still, she could not throw them away. She was intrigued by their curious design and handles worn smooth with use. She'd hang them and the sickles in the barn.

She'd also rescued the labelling machine, which she felt must surely be restorable, and a wood-burning stove (slightly rusty, but she could fix that). She kept anything serviceable: at least a thousand flower-pots (a couple of hundred of them perfect old clay ones), sacks of fertilizer, chemicals, compost, sharp sand, moss and grit, even eight bags of peat, a legacy from less environmentally aware times.

There was just one object in the office she could not budge. The office safe stood breast-high and was a good two feet across. She wanted to get rid of it – she needed the space for a decent filing cabinet. But she wanted to check its contents first. Also, since it was obviously old – Edwardian at the latest – she thought she should not just have it carted away. Mr Keegan might want to keep it. Or sell it. Or maybe it should be in a local museum.

She crouched down and wiped a damp cloth over its surface. It was certainly made to impress would-be thieves with both the value of its contents and the impossibility of getting at them. The door was embossed with the maker's insignia, a moulded badge of a snarling lion's face with a brass banner underneath carrying the words 'Bulstrode and Company Limited, Lockmakers'. The edges and corners of the safe were reinforced with heavy metal strips and caps. The door had two keyholes, both with brass covers to them, one of which was bent. Lotte could not swing it away to reveal the keyhole. She'd need a hammer to do that.

She thought of the tray of keys, many rusty, none labelled, that she had taken into the cottage to sort. Some of them were old and beautiful and she had an idea that Christo might like to polish them up and make a collection of them. She'd have to clean and oil the likely keys before she even tried them in these great locks.

'And then I'd better ring Terry Simons and ask him what to do with the safe,' she thought, heaving herself upright by pulling on the central brass handle.

The next second Lotte was sitting on her bottom, the door open in front of her. It had not been locked. She scrambled to her knees, her heart banging. But her excitement was shortlived. The safe had an inner door to the top compartment and a drawer beneath. And they were both locked.

That evening after tea Lotte started on the smaller keys, using wire wool and rust remover to clean them. She dried them on top of the Aga, then sprayed them with WD40.

Annie flopped down on the chair opposite her. She took no notice of what her mother was doing, but slouched in the chair, picking the nail-polish off her fingers.

Lotte said, 'Darling, there's some nail-polish remover in my dressing-table drawer. It would be quicker than picking at it.'

Annie didn't answer.

'Sweetheart, don't be rude.'

'What have I said that's rude?' Annie snapped with exaggerated hurt. 'I didn't say a thing!'

'Precisely,' replied Lotte.

But Annie was saved from an escalating row by the appearance of Christo. He inspected the keys on the stove, then hung over Lotte's shoulder, picking up the biggest ones from the tray.

'What are they all for, Mum?'

'Absolutely no idea. But there's a huge old safe in the office, which I can't get into. I'm cleaning the little ones in the hope that one of them might work.'

'Wow,' Christo said. 'Can I try the ones you've done already?' He dashed over to the Aga and picked up a key, only to drop it, yelping, 'Ow, it's hot.'

'Of course it's hot, dum-dum. It's sitting on a stove. Use the fish slice.'

Christo helped her to clean the rest of the small keys. When they were all dried and sprayed, Lotte said, 'C'mon, let's see if there's anything in there.'

She called up the stairs to Jo-Jo, who followed them, immediately speculating about gold coins and jewels and clamouring to be the one who tried the keys. In the end it became a game, with all of them – even Annie, whose curiosity had got the better of her determined boredom – taking turns to choose a key and try it, first in the upper lock, then in the drawer.

Annie hit the jackpot with her third key. It turned with ease and she pulled the inner door open.

Cries of triumph quickly turned to groans of disappointment. The safe was stuffed with folders and papers. Only Lotte was pleased. One look told her they were gardening records: there were faded lists of plant orders, diagrams of planting schemes, what looked like an engineering drawing of a boiler, and, best of all, six identical cloth-covered journals. All had 'Maddon Park Head Gardener's Log' embossed on the covers, with the volume number beneath the title. The volumes were numbered I, II, VI, VIII, XII and XIII. Lotte opened one at random and read:

May 3rd. 1866. Wisteria buds taken by frost. Some apple blossom damage, especially the new Beauty of Bath and Peasgood's Nonesuch. Seeded Western terrace proceeding well. No rye visible. Ordered 2 loads sharp sand for lawns and glasshouse. Cook complains of slug damage to radishes.

Absorbed, she didn't notice that the children had got the drawer open too. They had picked out the keys that looked like the one that had opened the top section and had struck lucky almost at once. Once more, however, Jo-Jo's hopes of treasure were dashed, while Lotte's heart beat faster. Inside the drawer were sepia photographs of plants, shrubberies and flower-beds, and a bundle of horticultural show certificates for tulips, roses, auriculas, peonies, leeks, onions, shallots, beetroots. Lotte stacked them all on her desk. Tomorrow she'd find some boxes and store them properly, so she could go through them carefully. She had a mental image of herself in the long winter evenings, cataloguing the garden's Victorian archive at the kitchen table. She might even start tonight.

Once back in the cottage, though, she was suddenly dog-tired. She had to force herself to keep going through the evening: she cooked some pasta, and thawed some frozen strawberries to eat with the ice-cream. After supper the children washed up while she ironed their school shirts and sorted out their sports gear. Then there was Jo-Jo's story, and twenty minutes with maths homework that Christo couldn't do.

But at last Jo-Jo and Christo were in bed, Annie was lost behind her head-phones and Lotte was free. She dragged herself upstairs, ran a bath and – to hell with the expense – poured a great slug of Myberg's Pine Essence into it. She watched the lurid green liquid hit the water, turning milky. The stringent clean smell of pine filled Lotte's head as she sank into the water. She closed her eyes, thinking that she wouldn't swop this moment for anything. Not even for a lover.

She shampooed her hair, then sank right under the water, rubbing her face with her hands. It felt marvellous. She smiled at her skinny form, unfamiliar and otherworldly in the green water. She'd lost weight recently. If you didn't look too closely, her body could be an adolescent's. She stretched out her hands and examined them. Despite the protection of the gloves, they were beginning to look like a gardener's hands. Two nails were broken, there were red patches that threatened calluses, and her fingers were truly filthy, with grime in every crevice and under every nail. Even shampooing her hair hadn't cleaned them. When she went downstairs she'd have to scrub them in bleach.

Her back ached, but pleasantly. She had done, she knew, more heaving, lifting and lugging than most strong men did in a day. She'd really pushed herself. Partly because she so badly wanted the background sorted so that she could get to the real job — the gardening. And, she hoped, the research and restoration.

But partly, too, she'd gone at the clean-up like a madwoman because she was proving something: that she, middle-class, educated, an historian, an architect, a woman (a rather *small* woman), could shovel muck with the best of them. She was, she knew, proving something to Andrew, to Simons the land agent, and of course to Brody Keegan.

After she'd gone round the house that night, checking on the sleeping Jo-Jo and Christo, telling Annie to switch off her music and go to sleep, turning out the lights, Lotte suddenly slipped out of the front door and padded the few yards to her office. She picked up the photograph that had caught her eye before and returned to the house with it. She climbed into bed and lay propped against the pillows with the picture against her knees.

It was of a bearded man wearing plus-fours, a tweed jacket and tie. He was tall and thin, his expression severe. In one hand he held a flower-pot containing an auricula sporting a single perfect bloom and in the other a Royal Horticultural Society's certificate. Round his neck hung the RHS Gold Medal. The picture was captioned: *Angus Ferguson, Head Gardener to Sir George Quentin, Maddon Park, Oxfordshire, with Auricula 'George Lightbody', winner of the RHS Gold Award, 1870.*

Lotte was spellbound by the picture. She knew that auricula: she'd noticed 'George Lightbody' in a catalogue because of the unusual grey margin to the petals. She felt this photograph was a direct line connecting her, Lotte Warren, with the Victorian Angus Ferguson, and stretching out behind him to his predecessors too. It occurred to her for the first time that she was the last in a long line of head gardeners serving not so much a boss as a garden. Owners, and head gardeners and their underlings, had come and gone over the centuries, but Maddon Park was still here, a little in need of a face-lift, but as demanding and engrossing as ever.

She switched off the light, thinking, goodnight, Mr Ferguson. I'm going to get to know you much, much better, very soon.

5. Summer

Dark creeping Ivy,
. . . bloom of ruins, thou art dear to me,
       When, far from danger's way, thy gloomy price
Wreathes picturesque around some ancient tree
       That bows his branches by some fountain-side;
Then sweet it is from summer suns to be,
With thy green darkness overshadowing me.

John Clare (1793–1864), 'To the Ivy'

Brody got out of his Jaguar and sprang up the steps of Threadneedle Chambers. He was pleased with himself. The morning negotiation had gone brilliantly. In another week *going-going-gone.com* would be his. The IT geeks who had started it were way over their heads. They knew all about computers but nothing about running a business. They just wanted out. Nineteen million would buy the company, the geeks would go away richer than their wildest dreams to start another IT miracle, and he, Brody, would make serious money from *ggg*.

He knew exactly how he'd fit the two businesses together. There would be huge savings in office space and staff – he'd move *ggg* down to Oxfordshire within a month

– and he'd be able to sell its services to the clients who used *find-on-line* and vice versa. It was a star deal.

He was eager to bring Leslie Cohen into the loop. They went back a long way, the two of them: Leslie used to buy his lunchtime bagel at the shop where Brody was a seventeen-year-old baker's boy, as Irish as Leslie was Jewish, and each as green as the other. Leslie had been Brody's money-man since he set up his first business, a spicy chicken takeaway, when both of them were still dead skint. Leslie wasn't even qualified then, but he did Brody's books for him in the evenings.

Brody lost patience waiting for the lift and set off up the stairs, two at time, pulling off his mustard-coloured Armani jacket as he went. Just as well Leslie's only on the second floor, he thought. He's so rich now he could take the whole building if he wanted, but he would think that was flash. And Leslie was never flash.

Even when they'd sold Brody's Baps – by then a chain of over 400 stores, a dozen of them in Germany – Leslie had to be bullied into dinner at the Mirabelle and a flutter at the Barracuda. Brody smiled at the memory: Brody with a couple of grand's worth of gaming chips had made Leslie feel physically ill.

The contrast between the two men's looks was as great as that of character. Brody, in lightweight fawn trousers, loafers and a collarless cream shirt, looked expansive and confident, lounging sideways in his chair. He held his coffee cup by the bowl, not the handle, and he was grinning.

Leslie Cohen was small, neat and grey-haired. He was only forty-five but he looked closer to sixty. He wore a three-piece pin-striped suit and had a deep red rose in his button-hole. He looked almost exactly like his father, who had founded Cohen and Cohen and whose portrait hung behind him. Leslie's only departure from his father's formal dress was a striped blue and white shirt (his father's was white) and a dark red tie. His ties, Brody had noticed, always matched his button-hole, and he always wore one. Yellow rose, yellow tie; pink rose, pink tie. He sat neatly, both hands resting on the blotter in front of him. When he picked up his coffee cup, it would be by the handle.

Leslie took off his heavy spectacles and polished them with a crisp white handkerchief. He shook his head. 'Brody, I don't like it,' he said.

'Leslie, don't be such a worry-guts. I can afford it. I'm seriously loaded. *find-on-line* has a market cap bigger than British Airways. I'm rolling in the stuff.' Amusement, almost devilment, shone out of Brody's eyes.

'You're well off now, certainly. But you're in a volatile business. You must know there is a danger that Internet stocks will not hold their value. A crash could take you with it.'

'Sure. The bubble's going to burst. But not for all dot.coms. Not for business to business services like *find-on-line*.'

Cohen raised a questioning eyebrow, and Brody leant forward to say, '*find-on-line* is not a wild idea with a couple of spotty youths behind it and a lot of greedy backers who don't understand the Net. We're already making pots of real money from real businesses, because we save them time and money. And the customer list is growing faster than our costs.'

Cohen looked sceptical, but said, 'Go on.'

Brody's enthusiasm grew as he spoke. 'We have all their suppliers' inventories, in real time. No more ringing round all day to find the right widget. They just tap in Blue Widget No. 28 or whatever, and up comes a list of every supplier with the thing in stock, plus prices. See?'

Brody smiled encouragingly at Leslie, trying to make him see what to him was clear as gin. But Leslie, as if mentally as well as physically strait-jacketed by his three-piece suit and sober tie, wasn't susceptible. His brow concertinaed in anxiety.

'At the risk of your calling me pompous, Brody, I must say that to me the Internet stocks boom feels just like every other stock-market bubble. And bubbles always burst.'

Brody stood up and came round the polished table. He sat on it, close enough to Leslie to put a hand on his shoulder, dwarfing him.

'Believe me, Leslie, you are a great accountant. You know every tax dodge in the book and a few besides. But you know nothing of the Internet and I know heaps. Trust me. I'm going to stay rich.'

Leslie glanced up at Brody, his eyes still concerned. He looked more like a sorrowful father than a professional advisor.

'Whatever the health of your company, I am advising you, as your accountant, to stop spending money on more madcap investments. At least put the bulk of your fortune beyond the reach of the receivers.'

Brody burst into his barking laugh. 'Receivers! Oh, Leslie, ye of little faith!' He straightened his face and stood up. 'OK. I can see I need to explain stuff so you can sleep at night. Listen, here come my guiding principles when investing in a dot.com.'

Brody declared that most on-line companies were heading for the pan because they relied on advertising, telephone charges or selling things to make money – three sure roads to disaster. Advertising didn't work because no one read the on-screen ads, telephone profits would be shortlived because competition and deregulation would make call charges as cheap as in the States, and a business selling stuff on line to the public cost a mint to set up and years to turn a buck – by which time one of the big boys, with millions of customers already, an existing distribution network and the wherewithal to play the waiting game, would come in and kill you.

'In short, don't invest in any dot.com that depends on advertising, phone charges or providing new services to new customers. Dot.coms that will stay the course are the ones that do something that already happens, but much cheaper. Like *find-on-line*. Got it?'

Leslie looked mildly comforted by this, but he wasn't about to give up. 'OK. But that doesn't mean you should buy another Internet company.'

Brody put both hands on the desk and leant into Leslie's face. He launched into another earnest speech, explaining that *going-going-gone* was a brilliant add-on to *find-on-line*. It allowed a buyer to auction the contract for a year's supply of something, and find the best and cheapest supplier. It worked for almost anything: spare parts for a car manufacturer; New Zealand butter for a chain of restaurants; screwdrivers for a DIY retailer. In a few minutes – at most a couple of hours – the buyer could let the contract without trawling through catalogues, investigating suppliers or negotiating with them, and all without leaving his desk. In fact he needn't even be there. *going-going-gone* would do it for him.

Leslie gnawed away at everything Brody said, questioning, probing, picking holes. 'But how does the buyer know the bidder is not a cowboy? That he will deliver the goods?' asked Leslie.

The beauty of *ggg*, Brody insisted, was that they did the checking for the buying company. Would-be suppliers had to register and their fee covered the costs of the whole 'due diligence' thing: making sure their factory didn't use child labour; what their capacity was; their size; their finances; their quality control; everything.

Brody veered between zealous persuasion and near-fury that Leslie could not see what he could see.

'Look, it's simple,' he said. 'When Volvo or Ford come along, wanting a year's supply of fan-belts, all they have to do is set the specification and estimate their likely need. *ggg* then sets up a reverse auction, inviting only the companies registered with them and who can meet the spec. The suppliers sit in their offices in the Far East or Europe or South America or wherever and enter their bids for the fan-belt contract. They bid against each other in real time and see each other's bids on screen.'

To Brody it was clear as daylight. Simple and beautiful. He punched his fist into his palm. 'The bidding stops when no one wants to go any lower. And *ggg* gets a fee from both buyer and seller, and a cut of the savings the buyer makes on the seller's list price. Neat, isn't it?'

Leslie was silent for a moment, thinking. 'But what's to stop the suppliers forming a cartel?' he said.

'They don't know who they are bidding against. Only the offers come up, not the bidders' names.'

In the end Leslie raised both hands, open-palmed in an I-give-up gesture, and Brody swung round the desk and half hugged, half shoulder-clapped him. The little accountant rocked under the assault. He smiled, a touch nervously.

Brody said, 'Come on then. Let's go to the Irish pub and down a Guinness. I want you to tell me how to raise the money. Do I use my own or have you got some cunning scheme to leave that in Jersey and borrow someone else's?'

Brody had persuaded Jade to have supper with him in the rowboat on the lake. It was a motionless evening with purple loosestrife and bulrushes perfectly reflected in the water and giant water-lilies retreating into waxy buds as the light faded.

It should have been idyllic. There was champagne in the basket between their feet, and the chef had made a sort of crumbly smoked salmon pie that you could eat in your fingers. It was still warm, and delicious. Brody wrapped a lettuce leaf round a slice, and handed it to Jade.

'Go on,' he said, 'it's really good.'

'Too fattening,' she said, taking the offering and unwrapping it. She ate the lettuce leaf, then broke the pie into pieces and threw a bit towards the swans, gliding slowly on their upside-down reflections. Within seconds the reflections shattered as half a dozen birds headed for the boat. Jade, pleased, dropped her bits of pie into the

68

water for them. They ducked and gobbled in unseemly haste, then sailed closer to the boat, expectant. Suddenly they seemed more threatening than decorative, stretching their necks over the side and shaking their heads, their beady eyes fixed on Jade.

'Brody, make them go away. I don't like them.'

Brody took a couple of pulls on the oars, and for a second distanced them from the swans. But they glided serenely behind the boat, and when it stopped, there they were again, close, demanding.

'Can't you do something, Brody?' Jade flapped her hands in panic as the birds surrounded her. 'Ugh, go away! Go 'way!'

'Keep calm, sweetheart. They aren't dangerous. They must come from somewhere where the public feeds them or something.'

'Well, I hate them. Chase them off, Brody.' Jade shrank away from the birds, her eyes wide and her lips drawn back.

Brody wondered for a second if she was acting or genuinely scared. 'OK. But hold tight, this could wobble a bit.' He stood up, his feet straddling the bottom of the rowboat. He waved an oar at the swans to make them back off a little, then slapped it smartly into the water to send a fountain of water splashing over them.

'Brody! Don't. We'll go over!' Jade shouted, alarm making her voice sharp.

'No, we won't!' Brody laughed, hitting the water harder. He was enjoying himself. 'Just hold tight.' He kept it up, drenching the birds, until they flipped their wings in indignation and sailed to a safer distance.

Brody had to work hard to brighten Jade's mood after

that. She had been upset by the birds, scared of capsizing, and she'd got splashed. And, Brody knew, she hadn't wanted supper on the boat anyway. Not that she'd had any. After the swan incident she'd had a glass of fizz and a few strawberries, but nothing he'd count as food.

'Come and sit beside me,' he said, shifting up on his bench to make room for her. The boat wobbled as she stood up, and he put his arm round her to pull her in beside him. 'I want to talk to you about our plans for Maddon.'

Jade looked at him expectantly. Almost politely, thought Brody, as if the matter didn't concern her. He went on, 'About your gym and pool. I've had an idea.'

Jade's eyes hardened. 'Brody, don't go back on . . .'

'No, sweetheart. Just listen, this is a better idea. How about we convert one of the cellars into a gym? And put the pool and sauna down there too? Then you can work out without having to trek across to the walled garden.'

Jade considered this, then smiled her perfect smile. 'You know,' she said, 'that could be really cool. We could have a sauna down there and a treatment room too. There's oodles of space.' She kissed his cheek. 'I'll ring David in the morning, maybe he can come down this week and we can –'

'Darling, David is a decorator, not an architect. I've asked Lotte to have a look and she's . . .'

'She's the bleeding gardener, Brody!'

Brody won the argument, but not without difficulty. He had known that Jade's instinctive dislike of Lotte could prejudice the scheme if she knew the idea of a gym in the cellar had been Lotte's. So he'd pretended it was his.

Lotte had been desperate not to have a leisure and sports complex in the middle of her walled garden. She'd come to him with a rough sketch of what she thought all the tumbledown buildings in the walled garden might once have been – melon houses and tool sheds and God knows what. She'd begged him to give her time at least to investigate them before he made a decision. She said she wanted time to explore the Maddon Archive in St Aldwyn's College, to see if there were any references to the walled garden. He had refused: what was the point of learning about a collection of derelict sheds?

Three days later Lotte was back with her basement plan. She must have surveyed the cellars in the two days he and Jade had been in London. You had to hand it to that little mouse. She sure didn't give up easy.

Brody tried to give Jade an oar but she declined to row. 'No, you do it,' she said, moving back to her seat opposite him. 'You'll get us home quicker.'

Brody pretended he hadn't heard this, and instead rowed slowly round the lake, keeping a weather eye on the swans. He tried to interest Jade in his plans for the garden and estate, but she listened impassively. She was mildly interested in the new tenant farmer's plan to go organic, to turn some of the arable land into a market garden and the old threshing barn into a farm shop. But she was indifferent to Brody's talk of a maze and a sculpture trail.

'What for?' she said. 'Who will ever use them?'

Jade's lack of pleasure in Maddon, in him, in this little boat ride, clouded Brody's pleasure. I so want to involve her in everything, he thought. But somehow I can't. Maybe

Maddon Park is just a posh address to her. And business bores her rigid. She turns right off if I talk about *find-on-line* or *going-going-gone*.

He made a final effort. 'Darling,' he said, 'is this not heaven?' He waved his arm at the setting sun, glowing red behind the trees to the west and casting the Chinese bridge over the stream, the summer-house on the island and the weeping willows behind the lake into silhouette. Then he swung the other way and pointed to the bank behind them. 'I've no idea what all those plants are, but they do look good, don't they?'

Jade looked at the purple loosestrife and yellow ligularia perfectly reflected in the absolutely still water, black and shiny now in the evening light, and agreed it was pretty.

'Maybe we should build a patio on the island with a little swimming-pool. And turn that Chinese hut thing into changing-rooms,' she said. 'Then there would be some point in coming down here. People could swim. And we could have barbecues.'

Brody, glad to have stimulated some enthusiasm, nodded.

Pleased now, she said, 'Yeah. We could have a themed Chinese ball or something. With Chinese food, and Chinese lanterns. And fireworks and stuff.'

Lotte had given the children some supper and left them doing their homework. One of the joys of summer was this freedom to walk in the evenings – she could never have left them alone in the house in London. Now, though she always carried her mobile phone in case they needed her, she knew they were safe.

The children seldom came with her. Annie still liked to take advantage of her mother's absence for hour-long calls to Lynette in London or her new friends from school. Christo preferred a book or his computer. Jo-Jo would have been willing enough – if only to dodge her 9 p.m. bedtime. Maybe, once they broke up for the holidays, Maddon would get more of a hold on them, Lotte thought.

But she was glad to be alone this time. She hurried along the southern edge of the lake, her hand on Mr Ferguson's log book in her Barbour pocket. It covered the years 1874–6 and in it he'd described building a bridge and a summer-house. Lotte was sure these were the Chinese bridge over the stream that carried the lake overflow back to the river, and the Oriental tea-house or hut on the island. Proving it would be fun.

Most of the wood of the bridge was as sound as the day it was built – in October 1875 if this was indeed Ferguson's bridge. Only the timbers at ground level had rotted at all. Lotte pushed one of the end posts and it rocked very slightly. She frowned and took out her book. She opened it at her yellow sticker and read again:

Painted the new bridge with paint from Mssrs Dixons. But Lady Quentin declares it to not be a true Chinese red, and it must be done again. Mr Pangbourn will return to mix the colours next week. A great nuisance as much time will be lost. I will set the men to paint the frames and glasshouses in order not to waste their labour, which we are contracted for. Ordered 2 gallons white lead for this. Dixon's man will deliver in the morning.

Lotte turned the pages carefully to an entry six days later:

Both bridge and Chinese tea-house completed today. Lady Quentin inspected same, and declared the colour satisfactory. But the finials for the bridge and tea-house roof are not yet placed, the workshop not having the drawings from Mr Pangbourn. They must now be painted in the workshop, and then fixed.

Am content with the work. The fallen oak from Grandon field has been put to good use. Six years seasoning has made the wood as hard as a nut. It will be sound a hundred years.

Well, if this is the bridge, you were certainly right there, my friend, thought Lotte. But red paint? The bridge was definitely oak, but it was a deep, weathered, unpainted brown. Lotte ducked under the edge of the bridge, taking care not to slip into the stream. She looked up into the corners and between the beams of the floor, thick as railway sleepers.

'I knew it!' she exclaimed. There were unmistakable traces of red paint in the middle of the beams on the protected undersides, especially in the corners.

She examined the construction with interest, wondering how such a long curved span could be unsupported in the middle. And then she saw that the wooden construction was reinforced underneath by a thick cast-iron frame, sunk into channels cut into the heavy beams. The construction was unmistakably Victorian, with heavy metal bolts securing the wood to the metal. So, thought Lotte, the bridge's longevity was not just due to seasoned oak. It had an iron heart. I wonder who designed it, she mused, a local blacksmith or a railway architect?

Exhilarated by the confirmation of her suspicions, Lotte walked back to the little canoe lying upside down next to the jetty, heaved it over and pushed it into the water. One day, she thought, we must build a Chinese-style boathouse to make going on the water less of a performance.

She paddled easily across to the island and forced the canoe through the bulrushes so she could clamber out without getting wet. She pulled the boat up the bank and tied it to a willow branch.

The tea-house had been painted Chinese red too. There was little of the paint left on the west and south sides, where the sun and the wind had baked and stripped it. But on the sheltered eastern side there were whole red sections. The building was octagonal with open latticed windows, now hung with festoons of dark ivy, on five sides. The remaining three were fully open for a perfect view of the house and park. It was not as solidly built as the bridge, and would need major repairs, if not complete rebuilding. The tiled floor was being lifted by the ivy which had also made inroads into the roof, dislodging the oak shingles.

But Lotte liked the place as it was. The ivy curtains gave it a gothic, theatrical look and ensured the interior was cool and dark. She went inside and sat down on the one safe piece of slatted seat, thinking she'd watch the sun go down and continue with Ferguson's log.

Absorbed by the gardener's diary, she was unaware of the Keegans' presence until she heard their voices at the jetty as Brody heaved the upturned rowboat right side up and manhandled it into the water. Then they were clattering into the boat. Lotte stood up, slightly flustered, thinking she ought to announce her presence. But then she thought, Oh God, they've got a picnic basket and champagne in a bucket. Jade will definitely not appreciate my presence here. Nor will Brody, come to that.

It was too late to emerge now. If she hadn't been reading, she'd have seen them walk across the park and she could have paddled the hundred yards back to the jetty before they even reached it and then given them a cheery hello and goodbye as she passed them on the path.

She sat tight, just hoping they would not want to land on the island. She didn't think she could be seen – she was far back in the gloom of the summer-house. She watched them, feeling guilty but fascinated. Seeing Brody deal with the swan, she was torn between laughing and anxiety that he might fall in as he flailed about.

Lotte heard every word of their conversation – their voices carried across the still water with ease. Her shame at eavesdropping and the things she heard combined to send her on an emotional roller-coaster ride.

She was indignant at Brody's claiming her cellar idea as his own. And Jade's 'She's the bleeding gardener' hurt. But she was gratified by Brody's defence of her, reminding Jade that she'd been a top architect for years. She didn't appreciate the argument that won Jade over, though – that they would be getting an architect's work for a gardener's wages. Finally, she began to feel increasingly sorry for Brody, who obviously adored his shallow wife. But what an ass that woman is, she thought, as she watched Brody help her from the boat. Maddon is wasted on her.

As Lotte walked home along the overgrown path behind the lake, she saw a barn owl quartering the field and a fox loping along the edge of the wood. Circular expanding ripples on the otherwise still surface of the lake testified to trout rising. Crossing the meadow, she bent down to grab a handful of newly cut hay and held it to her face. The best of summer smells, she thought. The farmer would bale the mix of grass, buttercups, ox-eye daisies and clover, and next year the fritillaries, safely seeded now, would be better than ever.

6. Midsummer

Where my foot rests, I hear the creak
From generations of my kin,
Layer on layer, pressed leaf-thin.

Thom Gunn (1929–),
'The Garden of the Gods'

'Peter Childersley speaking.'

'Oh good, I've been trying to get you. My name is Lotte Warren. I understand you have the pre-war archive for the Maddon Park estate.'

There was a silence. Either he was thinking, or he was not going to answer. Lotte asked, 'Is that right?'

His voice was dry. 'Yes. That is correct. May I ask what your interest is?'

Lotte explained that she was researching the history of the Maddon garden. 'I'm the head gardener there.'

Another pause. Then, 'I'm sorry, but it is not fully catalogued.' He seemed to think this was sufficient reason not to continue the conversation and Lotte began to panic that she would not even get over this first hurdle.

'But, perhaps I —'

He cut her off. 'And I am afraid we only allow accredited scholars to research the archive.'

'But I'm a serious student. I've got a degree in horticulture and garden history . . . And one in architecture . . .'

'We only allow academic study. Are you writing a thesis? Or doing a doctorate?'

Lotte could feel the door closing and she said quickly, 'At least let me come and see you. I can explain what I'm trying to do.'

'I am very busy, Mrs Warren . . .'

Lotte began to lose patience. 'But what are records and archives for, if not for people with a legitimate interest to consult?'

There was a brief pause, and Lotte thought she'd blown it. But when he answered his voice was noticeably warmer.

'I think you have a point. By all means come and see me.'

'Oh, thank you . . .'

He cut in, once again formal and dry. 'But I can't promise you access. You do understand that, don't you?'

Lotte had imagined a grey bureaucrat, probably in his late sixties. But Peter Childersley, archivist at St Aldwyn's College, Oxford, was fifty or less, and looked as though he'd slept in his clothes. He had a high domed forehead which sloped smoothly back to the top of his head, at which point his crinkly dark grey hair burst out like a halo. It had a hedge-like vigour, as if compensating for the baldness on his pate and temples. His eyebrows were vigorous too, bushy and unkempt. And beneath them were deep-set, worried eyes, framed by heavy, old-fashioned glasses. He wore a crumpled blue cotton shirt and shapeless fawn trousers. His shoes, black brogues, seemed to belong to some other, more formal, outfit.

Lotte liked him at once, in spite of her earlier reservations and his obvious suspicion of her. His brow was furrowed and his long thin fingers tapped his head, fingering a non-existent forelock.

'I don't want to be unhelpful, but you see, we need to be sure of the credentials of the people we let in to see the documents. We haven't the resources to supervise researchers, you see. Anyone could . . .'

'I quite understand,' said Lotte, smiling. 'I'm sure I can provide you with referees to testify that I won't deface or steal anything.'

Childersley was definitely friendlier now, but he still seemed to be waiting for more convincing credentials. Lotte didn't have any, so she tried the truth, telling him of Brody's plans for development and her plans for restoration, her conviction that under the woods lay lost ponds, maybe grottoes and who knows what else? She ended with a straightforward plea: 'Please let me study the archive. If you just saw how lovely the place is, you'd understand at once how crass it would be to turn the walled garden into a sports centre and put a conservatory on the terrace. You've got to help me.'

Childersley seemed to relax. 'Yes, well, why not? It could be interesting. To be honest, I am already intrigued. I had a preliminary look last night, after you called. I've done a little sorting.'

'You haven't!' Lotte exclaimed, her eyes flashing at him. 'So you were intending to let me see it all along! Why were you so, um, frosty, then?'

Childersley, now shyly pleased with himself, replied, 'Well, providing you were *bona fide*, I did intend to let you see the archive, yes. But if I'd thought your enquiries were frivolous, or you were one of those irritating amateur genealogists tracing their roots, well then, it would have been no.'

He pulled out a chair for her. 'Wait here. I will bring the papers.'

Lotte looked out of the narrow stone window. Below her the quad lawn was almost empty. A couple of young tourists, toting backpacks and hanging on to each other's necks, stopped in the middle of the path to kiss, completely unawed by the mediaeval cloisters, the aura of academe, the gravitas of an Oxford college.

They pulled apart, laughing. Something of their carefree mood infected Lotte, and she found herself smiling. I used to hate seeing happy people, she thought. I wanted the whole world to be miserable because I was miserable. Today she was happy. Maddon was becoming increasingly addictive. She loved almost all aspects of her job, even the physical work. She liked the fact that she could keep going alongside the other gardeners (all male) in trimming the pleached hornbeams from a fourteen-foot wire scaffold, wheeling heavy barrows of gravel, double-digging a bed or hand-weeding the terraces.

It was the hand-weeding that had finally brought old Andrew round. It had been raining for a week and the grass was too wet to mow. Perfect weeding weather, she'd said, and asked Andrew to join her on the terraces. They worked side by side, prising the grass, dandelions and clover loose with a knife and pulling them from between the paving-stones with their fingers. Lotte squatted on her hunkers to work, but Andrew, whose knees were no longer up to squatting, bent over. It was back-breaking work and when they stopped for coffee at ten-thirty Lotte's hands were sore and red from the rough edges of the paving-stones and the grit between them.

After coffee, back on the terrace, she tossed a pair of surgical gloves into Andrew's weeding bucket, saying, 'Here. I don't know about you, but my fingers are killing me.'

He took no notice of the gloves but said, 'Aye, it's nae work for a lassie,' and continued loosening and pulling the weeds. Lotte shrugged. If he wanted to be a martyr, fine.

They finished the main terrace just before 4 p.m. Lotte went across to where Andrew was clearing the last few inches and said, 'Look back, Andrew. Doesn't that look good?' He didn't answer, but they stood side by side admiring their handiwork. The colours of the rock roses, pinks and thymes glowed in the gentle light. Freed of the intervening weeds, the plants looked wonderful against the damp stone.

'Aye,' said Andrew.

'So congratulations, then,' said Lotte, flexing her stiff back and picking up her bucket.

'Aye, and to you, too.'

Lotte could not believe she'd heard him right. She looked at him sharply and saw him peeling a glove off his left hand. 'And thanks for this,' he said. 'It was kind of 'ee.'

Lotte smiled at the memory. Yes, she thought, the job is fine, even the curmudgeonly Andrew. Most of all, Brody was good to work for. He was full of praise for what she'd achieved so far: the returfed, neatly edged lawns, the disappearance of the stumps in the drive, the satisfying thickness of the new gravel, the clearing of the ivy from the house, the smart new five-bar fencing round the park, the redug ha-ha. He let her spend his money like water, never querying the hiring of machinery or extra labour, the purchase of miles of fencing, the lorry-loads of gravel.

So far the garden work had all been straightforward repairs or maintenance. She'd done nothing remotely creative in it. Only the building works in the cellars had her stamp on them. But that suited her: she wanted to take the garden slowly. She felt that if she understood its history and spent time just being in it, it would somehow speak to her. Tell her what to save, what to restore, what to bulldoze. And that would be the time to do battle with Brody. Which was why she needed the co-operation of this odd-ball archivist.

In ten minutes he was back, pulling an ugly metal trolley laden with several boxes, leather-bound books and cloth-covered ledgers. On the bottom shelf there was a roll of parchment tied up with brown tapes, and a larger cardboard tube.

Lotte put her hand on the top volume, a dark brown, almost square tome about two inches thick. She stroked the old leather, cool and smooth, momentarily absorbed by the thought that in this book long-dead scribes had recorded the minutiae of long-dead lives. She slid her hand to the edge of the volume, her fingers curling to lift the cover. But Childersley stopped her.

'I'm afraid you must wear these,' he said, producing a pair of white cotton gloves.

Lotte looked up, embarrassed. 'Oh, I'm sorry. Of course.' She pulled on the gloves and said, 'I'm dying to know. Tell me where to begin. What have we got?'

'Some good stuff, I think. I've only had a cursory look, of course. I knew the Maddon Archive was here, but as the College no longer owns the property, there's no call for it. Or there wasn't until your enquiry. I'd guess some of these documents haven't been opened for a hundred years. Maybe more.'

She looked up. 'Really? Has no one examined any of this?'

'Doubt it. I looked at the earliest references last night, and the very last ones. But apart from that, no.' Lotte felt the same sort of interior flutter she'd experienced when she saw the house across the lake that day with Brody.

'How far back does the archive go?'

'1539, I'm fairly sure. Look.'

He pulled on his gloves and took a large thin package from the trolley. 'This archival envelope is modern. Well, early twentieth-century. We still use similar folders to conserve things.' He gently slid out a yellowed parchment document and used both hands to open it carefully. It was rectangular, folded in half, with a knobbly seal inside. The seal was on a strip of parchment threaded through neat cuts at the bottom of the deed.

'This is quite something,' he said, looking up at her, his eyes reflecting her excitement.

Lotte felt like a child kept waiting for her birthday present. But Childersley could not be hurried. She peered over his shoulder, breathing in the faint waxy smell of old parchment. It was a grand-looking document, full of colour and curlicues, and closely inscribed in an even, elaborate hand.

Childersley adjusted his glasses. 'It's in Latin,' he said. 'Shall I translate?'

Lotte could not make out a word of it. 'Even if it was in English, the script is indecipherable,' she said.

'I know. It's called "secretary hand". But it's easy when you know how. All the important words are twice the size of the others for a start. This is a Letters Patent. It records the gift of the land and forest, "to make a park for the hunting of beasts and a fair pleasaunce (that's a pleasure ground) by His Gracious Majesty King Henry, to The Earl of Axtrim, he that was known as Sir Francis Robert Maydowne ere his Sovereign Lord did choose to honour that Knight with much lands and noble title, he being a loyal courtier and brave General in the service of the King."'

He read and translated the text as though he was reading *The Times*, with barely a hesitation. The remaining text dealt with the size and compass of the land, its woods, streams, river and boundaries, and with the obligations the new earl must now bear: mainly to build and maintain a hunting-lodge to entertain the royal party whenever the King wished to hunt his loyal subject's deer.

Childersley looked up. 'It's almost certain to have been confiscated from a religious order or Catholic family during the dissolution of the monasteries. Henry was liberal with his spoils.'

Lotte couldn't believe her luck. 'Mr Childersley, it's fantastic . . .' She stopped and shook her head. 'Look, I can't call you Mr Childersley. May I call you by your first name?'

'Well, yes. Of course. It's Peter.' He looked embarrassed but pleased, nervous fingers tapping his brow.

'Good. And I'm Charlotte. Lotte.' She looked down at the parchment, her heart banging. 'Peter, what a miraculous start. Wonderful.'

'There's more,' Peter said, smiling with a mixture of shyness and triumph. He picked up a parchment roll and undid the ties. He unrolled a little of the document and then allowed the top end to recurl as he unrolled the bottom, so exposing no more than six inches of text at a time. He explained that the brittle skin might crack if flattened completely. When he found the entry he wanted, he used cloth-covered oblong weights to hold back the rolled-up ends.

'Look,' he said, 'there's a scullion here being fined for poaching fish out of the stew-pond. The entry is April 1660.' He found the entry and his gloved finger hovered over it. 'So we know there was at least one pond.'

'I knew it!' Lotte exclaimed. 'I knew there were ponds.' After a moment she said, 'Aren't there any maps? A plan of the estate would resolve everything.'

Childersley gave her a wry smile and said, 'You don't ask a lot, do you? The answer is no, I don't think so.' He concentrated on securing the court scroll for a second or two. 'There might have been an estate map or survey, but we don't have it. Because they can be pretty big, we keep them together in the map drawers. So it was easy to check. Nothing, I'm afraid.'

Lotte watched his thin hands expertly tying the tapes in spite of the handicap of gloves. When he'd done this, he put the scroll on the bottom shelf of the trolley and picked up a wide leather-bound book, positioning it care-

86

fully on a V-shaped, foam-lined cradle that would allow it to be opened, but not so widely as to crack the ancient spine. When Lotte lifted the cover, she released the smell of old paper, foxed at the edges, bent and crackly. It was a rent book covering the period from 1751 to 1796 and was filled in on quarter days – Lady Day, St John the Baptist, Michaelmas and Christmas – with the tenants' names and amounts paid recorded in the same precise hand until 1785, when a different, bolder script took over.

Lotte was mesmerized by the neatness and accuracy of the record-keeping. Every person in this book, she thought, and both the scribes whose sharp quills had so slowly filled these pages, were all long dead, and no one had given them a thought for hundreds of years. But they were vivid to her. She said, 'Just think, for over thirty years or so this same bailiff opened up this book four times a year and filled in half a page or so, a line for every tenant. Can't you just see them sitting opposite him in their Sunday best, cap in lap, proud to have managed the rent, glad to see it recorded?'

Childersley looked a little taken aback, but pleased. 'Yes, yes. That's exactly what archives do. Bring things alive.' And then, as though embarrassed by his enthusiasm, he tapped a long narrow book covered with rough calf and said, 'This is a Long Book. It was used for accounts. Expenditure only. And this' – he lifted a large flat volume, wider across than from top to bottom, and opened it on the table – 'is the Lease Book.' Lotte saw more even writing, line upon close line, with never a mistake.

Childersley said suddenly, 'I'm curious too, now. I wish I could stay and help you.'

'Can't you?' Lotte suddenly wanted him to. She was right out of her depth. This was going to be a world away from studying great gardens at college, where all her sources had been read, translated, interpreted and sorted out by previous historians. She wouldn't be able to read half these papers and she wouldn't understand the arcane language, the references, the background. 'It would be wonderful if you could.'

'No.' He looked genuinely sorry. 'I just haven't the time.' His hand flitted across his bald pate. 'We are very short-staffed.'

Lotte wondered if she could ask him to help her another time. Or would he expect to be paid? She couldn't possibly pay him.

He went on, 'But I did look at the most recent documents we've got on Maddon Park. Not very interesting, but there's a record of the College's sale of the property after the war.' He reached across the table and pulled out a clothbound ledger. 'There was a feeling then that we should be concentrating our resources in Oxford, and on academic buildings. Look, here it is. 12 March 1947. For two thousand pounds.'

'Two thousand pounds!' Lotte laughed. 'The present owners paid eight million for it!' She looked up at the bespectacled archivist. 'And if you don't help me, they'll spend another eight ruining the place.'

That evening the telephone rang while Lotte was stuffing rubbish into the wheelie-bin. Jo-Jo answered it and leant out of the kitchen window to yell, 'Mum, it's for you,' and then, even louder, 'It's a *man*!'

Lotte took the receiver from her through the window, hoping whoever it was hadn't heard that. She frowned at Jo-Jo. Did she need to broadcast to whoever it was that 'a man' was such a rarity?

'Hello?'

'Er, hello. It's Peter. Um, Peter Childersley. We met today at St Aldwyn's. I'm the archivist . . .'

Lotte laughed. 'Peter, of course I know you. It's only been . . .' she looked at her watch, 'five hours. Even I can remember . . .'

'Oh, I didn't mean that! Yes, of course you can. Oh dear. Anyway. Forget that. I'm ringing because you said . . . I've been going through some of the Maddon Park documents and . . .'

Lotte interrupted. 'What what have you found?'

'Well, there's lots of interesting stuff. There was a smithy and an ice-house. They must have been very grand to have had an ice-house. But that wasn't why I rang.'

'An ice-house! Where?'

'I don't know yet. But in 1800 it was enlarged, at a cost of nineteen pounds fourteen shillings and sixpence.'

Lotte turned her back to the window and leant against the wall. 'But that's wonderful, Peter. I wonder where it is . . .'

'Lotte, that's not why I rang. I rang to ask you . . . er . . . well, to see if you'd like to come to dinner. Maybe one evening in Hall? You know, at High Table. It's rather stuffy, and the food's terrible, but the Fellows are mostly interesting and . . . well, you never know . . . But if you don't want . . .'

Lotte had a mental picture of Peter at the other end of

the line, looking anxious, tapping his forehead. She said, 'I'd love to.'

'Oh!' He sounded nonplussed. 'You would?'

'Yes. Thank you.'

As she went back to cramming the rubbish into the wheelie-bin, Lotte thought, things are on the up. I've got a date. With a very nice chap.

But better still, he was going to help her. All evening her thoughts had hovered round that daunting archive. She'd get completely bogged down, or distracted. She was supposed to be the gardener – she wasn't being paid to write the history of Maddon Park.

I need a colleague, she thought, someone I really like but am not remotely attracted to. A mate, a fellow enthusiast. Peter Childersley would do nicely.

As Peter introduced her to the half-dozen men and the two women who were to be her fellow guests, Lotte realized she'd got it wrong: neither of the other two women had taken any notice of the 'black tie' instruction. One, a scientist, was wearing a shapeless navy top and trousers, no make-up and flat shoes, and the Master's plump wife was in a Laura Ashley floral dress.

Lotte would have been more embarrassed by her party gear if the men hadn't been so obviously impressed. Peter came in for some ribbing – it seemed he had never brought a guest to dinner before. Once she'd got a glass of champagne inside her, she was glad she looked as good as she did. She was wearing a full-length black skirt, just short enough to show off her Emma Hope strappy shoes, and a filmsy black and white striped top, sleeveless and with a neckline that allowed a good bit of cleavage. She wore no jewellery but on her shoulder was a huge, floppy fake red rose.

The food was execrable, as Peter had warned her it would be. Old-fashioned, cholesterol-laden and with a reheated flavour to everything. The starter was a puff pastry vol-au-vent with chopped-up chicken in a heavy cheese sauce. The main course was a large overcooked fillet steak on deep-fried bread with a thick layer of tinned pâté and fried mushrooms separating the two. This came with leathery roast potatoes and yellowing broccoli under a blanket of Hollandaise sauce.

Lotte managed about half of each of these courses, and refused the pudding and the savoury altogether. She watched in amazement as her fellow diners polished off meringue baskets filled with banana and ice-cream and then Scotch Woodcock – which turned out to be scrambled eggs on toast with a couple of crossed anchovy fillets on top – before getting stuck into the port and cheese.

'They don't do this every night, do they?' she whispered to Peter.

'Some of them do,' he said. 'You can tell which by their waist-lines.'

'I heard that, Childersley,' said Lotte's other neighbour, a portly and flirtatious historian of about seventy. Lotte found him engaging, if self-satisfied. On hearing about Maddon Park, he said, 'At some universities you can get degrees in garden history, or landscape studies, or some such damned nonsense.'

Lotte smiled. 'I know,' she said, 'I've got one.'

'Oh dear.' He was unabashed, though. 'Which one?'

'Wroxham Countryside College.'

'Good God. That's not a university, is it? I thought it taught farmers' sons how to rotate crops!'

Lotte laughed. 'I guess it does. But it has degree-awarding powers.'

He shook his head in feigned disbelief. 'I don't know what the world is coming to,' he said. 'Gardeners at High Table! It was bad enough letting the likes of you in, Childersley. Archivists and librarians were strictly "lower orders" in my day.'

'They still are in most colleges,' said Peter. 'St Aldwyn's is still the only one enlightened enough to make the archivist a Fellow. And I bet that's only because I used to be Faculty.'

Lotte wanted to know more, and when her neighbour turned away, she pumped Peter. 'So how did you get to be the St Aldwyn's archivist? I can't imagine a sixth-former saying, "What I really want to do is spend my life in silent rooms looking at ancient bits of paper."'

Peter's fingers were tapping his brow. 'I think I was always happiest with my nose in a book, even as a lad. I grew up with books piled on every stair-tread, in every room, on every shelf.'

Lotte gradually extracted reluctant facts: Peter had never known his father, who had died when he was a baby. He'd spent his childhood, he said, between the stacks of the Evesham Library where his mother was the head librarian.

Lotte frowned. 'How sad.'

'Not at all.' His smile was tentative, even shy. 'I graduated from the Children's Section to History, via Novels, Magic and Pornography – or the closest the Evesham Library came to pornography.' He gave an embarrassed laugh.

He's nice, thought Lotte, laughing too. 'And then?' she asked.

'Nothing to set the Thames on fire. Boring academic life really. Confirmed bachelor. Nothing worth telling.'

'Rubbish,' said Lotte. 'I want to know. Where did you go to Uni? Where did you work before coming here?'

'Medieval history at Cardiff. PhD here, at St Aldwyn's. Taught for a while at Radley, which frightened the life out of me. I imagined university students might be easier, so I applied for a job here. Did that for four or five years, but I wasn't a brilliant teacher. I'm OK in a tutorial, hopeless in a big lecture theatre. So I retrained as an archivist. I've been in the job for eighteen years. Suits me fine.'

Lotte tried to absorb this compressed history. Peter obviously hated talking about himself, which made a change from most of the men she knew.

Dinner, including the port, was over by 10 p.m., and Peter and Lotte walked through the Fellows' Garden to Peter's car.

'Can you smell that?' asked Lotte, stopping by a flower border. The starry white blooms seemed luminous in the dusk.

Peter bent down and sniffed. 'What are they?'

'*Nicotiana sylvestris.* The tobacco plant,' said Lotte, closing her eyes and breathing in deep draughts. 'Heaven, isn't it? The smell of summer.'

When they got out of Peter's car at Lotte's cottage it was almost dark, and Peter said, 'Now, what is *that* smell? More tobacco plant?'

'No, that's *Matthiola bicornis*. Night-scented stocks.' Lotte picked a flower from a clump under the kitchen window. 'Here.'

Peter bent his head over the flower, and Lotte said, 'If I brought us a night-cap out here, we could smell the stocks and babysit at the same time.'

It took a while to pay the babysitter and see her off, and by the time she'd done that, and got a beer for Peter and a glass of wine for herself, and lit the bug-control coil, she half regretted her invitation. It had seemed natural at the time but now she feared Peter would think she was after him. Which was ridiculous: the man was very nice, but he was fifty-three and he didn't make your heart beat faster. But once they were sitting on the narrow bench outside the kitchen window, they fell into easy conversation again, and Lotte found herself responding to his questioning, telling him about Annie's sulks and Christo's fears.

'But are you happy here?' he asked, turning to look into her face.

'Yes, I think so. I feel for the first time there's hope of a real Lotte Warren emerging. All those years as a wife and mother, that is what I mostly was – wife and mother. And at my architectural practice I just went to work, designed these minimalist steel-and-glass constructions in the Richard Johnson style, and oversaw their construction. None of it had much to do with me, really.'

'But don't you miss married life? How long were you married for?'

'Fifteen years. Yes, of course I do. I miss being a proper family. I resent the loss of a husband and father. But I don't miss Sam as Sam any more.'

'You must have at first?'

'No. Not at first. I was too angry to admit I missed him. I was so raw, so outraged that he should fall in love with someone else when I had done all the home-making, child-rearing, etcetera. And he left me for his researcher. It hurt like hell.'

Lotte twirled her glass round and round in the darkness, trying to be honest. 'But of course underneath all the fury I missed him dreadfully. I think the truth is that Sam lost interest in me because I'd changed. When he married me, I was an ambitious architect, I could hold my own in most conversations, and I was fun — always positive, keen to have a go, intellectually alive. We used to have a lot of fun and a lot of conversation. But I got serious, exhausted, deeply absorbed in the children and much more interested in gardening books than in my job. I was too tired, and we were both so busy. We stopped having proper conversations. We never talked as you and I are now. I'd long since stopped asking him about his work, and he didn't ask me about mine because all I did was complain about it.'

It was pitch dark now and she couldn't see Peter's expression. Somehow, that was helpful. Like therapy, she thought, or the priest behind the grille: because I can't see him, confession is easy.

She started to talk about Sam's infidelity, of the pain of finding he was cheating, of forcing him to choose. And the far worse pain of him choosing Frances. Peter prompted her with the odd question but he didn't press her.

'It's been three years now. And I'm over it. I think.' She smiled towards him in the dark, not wanting him to be sorry for her. 'At least I don't wail and gnash my teeth any more.'

Peter didn't say anything, and Lotte had a sudden fear that she'd been boring and maudlin. She looked at her watch.

'God, Peter, it's two in the morning! I'm so sorry, I've been droning on with my life-story . . .'

'Is Sam happy, do you think?'

Lotte thought about this. The truth was she didn't know the answer.

'He's an honourable guy,' she said, 'and he feels guilty. And I'm sure he misses the children, especially Christo. But yes, he's happy. Frances gives him what he needs. She's very bright, shares his interests. No children. They are very wrapped up in each other and in politics. He's a senior civil servant at the Treasury. In line for the top job.'

Peter touched her bare arm and said, 'I should go. You're getting cold.'

They stood up and walked the few yards to the front door. Peter's awkwardness seemed to return to him in the light of the doorway, and his hand fluttered to his head as he said, 'Goodnight, Lotte. Thank you for coming.'

Lotte put her bare arms briefly round his neck and hugged him. 'It was a lovely evening. And thanks for letting me go on so. I haven't talked to anyone about all that for years. Not since the start, when I'd burst into tears and tell hapless strangers my life was in ruins!'

Peter bore the hug, his body rigid, his hand stiffly patting her shoulder. He said, 'I enjoyed listening to you,' which can't have been true, Lotte thought. All the same, I hope I haven't driven him off. I'd forgotten how good it is to have a friend.

Late one July evening Sam collected the children for a weekend in London and Lotte waved them off with unforced smiles. She even managed a more or less affectionate kiss for Sam. For the first time, his taking them felt like liberation, not deprivation. Feeling cheerful and free, Lotte set off for the West Woods to continue her search for the famous old Pond Yards.

She walked slowly across the park, revelling in the freedom to enjoy it. All day she'd felt the strain of pushing everyone, of jobs half done or not started, of paths not weeded, beds not dug over, borders not cut back or dead-headed, compost heaps not turned, brush not shredded. Once upon a time gardening, she supposed, had been a fairly peaceful occupation. Now there was no slack at all. She carried a mobile phone and a pager, just as she had as an architect, in case one of her staff or the Keegans or the land agent needed her. So much for the peace of the countryside.

At the edge of the woods, she suddenly felt reluctant to leave the sun and plunge into the shade for yet another fruitless search for the ponds. So she sat on the grass with her arms round her knees, looking over the lake to her left and ahead to the house, across the park, trying to imagine it as it had once been.

The modern house was clearly Georgian, but she was

sure the cellars under the central octagonal part were much older. Maybe Elizabethan? They were stone, with arched barrel ceilings. Maybe Sir Francis Maydowne had originally built that hunting-lodge just where the present house was.

Lotte scanned the park, imagining where else you might put a house. But the obvious place seemed to be exactly where it was, in the lee of the hill, with a magnificent view down the valley, sheltered by woods on the windward side. Except, of course, the woods might not have been there then.

At some point, certainly, someone had dug some fish-ponds somewhere. And fish-ponds would have been near the river. The area called 'Old Pond Yards' on her 1934 map must have been the place. Of course, the earliest pools might have existed even before Sir Francis's game lodge or mansion. They could have replaced older ones. If Peter was right and the land was confiscated from a Catholic order, they could have been stew-ponds for a mediaeval nunnery, or an abbey or priory.

Lotte took out her old Ordnance Survey map and unfolded it on the grass. The words 'Old Pond Yards' drew her like a magnet. Surely some evidence of them must remain. Modern maps made no mention of them at all, just showing the area as forested. But in 1934 when this map was printed, enough of the ponds must have remained to justify the words. The trouble was, pin-pointing their position was well-nigh impossible: 'Old Pond Yards' covered most of the eighteen acres of woods. The ponds could be anywhere.

Lotte had made frequent forays into the woods, hoping

to find something. But brambles, impenetrable laurels and waist-high nettles made anything other than sticking to the few narrow paths impossible. She was beginning to think she should cut her losses, and encourage her boss to bring in his bulldozers and build his wretched sculpture trail.

She needed a helicopter, that was what, so she could look down from above and see where the woods grew thicker and greener, indicating a spring or underground river. But Brody had flatly refused to take her up in his chopper. She suspected he knew very well where any stream had run – he flew over his park several times a week on his way to London. But he was set on planting modern sculpture along a twisting path through the woods, and wasn't going to give Lotte's ideas any oxygen. She wrapped her arms around her knees and gazed across the park. There had to be a way to persuade Brody.

Suddenly Lotte's heart skipped a beat. Her face became rigid, her eyes staring towards the house. Then she stood up quickly and hurried along the edge of the woods, her face turned intently towards the house all the time. She was looking at three oak trees in the park: trees she'd seen a hundred times and whose girth and breadth she'd frequently marvelled at. But she'd never looked at them from this angle. As she half ran, half walked, her conviction strengthened. When she'd gone perhaps fifty yards, she let out a triumphant shout: 'Yes, that's it. That's it!'

The trees were planted in a perfect line. Lotte knew with utter certainty that they were the remains of an avenue, a grand eighteenth-century avenue of oaks, leading the gentry in shaded seclusion to the water gardens. Such avenues were classic. She'd seen them many times on old estate maps. Lined up as they were now, they were an arrow to where her old Pond Yards were. She was sure of it.

7. Late Summer

Rubbish smokes at the end of the garden,
Cracking its knuckles to pass the time.

Craig Raine (1944–), 'Karma'

That's the first time, Lotte thought, that Jade has smiled at me with genuine warmth. She looked at the young woman's startlingly pearly teeth and full lips. It was a wide, toothpaste-commercial smile, but above it the eyes were real: excited and pleased, quite unlike her usual slightly scornful gaze.

'But would we ever get planning permission?' Jade said.

'I don't see why not. It doesn't interfere with the oldest cellars.' Lotte shuffled the plans to pull out the one she wanted. 'What it amounts to is flooding the largest of the later ones. It's deeper than the rest, though we may need to dig down a bit more. And it has a curved end wall to support the bow-front to the library above.' She used her pencil, poised above the drawing but not touching it, to trace the curve of the wall. 'And with a pool in there and good lighting of the vaulted ceiling, you'd show off the stonework beautifully. We'd be restoring and displaying, more than desecrating.'

'Yeah,' cried Jade. 'It will be brilliant. And the sound

down there is fantastic. We could have a great sound system.'

Lotte was pleased. She hadn't thought Jade, who tended to block her ideas if she could, would be so enthusiastic. But then she remembered that Jade thought this was all Brody's idea.

She gathered up her sketches and plans and said, 'Of course it will cost an arm and a leg.'

'No problem,' Jade replied.

And indeed there wasn't. At least, not over the money. Brody, as usual, took the project over, and had labourers digging up the cellar floor within two weeks. Lotte, a little put out at being sidelined from her own design, left him to it and got on with the garden.

One afternoon she found a builder's skip parked on the camomile lawn she had just planted. A conveyor belt was trundling soil and rubble up from the cellar through the old coal chute, dropping it into the skip.

Lotte stood with her mouth open, appalled. 'The unthinking bastard,' she muttered. 'How could he?' At least 200 plants were under the skip and quite as many around it were being churned into the ground by the builders. Her heart thumping with anger, she went in search of Brody.

She found him in the cellar with the builder, Barry. Barry was looking anxious and Brody was laughing. 'Of course I know I haven't got planning permission. And I'm not sodding going to apply for it either. What can they do if they don't like it? Ask me to restore the cellar to an unusable hell-hole?' He clapped Barry lightly on the back.

Barry opened his mouth to reply, but Brody converted his back-slap into a brief hug and said, 'Don't you worry, my old son. It will be fine. If a man can't dig up his own cellar . . .'

Brody caught sight of Lotte, and his smile broadened. 'Well, Lotte, what do you think?' He came towards her, his eyes alight.

She stared angrily back. 'I think it's criminal to put the skip on my newly planted camomile lawn. Brody, how could you?'

His chin went up. 'What are you talking about?'

'I'm talking about six hundred camomile plants. Extinguished under your skip, or being trampled to death all around it.'

'Camomile lawn? Whatever's that?' He didn't look particularly contrite, but he ended with, 'Let's go see.' And Lotte followed him up the stairs, mentally muttering, 'Bastard' to herself again.

Brody looked at the muddied plants. 'Are those something that matters? They look like weeds to me. And anyway, this was a flower-bed, right? We had those great red things, dahlias, in here, didn't we? I assumed you'd cleared everything out and were about to put some more in.'

'Brody, you can't have thought perfectly raked tilth, and little plants all in rows, all carefully watered, were weeds!'

'Were they in rows? Or watered? I didn't notice.' He was smiling, and Lotte had the feeling he was teasing her. He said, 'OK, I'm sorry. But it doesn't matter, does it?'

Lotte looked at the remains of her camomile patch,

gritting her teeth. 'Yes, it does,' she replied. 'It matters because Andrew and I worked all yesterday at it. It matters because you didn't consult me . . .'

'Hey, Lotte, be fair, I don't have to ask the gardener's permission to bring a skip into my own garden, now do I?'

Lotte wanted to say, yes, you do. Instead she said, 'No, but it would help if you liaised with me. This was to have been a mown lawn. Camomile smells wonderful when you walk or sit on it. And the green would look much better than flowers against the stone.'

Brody put his hands on her shoulders. 'And how about you liaising with me? Maybe I don't want a what-ever-you-call-it lawn. Have you thought of that then?'

Lotte was silent, seeing the justice of this, but still resenting it. She also resented his hands on her shoulders. What was this, *droit de seigneur*?

He shook her slightly, trying to make her look at him. 'Poor Lotte. Don't be mad at me. (a) I didn't mean it. And (b) it's not the end of the world, there must be more where those came from.'

Lotte wanted to maintain her anger, but it was leaching away. Brody was like a clumsy child, you had to let him off. She tried to be professional. 'But if you don't want a camomile lawn, we won't need any more. I suggest we leave decisions until the builders are gone.'

She sounded petulant, but she couldn't help it. She turned abruptly so he had to drop his hands, and said, 'I'll get a barrow and see what I can rescue. We might use the plants somewhere.'

As she walked away she was conscious of his gaze, and

she knew he was smiling. Unthinking oaf. How can he prefer pom-pom dahlias to a cool green camomile lawn?

Jo-Jo was standing on a wooden box so she could stir the white sauce comfortably. Lotte was teaching her to make lasagne.

'It's bubbling, Mum.'

'OK, then. Now take it off and put it on the table. And stir in the cheese.'

Jo-Jo brought the saucepan carefully to the table, and before Lotte could stop her she had dropped a half-pound slab of cheddar into it.

Lotte grabbed a pair of tongs and fished out the cheese. 'Jo-Jo!' she said. 'Read the recipe first, remember?'

'What? What's wrong?' wailed Jo Jo.

Lotte rinsed the cheese under the cold tap, dried it on a paper towel and handed it back to Jo-Jo.

'*A hundred grams of grated cheese* is what it says, dum-dum, not two hundred and fifty grams in a lump.' Lotte kissed the nine-year-old's head and said, 'Try again.'

Jo-Jo picked up the grater and, solemn with concentration, started to grate the cheese.

Christo came in. 'I'm starving. When's supper?'

'Seven-thirty. Peter's coming.'

Christo groaned. 'Why can't he come earlier? We always have to wait hours and hours for him.'

Lotte started to explain that Peter only left work at six, and liked to get home and change into something casual, but Jo-Jo silenced her with, 'I suppose you're going to marry Peter. Then he can live here, and we can have supper when we want.'

'She can't marry Peter, stupid. She's still married to Dad,' said Christo. 'Aren't you, Mum?' His voice was confident but his eyes were anxious.

Lotte ruffled his straight blond hair, feeling it flick coolly through her fingers. She pulled him to her and said, 'That's right, darling. We're still married. And no, Jo-Jo, I am not going to marry Peter! What on earth gave you that idea?'

'He likes you a lot. I can tell,' said Jo-Jo. 'And you are always ringing him up. And asking him to supper and stuff.'

It was true. Peter had got into the habit of coming to supper at Gardener's Cottage twice a week. He'd bring his latest discoveries from the Maddon Archive, and after supper he and Lotte would work on them together at the kitchen table.

Lotte explained that she saw a lot of Peter because he was helping her with the history of Maddon. 'And he's a good friend,' she said. 'I like him. Don't you?'

'He's OK. Only he's very old,' said Jo-Jo. Christo offered no opinion but his gaze was still intent and anxious. Oh God, thought Lotte, I don't want to cause them any more hurt. She said, 'But I suppose it's possible that Dad and I will get a divorce some day. Dad might want to marry Frances, don't you think?'

Christo frowned but didn't pursue it. And mercifully Jo-Jo's lasagne claimed her attention. 'Can I do the layers now?'

Lotte left Christo supervising Jo-Jo's efforts and went into the garden for the salad. It was a cloudy evening, and cool, but she dawdled over her task, rinsing baby beetroots under the tap, pinching out the tops of the basil plants to stop them flowering, and winnowing the dried-up chives from the green and perfect ones. She held the cut bunch by the top and gave it a gentle shake to dislodge the shorter dead leaves. Then she spread the rest on her palm and picked out those already striped or tipped with brown.

Of course the idea of Peter as a mate had occurred to her. Once or twice she'd even fantasized about a long-term deal. But she wasn't ready to consider the question out loud. The relationship was nowhere near that. Peter had never kissed her, not even on the cheek, nor hinted at anything beyond friendship. But the friendship bit was fine. He was good company, easy and relaxed.

And he'd proved a godsend on the archive. His research was meticulous and methodical. He would go through an account book or a rent book, reading every line and noting anything interesting in a plain bound book, recording the source and date before each entry. He colour-coded his entries too, so that later he could easily pick out all the references to the tenants' cottages, for example, or the productive garden, or the main house.

Lotte's method was more instinctive and haphazard. Excited by something in one of the Ferguson journals – she'd taken to reading them in bed before she went to sleep – she'd roam the estate, searching. She'd guessed the mount Ferguson had been mowing in June 1860 would be the overgrown hill on the western side of the house, just in the park. It had always looked too surprising, too high, too perfectly positioned, not to be man-made. She persuaded Peter to explore it with her. They clambered up the steep sides and found the remains of the corkscrew path winding to the top. The path had been solidly built. It was cut, like terracing, into the side of the hill, with brick and stone foundations under the once grassy path – a perfect snail mount, probably built in the seventeenth century, maybe even the sixteenth, to provide a vantage point for viewing the lake or looking down on elaborate terraces.

Brody had got very excited about the mount, and was, as always, impatient for results. 'But Lott, why can't we clear the rest of it now? Why wait?'

'Because I can't spare the labour. We are flat-out mowing and dead-heading and trying to keep the gardens looking good. That mount is a massive job. It may not look so big from here, but the path is nearly a third of a mile long, and it's all overgrown.'

'Well, hire some more labour, woman!'

Lotte took Brody at his word, and employed a young woman, tired of working in Tesco, and an older builder with a background in agricultural drainage. They were a terrific pair: the builder, Robert, behaved like a foreman and the girl, Molly, did what she was told. She used loppers and secateurs, and he wielded the chain-saw.

Within a fortnight you could see the whole shape of the old mount. They had cut away all the saplings and bushes and strimmed the grass, revealing the shape of the hill. The path was a good five feet wide, edged with the square blocks, and it hugged the hill tightly, spiralling shallowly to the top.

Now they were grinding or digging out the roots and rebuilding broken sections of the path. Lotte had wanted to suppress the weeds for a year with black plastic, and reseed the spring after next. But Brody always scoffed at her eco-friendly instincts and insisted she spray the whole hill with Roundup, then get a turf contractor in.

The pursuit of Maddon's past was becoming a mutual obsession for Lotte and Peter, but as yet Lotte had failed really to draw Brody in. He liked the drama of the mount, even speculating about Victorian ladies with crinolines and corsets, parasols and pretty boots sweating their way to the top, but he thought that searching for ponds so derelict and overgrown that no one knew they were there was ridiculous. And when they'd found the remains of the ice-house mentioned in the archive, and Lotte had taken him to see it, he had been completely baffled.

'This is it?' he said.

Lotte showed him the low wall, now part of a rockery in front of the tennis court. 'Look,' she said, 'I've dug down a bit here and you can see where the perfect dry-walling is going. It's half under the tennis court, I think. And I'm sure it goes much deeper. Ice-houses used to be —'

'Lotte, you lunatic,' Brody interrupted, 'I don't see an ice-house. I see a bit of busted wall and a rockery and tennis court. The last thing we need is an ice-house! No one, since the invention of electric refrigeration, has needed an ice-house!'

On reflection, even Lotte could not see the point of excavating it. She was keen to direct Brody's attention, and his money, towards the garden, and to the Old Pond Yards. The ice-house could wait.

Lotte looked at her watch. Peter would be here any minute. She tucked the chives into one end of her trug, then rapidly picked some runner beans to go with the lasagne and a bunch of the last sweet peas for the table. She was looking forward to seeing him.

That evening at supper Annie announced, 'Peter is going to teach me to ride his bike.'

Lotte lowered her forkful of lasagne, her mouth open. After a second she said, 'He most certainly is not.' She turned to Peter. 'How could you suggest that? She's only thirteen.'

Peter's hand flew to his high bald crown. 'Oh dear,' he said. 'Is that bad? I didn't mean . . .'

'It's not legal. She's a child.'

'It's just an idea. Annie is interested in bikes. She knows a lot . . .'

Lotte snapped, 'And anyway, it's dangerous, and I'd never allow it.'

No one said anything, and Lotte looked from Peter's troubled eyes behind his glasses to Annie's pink face, set in resentment. Then Peter said, 'It wouldn't be dangerous if we went slowly. We were only discussing whether we could ask Brody —'

'What has Brody got to do with it?' Lotte interrupted. Before Peter could answer she turned to her daughter. 'Annie, what is all this nonsense?'

Annie raised her eyes to the ceiling and then shut them as she gave an exaggerated sigh. 'Don't freak, Mum. Peter just thought that since Maddon has miles of private roads and lanes he could teach me on them.'

'You can get killed on a private road just as quick as on a public one,' rapped Lotte, looking not at Annie but at the beleaguered Peter.

'Oh dear,' he said again, his fingers still tapping his forehead. 'Maybe we should just forget it . . .'

Immediately Lotte felt like a bully, and said, 'Oh Peter, it's a nice idea. But I really don't think . . .'

Annie saw her mother weakening and was in like a knife. 'Mum, please. PLEASE. I won't do anything stupid. I'm not an idiot. I don't want to kill myself, you know. Even if living in the country is dire. But it would be something to do.'

In the end Lotte gave in, with conditions: no faster than thirty mph; hard hats; never without Peter on the pillion.

As Lotte washed up that night, she found she was humming. It had turned out a really nice evening, with the children talkative and relaxed. Peter was good with them. And he was such a nice guy. He'd eaten two helpings of Jo-Jo's lasagne. And taken the sweet peas home with him, saying she could pick some more, but his garden didn't sport such luxuries.

8. Early Autumn

And after having remained at the entry some time, two contrary
emotions arose in me, fear and desire, fear of the threatening
dark grotto, desire to see whether there were any marvellous
things within it.

Leonardo da Vinci (1459–1513)

Lotte and Peter looked down at a square sheet of thick
paper laid on the table in the St Aldwyn's library. The
edges were ragged and worn, and the writing, in ink, had
faded to a pale lilac. But the words 'Madden Pools' and
the date '1740' were clearly legible.

The two pencil drawings which occupied most of
the page were as clear as though drawn yesterday. The
smaller one was a sketch of a rounded grotto with a
stepping-stone path to it across a rock-fringed pool. A
waterfall splashed into the pool on the right, and a sculpture of a seated merman adorned a large overhanging rock
to the left.

The larger drawing was of the interior treatment of the
grotto, showing a wide stone seat jutting out of the rock,
with the whole wall behind studded with an inlay of
pebbles and shells. Swagged garlands of bunched-together
shells decorated the top of the wall and surrounded what

looked like two inset mirrors, each side of the seat. Under this drawing was a pencilled 'E.F.'.

Lotte whispered, 'It's wonderful. Perfect.' She looked up at Peter, her eyes round. She said, 'Oh, we've got to find it. We've just got to.'

'Your voice is shaking,' said Peter.

'I'm shaking all over.' Lotte laughed and darted round the table to hug Peter. 'Oh, you are such a clever man. You've unearthed . . .'

Her chatter was extinguished by Peter's response. Usually he bore her affection with stiff awkwardness, but now he pulled her into his chest.

Lotte drew back to look into his face. His big glasses obscured his eyes and she could not see his expression. But he tightened his hold, and Lotte could sense his desperation.

Suddenly sober, she said, 'Hey, what's this? Let me go.'

Peter held her gaze as he swallowed and shook his head. 'I can't. I can't let you go. Not ever.'

This close, Peter smelt tweedy and warm. It was somehow comfortable. Even tempting. But she looked over his shoulder and said lightly, 'Darling Peter, you'll have to. Two of your scholars have just come in the door.'

Walking back to her car, Lotte was still astonished at Peter's declaration. He was such a teddy-bear of a man: shy, nice, undemanding, not at all sexy. She tried to tell herself that such uncharacteristic behaviour was the result of shared excitement over the discovery of the archive drawings, that it was a spur-of-the-moment thing. That, in retrospect, he would be relieved that the arrival of the students had put a stop to whatever was going on, that he would be as keen as her to forget it ever happened.

And indeed what had happened? Nothing really. She'd hugged Peter. He'd hugged her back. And then talked some nonsense about not letting her go.

But was it nonsense? And was she keen to forget it? For a second, even as she told him to let go, she'd wanted to kiss him instead. To wipe the anxiety and desperation off his face by just giving him what he wanted. Why not? They were good together. She liked him. She could easily love him.

She already depended on him. Their Tuesday and Friday ritual of supper and poring over documents had first been welcome therapy that stopped her feeling sorry for herself. In London and at horticultural college, she'd kept self-pity at bay by constant work and permanent exhaustion. And she had friends in London, which helped.

But the first three or four months at Maddon had been harder in some ways. Of course the job was wonderful, but it had not been unadulterated bliss. She'd been keenly aware how much the children, especially Annie, missed their London life.

And Jade's near-hostility increasingly upset her. Last month, Lotte had been at the top of a sixteen-foot ladder, cutting back *Rosa banksii* on the side of the house, when Jade had appeared at the bottom.

'Lotte,' she'd said. 'I need my car washed and polished. By twelve. Will you see to it?' She didn't wait for an answer, but disappeared back into the house.

Irritated, Lotte climbed down the ladder. Why couldn't

Jade just pick up the phone to the chauffeur? – all the senior staff wore pagers at their belts. She was tempted to follow Jade into the house and offer to call him herself.

Instead, she walked the few hundred yards to the stable yard. There was no one in the old barn, now used as a garage. Jade's red Porsche crouched next to Brody's jeep. It was streaked with mud.

Lotte looked at her watch. Nine-thirty. Plenty of time for Duncan to get the car done. She went into the workshop and found a pen and paper. She wrote: 'Mrs Keegan wants her car washed by noon.' She picked up the workshop telephone and left the same message on Duncan's pager. Then she went back to cutting the fountain of fronds from the climbing rose.

Her mood lifted as she worked. Trimming the rose flat to the wall was very satisfying. The new growth was vigorous, green and glossy and, best of all, thornless. It was easy work, and she liked being high up and alone. The only danger was of the ladder slipping. But she was careful to jam the legs between the paving-slabs each time she moved the ladder to the next section of wall.

She was nearly done, the terrace heaped with piles of prunings, the wall looking neat and orderly, when Jade appeared again. 'For Christ's sake, Lotte. I told you to clean my bloody car.'

Lotte looked down at Jade's furious face. 'I left two messages for Duncan. Didn't he do it?'

Jade shook the ladder, and Lotte half climbed, half jumped down. She didn't think Jade meant to dislodge her, but she wasn't going to chance it. Jade shouted, 'Of course he bloody didn't. He's got the day off to go to a funeral, which is why I told you to do it. Duncan's just rung to say he got a message on his pager. Why can't you just do what you're fucking told?'

Lotte felt anger and shock flood her face. She turned away for a second, struggling not to explode, then turned back and said as levelly as she could, 'Look, Jade, if you had explained the problem, I probably would have washed your car for you. But since you just told me to get it done, I assumed you meant give the message to the chap who is paid to do it.'

'Are you refusing to wash my car?'

Lotte was about to say, yes, too right I am, when she caught the look of triumph in Jade's eyes. No, she thought, I'm not falling into that trap. She said, 'No, I'll do it now, madam.'

She walked away swiftly, feeling a momentary flush of triumph. That 'madam' had been insolent in the extreme, but Jade could hardly object.

Relations had improved, especially since Jade was to get her cellar gym and pool, for which Lotte had somehow reassumed responsibility. She bugged Lotte a bit about whether the builders would be finished in time (she was planning a celebrity launch in a month) but she hadn't been rude in weeks. Sometimes Lotte almost liked her.

But Lotte had to admit the main reason for her in-creased content was Peter.

Since she'd met him in August his presence, and his interest in Maddon's history, had made a huge difference. Now, if Sam and his betrayal of her invaded her thoughts, which to her shame sometimes still happened, Lotte could push them out, just by thinking about the archive project.

She wanted to keep Peter's friendship, and she didn't want to jeopardize it with a love affair.

The sight of her car in the car park pulled Lotte back to the present. As she threw her canvas hold-all into the back seat, she glanced at the parked cars, half fearing some College functionary would challenge her right to park there. Peter, who went about on his motorbike, had given her his sticker. But there was no one about, and she slipped into the driving seat with relief.

Lotte flicked on the radio and concentrated on getting through the traffic. She collected the chain-saw and strimmer she'd left at the repair shop in Fyfield, and headed home. As she drew up at the humpback bridge over the Isis and waited for the oncoming traffic, her thoughts were still on Peter and his curious mix of scholarly pursuits and schoolboy enthusiasms, the way he'd never notice if she was in jeans or her party best, yet he'd exclaim over a jug of flowers or the basil in a salad dressing.

Lotte didn't see Brody in his open Jaguar until the last second, when he was almost level with her. She just had time to catch his wave and flashing grin, and he was past her and gone.

She found she was smiling. What an idiot that man is, she thought, driving around with the top down in chilly October. What was it with men? Brody was seriously rich, and successful at whatever business he touched, yet he was never happier than when playing with his toys: customized X-type; helicopter; ludicrously huge Jeep; he even liked driving the gang mower, though Lotte disapproved because he went too fast and the rotary units jumped and failed to mow evenly.

And even Peter, scholarly, nice, eccentric archivist, was in love with motorbikes. Last night he and Annie had been discussing the relative merits of the Harley Davidson and something called a Ducati. Annie had listened to him expounding on torque and speed with the look of a doting disciple.

The following day Lotte was shredding the brush from the mount, adding it to the pile which would be next year's coarse mulch for the hosta beds and cutting garden, when someone tapped her shoulder from behind.

She swung round to see Peter, looking anxious. He was in a suit, and his fingers, as always when he was nervous, were massaging his brow. In his other hand was a briefcase.

Oh dear, thought Lotte, pulling off her goggles and ear-cans, and flicking the switch to silence the deafening din of the shredder, that little scene in the library is going to spoil everything. If he's here in the middle of a working day to apologize it will make a mountain out of a molehill. Worse, maybe he was going to tell her he loved her.

'What's up?' she said, kissing him lightly on the cheek.

'I couldn't wait, Lotte,' he said, 'I have to tell you.'

Lotte steeled herself for a declaration. She was touched, but she'd much rather he didn't say anything. She stalled with, 'Peter, look, I'm not ready . . .'

But Peter was waving his briefcase. 'Can we sit somewhere?' he said. 'I've got to show you this.'

Intrigued, Lotte led him to the mess-room, where she and the other gardeners took their breaks. It was a big room with a wood-burning stove, an old deep sink and half a dozen arm-chairs, stained and old, but comfortable.

They sat down and Peter looked dubiously at the none too clean coffee table between them. Lotte got a J-cloth from the sink and wiped the surface. He said, 'Sorry, just habit. Taking papers out of the archive and reading them in a gardener's snug is probably a sackable offence.' He flipped the case open, extracted a big manila envelope and slid its contents on to the table.

'Remember the E.F. on the drawing? The initials under the interior sketch of the grotto? Well, that rang a bell. And the sketch was dated 1740. So it was easy. I knew there were some eighteenth-century letters, and I looked through them for the period. Twenty or so are to Emma Fernley, daughter of the house. And guess what?'

Lotte's eyes were wide with expectation, and her heart started to thump hard and high in her chest.

'What?'

Peter opened one of the letters and said, 'I think they are from an aunt or cousin. Anyway, a female relative, Winifred Maud. It's not dated, sadly. But listen:

It is wise to decide before you begin, whether the grotto is to be adorned with crystalline minerals or with sea-shells, or with both together, and whether the style is to be formal, or natural. You must consider too, whether it is primarily for the interest of men of scientific leaning and as a stage for your father's collection. Think also, whether you wish to use formers to make stalactites for the roof. This would use the quartz, feldspar and gypsum most handsomely to give the effect of a limestone cave.

But perhaps it is for the delight of the ladies, to go into a

119

gothick cave, charmingly clothed in shells and crystals. If the latter your endeavour must to be make it pretty, and amusing, and to look well.

Peter looked up, his dark eyes intense behind his glasses. 'Good, isn't it?' He passed her the letter, saying, 'Perhaps Emma Fernley did her drawing as a result of this letter. If so, she seems to have taken the pretty option.'

Lotte was too astonished and delighted to speak. She looked dumbly at the careful, educated writing with its long s's looking like f's and its underlined abbreviations. Then Peter was saying, 'There are two more references to the grotto, in letters from the same woman – the first two years later, and the last seven months after that. The grotto must have been built around 1741, because this advice was obviously given before Emma began to decorate it, and by the next reference, in 1743, she's hard at it.'

He read the first passage to her:

I rejoice that the shell-sticking is going well. Do not finish the whole roof before I can come and make at least one small corner my own. Ammonites are best on the floor I think, and Mrs Delany's technique of setting her shells on their edge, and using them to make swags to resemble flower garlands is most effective. You are wise to seek her counsel.

Lotte shot forward. 'Mrs Delany? Mary Delany?' she said.

'No mention of Mary. Why? Does Mrs Delany mean something?'

Lotte almost shouted, 'Mean something? She most certainly does. She's the eighteenth-century queen of shellwork. If we have a Mary Delany grotto in the woods, we *have* to find it. Oh, Peter, I can't believe it.'

Peter sat forward in his chair, carefully unfolding the last of his letters. 'The only other reference I could find was this: "*I weep for you, dear Emma, at the loss of the* Esmeralda. *Your father must be much distressed. To have five hundred guineas of shells, already paid for, returned to the watery deep, must be very vexing.*"'

Lotte looked into Peter's face. 'Grotto builders imported shells from the West Indies. They paid a fortune for them . . .'

'And the *Esmeralda* must have sunk with the Fernleys' haul on board,' Peter finished for her.

They looked at each other for a moment, then Peter said, 'In the first letter, Winifred mentions the father's collection, doesn't she? And then ammonites. Maybe he collected shells and fossils as well as rocks.'

Lotte leant back in her chair, her face excited and happy. 'We have to find that grotto,' she said, 'or we'll never know.'

When Peter went back to work, and Lotte returned to her shredder, neither had mentioned the scene at St Aldwyn's the previous day. Lotte was glad. But some perverse bit of her was pleased it had happened, too. It was good to be desired.

Within weeks, Peter and Lotte knew a lot more about Maddon. Lotte's cache from the safe contained a receipt for mosaic tiles in 1872, with a pencilled 'Persian pool' written across the top in Ferguson's hand. The journal for that year was missing, so Lotte could not establish if the pool had been built then. But a trawl through the Ferguson log for 1874 contained the entry:

Lord Quentin has determined to sell the merman statue, and replace it with an Arabic vase, not yet purchased. Until such time we are to plant ferns on the rock and buy more tiles to complete the space.

Peter also married drawings from the safe for the melon and pine houses to a plan for the kitchen garden, which already showed the orchid house, heated walls for espaliered fruit trees, and sloping glasshouses for vines and figs.

Lotte now knew exactly what the nineteenth-century walled garden had looked like. It pleased her to think she was occupying the house of her Victorian predecessor. There was not one word about Ferguson's wife or family, but as she read his log she began to understand his professional life.

Ferguson had ruled a team of twenty-five. Lotte imagined him making his rounds, giving instructions to his three foremen in charge of fruit, vegetables and flowers respectively. He would oversee the lighting of the fires to warm the fruit-tree walls, the stoking of the big boiler that heated the forcing-room, the tying of asparagus bunches with raffia for the cook, the dispatch of perfect peaches to the big house, the growing of orchids in pots for the jardinières; the provision of fresh vegetables to be put on the train for London. He'd never address anyone as lowly as an apprentice or journeyman gardener, much less one of the weeder women paid by the basket to weed or pick stones out of the ground. He must be turning in his grave, thought Lotte, to see a woman in his job.

Lotte wondered who the gardener was in 1740, when Emma Fernley was making her grotto. Did he disapprove of such frippery, or did he regard the daughter of the house as a creature from a higher planet, almost a goddess?

9. Autumn

In all, let Nature never be forgot.
Consult the genius of the place in all.

Alexander Pope (1688–1744),
'Of Taste'

Brody always enjoyed his monthly meetings with Lotte, but he was particularly looking forward to this one. He wanted to see that obstinate woman approve of something he wished to do for a change. This time she'd have to, since his plans were the kind she might have thought up herself: historical, old, traditional. Maybe her obsession with garden history was catching. He'd never agree to her mad ideas about the ponds of course. But he did like the mount. Once it was returfed it would look amazing, like a giant green jelly-mould rising out of the park. Jade wanted to put a gazebo on top of it but of course Lotte disagreed.

Brody scrolled through his 'tasks to do' on his computer, and frowned at the 'Ring Leslie' entry. His accountant would give him an earful about the money he was spending. You'd think he was my mother, Brody thought.

Nevertheless, he brought up the Maddon Garden spreadsheet and ran his eye down the left-hand column: projects already done or committed to included the mount, restoring the largest of the greenhouses, the dry-stone wall round the west boundary of the park, the fencing round the whole estate, the restoration and replanting of the drive and the relaying of the entire terrace. To say nothing of the day-to-day expenditure on gardeners, machines, materials and plants.

Brody scrolled down to see the projected total for the year. His eyes widened at the total: £1,402,240, and that was before he put his new garden plans into action. And before adding the work on the house.

He pressed a few keys and the Maddon House spreadsheet appeared. Jade's cellar was going to cost £420,000, give or take a few grand. Then, if they carried out the house plans Jade and the fancy decorator were plotting, that figure would double. And restoring the stable yard and turning the old grooms' quarters into guest-rooms would cost another half a million at least.

Leslie was right, a country estate needed a bottomless purse. Brody leant back, smiling. Lucky I've got one then, he thought. And anyway, it's only money.

He continued the debate with his accountant in his head: just as well I can promise Leslie that Jade's birthday present is a sure-fire investment, he thought. We can always hock it if things ever get tight.

Brody hadn't told even Lotte about this, although it was Lotte who had first suggested it. The *pièce de résistance* which was to complete the basement works was a surprise, to be unveiled at Jade's party next month. She was going to love it.

His wife seemed a lot happier, looking forward to her party. And since last week's trip to France, she was at last showing an interest in the grounds. The sooner they got on with their new ideas the better.

Brody dismissed the spreadsheets with a click of the mouse and stood up.

Where the hell was Lotte? It was unlike her to be late. He took the two booklets he needed from his briefcase, then walked over to the window. And there she was, walking fast, hidden under a golf umbrella. All he could see were her rain-glossed black Wellingtons glinting as she hurried across the gravel.

Brody's study window looked on to the porch, and Lotte, busy shaking the water from her umbrella and kicking off her boots, didn't see him, two feet away. He watched her wobble on one foot and then on the other as she pulled on her moccasins, and then, as she waited for someone to answer the doorbell, she put her fingers under her hair and fluffed it about, pulling a few bits of fringe over her forehead. Brody, his hand raised to tap on the window, brought it down and turned away. He suddenly felt he'd been spying on her.

Lotte came in smiling. 'Oh Brody, I'm so sorry I'm late. I was deep in a mower maintenance lesson, and completely forgot the time.'

'Are you learning mower maintenance?' Brody said, his eyebrows shooting up in surprise.

'No, I'm teaching Andrew and the two students. Andrew is not one of nature's natural mechanics, it has to be said. But he's getting there. The lads have more of a clue.'

'But why don't you send the mowers to the workshop?' Brody asked.

'Because, if Andrew would only look after the things,

they'd need to go in less often for major surgery. And when it's tipping down like today, he might as well be doing something useful.'

'I'm impressed,' Brody said. 'How about some coffee? You must be freezing.'

'I'm fine. But I'd love some coffee. Thanks.'

Brody picked up the telephone to buzz the kitchen and said, 'Oh, hello, darling, what are you doing there? I was looking for Jean-Christophe or Mark or someone to make us some coffee. Oh . . . Well, sweetheart, how about you do it? Come and join us. I'm going to explain our Villandry scheme to Lotte.' There was a pause and then he said, 'Fine,' and put down the telephone.

Brody felt a moment's disappointment. He found he didn't want Jade in on the meeting. She always seemed so hostile to Lotte. He said, 'Jade's making the coffee and coming to join us.'

He pulled his booklets towards him. 'You know Jade and I have been in France? Well, you'll be pleased to hear we've been visiting gardens. To get ideas for Maddon. We went to Versailles, and to Villandry, and to half a dozen other French châteaux on the Loire whose names I'll never remember.'

He paused, waiting for Lotte to be impressed. But she said nothing. She just looked faintly alarmed. Brody leant forward across the desk.

'Anyway, the upshot is, we've decided to have a vegetable garden like Villandry's in the walled garden, and fountains on the terrace – we'll have to extend it of course. And then a maze in the park, just the other side of the ha-ha.' He sat back, sleek with satisfaction.

But Lotte still didn't respond. Too surprised, Brody thought. It's quite a lot to take in at once.

Then Lotte said, 'You want fancy-shaped beds and box edging and gravel paths and decorative veg in the walled garden?'

'Yes, exactly. Have you been to Villandry? Well, you must have or you wouldn't know all that. It's fantastic, isn't it? Amazing. They've got these amazing purple and white cabbages. And some frilly sort of kale. Not to eat. Just to look at.'

Before Lotte could answer, Jade came in carrying a tray. She sat down and set a mug of coffee in front of Brody and another in front of Lotte. 'I hope you like sugar.' She said this with finality, take it or leave it.

Brody winced. No good morning. No hello. He said, 'Lotte, do you take sugar?'

'Actually, I don't. But don't worry. I'm fine.'

Brody said, 'No, don't be silly. Jade will get you another, won't you, darling?' Oh, Christ, he thought, I bet she won't.

Jade pushed her own mug at Lotte and said, her voice sulky, 'Here, have mine. It hasn't got any sugar in it. Or any milk for that matter.'

'But don't you want –' Lotte began.

'For heaven's sake, just drink it, will you?' snapped Jade. Brody shut his eyes for a split second. Lotte cut in quickly. 'To get back to Villandry . . .'

Brody flashed her a look of gratitude and turned to Jade. 'Darling, I was explaining about our plan for a Villandry-style vegetable garden in the walled garden. Lotte has been to Villandry, so she knows what it's like.'

He opened the booklet in the middle, and across the double-page spread was a plan of one of the Villandry gardens with complicated patterns of box-edged formal beds. Each bed contained orderly rows or blocks of vegetables. The paths were of gravel, perfectly raked.

'And what's the verdict?' Jade asked, tipping her head back so her hair slithered past her ear as her chin came up.

'What do you mean?' Lotte sounded hurt and puzzled, Brody thought.

'Well, we all know Brody here won't make a move without your say-so. Never mind what I want. Or even what he wants. It's all, "We must ask Lotte", "Lotte will know" . . .'

'Jade,' Brody interjected, 'don't be daft. You and I decided on the Villandry vegetable garden. Not Lotte. I'm just confirming with Lotte . . .'

'Well, answer the question then, Lotte, and let's see.' Jade's eyes held Lotte's mercilessly. 'What do you think of the plan?'

Brody could see at once that Lotte was trapped. She wanted to confound Jade by agreeing it was a great idea, but she obviously didn't like it. And if Brody knew anything about Lotte, it was that she wouldn't just agree with the boss, like a good gardener should.

'Well?' Jade pressed, seeing her advantage. 'You don't like it, do you? And what Lotte doesn't like, Jade doesn't get. Right, Brody?' She stood up. 'But what the hell. I never cared that much anyway. Just don't give in on the fountains, Brody. I really, really want the fountains.' She walked fast across the room, both of them watching her swaying model's walk, the toss of that long blonde hair. She shut the door with an unnecessary jerk.

There was a short silence, then Brody said, 'Look, Lott, I'm really sorry. I don't know what's up with her. She's been upset ever since I told her – which was dead stupid of me – that the cellar scheme was your idea.'

It was true. Jade had promptly reverted to her old dislike of Lotte after being fine for weeks. He just didn't understand her. She was so capricious, it maddened and confused him.

'It's almost as if she was jealous of you,' he said, 'which is completely ridiculous, isn't it?'

As he said it, Brody realized that this wasn't the most tactful thing to say, but it was too late now. And Lotte would be too sensible to take offence, surely. She helped him out again by saying, 'She's quite right, though. I do think the vegetable parterre is a bad idea. Do you want to know why, or should I just bottle it?'

Brody was relieved she was smiling, but at the same time he felt childish disappointment. What was it with women? Why couldn't Lotte just agree with him? He was the guy spending the money. But he said, 'Go on then. What's wrong with Villandry?'

She told him, and he had to admit that she had a point. Several points. Flat patterns in a garden were best seen from above. Villandry's gardens were laid out under the châteaux's windows. No one in their right mind would put a decorative parterre hidden half a mile away from the house. The only beneficiaries at Maddon would be Lotte and her children. From the upper floors of Gardener's Cottage, they'd have a great view.

And then Villandry had thousands of visitors every year, so growing acres of unwanted vegetables destined for the compost heap made sense. The entrance fees paid for the labour and justified the waste.

Also, at Villandry they had lovingly restored what had been there once before. Maddon's walled garden had its own story, just as fascinating, and if they restored that, it would be beautiful too.

Brody didn't enjoy being put right, but he had to hand it to Lotte. She marshalled her arguments pretty well.

'OK. I'll think about the vegetable garden. But you'd better not kick up a fuss about the fountains. I've got it all worked out. We could pipe the water up from the river, and install a bloody great pump to get the pressure. Those fountains at Versailles go hundreds of feet into the air.'

Lotte was shaking her head, however, and Brody could feel irritation growing. Why did she have to object to everything? He said, 'Oh God, you're going to be boring again. Full of rational objections. As usual.' Her hurt face gave him a vicious little stab of pleasure.

In a neutral voice, Lotte replied, 'It won't work, Brody.'

'It will,' he said. 'I'll make it work.'

Lotte, eyes down and voice calm, moved Jade's undrunk coffee two inches to the left and said, 'For a start, we'd never get permission to take water out of the Isis.'

'Bugger that. I'll win them round, no trouble.' He flung himself back in his chair, head up. 'Any other objections?'

'Only that Versailles was a royal palace. I assume we are going to scale down the plan a bit to suit a modest Georgian manor house?' She lifted her eyes to meet his, her tone still polite, cool.

'You think I've got ideas above my station, do you?'

Lotte's silence gave him his answer, and he leant forward, his face alive with energy. 'Well, too right I have! I believe in ideas above one's station!'

There was another silence then while Lotte shifted the coffee mug back again. Brody stood up and walked round the table to sit on it above Lotte. She watched him as he moved round but dropped her eyes before he started speaking. This got to him too. If she'd only look at him, he'd persuade her. 'And I suppose you don't want a maze in the park either?' he challenged.

Lotte opened her mouth, then shut it again.

'Go on then, spit it out,' said Brody.

At last she looked up at him, and to his surprise her face was soft and open, not cold at all. 'Oh Brody, it's wonderful that you love Maddon so much. And that you want to do all these things. But you don't understand. It's so easy, so criminally easy, to spoil what has taken generations to achieve.' She stopped, and for a second, as she went back to delicately swivelling the coffee mug, Brody thought she'd finished. But she went on, 'Alexander Pope summed it up three hundred years ago: *consult the genius of the place in all*. In the first garden I ever had, when Sam and I were just married, I chopped down a *Deodara cedrus* – a cedar – because I'd decided I didn't like conifers. Now every time I see one, with their bright pendulous tips to every branch, I think how beautiful the one I chopped down would be by now, so accurately placed to give that ordinary suburban garden shape and interest.'

Brody said, 'Lotte, I'm a risk-taker. Nothing ventured and all that. I'm not into boring restoration – excavating ice-houses and rebuilding derelict ponds to hold fish no one is going to eat. Which is why I want a sculpture trail in the woods . . . Maybe you are right about the walled garden. About it's being too far away from the house for all that Villandry stuff. But those French fountains were something else! And Jade loved them. And I did think you'd like the maze idea. Surely that's conservative enough for you?'

Lotte's head jerked up. 'Oh, Brody, I've no objection to a maze if you want a maze. But not in front of the house! That park is a gem, and a maze slap bang in centre view would wreck it. I don't know who laid it out. Not William Kent or Capability Brown or any of the famous ones or we'd know about it. But whoever did it knew what they were about.' She jumped up suddenly. 'Let's stand on the terrace. I'll show you.'

'I know what it looks like . . .' Brody started.

'Please,' she said, her hand on his arm, her eyes urgent.

And then, somehow, she talked him right out of the maze project. They stood on the covered part of the terrace, looking out on to steadily falling rain, and Lotte talked with a sort of suppressed passion. As if she owned the place, Brody thought.

'Brody, don't you see how perfect it is? How the park, so open except for carefully placed clumps of trees, sweeps down to the lake and up to the woods?' She gestured with one arm, as if stroking the landscape. 'And how the lake, gently serpentine, draws your interest to wonder what is round the corner, beyond the bridge?'

She was silent for a second or two, then went on, 'And the planting is brilliant, with wonderful shapes, tall at the back and in great bold clumps. And the colour – just look at the reds and clear yellows and deep browns. Whoever planted those woods behind was thinking about all this for autumn, and the froth of white amalanchiers in front for spring, and that group of Norway spruce and the yellow and red *Cornus* at the water's edge for winter.'

She seemed oblivious of him, he thought, so absorbed in what she was looking at. Then she turned to him, her face alight. 'And don't you think the Chinese tea-house on the island gives a little focal point, like a figure in a painting? Nearly all landscapes, I think, are the better for a bit of human intervention.'

She put her arm on his sleeve and said, 'In the eighteenth century they talked a lot about "borrowed landscape" – meaning incorporating the view into your plan for the garden. Someone did that brilliantly here, with the ha-ha providing the invisible join. You cannot stick a maze in the park, Brody. It would ruin everything.'

That afternoon, Brody e-mailed his head gardener:

Damn it, Lott, you're right. We'll go visit some modest manor houses before we decide. OK? Happy now? Brody

10. Winter

My very heart faints and my whole soul grieves
At the moist rich smell of the rotting leaves,
    And the breath
    Of the fading edges of box beneath,
And the year's last rose.

   Alfred, Lord Tennyson (1808–92), 'Song'

'But why couldn't I? You could have asked, at least.' Annie glared at her mother's reflection in the bathroom mirror.

Lotte went on applying mascara to her lashes as she answered, 'I told you, sweetheart. They are not inviting any children, and the caterers are from London. I could hardly ask them if my under-age daughter could be a waitress because she wants to gawp at pop stars.'

She immediately regretted her tart reply – it was natural for teenagers to want to be near fame, and the gossip was that Jade's party guests were to include Posh and Becks and a host of singers and models that Annie knew all about and Lotte had never heard of. And one of the Pop Idol lads and his band would be playing after supper.

As Annie's stomping progress down the stairs and into the kitchen echoed through the house, Lotte leant her forehead against the bathroom mirror and closed her eyes.

Oh God, she thought, I have never in my life wanted to go to a party less.

Half an hour later, Lotte was standing against a wall, glass in hand. The basement echoed to the sound of a lot of people well lubricated by good champagne. It was every bit as bad as she'd imagined.

She felt horrible in these ridiculous beach swimming things. Twelve years ago she'd known she looked great in this bikini. The top had pushed her meagre bosom up into something worthy of notice, and the bottom half had shown off her tight bum and flat belly. But at forty-five? She should have worn a proper one-piece. She'd bought one from M&S in Oxford but it was so matronly it seemed to signal a death-knell to carefree days on the beach. She'd taken it back.

She draped the sarong to cover as much of her legs as she could, and accepted another glass of champagne. If she got enough alcohol in her maybe she wouldn't feel so awful.

It wasn't just the bikini. Lotte looked from one female guest to another. They'd all be at home in a swim-suit commercial. Indeed, she thought, many of them made their money in swim-suit commercials. No sign of cellulite on any thigh, no slackening of the flesh under the bikini bra-straps. Those tans were all real, from sojourns in the Bahamas, not out of a bottle like hers. It was true that the summer spent labouring in the garden had given her a real enough tan on her face and arms. But her colour looked coarse, she thought, accentuating faint freckles she didn't know she had and reddening her skin, whereas everyone else's had that honey glow of the ski-slope or the sun-lamp, the look of the truly rich who spend £300 on a bottle of face cream. These women's well-toned bodies were kept in shape by a personal trainer, not by double-digging in heavy clay.

Some of the guests were famous as well as rich. Lotte watched as people she'd only ever seen on television sought one another out. Without exception their eyes, on the hunt for other glitterati, flicked past her, not pausing for a second. Was it so obvious that she was nobody?

The South London voice of Clive Burnett, Jade's agent, rose above the party hubbub, and Lotte forced herself to leave her corner and join the crowd round the pool end.

Clive swayed slightly on an upturned champagne crate, a bottle in one hand and a glass in the other. 'Right, guys, I'm landed with the thank-you speech. Which I'm more than happy to do: it's no secret that Jade Allen is my best client, and when Jade here,' he put his hand on Jade's bare shoulder, 'says jump, believe me, boys, I jump.'

'Too right. Who wouldn't?' someone called. Clive acknowledged the interruption with a thumbs-up and raised his glass. 'So this is to thank Jade and Brody for a great weekend party. I'd no idea the country could be such fun. For one thing, I thought nose candy could only be had in SW1. How wrong can you be?'

He paused for the laughter, pleased with himself. 'Tonight's occasion is the nipple on the tit, if you'll excuse the expression. The Jewel in the Crown. The Pièce (he pronounced it pee-ace) de Résistance. We are, here, not just to scoff our hosts' champagne but to sprinkle some of it on to and into Jade's new pool and gym, disco, bar, massage parlour and general underground cavern of fleshly delights.'

He held his glass unsteadily aloft and said, 'To Jade and Brody, long may they play in her.' To the sound of clapping and echoes of 'Jade and Brody', he poured the contents of the champagne bottle into the pool. Lotte watched the pattern of the tiles on the bottom disintegrate, then regain its blue and green Islamic intricacy, wobbling back to stillness.

Well, that's over, she thought, maybe I can go home now, without having to get in there and swim. She stood up, pulling the sarong more tightly around her. But as she turned to go, she heard Brody's deep Irish brogue from across the room.

'Not so fast there now,' he said, gesturing to Clive to give way to him on the champagne crates. 'Just before anyone follows the bubbly into the water, there is someone Jade and I would like to thank.' He looked around, and Lotte felt his eyes fix her to the spot. 'And that is Mrs Charlotte Warren, chief architect of this basement venture, procurer of authentic de Morgan tiles, doughty battler with the builders and designer of everything: the gym, the lighting, the pool, the decor. It was Lotte who thought of flooding the lower cellar wall to wall, and Lotte who persuaded those bureaucrats at the Council not to prosecute when we took it down a few feet without asking them. Without Lotte, this would surely be the dank cellar it was a few months ago. Lotte, come here.' He lifted an enormous bunch of flowers towards her so that she had no option but to weave her way through the crowd to him.

She tried to take the flowers from him without joining him on the improvised podium. But he grabbed her hand

and pulled her up, and she let go of her sarong in the process. As Brody pulled her to him and kissed her cheek she felt the thin cotton slither to her feet. She could feel Brody's fingers in the soft flesh of her waist and Jade's eyes, everyone's eyes, on her white stomach and thighs. She made a scuttling escape, trailing her sarong and barely pausing to force a smile of thanks.

Mercifully, all eyes returned to Brody as he lifted his voice to say, 'And the fun is not over yet. Today is Jade's twenty-sixth birthday.'

Lotte, safely at the back of the crowd, turned to watch as clapping and a half-hearted attempt at 'Happy Birthday' broke out. Brody silenced this with an uplifted hand and went on, his eyes on his wife, 'Don't scowl, darling. When you are as old as your husband, twenty-six will seem like sixteen. Anyway, I've bought you a birthday present.'

He paused, and Jade, standing at his side, looked up at him, her frown vanishing in expectation.

'I know you wanted a Lamborghini, but hey, tough, here is a Rodin instead.' He waved to the far door, and everyone turned in that direction. No one knew what to expect. They all looked puzzled and curious, craning to see.

But suddenly, Lotte knew exactly what it was. Brody had bought a real Rodin, a lifesize standing female nude, carved from the purest Carrara marble. Lotte knew because she had suggested it. He'd picked up a gardening magazine from her desk, and she'd shown him a picture in it of a pool in a Roman garden, with a Rodin in an alcove at the end of it, and joked, 'Just the thing for your basement pool, Brody. Only eleven million.'

In a flash, Lotte understood what the platform at the far end was all about. Brody had never explained, but two weeks before, when the pool tiling was nearly complete, he had suddenly demanded she build a stone console on the far wall, its wide surface to be five centimetres below the level the water would come to. And he'd ordered a hook in the ceiling above it, strong and heavy enough to hang an elephant, he'd said.

At the time, Lotte had been miffed by Brody's secrecy. The cellar project had been her design and she resented what she suspected would be some awful hanging mobile or horrible water feature. But as always, when it came down to it, Brody called the shots.

And now she understood. He'd wanted to keep his present to his wife a total secret. Lotte looked across the pool and for the first time noticed a nylon rope and pulley attached to the hook in the ceiling. For hoisting the statue, obviously, but how would it get there? The pool had no surround, no pathway to carry a statue. Just a wide floor at this end with steps into the water. The two side walls and the curved end one were sheer from the tiled pool bottom, five feet down, to the vaulted ceiling.

There was a hush as five men came in, straining under the weight of the marble nymph. Two of them were Lotte's student gardeners. The nymph wasn't wrapped, but she had a nylon rope tied firmly round her body, under one arm and round her neck. All the men were wearing bathing trunks and Brody directed them as they carefully stepped into the pool, down the wide curved steps at the shallow end.

It was an amazing scene. The guests stood silent as the

men, walking slowly, only their heads and necks above water, carefully carried the naked statue on her back across the glowing blue-green pool. She seemed to swim like Ophelia, serene and oblivious.

When she'd been hoisted into place, to a great deal of cheering and clapping, the room fell briefly silent. She took your breath away. Brody had calculated the levels perfectly so that she seemed to be standing on the water, framed by the curved wall behind her, gazing across the expanse of pool. She had a goddess-like serenity coupled with a very womanly sexiness — as if conscious of her beauty and indifferent to its effect. You could not take your eyes off her.

Once the hubbub of talk resumed, and a few young women were in the pool, Lotte suddenly felt hungry and went in search of food. Jean Christophe, the chef, had set up a buffet along the mirrored wall of the gym. As she waited for him to help her to *risotto al porcini* and rocket salad, she looked at herself in the mirror. A lot better with the sarong, she thought. You might pass for thirty-five in this light.

'Pretty good, don't you think?' It was Brody, and for a wild second she thought he was talking about her. But just as quickly, she knew he meant the party, or the food, or the Rodin.

'It's all wonderful, Brody. Congratulations. Jade must be thrilled.'

Lotte noticed, not for the first time, his chipped tooth, and how his eyes shone when he was excited or pleased. He looked so young when he was happy — nearer thirty than forty. He said, 'She'd better be! This little lot's cost a shed-load of lolly, that's for sure.'

When Jean Christophe had filled her plate, and Lotte

put out her hand to take it, Brody said, 'I'll take the plates, you grab us some wine from over there. Get a bottle, Lott. I'll find us a place to sit.'

Surprised, and certainly flattered, Lotte got two glasses and a bottle of red, and then followed Brody's back as he weaved through the throng, smiling and chatting, but refusing to be held for long. He led her to the little ante-room outside the sauna, which was empty, kicked the door shut behind them, and sat down on the sofa.

'That's a bit of luck. Damned if I'll have my dinner sitting on an exercise bike or a trampoline,' he said. 'Lot quieter, too. I'm too old for that rap stuff.'

Lotte was uneasy about Brody and her being alone in the little room. She knew Jade wouldn't approve, and she thought the host should be out there with Kate Moss or Elton John, not having supper with the gardener. Besides, she was still conscious of her bare legs and shoulders. There was something so overtly masculine about Brody – you could not ignore his sexuality. She kept her eyes on her food, trying to avoid the sight of his stocky brown legs stretched out in front of him, or of the hair on his chest – curly and reddish-brown – visible inside his horrible Hawaiian shirt.

But as he talked she forgot all this, and found herself listening, fascinated, to his enthusiasm for the Internet, and how he got into the business.

She said, 'Thank you for the speech and flowers, Brody. You needn't have – I loved doing the work.'

'Well, you are very good at it. But do you like the rest of the job? Did you make the right decision, leaving architecture?'

'Absolutely!' Lotte looked into his face. 'I love my job. Really love it.'

And then Brody said that loving one's work was as important, maybe more important, than loving one's mate, and that he'd loved most of the jobs he'd ever done. He leant against the squashy leather of the sofa and talked of his days as a baker. How he'd arrive at the bakery at dawn, take the dough from the prover where it had been swelling slowly overnight and manhandle it into the mixer to be kneaded. Then he'd cut lumps off it to exactly the right weight, shape them by hand, plonk them in the tins, and then go down the rows slashing a long slit down the middle of each one. 'That's what makes the double farmhouse crust,' he said. 'It was hard work, but I loved it. And all the time, you know, I was dreaming,' he mused, 'like only Irish boys can dream. Of going to America. Of being a pop star. Of being a demon trader in the City. Always, always of getting rich.' He caught her eye and smiled.

He told her how he used to nick milk, sugar and raisins, and some of the unsold bread destined to end up as dried breadcrumbs which they sold in packets. He'd get in really early, or sneak back when everyone had gone home, and make bread pudding for his market stall.

'It was my first business and I was a great salesman,' he laughed. 'I used to tell the customers it was my nan's recipe. Which was a joke, since the only grandmother I heard tell of died of the drink before I was born.'

Lotte noticed how his accent broadened into a proper Irish brogue. She twirled her near-empty glass round in her fingers and asked, 'But didn't you ever get caught? Didn't the baker twig what you were doing?'

Brody laughed. 'I did and all! But he didn't call the rozzers. He just gave me a pasting and demanded a percentage of the take. Fair enough, I thought.'

He reached for the bottle on the floor and filled Lotte's glass, saying, 'Anyway, I saved what I could, and then borrowed the rest to open a cooked chicken takeaway. God, I was proud of that shop! We grilled the chickens over charcoal with a marinade of chilli and garlic. Mild, Hot, and Blow-Your-Head-Off. We sold the chickens whole or by the quarter. But of course we sold more breasts than legs, so I put my baking skills to good use and made baps, which we sold filled with all the leftover leg meat. Quite soon demand for the baps was greater than for the chickens.'

Brody must have told that story a hundred times, Lotte thought. But he tells it as if still amazed at his own success.

'And that was the start of Brody's Baps?'

'It was and all. And the Spicy Chicken Bap is still the best seller, although the new owners make all sorts of fillings we'd never heard of. I went into the Covent Garden store the other day and they had upmarket stuff like Thai Crab and Coriander, and Grilled Peppers and Tapenade. The customers were pretty upmarket too. Jade wouldn't have looked out of place in the joint! No more sausage and beans. We used to do fried egg and bacon. We even did one with chips and tomato ketchup in it. Delicious!'

Lotte pulled a face. 'Urgh,' she said, 'why did you sell the business?'

'Easy. We were offered about twice what it was worth. And I'd had enough, anyway. We had four hundred stores, and we'd gone public a few years before and I hated having shareholders.'

'Why?' asked Lotte.

'Oh, our shareholders were mostly City institutions full of pin-striped clones who couldn't run a whelk stall. And you had to deal with analysts and fund managers who think the *Financial Times* is Holy Writ – all telling you how to run your business.'

Engrossed in his own story, Brody picked up Lotte's glass from the floor between them and took a couple of gulps before putting it back. Lotte said nothing, not wanting to break his mood.

'The high-street restaurant business is tough enough without shareholders expecting double-digit profit growth year on year. It's unbelievably competitive.' He started to tick off the retail-chain problems on his fingers. 'You have to fight Costa Coffee and Prêt à Manger for every site; you're desperate for staff; the environmental health officer makes your life a misery; regulation and bureaucracy take the fun out of the business; the public want new gimmicks all the time. It sucks, Lott.'

He reached for her wine glass again, realized his mistake and said, 'Oh God, Lott, I've been drinking your wine. I'm really sorry.'

She poured the rest of the bottle into both their glasses. 'Don't be silly. I don't care. I'm not the environmental health officer.' They smiled at each other. 'So you took the money and ran?'

'Yup, or rather, I took the money and bought *find-on-line.com*.'

'And lived happily ever after?'

'Sure. Who wouldn't? I've got everything anyone could possibly want. Don't you think?' He paused for a second then added, 'Except kids. I want some kids. But they'll come. Jade is only twenty-six.'

Lotte walked home fast across the park, her winter coat and Wellies disguising her ridiculous bathing gear. She was upset. Not because Jade had dragged Brody away, but because he'd gone so willingly, and because he'd said, 'OK, darling, I'm with you. I just needed refuelling. I can't eat standing up. Old farts like me and Lotte here need a little sit-down between bouts of partying.' She knew he'd been joking, but 'old fart' was a bit steep. Her mood of embarrassment and awkwardness, which had vanished during their conversation, returned.

Cross with herself for minding, she gnawed at it. What was wrong with her? She had every reason to be happy. What did it matter if a lot of strangers had seen her unlovely body? And she'd always known Brody wasn't tactful. And it was good of him to make that speech and give her this monster bunch of flowers. And to spend all that time with her.

And the gym and pool had really worked. Especially the pool. A balmy satisfaction warmed her briefly as she thought of it: the walls sand-blasted to a pale biscuit; the way they dropped sheer through the water without even a handrail; and more than anything, the floor tiles. Everyone had exclaimed at the de Morgan tiles. The lighting had worked exactly as she'd planned, underwater strips irradiating the rich blues and greens on the bottom and emphasizing the uneven stone of the walls, and the uplighters showing off the ceiling and the apse-like end wall. She'd done a good job.

But counting her blessings didn't lighten her mood for long.

The flowers were heavy, weighted by their cellophane bag of water. Lotte dumped them with relief on the kitchen table and sat down. She slumped back, her gaze fixed, unseeing, on the Aga.

I know what's wrong with me, she thought. I'm jealous, that's what. I'm put out because Brody's Rodin stole the show. That sculpture looked so wonderful, and the whole drama of installing it was so perfectly stage-managed. My beautiful pool became a mere backdrop for Brody to display his love for his wife.

Suddenly, Lotte felt a great tide of yearning. Oh, I want someone to love me like that. Extravagantly. Completely. In spite of all my faults.

Bloody Jade. Shallow, spoilt, thick. What has she done to deserve love like that?

11. Late Winter

Now there come
The weak-neck snowdrops
   Bouncing like fountains
         And they stop you, they make you
  Take a deep breath
       Make your heart shake you

      Ted Hughes (1930–98), 'New Year Song'

Brody was cold and cross. He'd left his nice warm office early, not to go to his nice warm house, but to have this meeting with Lotte while it was still light. Not that she'd appreciate the effort he'd made. She seemed perfectly indifferent to the cold, standing there with the rain running off the back of her hat, her trousers tucked neatly into her boots. The rain was getting into his collar. And his fingers, struggling with the zip on his Barbour, were so cold they hurt.

'This is bloody useless, Lotte. Nothing has changed in months! What are you guys playing at, for Christ's sake?'

Lotte didn't answer. She just looked at him in that superior, patient way she'd developed, as if he was being unreasonable. It really got to him, that look. No wonder Jade said she was insolent.

'Lotte, I'm paying an army of your people. And we could have bought that digger-hire company for less money than we've spent with them.' He glared accusingly at the lake edge, scraped bare of weed and grass.

The mud gleamed flat and greasy for 100 yards into the field and all along the lake. Blue irrigation pipes lay in waterlogged channels, the jets for the fountains could be seen above the lake's surface, and the new pump-house, disguised as a Chinese pagoda, was in place. At least the woman had got that much done. But the whole site was a mud-bath, nothing had been planted, and she just stood there, saying nothing.

Irritated by her silence, Brody said, 'This place looks like the Battle of the fucking Somme, Lotte, and it has all winter. And now you tell me we've been refused bloody planning permisson.' He paused fractionally. 'For God's sake, do me a favour and answer.'

She turned to him then, and her face was calm. 'OK. Actually, the cost of the diggers is on budget. The staff bill is slightly under budget: the college students come pretty cheap as they're on work experience, and we laid off Robert and Molly as soon as they'd finished the mount.'

She crossed her arms over her chest, her hands pushed up into her armpits. She seemed to bounce slightly in her rubber boots. 'I can't help the weather, Brody. We can't plant until the rain stops. And we can't finish the installation either. The machines just get stuck in the mud.'

Brody stamped his feet, trying to get some warmth into them. Her reasonableness was as maddening as her silence. He said, 'And I suppose the rain stops planning permission too, does it?'

She smiled as if he'd made a joke. 'No, but I told you Thames Water would never let us help ourselves to water from the Isis. But in fact, we don't need to. Jade can have her fountains, and you can have your cascades, and maybe I can even get the lawns watered, without tapping the river.' She looked, Brody thought, amused, even a bit smug. Like someone dangling a bone in front of a dog.

'How?' he asked.

'We'll pump the water out of the lake.'

Oh bugger, he thought. She's not as clever as she looks. For a moment there I thought she had a solution. 'We can't do that,' he said, 'as it is, the lake stinks when the water drops in the summer. If we take any more out of it . . .'

'It's OK, Brody, I've thought it all out. I've had some irrigation people look at it too, and it's feasible.'

Brody shook his head. 'We've got to get an OK to tap the Isis. It's the only solution. Lotte, the truth is you didn't make enough effort. You have to schmooze these bureaucratic clones. You think being nice to people is bribery, and because you don't want the fountains, you just didn't try, did you?'

Well, at least that got a reaction. Brody watched Lotte's face redden, and her eyes glared at him.

'That's not fair,' she said, 'and you know it. I knew we'd never get permission.' Placing her hands on her hips, she leant towards him, her chin up. 'I told you so. But you insisted, and I did everything correctly, and with energy, and on time. But they'd advised us at the outset it was hopeless. And they were right.' Her voice cooled and hardened. 'And used fivers for the Chairman of the Planning Committee would not have made any difference.'

'How do you know? You didn't try.'

Immediately, Brody regretted this. For some reason he would rather Lotte thought he was above bribery.

'Of course I didn't. I thought you were joking.'

Brody said quickly, 'Sure, I was joking. About money. But a few smiles and general friendliness might have helped.'

Lotte turned her gaze to the lake, her jaw tight. Brody caught the infinitesimal shake of her head. Then she swung back, 'And it's not true that I don't want the fountains. I think they'll be fine – now they are no longer on Louis Quatorze scale. Why else would I have been working on an alternative solution?'

Brody felt a little chastened by this and said, 'OK then, let's have it?'

Lotte's plan, he realized with quick but reluctant admiration, would work. It was simple and clever. They would dig a deep reservoir to the left and slightly behind the lake, masked from the house by new planting. During the winter the huge surface of the lake would act as a catchment area, and the surplus lake water would flow into the reservoir. During the summer the flow would be reversed, the water pumped from reservoir to lake.

'We'd then be able to keep the lake level constant,' concluded Lotte, 'which means that the marginal planting will not dry out in summer and we can have sheets of bog primulas and mimulus. We can pump water up to the house to water the garden and feed your cascades, and we can use the same pump to get the pressure for the fountains in the lake.'

Brody had the familiar feeling that he had once again

been bettered by Lotte. He put his arm over her shoulder, briefly hugging her to him. 'You're OK, young Charlotte. Brains as well as brawn, hey? I guess I should stop arguing with you and start trusting you?'

This was a mistake. Smiling up at him, Lotte promptly pressed her advantage. 'That would be great,' she said, 'especially if that means I can hire a couple more students for the summer to find the Old Pond Yards. What do you think?'

Brody shook his head, amused. 'Don't push your luck, lady. That's one argument I am going to win. I want a sculpture trail through those woods, and we aren't going looking for trouble. If you find some crumbling ruin, we'll have English Heritage preventing me bulldozing a trail through my own land —'

'No, we won't . . .' interrupted Lotte, but her voice trailed off as Brody clapped her shoulder by way of farewell and set off for the house.

As he squelched back through the sodden park, Brody thought how often Lotte did get the better of him. It used to be that only Jade got her way, but now, he mused, Lotte beat him with reason while Jade did it with the more traditional armoury of fury and sex. Jade's sex appeal was drenching, and as hard to resist as Lotte's logic.

Jade was not in sex-drenching mode. She was tight with anger. She flung her hair-brush on the bed and shouted over her shoulder, 'I'm not going on holiday with her.'

Brody followed her into the bathroom and took her by the shoulders, holding her so she faced the mirror. Her reflection glared at him, alive with fury. He was tempted to turn her round so he could kiss the flashing eyes, the tight-lipped mouth. But he held her reflection's eyes in his.

'Listen, my beautiful one,' he said, 'it's not a holiday. It's a three-day plane trip to see a couple of gardens. It's a research trip. And Lotte has to be there because she's the expert. She knows what we should see. Think of her as a tour guide.'

Jade glared back at him, unforgiving. He dropped his head and kissed her neck and bony collar-bone. She pulled out of his grasp and reached for her electric tooth-brush. She clamped her lips around it and turned it on. Its whirring stilled both conversation and Brody's desire. He shrugged slightly, and left her to it.

He went across the landing to his study where he poured himself a Jamieson's. Once, he'd drunk Scotch or champagne, because they were posher. But now that he'd made it and had no need to impress anyone, he drank the drinks of his young days in the Wicklow Hills: Murphy's, Guinness, Irish whiskey.

He'd thought a lot about County Wicklow lately. He'd been brought up by his da, his mother having died when he was a baby. His father worked on the Powerscourt estate, mostly with the horses, later buffing up the cars for the gentry. Da, for all he was so Irish the English guests couldn't understand a word he said, didn't talk much. No Irish charm or blarney, no folk songs round the peat fire. But the Irish tradition of boozing ran thick in his veins, and by the time Brody was twelve, a lot of his nourishment came in liquid form. Johnny Fox's, high up and in the middle of nowhere, was young Brody's idea of heaven –

where everyone got plastered, everyone knew the words of all the songs, and the girls danced jigs with their arms stiff at their sides, backs ramrod-straight, feet flicking back, eyes alight. And with their tits jiggling about under their shirts like ferrets in a sack.

As he swirled his whiskey round the glass and stared at his polished brogues crossed in front of him on the desk, Brody thought how curious it was that he had loved Powerscourt so much. He shouldn't have. He was under-fed, often walloped for no reason, ill-educated and badly clad. But somehow he'd been fine. His da loved him, he knew that, and he had the run of the place. No one caught him poaching in the woods or fishing in the river. No one minded if he and his mates climbed up the waterfall or swam in the lake. And no one had any idea how he dreamed of owning Powerscourt one day, with armies of gardeners, chauffeurs and cooks to order about.

Brody smiled. Of course he'd never own Powerscourt now. It belonged to the Slazenger family and they'd turned it into a visitor attraction. But it would be good to see the place again. Maybe he'd take Jade there. Show her a slice of Irish life.

Brody's thoughts turned to his gardener. He was glad she'd come round about the fountains, even if she'd persuaded him to put them in the lake rather than on the drawing-room terrace. She was right of course. There was more room in the lake for really tall jets, like at Versailles. And he and Jade were agreed that puny little dribbles would not do. Feeble fountains were worse than no foun-tains at all – like back-garden fireworks sporadically startling the sky. What one wanted was unremitting orchestrated professional explosions set to Beethoven. I wonder, he thought, if you can get fountains to dance to music. I bet you can.

This afternoon, out in the cold, he'd expected Lotte to return to their conversation of the previous day, but she'd been doing her cool, silent act. Yesterday she'd telephoned and said, 'Brody, I've got an idea.'

'Uh-huh?' He could hear her taking a deep breath. He imagined her squaring her narrow shoulders, bringing her chin up. He smiled, amused.

'I thought we might start a community project to look for my water gardens in the woods. Get young people clearing the undergrowth. It can't be done by machine because we might drive over something important, or damage a grotto or a canal. We could advertise on the Net for volunteers, get some local youth groups . . .'

Brody could hear her enthusiasm mounting. Her voice went up as she talked faster. It was sweet, really.

He laughed. 'Don't be silly, Lotte. Charity is all very well, but it doesn't begin at home.'

She didn't reply for a second, and her voice was flatter when she did. 'What do you mean, charity doesn't begin at home?'

Brody smiled into the telephone, pleased with his joke. 'It means I don't want a lot of no-hopers and druggies inside the estate walls, that's what it means. They'd be shooting up in the shrubberies and gawping through the windows, hoping to see the famous Jade.'

Lotte replied coolly, 'I could see that they didn't.' And then she said, 'Brody, I don't understand you. You are obviously concerned about the money we are spending, but you won't entertain an idea which could save us some.'

'No you don't, Lotte,' he said. 'Don't try that tack. I'd not be saving money, because I haven't agreed to investigating those damn woods at all. I've got them earmarked for a few grassy tracks and a sculpture trail. You can't save me money on a restoration project I've no intention of doing.'

She'd said, 'OK, fine, just an idea,' but he'd been put out when she hung up. She had this ability to put you down without doing or saying anything you could point at.

Of course Jade did plenty of pointing. Brody's brow creased as he considered Jade's many complaints about Lotte. The chief one was that he spent more time with the gardener than with her, but there were plenty of more specific ones: Lotte had refused to run some errand for Jade; Lotte's children hogged the tennis court; the fat, sullen one drove that motorbike like a madwoman; Lotte kept her mobile switched off and didn't respond when Jade rang her; and on and on.

Some of all this was true. Brody quite often went to work late or came home at lunchtime so that he could discuss some project with Lotte. And at weekends he liked to walk about the estate. He so wished Jade would join him, would at least give it a go. Since he'd owned Maddon, he'd found a whole new world of detail that he'd never noticed before, and some of that was Lotte's doing. She'd made him see the magic of frost-edged leaves or snow-drops cracking through the snow, discoveries he wanted to share with Jade. But she stayed indoors feeling neglected.

His sympathies, if he were honest, were with Lotte. He'd been all prepared to tick her off for behaving like a trade union official when she refused to collect something from Oxford for Jade. But Lotte said she'd no objection to running errands, only she'd made an appointment with some fancy professor, a plant pathologist from the Botanic Gardens, to come and diagnose some sick tree.

And it was he, Brody, rather than Lotte, who had encouraged the children. And he didn't think it unreasonable to have your mobile off on Sunday mornings.

But he knew defending Lotte was a bad idea. Jade wasn't rational about her. Actually, Jade wasn't rational at all. Which was, he supposed, part of her attraction. Her irrationality, her spoilt-child capriciousness, her moodiness – sultry indifference followed by demanding randiness – were part of the challenge of her. He didn't understand her, which he didn't mind too much. But he did want to master her, to have the upper hand. But she eluded him, taking her rangy beauty off when he wanted her most.

Brody swung his chair round to look at the giant framed poster of his wife on the wall. It was the famous one of her on the Harley Davidson, her hair as wet and shiny as her leather trousers and high boots, her small breasts trussed in some designer bondage gear, her slim belly supporting a metal chain and padlock.

As always, the picture stirred his desire. It was the way she sat on the enormous bike, like a child riding a tiger. She was tipped forward in the seat, her rounded bum thrust up, her back arched, her pubic bone on the saddle. Her mouth was half open and her eyes half closed, the picture of lust. You could feel the vibrations of the bike.

When he'd first put the poster up, he'd made love to

her on his desk, talking sex to the real Jade with his eyes fixed on her photo. It had been an amazing turn-on, like looking at the porno mags of his adolescence while risking blindness and hell-fire by doing what Father O'Connell called Defiling the Temple of Jesus. Jade had been turned on too – by Brody's whispering, his hands all over her, the hardness of the desk against her back, but mostly by the narcissism of her image on the wall.

We are both in love with Jade, Brody thought. Maybe it would be better if she were more in love with me.

And then he thought, the hell with that, I want her, that's enough. He swung his feet off the desk and stood up abruptly. He knew exactly what he'd do. He'd pull Jade out of bed and stand her in front of the long mirror. He'd stand behind her and undress her in front of it, make her watch his brawny arms and large dark hands against her white belly. They'd both watch her nipples harden and rise and her eyes would go soft with desire. He'd tell her to kiss herself in the mirror, and she'd do it, closing her eyes and moaning very softly. And then he'd lead her gently to the bed, and have her.

12. Late Spring

We know that even God could not imagine the redness of
  a red geranium
nor the smell of mignonette
when the geraniums were not, and mignonette neither.

D. H. Lawrence (1885–1930),
'Red Geranium and Godly Mignonette'

Lotte had planned the three-day garden tour with great
care. Fountains for Jade at Alnwick Castle, restored Victorian kitchen gardens at Heligan for her, and a visit
to Powerscourt for Brody. They'd done Alnwick that
morning, and they'd all loved it. Even Jade had said she
was beginning to see the point of gardens. Now they were
heading for Cornwall and Heligan.

Brody, in the pilot's seat, turned round and took off his
ear-cans. His face was bright with pleasure as he shouted
above the din, 'You two OK? You look a bit green, Lotte,
don't you like it?'

'I'm fine,' Lotte yelled back, but she wasn't. She did
feel sick, and she was frightened. She hated the way the
little plane bucked and bumped. She shut her eyes against
the dipping horizon, swirling sea and heaving land.

The noise was deafening and she could not persuade

her mind that the engines would not fail. And the way the co-pilot kept peering out of the window as though looking for landmarks and then studying his map was not reassuring. She wished Brody would let the man fly his plane. But Brody always flew hired planes himself. He said it was to keep his flying hours up for the day, coming soon, when he'd buy a fixed-wing plane to go alongside the chopper. But the truth is, Lotte thought, he's a control freak. And he loves it.

Brody reached back between the seats and squeezed Jade's knee. Jade looked up from *Hello* magazine and smiled at him, then returned to a Britney Spears picture spread. Lotte silently willed Brody to concentrate on the controls and was relieved when he faced front again.

At last they were banking over St Mawes. The flight from Alnwick had taken nearly two hours and Lotte was wrung out. She was anxious about the children and guilty about Peter. She knew that she was taking advantage of him, using him as a babysitter. He was happy to do it, of course – he'd insisted. But should she have accepted?

She'd done so because she so badly wanted to go on this trip with the Keegans, but Peter might read more into it than she meant, and who could blame him? They were so close now – to all intents and purposes they were a couple, except that they didn't sleep together.

Annie was a different girl, largely due to Peter and his motorbike. Even Christo was relaxed with him now. Peter had bought him an old Pentax camera, which Lotte should have disallowed, but didn't. The pair of them had turned the cupboard under the stairs into a dark-room.

One Sunday afternoon, when they'd all been out walking, Peter and Lotte had swung Jo-Jo between them, and Lotte had suddenly felt a rush of content, of being a family again. She'd not said anything though, and had refused Jo-Jo's pleas for more swinging.

Maybe Peter was just what they all needed. He was so comfortingly old-fashioned. He wasn't interested in digital cameras and cropping pics on screen. He liked his old-fashioned Hasselblad plate camera, and his old-fashioned Harley Davidson. And old-fashioned romance, Lotte thought: no hurry, no stress, just reliable affection, steady love. For ten months now she'd thought of him as her best friend. And what was wrong with that?

As they rode the short distance to the hotel, Lotte sat in the front next to the taxi driver and longed to be at home. She wanted to be with Peter and the children, eating baked beans on toast and maybe playing Monopoly. The last thing she wanted to do was eat a fancy dinner with her employers.

In the event, she didn't have to. As they checked into the famous Tresanton Hotel, Brody said, 'OK, girls? What time for dinner? Meet you in the bar at eight, Lotte?'

Lotte looked up from signing her name, intending to say, fine. But she caught Jade's frown and said at once, 'Would you mind if I skip dinner? I'm beat.'

Brody protested, but Lotte insisted, saying she was still sick from the flight.

Within five minutes of arriving at Heligan, Lotte was bewitched. She walked with Jade and Brody through the enormous vegetable garden, marvelling at the neatly raked soil, orderly rows of seedlings, apple trees trained over a tunnel of huge metal hoops, flowers bordering the paths, five or six gardeners bent over their tasks. The scale of it took her breath away.

They stopped to watch a woman gardener carefully fitting six-inch fabric mats round every newly planted cabbage seedling. She'd done about a hundred, with another fifty to go. She was planting along a string guideline pulled tight by metal winding stakes at each end.

Lotte crouched down to examine the elaborate ironwork of the stake top. 'Is this Victorian?' she asked.

The woman didn't stop planting, but she looked up briefly. 'No, but it's a Victorian design. They're made in the estate smithy to the old pattern. Easier to wind than a modern one.'

'And the mats?'

The gardener handed Lotte one of her mats to look at and said. 'They're modern. We get the fabric from the Doubleday Research place.'

'What are they for?' asked Brody. 'To keep the cabbages cosy?'

She smiled. 'Well, actually, yes. They work like a mulch, keeping the soil moist underneath. We hardly water here, you see. And when we do it's by hand, from hand-drawn bowsers, or by lugging cans to the dipping-pool. I'll do anything to avoid that.'

Brody looked baffled. 'Why not just use a hose?'

The woman used the flat of her hand to firm the ground round the last cabbage plant in the row, then stood up. 'Because this garden is an example of how things can be done with minimum stress to the environment. We grow everything as close to organically as we can, and we don't waste water. That way we can help commercial producers and the public who want to grow sustainably.'

Brody didn't quite raise his eyes to heaven, but Lotte could see he thought this was anorak-talk. She felt a little shaft of anger, but she couldn't challenge him in front of the Heligan staff and Jade.

Brody's interest in the buildings of the melon yard mollified her, however. She watched him covertly as they inspected antique tools in the tool shed, peered at pallid rhubarb stalks in the gloom of the forcing-room, and mastered the workings of the 'thunderbox' or gardener's privy, the unsavoury product of which was once used as fertilizer. Brody was clearly as fascinated as she was by the reconstruction of the melon house and pineapple pit, achieved by a mixture of archaeology, research and guess-work. Guide-book in hand, he examined the manure trenches running along the side of the main structure of the pineapple pit. He looked round, eyes alight.

'Where's Jade?' he asked. 'She's got to see this.' She was leaning against the potting-shed wall and Brody strode across the yard and pulled her over to join Lotte at the pineapple pit.

'Look darling, it's amazing. They shovel fresh horse shit in here, and as it rots it gets hot, and warms the pineapples growing in those pots inside the greenhouse. Neat, or what?'

Jade pulled her arm away with a little jerk. Lotte noticed the look of surprise followed by hurt on Brody's face. Jade looked from Brody to Lotte and back again, her eyes hot. 'Well, I can see you two get off on all this. Do you realize you have been gassing for an hour and a half about compost and mealie bugs – whatever they are – and horse manure and night soil – night soil, I ask you.' Her voice was rising, fuelled by indignation. 'That's human crap in most people's language. Well, I've had it.' She swung round, looking for a way out of the melon yard. Over her shoulder she said, too loudly, 'I'll see you in the restaurant. If they have such a thing.'

They both watched her stalking gait as she walked away. Lotte was too embarrassed by the sudden outburst to look at Brody. But Brody's voice was relaxed as he said, 'Poor Jade. None of this is her cup of tea, is it?'

'Shouldn't we follow . . . ?'

'No, better to let her cool down.' He grinned suddenly. 'Besides, she's bound to find the shop, and she'll like that a whole lot better. Let's go find this so-called "lost valley".'

A little uneasy, Lotte followed him through a newly planted orchard and down a shady track to a wooded valley floor, once an exotic garden of strange and wonderful jungle plants imported by long-gone squires. Reading the guide-book, she felt her pulse quicken as she realized that down there were pools and channels, fish-ponds and water gardens of the kind she dreamt of at Maddon. She'd brought Brody here for the vegetable garden, and hadn't known about the 'lost valley' – and she was suddenly nervous that he'd think she'd chosen Heligan to get him to take her Old Pond Yards obsession seriously.

She decided to say nothing. After all, he'd suggested they follow the signs to the valley, not she. The sun was warm on Lotte's back, and as they walked, she felt exhilaration take over from anxiety. This, she thought, is a real treat. Not like work at all.

'Gardening is a short-lived thing, isn't it?' she said.

Brody's face was a question mark. She explained, 'That productive garden – the veg garden and cutting garden and the melon yard – imagine what they looked like after 130 years of neglect: much like Maddon's walled garden, only worse. Everything sleeping under a blanket of brambles and ivy. Fully mature trees growing through the old buildings.'

Brody was looking at her intently. Encouraged, she went on.

'Four generations of Tremaynes lavished time and money on Heligan. And then the Great War put a stop to a hundred years of clearing, planning, building, planting and plant collecting. Half the Heligan staff died in the mud of Flanders, and death duties impoverished the family. They struggled on, understaffed, but in the end the brambles and laurels won.' She looked up at Brody, her eyes solemn. 'It's so sad.'

'Why sad?' asked Brody. 'Those plant-mad Tremaynes are all dead.' He put out a hand to help her over a slippery bit. 'But for the guys in charge now – it must have been good fun fixing it all, don't you think?'

'Oh, Brody, it must have been wonderful. So exciting. So interesting. The best job in the world. And they are still doing it. Tackling new bits of the old place every year.'

Brody smiled indulgently at her, as one might at a child raving about her Barbie doll, and said, 'It must be costing them a packet to do it authentically, and it will take forever. Why they can't cheat a bit, forget all the research and just make a new garden, beats me.'

Lotte frowned at his dismissive tone and his deliberate

refusal to see the point, and she felt a flicker of irritation. Keeping her eyes on the ground, she said, 'Can't you see any romance in what they are doing? Doesn't the dream of it stir you at all?'

'Romance? Dream? I see an endless slog to restore a garden which could be made just as delightful with little or no reference to the past. At half the cost, too, I bet.'

Irritation was in danger of licking into anger. 'Oh, you'll never understand, Brody. You are such an instant, pay-for-it-and-get-it-done-yesterday sort of guy. I can't believe you've so little feeling for the past. And take no pleasure in the careful uncovering of old secrets.'

Brody's hand gripped her shoulder, stopping her on the path. 'Hey, Lott. Cool it. It's only a garden. And someone else's garden at that. No need to get so steamed up, chicko.'

Suddenly she felt foolish. Why was she getting emotional about Heligan? Brody was right, it was someone else's garden. But she did want him to understand. As they strolled between the pools in the valley and made their way back up the woodland walk to the restaurant, she tried hard to keep her voice cool as she explained that what she loved about the Heligan project was the way it went on, year after year, gradually revealing more of the old garden. And the way it worked on a local level, with volunteers excavating, digging, planting and weeding. And with the produce ending in the restaurant kitchen, the fruit used for jams sold in the shop.

She ended lamely, 'It's not just a rich man's folly, you see. It's a whole eco-system. And it's for everyone.'

Brody had listened to all this in silence, but now a burst

of laughter escaped him. 'Oh Lott! Eco-system indeed! Where did you learn such greenie-babble? If they could afford to do without the public and without the volunteers, you can bet your sweet life they would. The only reason —'

It was too much. Lotte felt the blood charge into her face. She cried, 'It's not greenie-babble! Can't you see there is something right, something satisfying about the inclusiveness, the community aspect of the thing? That local craftsmen . . .'

'Lott, Lott!' Brody interrupted. '"Inclusiveness", "community aspect"! I didn't have you down for a touchy-freely new-age babe.' He put his arm over her shoulder, pulling her to him, laughing.

The familiarity of the hug, the teasing voice, the laughing, the deliberate non-comprehension, combined to ignite Lotte. For a second what she felt was pure hatred. She flung her arm up to remove Brody's hand and snapped, 'Oh, belt up, Brody. You'll never understand. I shouldn't have bothered.'

She quickened her pace, leaving him standing stock-still on the path. Tears burnt hot behind her eyes, but she forced herself to walk with her head held high. She would not be childish as well as over-emotional. She would just stay ahead of Brody and pull herself together.

He didn't call after her or try to catch her up. They were not far from the restaurant, and in five minutes she was there. She didn't look back, but walked on to the Ladies, giving Brody, she hoped, time to get to Jade before she did. If Jade was there, they could not continue the conversation.

Lotte looked at her flushed face in the washroom

mirror. As she stood there, shame crept in to replace the anger. Shame at losing her composure, at showing so much of her feelings to a man who didn't care a scrap for them. Shame at her own humourlessness. Brody had hit on a side of her that could not bear teasing. Why am I so earnest and moralistic, she thought. Why can't I just go with the flow?

It was the righteous side of her, at least in part, that had made her leave her last job: she'd come to believe the elegant buildings they designed were there to flatter corporate egos and governments and to intimidate ordinary mortals. She'd have liked to design less grandiose, friendlier, more human-scale architecture, but that wasn't the Richard Johnson style. So she'd left. An extreme reaction. Just as her minding so much that Brody didn't agree with her was extreme. Underneath this usually controlled exterior, she thought, lies a madwoman.

All Brody said when she joined him and Jade at the restaurant was, 'Well, that was quite a morning. Both my women stomping off in a huff.'

Lotte found herself smiling. Only Brody could be so insouciant. And she didn't mind – though she should – being included in that 'my women'. But Jade minded a lot, you could see. And not about Brody's possessive 'my'. What she minded was sharing the space with Lotte.

13. Late Spring

But come ye back, when summer's in the meadow
Or when the valley's hushed and white with snow.
It's I'll be here, in sunshine or in shadow.
Oh Danny Boy, oh Danny Boy, I love you so.

Fred Weatherly (1848–1929), 'Danny Boy'

In the afternoon they flew to County Wicklow. Again it was a long ride, and a little bumpy over the sea. Lotte had stuck an anti-seasickness patch behind her ear and was feeling fine. But Jade was silent, whether from sickness or the sulks, Lotte could not tell.

Lotte was relieved that Brody, for once, had surrendered the controls to his co-pilot. As they flew over Powerscourt, he swung round to point things out to them, jabbing the window with his finger.

'Look, can you see the terraces, Lotte? Great green steps in the hill? It took a hundred men twelve years to make those. Fantastic, isn't it?'

Indeed it was. Four pairs of curving giant steps were cut into the park above the lake. Each pair met the central backbone of cascades running down to the lake. They formed a huge amphitheatre with the water as the stage.

Brody was jabbing the window again. 'I've climbed up

that waterfall,' he said, grinning at the memory. 'And poached in those woods, and swum bollock-naked in that lake.'

His face tense with excitement, Brody remained glued to the window as the little plane circled, only straightening up when the view of Powerscourt disappeared as the plane dropped down to land. Lotte watched him, intrigued. So you're not as immune to the pull of old gardens as you'd have us believe, she thought. I'll have you yet, Brody.

Brody insisted they give the hotel dining room a miss and eat at his old haunt, Johnny Fox's. They took a taxi, and the driver wanted to charge them £40 for the ten-minute trip.

Lotte, who was sitting in front and about to pay, was taken aback. 'Forty pounds?' she said. 'Surely not? We've only come from Enniskerry. It can't –'

Brody interrupted from the back. 'I'll deal with this, Lotte. You and Jade go inside and bag us a table.'

Lotte was relieved. She hated squabbling over money. She jumped out of the taxi. 'Thanks, Brody,' she said. 'Shall we go, Jade?'

As the two women walked to the door, they heard Brody's raised voice. 'Be-Jasus, man. What do you take me for? An ignorant English tourist, ripe for the plucking?' His accent was a good deal more Irish than Lotte had ever heard it.

The two women had hardly sat down at the only table they could find – against the wall with two couples already at one end of it – when Brody joined them, shunting Lotte up to sit next to her on the bench. He looked very merry. He'd given the man a tenner and told him to count himself lucky.

'Didn't he argue?' asked Jade.

Brody grinned. 'Of course not.'

Wise taxi driver, Lotte thought. I bet Brody was a bruiser before he got rich. He still looks as though he'd enjoy a scrap.

She looked round the pub, eyes round with amazement. She caught Jade's eye across the table and was glad to see that for once her cool had failed her. She responded to Lotte's look with, 'Well! Who would have thought there could be such a joint out here in the boondocks.'

The pub was indeed astonishing. For all it was high up on the hills in the middle of nowhere, it was huge: a warren of dimly lit interconnecting rooms, each one crammed with old wooden tables, all packed with customers. Behind the great double-sided bar half a dozen staff shoved over-flowing pints of Guinness to the three-deep crowd jostling for attention.

Every inch of wall space, every beam and ledge, was crammed with ancient bric-à-brac. Old farming clobber like scythes and buckets competed for space with domestic bowls and jugs, fishing tackle, guns, Fifties advertisements, anything and everything.

Brody grabbed a passing waitress by her waist. Unfazed, she fished out her order pad and smiled. He shouted above the din, 'We'll have three grilled lobsters and a big bowl of chips, and three pints of Guinness.' He glanced at the women, and said, 'OK, girls? That's what they do here – seafood. And it's the best.'

Jade started to protest that she didn't want chips or

beer, but Brody heaved himself half over the table to kiss her, saying, 'Nonsense, darling. In Johnny Fox's everyone eats chips and drinks Guinness.' This was patently untrue. There were bottles of Sauvignon Blanc and Ballygowan water on the next table. Jade must have caught something of Brody's pleasure in the place, because she smiled back at him and didn't argue.

Half the place seemed to be a restaurant, with a few tourists and many more well-heeled Dubliners or couples from Bray eating enormous pyramids of seafood. But in the rest of the pub serious drinking was going on, with no culinary distraction.

Within seconds Brody was talking to the couples at the other end of their table, and a handsome, slightly unsteady young man was chatting Jade up, or trying to. Lotte sat back and let the hubbub of soft Irish voices wash over her. It felt pretty good.

And the food was wonderful. Lotte had never been served a lobster of that size or succulence in all her years of stylish dining in London. It came with a jug of home-made Hollandaise sauce, which she tried to resist, but couldn't. And the Guinness went down smooth and rich, warming her like a blessing.

To her surprise, and Brody's obvious pleasure, Jade ate everything too. She'd looked dismayed at the cholesterol-laden chips and the Hollandaise, but had yielded to Brody's demands that, for once, she enjoy her food.

For pudding Brody ordered apple cobbler and custard for them all, again without consultation. He was still fired up, delighted that the pub was as he remembered, and gratified by Jade's pleasure. He spoke with proprietary pride, telling them how mates working behind the bar used to slip him drinks, how he joined the Irish jig sessions to get to meet girls.

'And the room down there, on the end, that was where the local sympathizers met the IRA boys from the North. They never had to pay for anything.' He leant back and chuckled. 'Those guys are probably wearing suits and talking about the peace process now. In those days we thought we'd get knee-capped if we opened the door.'

Lotte listened, trying to imagine Brody too timid to open a door, or too poor to buy a drink. 'Did you work here, Brody?' she asked.

'I did and all. But I wasn't supposed to. You had to be eighteen. But I'd been sleeping on one of these benches while my da got drunk for so long, I guess they regarded me as family. I started cleaning the yard and washing up. But I was away to England and a job as a baker before I was old enough to pull a pint.' He looked, Lotte thought, wistful, almost sad.

Jade lifted her hair off her face with the back of her hand and said drily, 'Good thing too. Or you'd have followed your father.'

Lotte expected Brody to take offence at this, but he threw back his head and laughed, showing pink gums and a couple of gold fillings.

'Too right, baby!' he said, tossing off the last of his Guinness. He lifted the empty glass at a waitress, holding up two fingers of his other hand to signal his order for two more. 'On the other hand, I might have ended up owning the joint. What do you think, Lotte?'

Lotte noticed that Brody's streaked, greenish-hazel eyes had huge dark pupils. It's the gloom in here, she thought, mine and Jade's must be the same. Then she focused on the question and answered, 'The latter, I think. But you might have got into gun-running as a side-line.'

The conversation was interrupted by the arrival of a bearded folk singer. As he set up his amplifiers in the corner, he joshed with the customers, obviously familiar with most of them. Soon he was prattling into the microphone in a soft brogue, introducing his songs, then singing in a lilting tenor.

Mostly he sang Irish folk songs, and Lotte was amazed at how many people knew the words. Gradually, encouraged by his gentle goading, more and more customers joined in until the whole pub reverberated to an old-style sing-along.

Brody knew all the words too, and sang in a deep vibrant bass. He leant back against the wall and stretched his arm along the back of the bench behind Lotte. Lotte, eyes shut to hear the music better, leant back without realizing his arm was there. As soon as she felt it against her back she leant forward again.

'Sorry,' she said, turning to him and smiling into his eyes. She felt relaxed and confident.

'No problem,' he said, 'feel free. This is Ireland.' And he gave her shoulders a hug.

At once Lotte looked across to Jade, who lifted a cool eyebrow at her. But somehow Lotte didn't care. She knew Brody was only being friendly, that Jade had no cause for jealousy. She was tired of stepping round Jade's innuendoes and bad behaviour. Maybe it was the effect of the

Guinness, but she decided that if Jade had a problem with Brody's arm on her shoulders, then tough.

In fact, Brody didn't keep his arm there, and for a split second Lotte felt the loss of it. He leant forward and signalled to the singer.

'How about something these English ladies can sing? Like "Molly Malone" or "Danny Boy"?'

The singer nodded his agreement and sure enough, soon everyone in the pub was singing 'Molly Malone.' Everyone except Jade. Brody stretched across and held her arm. 'C'mon, darling. I know you can sing.' He gazed into her eyes and sang, 'Cockles, and mussels, alive, alive-O'. But Jade shook her head.

So Lotte and Brody sang, smiling at each other and occasionally at Jade, as they belted out 'Danny Boy' and then a succession of ballads from 'Greensleeves' to 'Mrs Robinson' via the 'Skye Boat Song' and 'Scarborough Fair'. It was corny, sure, but wonderful: friendly and exhilarating.

Suddenly Jade got up, saying she needed the loo, and left them. Poor girl, Lotte thought. She doesn't know how to enjoy herself.

The singer took a break, and Brody was talking to the couple across the aisle about the Irish elections. Lotte took the opportunity to follow Jade to the cloakroom. There were a few women queuing but no sign of Jade. When Lotte got into a cubicle, though, Jade's pink and purple bucket-bag was visible under the partition between her compartment and the next.

Suddenly, she heard the unmistakable sound of retching followed by violent vomiting from Jade's side of the partition. Lotte didn't know what to do. Poor Jade, she thought, she can't be drunk. She's only drunk half her Guinness. She must be sick. No wonder she didn't want to sing. She called out, 'Jade, are you all right?'

There was no answer. Indeed, now there was no sound at all.

Lotte, concerned, tapped on the partition and called again, 'Jade. Are you OK? Shall I get Brody?' Still no answer. Lotte hesitated, her hand about to tap on the wall again. Then suddenly she realized what it was: Jade must be pregnant.

Lotte washed her hands at the basin, and dithered about leaving Jade. Women were coming and going, and it seemed heartless to leave her, feeling awful, with strangers gawping at her. But Jade was so difficult, and she obviously resented Lotte knowing she'd been sick, otherwise she'd have answered, surely?

Lotte decided to leave her, but changed her mind when she was half-way back through the crowded pub. She couldn't just abandon the woman to heave her guts up. She turned round and wove her way back to the cloakroom.

She found Jade cleaning her teeth at the basin. How efficient, Lotte thought, to have a toothbrush and paste in her bag in case she's sick! She was about to say something when a couple of seriously drunk young women recognized Jade. One said, 'Hey, you're that model off the telly, aren't you?'

'Yeah, tha's right. Jade Allen!' cried her friend. 'With the breakfast cereal and the cute guy with a hangover! That's a pretty cool ad.'

Lotte watched Jade in the mirror. She looked up from

the basin with a hunted look on her face. She stuffed the toothbrush into her toilet pouch and crammed it into her bag. Lotte noticed how bloodshot her eyes were and how pale her skin.

The young women, emboldened by alcohol, were each side of Jade now, elated at their proximity to fame. But Jade cut through their chatter with a furious 'Piss off' as she swung away from the basin.

The girls were stunned into silence for a second, then retaliated with loud jibes, as hostile now as they'd been admiring before. As they bumped out of the door, one of them shouted over her shoulder, 'The stupid cow is well past it anyway. She looks like shit.'

Jade still hadn't seen Lotte, although there was no one left in the room except her now. She had her back to Lotte as she dried her hands at the roller-towel. Lotte considered backing out unobserved – Jade would certainly not have wanted a witness to her unlovely exchange with the girls – when Jade put her face into the towel and burst into tears. She sobbed in heaving, ugly gasps. Lotte walked up behind her and put a hand on her shoulder.

'Jade', she said, 'don't. Nothing can be that bad.'

Jade sprang round, and Lotte again noticed the red eyes. That must be the vomiting. She asked, 'Are you preg –?'

'Why the hell are you still here?' snapped Jade. 'Are you haunting me or something?'

Lotte was momentarily silenced by her rudeness, then anger erupted like a geyser. 'What's the matter with you, Jade? For God's sake, I came back because I was worried about you. I knew you were being sick and I thought you might get mobbed.'

The two women stared at each other, and Lotte concluded, 'But I'll know better next time.'

Jade suddenly leant against the wall and closed her eyes. She looked gaunt in the harsh light. 'Look, I'm sorry, Lotte. I'm really sorry.'

Lotte immediately softened, saying a little stiffly, 'No problem. But is there anything I can do?'

Jade opened her eyes and looked at her with dead eyes. Lotte said, more gently, 'You're pregnant, aren't you? Does Brody know?'

Jade gave a short barking laugh, 'Pregnant! No chance. For starters, I'd never have kids, and anyway I've starved myself so much I can't have them anyway.' Her eyes had regained some life, hard and cold. 'Happy families are for people like you.'

Lotte forced herself not to react. Jade was obviously wretched. Lotte said, 'Maybe you're allergic to lobster? We should go back to the hotel and get a doctor.'

Jade's smile was wan. 'No doctor.' She rummaged in her bag for a brush and swiped it through her hair a couple of times. 'It's nothing. I'm used to it.'

She did look a little better. She wasn't so pale and the vulnerability had gone. She was back to her old unfriendly self.

'Is there nothing I can do?' Lotte asked.

'Not unless you've got a line of coke.' Jade stuffed her brush into her bag and bared her teeth for inspection in the mirror. She caught Lotte's eye and said, 'Oh, Lotte, don't look so shocked. It was a joke, I don't do drugs.' She held Lotte's gaze in the mirror and added, 'You could help if you had a cure for bulimia.'

Lotte saw at once that that was it. Jade was bulimic. The red eyes, the toothbrush kit, the avoidance of eating publicly. This was the first time she'd seen her eat a proper meal and she hadn't been able to avoid it. Brody would not have taken no from either of them – he'd practically forced the lobster and cobbler down them.

Jade was still speaking, her voice bitter. 'And since I'm sure you are dying to know: yes, I do raid the larder at night; yes, I do binge on chocolates, and yes, I do stick my finger down my throat.'

'Oh God,' said Lotte, 'how horrible for you.'

Jade picked up her bag and said, 'My shrink says I do it because I hate myself. Well, most people hate me. Including you. And Brody tells me you are always right. So maybe it's the correct judgment.'

Lotte put an arm round her bony shoulders and said, 'Look Jade . . .'

But Jade shook her off. 'You can't help. No one can. And anyway, it's the only way I know to stay at seven stone.' She walked out of the door ahead of Lotte, flinging over her shoulder, 'Only don't you bloody dare tell Brody.'

Lotte let Jade get back to the table first. When she joined them, she was surprised to see no trace of the desperate girl she'd been with in the loo. In her place sat the elegant, immobile, cool-as-a-cucumber Jade. She was sitting next to Brody now, where Lotte had sat before, and Brody's arm was round her waist.

Brody looked up and signalled to her. 'Get me a Jamieson's, Lott. I can't get out. And what about yourself? Make them doubles while you're at it.'

'And some mineral water. Fizzy,' said Jade.

As the barman put the bottle of mineral water and Brody's whiskey down on the bar, Lotte thought, why not? She ordered another double.

As she started back to the table, she heard Brody's voice, mellow and deep, singing solo at the microphone. Surprised, she stopped and watched him. She didn't know the song, it was in Irish, but it had a gentle, easy tune, so simple as to feel familiar. He finished the first verse, smiling confidently at his audience, and then lifted his voice to lead everyone in the chorus.

Lotte put the Keegans' drinks on a ledge and leant against the wall, sipping her whiskey. Brody sang the second verse, low and sweet. Lotte closed her eyes and let the sound fall round her. The words 'gentle rain from heaven' popped into her head.

Silly, she thought, that's *The Merchant of Venice* and it's about mercy, not music. I must be drunk. I ought to go and sit with Jade. Poor woman. I wish I could make a friend of her. She needs a friend. But the truth is, I don't like her.

Lotte watched the drinkers sway gently to the chorus, then once again let Brody's rich bass voice get to her, get inside her head and her body. This time she kept her eyes open. He looked terrific, brawny and fit, his eyes dark and alive, his hand steady as he held the mike, his feet just slightly apart, legs relaxed, one foot gently tapping to the rhythm of his song.

It was like a massage, or a warm bath. Brody's voice caressed her and stirred her. She thought of his arm against her back, and how if he hugged her again she might turn into his embrace. Have that stocky body up against hers, those strong legs against her thighs.

Brody's song was over, and he was bowing to claps and cheers. Lotte pulled herself out of her fantasy. She shook her head slightly in self-reproof and made her way to the table. She put the drinks down and said to Jade, 'Are you sure you don't want some whiskey? It might settle your stomach. Have this . . .'

Jade's eyes glittered hostility. 'Stuff what I want. What you want is plain as day. You want my husband, don't you?' she said.

Oh God, thought Lotte. Can she read minds? But she said evenly, 'No. No, I don't. Why do you ask?'

She was saved by the arrival of Brody, demanding congratulations and whiskey. Lotte, her face hot with shame, tried to provide them, while Jade sat silent.

Brody could feel the pent-up rage in Jade's back as he ushered her out of the lift. She stalked ahead of him down the corridor. He watched her high round bum in her shiny trousers and felt a mixture of irritation and lust. Why did she have to be so bloody difficult?

He was embarrassed for Lotte too. All evening she'd valiantly pretended that Jade wasn't sulking, and now the poor girl was trailing behind him as Jade marched in front.

Jade had no option but to wait for him at their door, because he had the key. He caught her up and turned to Lotte, already fitting her key into the next-door room.

'·'Night, Lott,' he said. 'Shall we say nine for breakfast?'

'Yes, fine,' said Lotte. 'And thank you for a wonderful evening. It was a fantastic pub. I loved it.'

As soon as Brody had shut their door, Jade flung her bag into the corner of the room and rounded on him.

''Course she bloody loved it. She was gagging for you. Why don't you just go next door and screw the bitch?' she said.

Brody had been expecting her anger. He was familiar with the signs. But he hadn't expected that tack. He frowned. 'Jade, darling, what are you on about? You cannot be jealous of Lotte!' He walked towards her, holding out his arms.

She swung away. 'Jealous! Who said anything about jealous? As far as I'm concerned, she's welcome.'

Brody knew what Jade was doing. She was trying to provoke him to anger so she could be in the right. But he didn't feel angry, only weary. A great evening was going to end in a row.

He watched his wife prowl around the room, flinging her jewellery on the dressing-table, yanking her clothes off as if they were the enemy. When she was down to her underclothes she swept into the bathroom and shut the door.

Brody undressed slowly and got into bed. He lay on his back, eyes open to the ceiling. Maybe he'd have to say goodbye to Lotte. Jade was becoming obsessive about her. She found fault with her attitude, with her work, with her children. And she was increasingly rude to her.

Why was Jade so jealous? Was she mad? He'd never been anything but friendly to Lotte, and Lotte was a mouse. Good enough looking, true, and with a feisty attitude you didn't expect. He liked the way she took him on about the garden. But physically, she was a mouse.

She's also amazingly tolerant with Jade, he thought. It must take some steel to turn a blind eye as she does – she gets crosser with me than with Jade. But I bet she minds. You only have to see her with those children to see how much heart she has.

For a minute or two Brody managed not to think of Jade by thinking about Lotte's children. They were good kids. His face softened. That Jo-Jo is great, he thought, a little bruiser in angel's curls. Lovely to have a daughter like that. And Christopher was clever. Going to make his mam pretty proud one day.

He mused on about Lotte, wondering what her background was. He'd never asked her about the father of her children. He presumed there was a man around somewhere, because the children seemed to disappear some weekends.

And that mad professor type, the historian who was helping with Maddon's history, he was always about. Wasn't he babysitting right now? Maybe she's having a roll in the hay with him?

Brody didn't like this thought, and shifted in the bed. He let his mind go back to the pub. It pleased him that Lotte had loved it so. He hadn't really expected Jade to like the place, but he thought she might have been jolted out of her London cool, and just let go and enjoyed herself. At first it looked as though she would. But no. He sighed, rolled on to his side and reached for the magazine on the bedside table.

But he found he was reading whole paragraphs without taking them in, all the while considering Jade. He wanted his wife to like what he liked – which included the simple stuff he'd grown up with, like a good Irish pub with bags of atmosphere, home-made food and friendly strangers.

And little Lotte had been a good sport, entering into the spirit of the thing. He could see her face now, face flushed and eyes dreamy as she sang.

Jade emerged from the bathroom in a dressing-gown, only sliding it off as she slipped into bed. When she was angry with him she didn't march about naked as she usually did. Now she said nothing, just turned her back and turned off her light. Brody knew he was supposed to woo her, but he couldn't summon the energy. And anyway, he didn't feel like it.

But in the night she moved up against his back and put her arms around him, whispering, 'Brody, I'm so, so sorry. I was such a cow.'

At first he lay immobile. But she laced her legs through his, climbed on to him, rubbed her warm body against his, sweeping her great curtain of hair across his chest.

Of course he gave in and made love to her. And told her it was OK, he loved her as he always had. But afterwards, when her steady breathing and total stillness told him she was asleep, he allowed himself the tired thought: this is crazy — we can't go on like this. I need some peace in my life.

14. Summer

When I see birches bend to left and right
Across the lines of straighter darker trees,
I like to think some boy's been swinging them.

Robert Frost (1874–1963), 'Birches'

'Why can't we go to Blenheim Palace, Mum? And go on
the little train?' Jo-Jo turned to Peter. 'Peter, please make
Mum give in. It will be so boring in Maddon Woods.
There's nothing to do.'

Peter pushed the folded picnic rug at Jo-Jo, saying,
'Sorry, sweetheart, but I'm siding with your mum on this.'

Lotte was tugging at the stuck zip of the cool-bag, and
she answered without looking up. 'It won't be boring. It's
a lovely day, and we can explore. And whoever finds what
we are looking for will get a prize.'

'Who'll get a prize? For what?' Christo asked as he
swung into the kitchen on his skate-board, swirling to a
practised stop in front of the Aga.

'Christo, get off that thing. There's no room in here.'
Lotte transferred Cokes and cans of lager from the fridge
to the drinks-cooler. 'We are hunting for some evidence of
my mediaeval ponds. Or the Persian pool. Or the grotto.'

Annie looked up from her book. 'Get real, Mum. You'll

never find them. And if you did, Brody wouldn't let you restore them.'

She's right, Lotte thought as she stacked the picnic box, rug, drinks-cooler and undergrowth-clearing kit – sickle, machete, loppers, secateurs, spades and gardening gloves – in the drive, but he can't stop me looking for them.

Annie didn't take her nose out of her book until Alex and Jamie arrived on their bikes, when she dived upstairs, presumably, thought Lotte, to change her black clothes for other black clothes. Lotte had invited the students to join them. Alex would be leaving to go back to college in the autumn, and Jamie had just arrived to spend a year at Maddon. She hoped to engage them in her Old Pond Yards quest. They were, after all, horticultural students, and might be – or should be – interested in garden history.

The lads loaded most of the gear on to their bicycles and Christo's. Everyone walked across the park, the boys pushing bikes and Jo-Jo skipping about, her earlier complaints forgotten. Lotte, Peter and Annie carried spades and loppers over their shoulders.

At the spot where you could look towards the house and line the three oaks up in a straight row, Lotte stopped.

'Here,' she said, 'here's my path. It gets overgrown as fast as I clear it, but we'll be able to get through OK. Only not with bikes.'

They divided the baskets and rugs between them. Alex went ahead into the green tunnel, machete in one hand, bush-whacking nettles and brambles out of the way. It was cool and dark, and Jamie, who was taller than the burly Alex, had his baseball cap pulled off by an overhanging branch. He didn't notice, and Annie picked it up and put it on her own head, backwards.

Jo-Jo, walking behind Annie, darted forward to whip the cap off her sister's head. Annie tried to snatch it back, hissing, 'Give it back Jo-Jo or I'll . . .'

'You'll what? . . . Cry?' Jo-Jo jumped about the narrow path, taunting her sister. 'I know why you want it – you're soft on –'

'Shut UP!' Annie wrenched the cap out of Jo-Jo's hand. The scuffle had stopped the others, and Jamie turned round.

'What's up, girls?' he asked.

Annie, her face beetroot, shoved the cap at him. 'Here. I picked it up.'

Jamie took the cap, looking puzzled. 'Thanks, Annie,' he said, returning it to his head.

'C'mon, guys,' Peter called from the back, 'less tom-foolery and more progress, please.'

After about 500 yards the laurels were behind them and the path came out into more open forest. They followed a trampled track through classic English woods of thorns, ash, occasional large oaks, holly and hazel. Nettles and brambles threatened the path, and fallen tree trunks and broken branches meant they had to duck and weave. But eventually they were in a stand of beech trees. Not much grew beneath them, and the leaf-mould was soft and springy under their feet. Some of the trees were huge, with elephant-grey trunks going straight up to a high filigree canopy, through which sunlight spattered the forest floor like gold coins.

'Pretty good, you've got to admit,' Lotte said, shaking out a rug.

'It's wonderful,' Peter agreed. 'Isn't it, Annie?'

Annie looked round, determined not to be impressed. 'What's so great about it? It's just a load of trees, and piles of dead leaves and stuff.'

'I think it's great,' said Jamie, his head thrown back to look at the slanting rays through the leaves. 'And I bet no one ever comes here. Like a secret wood.'

Lotte said, 'Years ago they used to rear pheasants in these woods, and then I guess there were poachers and game-keepers all over it. But Brody doesn't shoot, so no one comes here much. Except me.'

'Mum, can we have the picnic now? Before exploring? I'm starving.' It was Christo, rootling in the picnic basket.

But Lotte wouldn't give in. Lunch, she said, would be at one, when they had all gone off in separate directions for half an hour, allowing another half hour to get back. 'Here,' she said, handing each student and Christo a hiker's compass. 'Do you know how to use these?'

Jamie and Alex said they did, but Lotte, fearing adolescent male pride, explained anyway, pretending the explanation was for Christo's benefit.

'They aren't deadly accurate, but they'll get you back to within shouting distance if you get lost,' she said.

Annie raised her eyes to heaven. 'Mum, we are hardly likely to get lost. We can't be half a mile from home. This is Maddon Woods, not the Amazon jungle.'

'Sweetheart, it's extraordinarily easy to get lost in a forest. We may be half a mile from the edge, but there are fifteen acres behind us, and if you don't know . . .'

'OK, OK. I get the picture, Mum,' Annie interrupted,

glancing at Jamie, who just said, 'She's right, kiddo.' Annie scowled.

Lotte pressed on. 'Now, each child gets a grown-up for a team-mate. 'Who do you want to go with, Jo-Jo?'

'Alex,' said Jo-Jo, quick as a flash. 'He's got the machete.'

Christo, after a dragon-look from Annie, said he didn't care. Lotte caught the look and felt a pang for her churlish daughter, so obviously keen to impress Jamie and going about it by being as childish, rude and sulky as possible.

She handed Peter, Jamie and Alex spades. 'OK. So what we are looking for is any lumpy ground that isn't just roots. Anything that could be old buildings or paving cobbles. Or a big hollow that could have been a pond, or what might have been a stream or channel. If you find anything, mind you mark the way back so we can find it later.'

Peter said he'd go on his own, and they agreed on the quadrants each of the four parties would cover.

Lotte enjoyed her hour with Christo. He wasn't looking for ponds. He was climbing logs and kicking things. But she didn't mind: it was so nice to have him to herself. As he chattered away about the school photography club, and his chemistry teacher, Lotte thought how much happier, how much less stressed he was now.

And then suddenly he said, 'You know, Mum, I can handle it if you marry Peter.'

Lotte's heart missed a beat. Keeping her voice steady she replied, 'What made you say that? Do you want a step-father?'

Christo looked up at her quickly. 'No, of course not. I've got a real father.' For a second his eyes seemed to regain their old strained look. He picked up a stick and began pulling the dead leaves from the end of it. 'But Peter's OK. He's cool.'

'What makes you think Peter and I want to get married? We're just good friends.' She smiled at the trite phrase, and added, 'No, really.'

'I bet Peter wants to even if you don't,' said Christo. 'He wouldn't look after us while you go to look at gardens with the Keegans for no reason. And teach Annie to ride his bike, and me to develop photographs and stuff, would he?'

'Why not? Don't undersell yourselves.' Lotte put her arm round Christo and hugged him briefly. 'You're the best children in the world. And I think he's been rather lonely up to now, with only grown-up work colleagues to talk to. I bet you're more fun than me. All I think about is gardening.'

Christo smiled, relaxed. Lotte said, 'Still, I do like having him around. But no marriage plans, I promise.'

No one found anything, but everyone had enjoyed the attempt. Even Annie, it seemed, had got quite excited about a moss-covered straight ridge, but it had turned out to be a fallen tree trunk, half buried.

Lotte looked up at the trees above and around them. 'Peter, this open bit is all beech. Wouldn't that mean it was a man-made plantation?'

Peter nodded. 'Yes, I guess so. Beech was used, still is, to make furniture. Windsor chairs in particular. How old are these trees?'

'A hundred years. A hundred and fifty at the outside. Which means if this bit of the indigenous forest was cleared that long ago, the ponds would have been filled in then. But they are marked on the 1930 Ordnance Survey map.'

Peter handed round beers and Cokes. Jamie said, 'Couldn't they have just left the ponds, planted round them?'

'Maybe. But perhaps they avoided the ponds when they chose the plantation site. I've an awful feeling my ponds are in the thickly overgrown belt we came through.'

'So? Hello . . . o? Why are we looking here then?' asked Annie, opening her eyes wide and looking at her mother as though she were half-witted. Lotte considered telling her not to be rude, and then, as her daughter helped herself to a beer, telling her not to show off, that she was too young for alcohol, but then decided not to humiliate her in front of the young men, and said nothing. I'll get the can off her in a minute, she thought, and answered the question as though it had been asked politely.

'Because I've only just thought of it. And I may be wrong. As Jamie says, whoever cleared the older wood, or planted the beech, might have left the Pond Yards intact, or as intact as they were.'

'Or,' said Alex, 'the belt of laurel, planted at the edge of the park ages ago, just spread and swallowed your ponds.'

'Quite,' said Lotte, feeling depressed.

The Spanish potato omelette, made by Peter, was hefty and very garlicky with a cheesy-herby topping browned under the grill. It was still just warm, and they ate it wrapped in lettuce leaves. Lotte had fried a dozen sausages with mustard, soy and honey, and they ate them in fancy little dinner rolls from the covered market in Oxford. They disappeared in minutes.

Lotte thought how satisfying it was to feed young men. They were less picky than her children and they ate more, making appreciative noises, not complaints. They had cinnamony red berry compote with a layer of yogurt and crème fraîche on top for pudding. Lotte had made them in old yogurt tubs and she sprinkled a nutty crumble mix on top of each as she handed them out. After that she produced a plastic box of cut-up fruit, Greek style: large chunks of pear, melon, banana, and mini-bunches of grapes, plus a handful of cherries. They ate with their fingers, and ended with large squares of fudge, made by Jo-Jo and Christo.

Jamie licked his fingers and flopped backwards on to the rug.

'Wow, Lotte. That was great. I wish my mum cooked like that.'

'Peter did the only real cooking. He made the tortilla,' said Lotte, smiling over her beer can at Peter.

This clearly impressed the boys. 'Really?' asked Alex. 'My mother complains Dad doesn't know where the tea-towels live.'

Peter looked embarrassed, but pleased. His hand smoothed his scalp. 'Ah, but I've had thirty years of living on my own,' he said. 'Learning to cook beats a diet of takeaways.'

'Well, anyway,' said Jamie, 'that was an ace picnic. *My* mother's idea of a picnic is a sandwich from the supermarket and a Kit-Kat.' Lotte smiled at the compliment, but felt momentarily put out by the realization that she was, indeed, old enough to be his mother.

Annie lay down next to Jamie, wriggling to get a bit of the rug. 'Should have brought my CD player,' she said.

'No, you shouldn't,' said Jamie. 'Listen. That's a green woodpecker. Its call sounds like laughing. Do you hear?'

Everyone listened for a few seconds and the loud ringing call came again. Jamie said, 'Its other names are Yaffle and Rainbird.'

Annie looked at him wide-eyed. 'How do you know all this stuff?' she asked.

'Dunno. I like birds. And if you work outside, you hear them, I guess.'

Lotte hadn't planned more searching after lunch, but to her surprise Annie said, 'Jamie, if Mum thinks the ponds are under the jungle bit, shall we try one side of the path, and Christo and Alex can do the other?'

Her voice sounded a little odd, louder than usual, and Lotte looked up at her daughter. Annie's face was bright red, flushed and hot. Oh dear, thought Lotte, I forgot to drink half her beer.

When they'd gone, Jo-Jo clambered over a fallen tree at the edge of the clearing and then busied herself making a den under it, while Lotte and Peter lay on the picnic rug looking up at the soaring beech trunks and the perfectly fanned branches.

What bliss this is, thought Lotte. Not just the beauty of it, but the silence. No pop music, no children quarrelling, no tractors, chain-saws or strimmers. No mobile phone.

'"God's cathedrals". That's what my mother used to call beech woods,' she said.

Peter, dozing, said, 'Mmm,' and reached a hand out to touch her arm.

'Peter,' Lotte said, still looking up through the leaves, 'why are you so good to me?'

Peter fingered his forehead as he replied, 'We are good to each other, aren't we?'

'No. I mean, how come you take on all the boring bits, like my children, and cooking omelettes, and never make any demands? I'm doing all the taking, and none of the giving.'

Peter turned his head to look into her face. 'You mean, why don't I insist on sex?'

The light caught his glasses and Lotte could not see his expression. She leant up on her elbow.

'Well, yes. I suppose I do. We've been so close, a couple really, for a year. Except we don't sleep together. And I know that's my doing. But it's not just that. You do things for me all the time, but you don't expect me to do anything for you.'

'You mean, darn my socks or iron my shirts?' Peter smiled but his eyes were anxious. 'Anyway, you do. You collected my books from Blackwell's last week, remember?'

Lotte pushed him lightly in the ribs. 'You know what I mean.'

Peter looked up into the trees. He spoke slowly, carefully. 'Sex isn't everything. Of course I want you, Lotte. You know that. But I'd want you to be sure that it was for keeps. I'm too old, too conservative and too bruised to want to gamble with what we've got.'

Lotte felt a pang of remorse. Why had she started this conversation? It was the gentle cool of the forest, the beer. Her vanity. She was suddenly anxious that he'd want to know where he stood. And she didn't know the answer.

But he said, 'The truth is, Lotte, I've only ever been in

love once, twenty-four years ago, and that was with some-one else's wife.' He turned his head at last and their eyes met.

He told her the story softly, conscious of the proximity of Jo-Jo. Peter's lover had been the wife of the Bursar at Radley, the school he'd taught at. She had a two-year-old daughter, and she had not wanted to leave her husband, though Peter was desperate for her to do so. And then the husband had discovered the truth and forced the issue. She left her daughter with her husband and went with Peter to London, where he worked erratically as a supply teacher.

'But it didn't work,' he said. 'She missed her little girl. And then she became pregnant and I was overjoyed – I thought that might make it all right.' Peter's eyes were dark with the misery of decades ago. 'She went back to her husband. He forgave her, and brought up the child as his. I've never seen her or the child since. I don't even know if I have a twenty-three-year-old son or daughter.'

Lotte was silent, tangible sympathy running between them. After a little while she touched his arm and said, 'And since then?'

Peter, kneading his brow, forced a smile. 'Since then I've had a few, unsatisfactory, affairs of the body, none of the heart. All my friendships are – were – male, and bookish – until I met you.'

She wanted to put her arms round him, reassure him, tell him that she loved him and it would be OK. One day it would be OK.

But she wanted to tell him only the truth. And how could she tell him it would work, when she knew it might not? She stroked his arm and said nothing.

Suddenly they were both startled by distant shouting. And then by Jo-Jo, running to Lotte.

'Mum, someone's yelling. What's happened?'

Lotte sat up, her hand raised to silence Jo-Jo so she could listen. 'Someone's coming,' she said, jumping to her feet and facing the sound of breaking sticks and swishing branches. Peter was already running towards the sound.

Alex plunged out of a thicket, his eyes wide and frightened. 'Peter, Lotte,' he gasped, 'come quickly . . . Christo's fallen through . . .'

'What? What's happened?' Lotte shouted, running to him.

'He's fallen into a trap or a well or something. I think he's broken his leg. He can't get out. It's underground. He was ahead of me, and then suddenly he disappeared. I couldn't . . .'

'Quick, show us,' cried Lotte.

'What's happened, Mum? Mummy?' Jo-Jo's voice was shaky. Lotte turned to see her daughter's stricken face, eyes wide, mouth trembling.

She bent over and put her hands on each side of Jo-Jo's face. 'Darling, Christo will be all right I'm sure, but we must go and help him, OK?' Jo-Jo nodded. 'Just stay with us, don't get left behind.'

Lotte took her hand and started to run after Alex, already at the point where he'd emerged from the laurels. He crashed through the undergrowth, clambering over roots, ducking branches, with Peter close behind him. Lotte followed, sometimes hit by branches springing back as Peter surged after Alex. She dropped back to help Jo-Jo, calling, 'Alex, not so fast. We can't keep up.'

He stopped and waited, swirling backwards and forwards in anxiety and impatience. 'Hurry, Lotte, please. Christo is really hurt. And he's in this sort of cave. He can't climb out . . .'

Peter said, 'Look, Lotte, you go with Alex. I'll follow with Jo-Jo. You'll be quicker then.'

Lotte was about to agree, but Jo-Jo clung to her, screaming, 'No, Mummy, no, Mummy, please. Please don't leave me.' She gripped Lotte's tee-shirt with fingers of steel and her hysterical face was too much for Lotte.

'Oh God,' she said. 'Peter, I can't leave her. You go with Alex. Be as quick as you can. We'll follow you. Only break off fresh leafy branches and leave them in the path so we know which way you've gone.'

Peter remonstrated. 'Lotte, darling, this isn't Hansel and Gretel. No one is going to get lost.'

Lotte's control evaporated and she screamed at him, 'Peter, I know these woods and you don't and it is dead easy to get lost. Just do as I say, will you? Go with Alex and leave a trail. Do it!'

As soon as they had caught up with him, Alex plunged further into the woods, this time with Peter. In minutes they were out of sight, screened by a wall of greenery.

Jo-Jo had been silenced by her mother's shouting, and was now crying quietly, obviously terrified. Lotte crouched down by her and said, 'Look, Jo-Jo, I can't carry you. I need both hands to get through the branches. And you have to stop crying so we can get there quickly. OK?'

Jo-Jo sobbed, 'Mummy, what's he mean, Christo's hurt? Why can't he get out? He won't die, will he?'

'Of course not, darling. He'll be fine. But we need to be quick.'

Jo-Jo consented to be led by the hand and they set off after Peter and Alex. Lotte could hear the cracking of twigs, and she pressed forward.

She was glad to see that Peter was laying a trail: there were broken twigs and small branches every twenty yards or so. She pulled Jo-Jo behind her with one hand and wrenched branches aside with the other, so they could clamber through.

And then suddenly there were no more broken branch markers. Trying to control her panic, she went on, following what seemed to her a sort of track for another twenty yards or so, but then she knew they were lost.

Once again she bent down to Jo-Jo and said, 'Darling, we have to go back a bit. I think we've taken a wrong turning.'

She led Jo-Jo back the way she had come, but now she recognized nothing. They carried on for at least sixty yards without finding a single broken branch.

Lotte stopped and held her hand to Jo-Jo's lips to stop her crying. Jo-Jo made a brave attempt, biting her bottom lip and holding her breath. Her eyes, solemn and full of tears, were fixed on her mother's. Lotte stood still, listening intently. She could hear nothing. Nothing but the silence of the wood, which seemed to crowd in on her, pressing her to panic.

Lotte lifted her chin and yelled, 'Alex, Peter, where are you?'

She thought she heard a distant shout but wasn't sure which direction it came from. She yelled again. Nothing.

She didn't know what to do. Peter would come back for her, or send Alex, as soon as they'd found Christo. But when? And would Alex find Christo again? How far away was Christo? And would Alex or Peter find Jo-Jo and her?

She couldn't bear to stay still. She had to find Christo. The thought of his white face grimacing in pain, of jagged bones sticking through his pale skin, tortured her. She'd be able to go faster and cover more of this horrible wood if she left Jo-Jo. But she could not do that. And anyway, she didn't know which way to go. Frustration and fear swelled together.

She took a deep breath and tried to regain control. She crouched down to put her arms round Jo-Jo and said, 'Darling, this bit of wood, the thick green part, is only a quarter of a mile wide. If we keep walking in the same direction we will come to the open park. And if we call out all the time, the others will hear us. And we'll find poor Christo. OK?' She knew she was so frightened herself that she was not reassuring Jo-Jo, and her heart clenched in gratitude when her daughter nodded, trying hard not to cry.

Lotte checked her compass. They were going due west, towards the park and parallel to her hacked path, which must be just to the north. As they ducked and weaved under the branches and trampled over patches of brambles and nettles, Lotte kept an eye on her compass to keep them in a more or less straight line. She knew this might not be the way to Christo, or even Alex, but her instincts, even now, were to be systematic, not just to blunder blindly about.

But after ten minutes of struggling through the laurels and shouting for Alex, Lotte was in despair. Both her forearms were scratched and bleeding from the brambles – she had no gloves and no tools. Jo-Jo was crying again, and they were both out of breath. They stopped in a thinner part of the thicket, where the laurel gave way to thorns and blackberries. It was marshy underfoot, and the mud squelched over Jo-Jo's ankles. She lifted her arms to her mother, like a toddler, and wailed, 'I'm tired, Mummy. Carry me.'

'Oh darling, I can't. I told you I need both hands to push back the brambles and help you over them.'

Jo-Jo accepted this, and once more Lotte shouted, as loud as she could, 'Al . . . e . . . x.'

Immediately they heard an answering cry. A high boy's voice. Christo.

Mother and daughter looked at each other wide-eyed and Jo-Jo clutched Lotte's arm. 'It's Christo, Mum. It's Christo. Let's . . .'

'Shh, darling. Shh.' Lotte turned to the right and called, 'Christo, Christo! Where are you?'

Lotte would never forget the flood of relief, the benison of prayers answered as she heard the boy's answering shout. His voice seemed muffled and distant, but she knew it was his, and she and Jo-Jo scrambled towards the sound.

Finding him, following his shouts, seemed to take forever, but at last they splashed through a boggy patch and could hear his voice, close and clear. 'I'm here, Mum. Here.'

Lotte looked round wildly. She could see nothing but the bole of a tall bat willow, knobbly and covered in moss, growing against a slope. Christo's voice came again, tearful now. 'Mummy, where are you? Help me, Mummy. It hurts.'

His voice seemed to be coming from inside a large mound with an alder growing on it. Lotte leapt up the slope, holding on to the twisted trunk. She shouted, 'Oh darling, where are you, where, sweetheart?'

And then she saw the hole. It was like a huge badger hole, on the far side of the tree between the roots, broken through jagged rock, mud and moss. She fell on her knees and pushed her head into the hole.

'Are you there, Christo? Oh God, darling, are you all right?' But her body blocked the light and she had to pull back a little.

She saw then that Christo was lying at least eight feet down on the floor of a sort of cave. She could make out his pale shirt and bright hair, but she could not see his expression. 'Darling,' she said, 'what hurts?'

'My leg. Mummy, how am I going to get out? I can't move.' His voice shook and came between sobs. 'I'm cold, Mummy, and I can't get out of the water.'

Oh Jesus, thought Lotte, he's broken his back. She said, 'Christo darling, this is important. Can you move your feet? Bend them at the ankle so I can see . . . Do it, darling.'

Christo moved his left foot but not his right. 'I can't, Mum. It hurts . . .'

'Christo, listen to me.' Lotte's voice was commanding and urgent. Christo swallowed his sobs. 'Wiggle the toes of your right foot. You needn't move the whole foot. Just tell me, can you feel your toes against your sneakers when you move them?'

'Ow, ow . . . Yes, I can feel them. But my leg hurts, Mum. I can't bend my leg, it hurts . . .'

Lotte's relief was immediately washed away by a new thought. What if more of the roof fell in before she got Christo out? It seemed that the tree roots were all that was holding it up. Jo-Jo was lying on the slope, a little higher up than Lotte, trying to see into the hole.

'Jo-Jo, get down over there darling, we mustn't send more rocks and mud in on top of Christo.'

Jo-Jo slid down and asked, 'Mummy, what are we going to do?'

Lotte looked at her trusting face, the face of a child as yet unaware that parents are fallible. 'Oh darling,' she said, 'I don't know.'

Lotte was desperate. She longed to jump into the cave with Christo, put her arms around him, kiss him better. But that might cause more rock collapse, and she'd never be able to get Christo out on her own.

She said, 'We'll just have to keep shouting, darling. The others will hear us sooner or later.'

The next hour was a nightmare. Lotte shouted steadily, at the top her voice, to no avail. And then, realizing she would lose her voice, she rationed her shouting to three long 'H . . . e . . . l . . . p's every three minutes. That way, she figured she'd be heard by the boys when they were within earshot, and she'd not waste her breath in repeated yelling when they were not.

Each time she shouted with renewed hope, the answering silence, reverberating through the woods like a mocking echo, brought renewed despair followed by renewed panic. Christo had stopped crying but was moaning in pain. He was no longer answering her efforts at comfort. Lotte imagined internal injuries, her son slipping into unconciousness, dying.

She told herself this was fanciful. But horrible things did happen. Children got locked in abandoned freezers, they drowned in wells. Maybe Christo . . .

Oh, why hadn't she brought her mobile phone? She carried it everywhere when she was working, but this morning to be free of it had seemed a bonus, confirming the fact that she was off duty. Anyway, even if she'd had it, she could not accurately describe where they were. But at least she could have called out a search party.

It was ridiculous to be lost in such familiar woods. And trapped. If she could only leave the children, she knew she'd be in the park in no time, and she'd find her way back, she was sure. But could she trust Jo-Jo to stay with Christo? And what if Peter or the others came back and tried to get Christo out without her, and brought the earth and rocks crashing in on top of him? Or what if Christo needed her, started calling for her? No, she had to stay.

And then, at last, she heard, or thought she heard, an answering shout. She turned towards the sound and shouted, as loudly as she could, 'H . . . e . . . l . . . p! Here! Help!'

And then she listened again, and this time she was sure. It was a male voice, calling, 'Lotte, Lotte . . . Where are you?'

She could hear raised voices, calling to each other, getting closer. And then, yes, oh thank God, yes, the sound of feet in the undergrowth, and more shouts: 'Lotte, where are you?'

Standing now and clutching Jo-Jo, she shouted back,

'Here! Here!' And then she remembered that gaps between the words made shouting more intelligible to the hearer. She yelled, 'I . . . have . . . found . . . Christo.'

Suddenly they were all there – Annie, Peter and both the students. And Brody. And Brody had a rope slung round his neck.

Lotte ran towards them, words tumbling out, and then she ran back again to stop anyone treading on the raised slope that was Christo's roof.

'Lotte, Lotte. Stop, It will be OK,' said Brody, taking her by the shoulders. 'Just show me where he is.'

Brody took over. First he used the doubled rope to help lower Alex and then Jamie in through the hole. They dislodged a bit of soil but no rock. Then Alex put the loop of rope under Christo's arms and Peter and Brody pulled him out, with Alex and Jamie helping from below. As his legs scraped and bumped against the rock, Christo let out a high, agonized scream. And then suddenly he was silent, his head and arms flopped back, his mouth open.

'It's OK, Lotte, he's fainted,' Brody said as Lotte dropped to her knees and cradled Christo's head. He was pale as paper, looking drained and lifeless.

They laid him on his back and saw at once that there was something wrong with his left leg. The knee was distorted, the knee-cap lumpy and sticking out at the side of the leg, which was bent awkwardly.

'It's dislocated,' said Brody. 'I'm going to put it back while he's out for the count. Quick, Peter, hang on to his shoulders. I'm going to yank on his leg.'

'No, no,' shouted Lotte. 'Wait for a doctor . . . You can't . . .'

But Brody just said, 'Trust me, Lotte,' and then, 'Ready, Peter?'

Brody knelt beside the boy, gripping his ankle with one hand and cradling the knee-cap with the other. Lotte watched Brody's jaw tighten as he pulled steadily and hard on Christo's ankle. There was an audible click as the knee-cap went back into its socket, causing Lotte's stomach to rise to her throat. She clenched her teeth against a wave of weakness and nausea. Holding Christo's head in her hands, she prayed incoherently, not to God, but to Christo. Please, darling. Please, darling.

Christo's eyes fluttered open and met Lotte's, hazy with pain. 'Mum, please, it's agony.'

Lotte was crying too. Christo's leg looked normal now, but he was still in pain. Not being able to help him was terrible. He was soaking wet, his teeth were chattering, and he was weeping. And she could do nothing. Peter was kneeling beside her, his arm round her shoulder. Lotte, intent on Christo, seemed unaware of his presence.

Brody rummaged in his jacket and took out a packet of tablets and a plastic bottle of water. 'This is the best dope in the world, Christo. Don't get a taste for it. It's morphine.'

Lotte protested, 'Brody, no. The ambulance men will . . .'

Brody interrupted her. 'Relax, Lott. I know about this stuff. Jade takes it when she has to work with her back playing up. It's magic.' He popped a couple of tablets out of the card. 'And he's going to need it if we are to carry him to the ambulance.'

Brody cupped his hand under Christo's mouth and

the boy obediently opened it, accepted the tablets and swallowed them with a gulp of water.

Brody looked up at Peter. 'Better get the lads out of that hole,' he said.

But Jamie was already out, having climbed on Alex's shoulders. Now he was lowering the rope in for Alex. Peter helped him haul up the young man, now covered in soil and smeared with mud.

Brody pulled his mobile phone out of his trouser pocket. 'Ambulance, please.' He waited, then said, 'I ordered an ambulance half an hour ago to come to Maddon Park. Now I need to tell the men how to find us.'

Lotte watched him as if through a glass wall, as though she had nothing to do with all this. Everything seemed so calm now, so undramatic. The lads knew where Lotte's main path was. They set off to meet the ambulance men, who were on their way.

Jo-Jo was sitting between Brody's knees and Brody was talking to Christo as if a dislocated knee was a mosquito bite. The morphine was obviously working because Christo had stopped moaning and was drifting into sleep. Lotte didn't have to do anything except sit there, leaning against Peter and stroking Christo's forehead.

But she still felt faintly sick and weak. She kissed Christo's brow and stood up. She must pull herself together. She wandered over to the alder tree and looked down into the cave. She shuddered at the slick of water Christo had lain in. She lifted her eyes to the walls and saw shiny spots on the dark rock, like mother of pearl or crystals. And on the far side she could make out a slab or bench, dark with moss.

Laughter suddenly swelled in her throat and erupted. The release was wonderful. She leant against the tree, sobbing and hiccupping. She could feel the thing getting out of control, but she didn't care. She was carried along by hysteria and it was both frightening and exhilarating.

Peter's arms were round her. He tried to calm her by hugging her to him, but for some reason his anxious face set her off on further paroxysms. She pulled away from him, shaking her head and blurting, 'Sorry ... sorry,' between the gusts of mirth.

'Lotte. Stop that.' It was Brody, walking fast towards them.

But she couldn't. I'm hysterical, she thought, that's what it is. Hysteria. Any minute the masterful Brody is going to slap my face. Like in the movies. The thought was so funny, it brought on a renewed torrent of laughter.

Brody did slap her. She gasped, choked off a sob and said, 'Christo's won the prize.' She could feel the laughter mounting again, but she forced it down. 'He's found your grotto, Brody. We are standing on the site of Mrs Delany's grotto.'

15. Late Summer

Watching hands transplanting,
Turning and tamping,
Lifting the young plants with two fingers,
Sifting in a palm-full of fresh loam, –
One swift movement, –
Then plumping in the bunched roots,
A single twist of the thumbs, a tamping and turning,
All in one,
Quick on the wooden bench,
A shaking down, while the stem stays straight,
Once, twice, and a faint third thump, –
Into the flat-box it goes,
Ready for the long days under the sloped glass:

Theodore Roethke (1908–1963), 'Transplanting'

Brody said, 'Jade, I'm sorry, but no. It's crazy.' Then he held the mobile phone a little away from his ear, screwing up his face as his wife shouted at him.

Suddenly there was silence and he checked the display. Maybe they'd lost the signal. But no, Jade had hung up on him. Frowning, Brody flipped the mobile phone closed. Jade's ability to run through the limit of her credit cards astonished him. How can you run out of money when you are on a swimwear photo-shoot in Antigua and living all expenses paid in a beach-house? Easily, it seemed.

The joke is she's probably getting a £100K fee, he thought, but somehow it's my money she spends.

Brody was standing on the spot where he had berated Lotte for being slow and failing to get planning permission to pump water out of the river. Then his boots had been clogged with heavy clay from the churned ground, and the mud had been slick and slimy everywhere. Now Brody ran his eyes over the perfect turf, so green it looked unreal, the cascading water crashing down from the house, and the four fountain jets leaping straight out of the lake.

Absentmindedly, he tossed his mobile phone up and down in his big hand. Maybe he should ring Jade back, tell her he'd call the bank in the morning. After all, what did it matter? It was only money. He scrolled through his phone book and highlighted 'Jade', but then he scrolled on to 'Lotte' and pressed the connection.

Lotte had been away with the children, but they should be back now, and Brody wanted to see her. They had not met since the drama in the woods two weeks before, and though she'd written him a formal little note thanking him for all he'd done and telling him that Christo was fine, he felt a little more personal gratitude would not go amiss. It was the first time he'd seen Lotte vulnerable and not in control, and there was something satisfying in that.

And he was surprised she'd not come back to him about the grotto. Now that she'd found it, he'd expected her to be pestering him for permission to restore it.

He wanted to tell her she'd been right about the lake and the fountains all along. He smiled at the memory of her feisty response to his accusations of dilly-dallying and wasting money, and her determination to make him see sense, abandon his plan to take water out of the Isis and build a reservoir instead. The fountains were magical in the lake, far better than on the house terrace.

The telephone rang and rang. He hung on after he knew she wasn't going to answer, until eventually he heard her brisk 'Hi, it's Lotte. Please leave a message.'

'Lotte, it's Brody. Where are you? I'm down at the lake, which looks a dream. Congratulations.'

Indeed, the transformation from mud-bath to this was barely believable: the new reservoir, tucked out of sight, was keeping the lake level full and steady, the waterside planting, even after only one season, looked lush and natural, and the giant terraces they'd copied from Powerscourt enfolded the lake as he'd hoped they would. From the house you were unaware of them, but from down here they made a great green amphitheatre, with the central aisle a torrent of water, dashing over huge carved stone rills.

Brody walked along the curved edge of the lowest of the terraces towards the central cascade. He looked up at the house, now clear of ivy, the soft ochre stone meeting the formal lawn. The sun was on it, and Brody felt a small thrill of pride. It was beautiful, and it was his.

But immediately his thoughts clouded again as he thought of the cost. The fountains and cascades were going to exceed even the Rodin-adorned pool and gym for sheer breathtaking extravagance. When they'd come back from Ireland and decided to cut the sloping park in giant turfed steps, install the fountains and commission the sculptor Bill Pye to make the cascades, he'd been flush.

The cost then had been immaterial, but now it made him slightly uneasy.

So far, Bill had only made fibre-glass models of the sculpted blocks over which the water crashed, to test the flow of water and see how they looked. Brody thought they looked pretty good and was tempted to stop at that. They might not last as long as stone, but sure, they'd see him and Jade out. But he suspected Bill Pye would rather lose the commission than use fibre-glass. Besides, Jade was after the real thing, carved stone, inlaid with sinuous ribbons or rivulets of shiny steel.

Brody hated fretting about money, but just lately he couldn't stop, like putting a tongue into a sore tooth. *find-on-line* was still a sound business, still making fair profits. True, the purchase of *going-going-gone* had set them back a bit, but sales there were growing fast too and that business should break even within two years.

The trouble was that the crash of Internet stocks had more than halved *find-on-line*'s book value. It shouldn't matter because he and Jade owned the company and he didn't want to sell any of it, or borrow money against its value or float it on the stock exchange. But so many dot.coms had gone belly up he no longer had those options. And he wasn't used to feeling hemmed in.

Brody turned away from the lake and set off the way he'd come, his head down now, oblivious to the sheen on the new turf or the first tinge of autumn colour in the chestnut trees.

The following day there was still no sign of Lotte, and at 4 p.m. Brody went in search of her. He found her in the potting shed. He flung open the door, and said, 'Where the hell have you been?'

Lotte stopped shovelling compost into compartmented seedling trays with her plastic scoop and looked at him. 'In here since two. Before that, I was helping Andrew dead-head the herbaceous –'

'No, blast it,' said Brody, 'I meant yesterday. I was trying to get hold of you yesterday.'

Lotte resumed her task, shaking the trays to level the compost, smoothing the tops with her hand. She didn't look the least put out. She smiled confidently at him. 'I know,' she said, 'I got your message. Thanks. But I didn't like to ring you on a Sunday night. And anyway, it didn't need an answer, did it?'

Brody said, 'I'll be the judge of that. Next time I leave you a message, ring me back, do you hear?'

'Sure, boss,' said Lotte. She sounded equable but puzzled, Brody thought.

She picked up a pencil and dibbed it once into each seedling-tray compartment. Brody, still feeling vaguely put out, watched her absently as she took her penstemon cuttings out of the water, dipped the stems one by one into the rooting powder and then tucked them into the pencil holes.

Suddenly Brody laughed. 'What a pompous ass I am! "I'll be the judge of that", indeed. I'm sorry, Lott. It's just that I really wanted to tell you how good everything looks down there now. I wanted to walk round with you and ask you if you thought we could persuade Bill Pye to let us keep the fibre-glass cascades, rather than making the real ones. I'm beginning to feel queasy about the money.'

Lotte paused with her two forefingers lightly pressing each side of a cutting. 'You what? You worrying about money! Never.'

Her activity finally caught Brody's attention. 'What on earth are you doing anyway?' he said.

'I'm taking penstemon cuttings. Insurance policy. In case the frost gets the ones in the garden. If we have a hard winter we could lose the lot.'

'But can't we just buy more?' Brody asked, peering at the trays of cuttings as at an alien life-form.

'We could, but they'd be expensive. And we might not get the ones we want. Besides, I like propagating. It's satisfying. You get something out of nothing.'

He shook his head, and she went on, 'You should understand that, Brody, you used to make bread pudding out of unsold loaves, remember?'

Brody thought about that for a second, then replied, 'True, but I had no option. No money.'

By now Lotte had loaded her twelve plant trays, twenty cuttings to a tray, on to a flat board set across the wheelbarrow. She grabbed the barrow handles and said, 'Come on, I'll show you.'

Brody followed her into the greenhouse and looked in astonishment at the rows of tiny cuttings in trays, arranged with military precision on the shelves.

'Wow,' he said, peering in bewilderment at the white plastic markers, one marker per tray. He made an attempt to read them, slowly pronouncing *'Abutilon vitifolium album'* and *'Campsis tagliabuana Madame Galen'*. But *'Ceanothus thyrsiflorus repens'* defeated him and they both laughed.

'How do you know all this stuff?' he asked.

'You learn as you go, I guess. It's like a language.' She pointed to the abutilon. 'These are cuttings from the white-flowered plants on your terrace, in the lead pots. The campsis is the orange climber on the tennis-court fence. You know, they are out now – great clusters of trumpet flowers? And the ceanothus is the blue thing that flowers in the shrubbery in spring. There's masses of it.'

She was looking at him, he thought, as though she was almost pleading with him to recognize her children. But he hadn't a clue. He shrugged. 'Sorry, Lotte, I haven't noticed any of them. But I'll go and look, I promise.'

He continued his tour of inspection and helped her transfer the penstemon cuttings from barrow to shelf.

'It's amazing,' he said, peering up at the ornate Victorian ironwork and glazing. 'It's not just the plants. I thought we'd agreed to bulldoze this place and buy a modern one. It was a wreck.'

Lotte's expression was one of quiet triumph as she lifted her chin to follow his gaze. She said, 'In fact it was mostly just filthy. Eons of lichen and moss. Andrew repaired the wooden staging and broken panes and scrubbed and painted the metal. Awful job. Lots of Jenolite and wire wool.'

'Jenolite?'

'Noxious stuff for getting rid of rust. Horrible job. Andrew surprised me. He's a better builder than a gardener.'

Brody picked up a handful of clay beads from a shelf. 'And what's this?'

He only half listened to her explanation about water

retention and the automatic irrigating system. He was thinking how pretty she looked, her face serious and professional, but with a hint of flushed excitement, like a child showing Daddy the cake she'd made at school.

Lotte had pulled her secateurs out of her jeans pocket and was now removing dead leaves from house-plants on the wide bench opposite the trays of cuttings. She had to roll on to the balls of her feet and stretch to reach the back row, and Brody's eyes slid down to the inch of flesh between her top and jeans. Her top hung away from her body as she leant forward and Brody had a sudden desire to put his hand on her belly.

She straightened up and said, 'Did you want anything, Brody? Do you want to see anything in particular? You know we are about to start on the rest of the plant houses – the forcing-rooms and the melon house, etcetera. Shall I get the plans?'

She started for the door, but he stopped her. 'No. No. You've shown me them already. Just go on, do whatever you are doing.'

Brody watched her as she worked methodically down the rows, bending her head to peer under branches before removing yellowing leaves and clipping back flowered shoots.

'Look,' she said, turning over a stripy green leaf to show him the dark purple underside. 'Isn't that amazing? It's the commonest house-plant, easy to propagate, easy to grow. But I love it. It trails so gracefully and will spread and root in neighbouring pots if you don't watch it – its common name is Wandering Jew.'

But Brody wasn't looking at the plant. His eyes were on

Lotte's soil-stained fingers, watching the tender – loving – way she lifted the trailing fronds.

He reached out and took the secateurs from her, laying them on the bench. He looked into Lotte's enquiring face and turned her hands over in his.

'Real gardeners' hands now, aren't they?' he said.

She tried to pull them away, saying, 'Yes, they're horrible.' But he hung on to them for a second, then suddenly jerked her roughly towards him and wrapped his arms round her. One hand on her bottom, one on her shoulders, he pulled her into his body and held her there.

'No, Brody. No.' Lotte's eyes, dark and desperate, looked into his. Then, abruptly, she stopped pulling away. Her eyes seemed to focus on his for a second, then her lids half closed and her eyes softened and he was kissing her.

She seemed dazed, immobile, but unobjecting. She just stood there, letting it happen. He put his hands on each side of her face and lifted her mouth to his. And then she opened her mouth, and lifted her arms and pushed her pelvis into his. Christ, she was delicious. He had his arm up her back now, under her top, and he spread his fingers to feel as much of her as possible. As he ran his hand round to her belly, turning her slightly so he could caress her rib-cage and push his fingers up under her bra, he thought how much softer, less bony she was than Jade. He wanted to stroke all of her at once and his movements became more fevered and desperate.

And then, unexpectedly and devastatingly, she wrenched out of his grip, gasping, 'No! No, Brody. We can't.' And she stumbled out of the greenhouse, briefly colliding with the wheelbarrow, leaving the door open. She slammed into the potting shed and then he heard the door bang and the sound of her quick steps as she hurried away.

16. Early Autumn

Now let forever the phlox and the rose be tended
Here where the rain has darkened and the sun has dried
So many times the terrace, yet is love unended,
Love has not died.

Edna St Vincent Millay (1892–1950),
'The Hardy Garden'

That evening Lotte was trying, without much success, to concentrate on the walled garden drawings, when Annie wailed, 'Mum, why can't you listen to me? It is the most important thing in my life.'

There was something desperate in her voice, over and above her frequent grumbling. Lotte put her pencil down and looked up at her daughter. Annie was leaning against the Aga, eating ice-cream out of a family-size carton with a tablespoon.

Lotte swallowed her instinct to whip the ice-cream out of Annie's hands and snap at her.

'I am listening. You were complaining that Rosie, who two weeks ago you told me was a cow whom you hated, had not invited you to her party.'

'Well, she is a cow. This just proves it, doesn't it? She's supposed to be my best friend, isn't she? But since she's got a boyfriend,' Annie said the word with exaggerated scorn, 'I'm out of her life.' She made go-away gestures with her spoon. 'Thank you and goodbye!'

Lotte pushed her plans and pencils to one side and said, 'C'mon, darling, sit down. Tell me what's up. It can't be that someone you don't like doesn't invite you to her party, now can it?'

Annie gave her mother a look of hatred, Lotte thought. 'I knew you wouldn't understand. You never understand.' She grabbed the tea-towel from the Aga rail and buried her face in it as she slammed out of the kitchen.

Lotte stood up to follow her, then turned and sat down again. Trying to get close to Annie was hopeless. Everything Lotte said seemed to enrage her daughter. But then, Lotte thought, she infuriates me too.

It drove Lotte mad that Annie would not wait for meals and snacked between them while complaining endlessly about her weight. But Lotte also feared these were manifestations of real unhappiness, and she longed to be able to comfort Annie, to make it all better as she'd once been able to.

Oh God, she thought, how am I to help her when she won't talk to me? What's happened to her in the last few months? It can't just be puberty. Lotte's mind went back to the picnic in the woods when Annie had been so relaxed and uncomplicated, enjoying searching for the ponds. Of course it had helped that the students were with them: Annie obviously hero-worshipped Jamie. But she'd been so mature about Christo's accident, taking charge of Jo-Jo when Lotte was with Christo at the hospital and making supper for everyone.

Recently, though, she'd been so unpredictable. Fine one minute, childish and sulky or explosive and rude, the next. Poor girl, she needs a father, they all do, she thought.

This led Lotte's mind briefly to Peter. Where was he? The knowledge that he'd be here any minute calmed her. He'd listen to her groan about Annie and would give her a glass of wine and tell her how wonderful she was, and, more importantly, how wonderful Annie was. Strange, Lotte thought. If he agreed with me that Annie was a nightmare, I'd hate him. The way to a mother's heart is through unlimited admiration of her offspring.

But then the scene in the greenhouse with Brody finally elbowed its way into Lotte's head. All afternoon she'd refused to think about it. And she knew she was avoiding it because she was ashamed of herself. Ashamed of the speed of her desire, the absolute flood of lust that had engulfed her, the greedy way she'd responded to Brody's kiss. If I hadn't bolted when I did, she thought, I'd have had him on the greenhouse floor.

But it wasn't just shame that she felt. It was an under-current of excitement, a feeling almost of triumph. Brody was charismatic, rich, attractive, a lot younger than her – and he wanted her! Of course it meant nothing, maybe he went for every female he met. But still. And though her own longing was shaming, it was rejuvenating too. She'd thought that that breathtaking, mind-blowing, over-whelming sexual drive was part of her much younger self, and had been lost forever. Died of neglect somewhere in the last years with Sam. It was frightening, but not altogether horrible, to find it had only been dormant.

Lotte stood up suddenly, shaking her head in a vain

attempt to redirect her thoughts. She walked to the window over the walled garden and looked out towards the greenhouse. But she did not see it. She was not going to be such an ass as to have an affair with her boss. She'd end up losing the best job in the world. Besides, that episode in the greenhouse had been pure lust. Brody was not her type: he was brash and ill-educated. And he always had to be so bloody masterful. Lotte thought with amazement of how, that day in the woods, she'd allowed him to reset Christo's knee and then stood by while he fed the boy morphine tabs.

How could she have been so feeble and irresponsible? And yet she'd been, and still was, deeply glad of Brody taking over that day.

Lotte turned round and sat down in front of her plans. She must finish the drawing of the walled garden. Or she should go and comfort Annie. Or make the supper. But not brood about herself or Brody. Or Jade.

Jade might be vapid and shallow, but she didn't deserve Brody cheating on her.

No one deserved that. Lotte's mind went back to that awful Tuesday when, quite by chance, she had seen Sam and Frances walking together out of the Curzon Cinema at 5 p.m. That little scene meant the end of her marriage and the beginning of years of torture. Sometimes she'd felt that if only she hadn't seen them, the rest would not have followed – Sam's admission of guilt, confession of love, ultimate rejection of her for Frances. Lotte knew now that she had not been entirely sane for two or three years at least after that. She would be blind with rage and utterly miserable by turns. Only the need to keep going for the children and the routine of her working day prevented her complete disintegration. And then it had taken another four years to get over the cruelty of being cast off, done with. If she was over it yet.

Was she? Maybe that sudden flood of longing for Brody was a sign that she was at last a new woman. Her own woman. Not Sam's reject.

The sound of Peter's motor bike coming down the lane reminded her that the sausages were still frozen and the spuds unmashed. And she hadn't finished her drawing either. They were going to do a last check against the historical information collated from Ferguson's notes and the drawings in the safe before going ahead with the restoration of the fruit-tree walls, the forcing-rooms and the melon house.

I'm not coping, she thought, I'm falling apart. I'm making a pig's ear of bringing up three children on my own. And then I behave like a whore in the greenhouse with my boss, and go on stringing poor Peter along like a spaniel. What's the matter with me?

She put the packet of sausages into the microwave and set it whirring. Then she tipped a splash of oil into the frying pan and lifted the middle lid of the Aga. She felt the blast of heat on her face as she slid the pan on to the hotplate.

Peter came in with Christo, who said, 'Hello, Mum, what's for supper?' Peter clapped his hands together, going, 'Brrr. It's cold.' Then he kissed Lotte on the cheek, one of his darting, shy kisses.

'I met Christo at the main gate, limping along on his bad knee. Gave him a lift.'

'Did you make him –?'

'Yes, I did. I made him wear a helmet.'

Lotte laughed a little shakily. 'How did you know I was going to ask that?'

'Because you always do.' Peter opened his bag and pulled out a bottle of wine. 'The whole summer with Annie on the bike, it was the first thing you asked: Did you wear your crash helmet?' He got the corkscrew from the dresser drawer and said, 'Red all right? It's Merlot. I figured it was too cold for white, whatever we're eating.'

Christo said again, 'What are we eating, Mum? And when?'

'Bangers and mash, and not for half an hour.' Lotte opened the microwave and felt the sausages. Half thawed. She pulled off the wrapping, eased the sausages apart and dropped them into the pan. A spray of hot fat spattered her jersey.

'Oh blast,' she said, inspecting the stains. Then: 'Go start your homework, and I'll call you. And Christo, check that Jo-Jo has done hers, will you?'

'Great kid,' said Peter as Christo swung out of the room.

Annie didn't come down for supper, which further upset Lotte. She wanted to go and remonstrate with her, but Peter persuaded her to leave her be. After supper, while Lotte was washing up, he put a hot sausage and some tomato sauce into a bread roll and sent Jo-Jo up to Annie with it. 'Say it's a peace offering from your mum,' he said.

Lotte turned round from the sink, about to protest, when Jo-Jo said, 'What's a peace offering?'

Peter replied, 'It's something one person gives the other when they don't want to quarrel any more. Your mum's hoping Annie will stop quarrelling with her.'

'No chance,' said Jo-Jo, heading for the door. 'Annie hates everyone. She never stops quarrelling.'

Lotte felt her throat tighten. She stared into the greasy water as she swished her brush round the encrusted frying pan. She could hear Peter clearing the things off the table so that he could lay out the walled garden plans. Suddenly she was too tired to pore over drawings of orchid-house boilers and pineapple-pit trenches. She just wanted another glass of wine, and bed.

She turned round. 'I'm sorry, Peter. I don't feel up to any more work tonight. Could we forget the garden, do you think?'

'I thought you'd never ask.' He smiled shyly at her and then, unsure, said, 'Oh, I'm sorry, Lotte. Do you want me to go home?' His fingers smoothed invisible hairs over his bald crown.

Lotte opened her mouth to say, yes, do you mind? and then found she didn't want him to. The truth is, she thought, I don't want to be alone, and I don't want just the kids for company.

She shook her head and Peter said, 'Great. We can watch television. Or listen to some music? I've got Handel in my disk player . . .'

Lotte put out a hand and pulled his sleeve. 'Let's see if we can kick the children off the TV.'

But the sitting room was empty, the steady thump from the room above testifying to teenage presence.

They watched *Who Wants to Be a Millionaire?*. Half-way

through, Jo-Jo appeared and pushed herself between them on the sofa, snuggling up to Lotte and flashing a grin at Peter, aware of her right to usurp his place. She said, 'Annie says sorry for quarrelling and thanks for the sausage, Mum.'

'Did she? Really?' asked Lotte. 'Did she really send you down to say that?' She felt pathetically grateful.

'Not exactly,' said Jo-Jo. 'I was coming anyhow and I asked her if the peace offering had worked, and she said it was OK, she supposed.'

Lotte stroked Jo-Jo's cheek with the back of her hand. 'And she didn't tell you to say sorry or thanks?'

'No, but she didn't say not to.' Jo-Jo looked up, her big eyes solemn. 'I said I'm going to tell Mummy you are sorry for quarrelling, and thanks for the sausage.'

Peter stretched his arm along the sofa back behind Jo-Jo and rested his hand on Lotte's shoulder, shaking it gently.

'Don't look a gift-horse in the mouth, Lotte,' he said. He dropped his head to whisper in Jo-Jo's ear, 'And you are a great little go-between.'

Lotte dropped her cheek on to Peter's hand for a second, touched that both he and Jo-Jo were working to the same end – peace between her and Annie. She knew she should chase Jo-Jo up to bed again, but somehow she didn't have the energy.

Between them, she and Peter knew the answers to get to a quarter of a million. Then the contestant, having used up all her lives, hesitated at the question: Which of the following is the botanical name for the variety of willow out of which cricket bats are made: *caerulea; tortuosa; vitellina; purpurea?*

Lotte had to make an effort not to shout at the screen. She growled, 'Go on, woman. It's *caerulea*. Go for it!'

But the woman took the money.

'Damn,' said Lotte. 'We might have gone on to a million.'

'You could play all the questions on their website,' said Peter, 'only you don't win the money.'

Lotte laughed. 'Peter, how do you know that? Don't say you log on to *Who Wants to Be a Millionaire?*! What a sad life you lead!'

'Actually, madam, I play it with your son. Christo and I are a hot team. Once we got to a million, even without your horticultural knowledge.'

Lotte digested this as Peter once more became absorbed in the programme. She knew he and Christo were sometimes on the children's computer together, but she'd assumed they were doing Christo's homework. Christo had slowly relaxed about Peter, accepting his presence without questioning it. And Peter had always got more change out of Annie than she did. Tonight's sausage business was typical. She normally took Annie on straight, drove her into a corner. But Peter let Annie have escape routes.

Lotte looked down at Jo-Jo, now fast asleep against Peter's side. It was nice sitting here with Jo-Jo between them, and Peter's fingers gently massaging her shoulder and the back of her neck. Like a family.

A warm wave of affection, even love, washed over her. 'Peter,' she said, 'do you think I treat you badly? Take you for granted?'

'No,' he said. 'No, I told you so in the woods that day. Stop worrying about me, Lotte.'

His eyes flicked down to the sleeping Jo-Jo, and then back to Lotte. They were very intense. His voice was a shade lower when he said, 'You've no idea how happy you've made me, Lotte . . . Even if you never . . .' He stopped, his fingers making little rubbing movements on his brow.

Lotte leant across Jo-Jo and took his hand off his head, and held it. 'Even if I never what, Peter?'

He was absolutely still. Even his usually fluttering hand, imprisoned in Lotte's, was motionless. His eyes held hers. 'Even if you never love me . . . I will love you till the day I die of course. All of you. I'm in love with the whole family, Lotte.' He spoke so earnestly that Lotte could not interrupt. 'I could not live without this now. Coming here, being allowed to be part of it . . . it's completely changed my life. I don't think I had a life before you came. Just books. And my bike. Dross, really.'

Lotte said, 'And is it enough?'

He smiled a quick, sharp smile. 'It might have to be, mightn't it? If it is, I'll be glad of what I have. If you don't love me enough to marry me, Lotte, that's OK. I'll live with that.' He sounded sad but determined. 'Only I couldn't handle you falling in love with anyone else.'

Lotte pulled his hand, still in her grasp, to her mouth and kissed the back of it. It was quite rough and hairy. And warm.

'Maybe we should sleep together before we talk of marriage?' she said. 'Should we?'

The following morning Lotte rang Brody's office. He'd gone to London first thing, his PA said, but would be back in the afternoon.

'Can I have half an hour with him?'

'Well, I think he's going straight home. You could catch him there after five, I'm sure.'

Lotte shook her head. 'No, I need to see him in the office. Could you ask him if he minds? Otherwise I could come in tomorrow.'

Lotte was sure it had to be the office. She'd be stronger there. It was more formal and she could say what she had to say.

At four-thirty, dressed in a suit, she parked outside *find-on-line*'s shed-like office in the business park. She flipped the sun-visor down to check her hair and face. She looked pale, and for a second she was tempted to use a bit of lipstick, but stopped herself. What am I trying to do, she thought. Attract the man or tell him it's no go?

But she was glad she'd worn the suit. It was grown-up City armour, the kind she'd used in her old life to impress clients or intimidate builders. As she followed the receptionist through an open office where young people dressed in jeans and sweaters sat staring at screens and talking into head-phones, she mentally squared her shoulders.

Brody was in shirt-sleeves behind a preposterously big desk, on which there was very little other than one of those irritating executive toys, steel balls that clicked together for hours if you set them off. Lotte felt a second's satisfaction at this confirmation of her prejudices. Her eyes flicked round the room, shying away from the expensive corner collection of her least favourite plants – orange bromeliads, multi-coloured coleus and gloxinias with multiple gaping scarlet and purple throats.

The door closed behind the receptionist as Brody, smiling delightedly, swung round the table towards her.

'Lott, I'm so glad . . . Did you get my flowers?' He didn't wait for an answer but opened his arms to embrace her, saying, 'Oh Lotte, you shouldn't have run away. I want . . .'

'No, Brody, no. Listen to me.' Lotte backed away.

But he didn't. He put one hand each side of her on the closed door and looked down at her. She tried to duck under his arm, but he brought both arms down and around her.

'Lott, my Lott,' he said, 'it's OK. It will be OK.'

For a second Lotte felt overwhelmed. Overwhelmed by the size and strength of him, by the warmth of his voice, by the smell and closeness of him, above all by the maleness of him. No one else calls me Lott, she thought, only Brody. The temptation just to give in, to succumb as she had in the greenhouse, to let him do whatever he liked, ripped through her like a furnace blast.

But then she summoned up some anger, indignation, some self-respect. She'd have liked to yell at him. Shouting would encourage her anger. But she was conscious of the open office beyond the door. She took a deep breath and said, not as calmly as she wanted – she was still tight in his arms and speaking to his chin – 'Let me go, Brody. How can you just assume I'm here for the taking?'

Brody's arms relaxed for a second. He looked down at her, then dropped his arms to his sides and turned away. For a moment, for a split second, she felt the loss, wanted him back. But she went on, more calmly now, 'I came to say yesterday was a mistake. I know it was my fault as much as yours, but it is not going to happen again.'

Brody swung round. 'But Lotte, I know how you felt

yesterday. We both felt it. And it's still there, I know. Don't try and pretend –'

Lotte interrupted him again, her voice flat. 'OK, I agree. I'm not above lust. But that's all it was. And it's madness. I don't want an affair. You are married to Jade and I am going to marry Peter Childersley.'

Until she said it, Lotte had not made up her mind to do any such thing. But now she knew it was true.

'And there's an end to it,' she said.

Brody said nothing. Lotte turned and opened the door. She shut it carefully behind her without looking back, and walked through the office, nodded to the girl at reception, went down the stairs and into the car park.

She slid behind the wheel of her car and closed the door. And burst into tears.

When she got home she found a long florist's box on her doorstep. She picked it up, walked under the arch and tried to cram it into the wheelie-bin. It wouldn't fit, and she fetched a knife and opened the box. Inside were twenty-four long-stemmed red roses and a bottle of vintage Veuve Clicquot.

'Oh Brody, don't, don't!' she cried aloud as she tipped the roses into the bin on top of the sausage wrapper and the remains of last night's salad. She picked up the bottle, intending to bin it too, but then she thought, what the hell, and lifted it out of the box. She used the knife to split the box and forced it into the bin.

As she slammed the lid, a little envelope fell to the ground. She picked it up and dropped it, unopened, into the bin.

17. Early Winter

Dead dreams of days forsaken
Blind buds that snows have shaken,
Wild leaves that winds have taken,
Red strays of ruined springs . . .

Algernon Charles Swinburne (1837–1909),
'The Garden of Proserpine'

A few weeks later Lotte was working alone clearing the entrance step to the grotto. She and Peter had already dug away the soil and leaf-mould from around the grotto, which had turned out to be solidly built against a sloping bank. The walls were of rustic rockwork and the arched entrance was surrounded by blocks of volcanic tufa, holed like a sponge.

Lotte had been here for four hours so far and had uncovered smooth stones, almost like cobbles, forming a narrow path, sloping down. After a few yards the path seemed to end abruptly, but the last stone slab was much bigger than the rest, stretching right across the path, and it seemed to be buried more deeply than the others.

She knew she should stop. Peter had taken the children skating in Oxford, and they'd be home any minute. But she wanted to know why such a heavyweight stone buried so deep ended such a small path.

She had to dig a sizeable hole to expose the stone, and it was heavy work. The deeper she got, the wetter and heavier the soil was. Her hands were wet and cold, but her back and face were running with sweat. She took off her sweater and put it on top of her Barbour, discarded hours ago.

And then her spade struck something solid at the bottom of the hole. Probably just natural rock, she thought, as she crouched down and cleared a section with her trowel.

But it wasn't natural rock. Gleaming dully from the depths of the hole was something blue and flat. Something man-made. Her hand was shaking as she scraped the mud away a little more. Tiny blue and orangey-brown tiles appeared.

Her tiredness forgotten, Lotte kept working. She had to make an effort to go slowly, carefully. The temptation to take the big spade to the job was almost overwhelming, and she did use it to take a foot or more of soil off the top, but then, because leaning into the hole was killing her back, she lay flat on the muddy ground and reached in with a trowel and paint-scraper.

She gradually exposed a mosaic of tiny Islamic-looking tiles. They were quite beautiful. Magical.

Eventually, when she'd cleared a good two square feet of perfectly preserved mosaic, she sat back, thinking excitedly that they would have to tell Brody now. Surely he'd be thrilled? It was the Persian pool Ferguson mentioned, she was positive of that. The ones the mosaic tile bill had been for.

Lotte had not told Brody that she and Peter were excavating the grotto in their spare time. Brody wouldn't object to her doing unpaid overtime of course. But restoring the Old Pond Yards had never interested him. So she and Peter, and sometimes the students or the children, worked in secret. Sneaking off for another bout of scraping, sponging and discovering had become an addiction.

But, she thought, if the Persian pool was anywhere near complete under here, it would have to be preserved. And as the earlier grotto was so rare, Brody must surely want to preserve them. They could be the first focal point of his sculpture trail, which could wind through the woods up to the ruined folly. That way it would start and end in the past, with Brody's modern works in between.

Yes, maybe she should tell him soon. When they'd uncovered the whole pool. She felt a warm ripple of satisfaction, thinking of Brody's face alight with astonishment. She smiled: just as long as he didn't try to take over, wanting it all done in a month, complete with fake rills and water features.

As Lotte walked home, she thought uneasily that her thoughts had been more about telling Brody than telling Peter. Which was somehow disloyal: Peter had worked almost as hard as she had on the grotto. And he'd be so thrilled at her discovery. I'll tell him tonight. Or better still, show him tomorrow.

One day in late November Lotte sat back on her heels and let her eyes sweep over the dozen square yards of mosaic. Their beauty and symmetry still thrilled her. It was astonishing how much of the Victorian tiling was intact. There were only a few missing or badly broken patches. Most of it was perfect, the colours as deep and rich as they must have been when the tiles were laid a century and a half ago.

Peter appeared at the grotto entrance, cleaning his glasses on a red spotted handkerchief.

'Lotte, aren't you freezing? Shall we call it a day?' He walked across to her, his boots squelching in the icy mud, and stood behind her, massaging her shoulders. 'Tired?'

'Whacked,' she said, leaning against his legs. 'And freezing. How's the grotto?'

'A mess. That hole in the roof made by your son is a bit of a challenge. We'll have to decide whether to remove the alder and do a massive restoration job – if we pull it out it will take most of the shellwork with it.'

'Maybe we could leave the roots and fill in around them,' Lotte suggested. 'Could be gothic and romantic. Eighteenth-century grotto builders often used old roots on purpose.'

'We'll have to call in some expert help. English Heritage, I guess.'

Lotte put out her hand for Peter to pull her to her feet, saying, 'The more moss you get off the grotto walls, the more certain I am that Mary Delany had a hand in it.'

'You know you are going to have to tell Brody, don't you?'

'Yes.' She smiled up at him. 'But there is an up-side. If it is a Delany grotto, English Heritage will slap a preservation order on it in two secs flat.'

They walked together round the pool, Peter peering closely at the mosaic. 'You've done a lot,' he said. 'It's 'tremendous, Lotte.' They had cleared about half of the floor, they thought, and had begun to believe that the rest of it might be intact – the ground was flat with little growing on it. The pool appeared to be rectangular with scalloped corners. One corner was badly broken where hawthorn roots had lifted the tiled floor, and they could only guess at how high the sides had been because none of the surrounding walls was complete.

'Thanks,' Lotte said. She felt good: pleased with herself for a successful day's work, and warm from Peter's 'tremendous'. Brody didn't dish out much praise, and Jade none. And it had been weeks since Lotte's lasagne, or chocolate cake, or roast chicken, got anything like 'tremendous' from the children.

They were silent as they trudged back through the yellowing autumn woods to Peter's car. Lotte was pleasantly, satisfyingly tired. My bones are singing, she thought. Not in pain, just a dull lament for steamy baths and whisky.

And then suddenly, without preamble, she made a decision. 'Peter,' she said, 'shall we spend the night together, sleep together, do you think? Tonight?'

Peter stopped dead, and a hand flew to his hairline, then down again. Lotte walked on, laughing. 'Don't look so appalled. I made this proposition before, remember? The night we watched *Who Wants to Be a Millionaire?*.'

'Of course I remember. I remember every word. You said, 'Maybe we should sleep together before we talk of marriage.'

Lotte slid her arm under Peter's and round his back. She burrowed her face into his jacket and said to his chin, 'And wasn't I right?'

She sensed Peter wanted to stop and kiss her, make a big deal of it, which would be OK, but somehow she didn't want that. Fortunately, however, he was encumbered by two spades over one shoulder and the tool-bag over the other. And she was lugging a rolled-up tarpaulin and a bucket full of brushes and sponges.

With his free left arm, Peter returned Lotte's hug, then released her as she pulled away. He said, 'Why now? What secret test have I passed?'

Lotte laughed. 'No test, or none other than being so patient with a lone parent of three. They do tend to make secret dalliances a bit of a challenge.'

Lotte watched Peter's fingers gently massaging his forehead and felt a wave of affection. The slightest stress – anxiety, embarrassment, confusion – brought his hand to his brow, like a thumb to the mouth of a child. He looked sideways at her from under his wrist and asked, 'And why is today the day, then?'

Lotte laughed. 'Because it's been a heavenly day. Blue sky and golden leaves and sharp autumn air.' She walked on a couple of paces, then added, 'And the children are all staying with their father, and they won't be back till tomorrow night.'

They piled the stuff into the boot of Peter's car and climbed in.

'God, it's got cold,' Lotte exclaimed, teeth chattering. 'Your place or mine? Which is warmest?'

They decided on Peter's house, but stopped at Gardener's Cottage for Lotte to collect some things. Peter stayed in the car while she raided the house. She put Brody's champagne, a frozen pizza, a packet of supermarket salad, a jar of home-bottled damsons and a tub of vanilla ice-cream into a carrier bag. That's supper, she thought. Now for afters.

She dashed upstairs and stuffed some clean underwear and her wash-things into her overnight bag. Oh God, she thought. Condoms. I haven't needed condoms for ever. What will I do? Have to discuss it with Peter, poor chap.

On impulse she picked up two huge scented candles, one green, one yellow, belonging to Annie, and a little jar of essential massage oil. She read the label: '*Add a few drops to the bathwater for a revitalizing experience*'. What tosh. But she put it into the wash-bag with the candles anyway.

'Pizza and ice-cream for supper,' Lotte said as she climbed back into the car. 'But unless you've got some condoms, we are going to have to be inventive.'

Peter's fingers explored the lines of his frown, but he was smiling. He said, 'Lotte, you gave me a month's warning. I've got condoms.'

They drove the seven miles to the village of Swinford, listening, or half listening, to Classic FM. Lotte used her mobile to ring Sam's number.

'Hi. Christo, it's Mum. Have you got a pencil? Good. Darling, just write this number down, it's Peter's, just in case . . . No, no, I'm just having supper with Peter. Your dad and I always leave numbers so we can get hold of each other if one of you falls under a bus. OK?'

She repeated the number to be sure he had it right, then said, 'Night night, darling. See you at the station tomorrow. Have a good time.'

'Isn't that just asking your ex-husband to ring you up?' asked Peter.

'No. He won't unless there's a crisis. But I'd lie awake imagining there was one if there was no way they could get hold of me.' She leant across and stroked his shoulder. 'I'm sorry. Just one of the prices you pay for having any truck with a mother. We are all the same. Neurotic.'

Lotte put the ice-cream into Peter's freezer and said, 'Can I have first bath?'

Peter replied, 'Sure thing. I'll do the man thing. Get logs. Make fire.' He grunted, Neanderthal-style, and Lotte laughed.

'And I'll do the lady thing and lie in scented bubbles with perfumed candles all about.'

First, though, she sat in the empty bath and shaved her legs and underarms and washed her hair. At home she'd have shaved and shampooed in her bath-water, but she didn't want to be caught swishing hairs down the plug, or risk Peter discovering them in his bath.

Legs smooth and hair clean, she cleaned the bath out and filled it, emptying a mini-bottle of bubble-bath under the tap. It smelt faintly of pine, but when she added a dozen drops of the 'essential oil' a powerful smell of rosemary wafted up with the steam.

She was about to step in when she realized she hadn't got a match for the candle. She was shivering, longing for the warmth of the water, but she was determined to have this bath as intended. She wrapped herself in a bath-towel and padded down to the kitchen.

Peter was coming in from the back, a basket of logs in his arms. 'Out already?' he said. 'I thought you were going to lie about like Cleopatra.'

'I am. That's still the plan,' Lotte said, holding the towel firmly round her, and hopping from foot to foot on the cold quarry tiles. 'I even pinched two scented candles from Annie, who spends happy hours lying in my bath with the place lit up like an altar. Only I forgot you need matches. Can I borrow some?'

Lotte lay in the bubbles and tried to relax. She'd have liked to ask Peter for a whisky to have in here too, but that seemed a bit unsociable. She'd have to wait.

She could hear Julie London belting out 'Cry Me a River'. It sounded muted and romantic coming from below. Then she went into 'Skylark' and Lotte sang along in her head.

> Skylark, have you anything to say to me?
> Won't you tell me where my love can be?

'He's right here, idiot,' Lotte said aloud to herself. 'Peter's wonderful and you are a lucky woman.'

And yet she felt unmoved, not as she wanted to feel when about to make love for the first time with the man she planned to marry. Maybe you couldn't expect swooning and palpitations when you were forty-seven and your lover-to-be was fifty-something. But if it had been Brody downstairs, how would she feel then?

Lotte scooped water into her cupped hands and rubbed her face vigorously. She must commit herself to Peter. It would buttress her against Brody. Make it easy for her to reject him. He'd been in America for three of the four weeks since the scene in the greenhouse, and she had not returned his calls. But he was home now, and he was so insensitive he wouldn't get the message unless it was written in yard-high letters. Marrying Peter was a mile-high message.

Lotte stared fixedly at the ceiling, her eyes wide open to circumvent tears. Peter knocked on the door. 'Can I come in?'

Lotte pictured him, eyes anxious behind his big glasses, fingers on his brow, waiting for a yes from her. And yes made sense. All right, she thought, I've made a decision, and it's a good one.

'Yes,' she said.

She watched the door in the big mirror opposite the bath. It opened and Peter appeared, not fingering his brow in anxiety as she'd expected, but smiling broadly and bearing the opened bottle of champagne in one hand and two tumblers in the other. She wanted to laugh. His hair, as usual, erupted on each side of his ears, and the harsh bathroom light shone on his glasses and his domed pate.

He looked down the length of the bath. Only Lotte's toes were visible above the meringue of bubbles.

'You look disappointingly decent,' he said.

He sat on the loo seat and put one glass on the window-sill. He filled the other, tipping the glass to a slope, and poured the champagne slowly to prevent too much of a head. He passed her the glass and poured the other. 'Sorry about the glasses. I don't seem to run to flutes.'

Lotte held the ice-cold glass against her warm cheek for a second and said, 'It would be welcome out of a tooth-mug. I was just thinking how much I'd like a drink, and here you are, the bathroom butler.'

Peter took a mouthful of his champagne. 'This is

delicious. I hope it was a present. Gardeners can't usually afford La Grande Dame.'

Lotte nodded. 'It was a present.' He didn't ask from whom, and Lotte, grateful, thought, he'll never be petty or jealous.

Peter looked round the bathroom and said, 'I don't think this place has ever smelt like this. It's wonderful. What is it?'

'The bubbles are pine, the bath oil – which promises to make me a new woman – is rosemary, and the candles are lemon and lime.'

'A veritable Mediterranean hillside.'

They drank the champagne, Peter keeping their glasses topped up, while the sound of Julie London's voice filtered upstairs. Lotte relaxed and a sensuous drowsiness crept over her. The warmth of the water, the alcohol, the music and the smells of candles and bath-water had her drifting blissfully. She shut her eyes and said, 'I'm being very unfair. It's your turn for the bath.'

'It's OK. I'm fine. Sitting here imagining your body under the foam.' She heard him shifting and opened her eyes a fraction. He was kneeling beside her. She thought he was going to kiss her, and she lifted her chin a bit to make it easy for him. But he took her arm out of the water and started to soap it with the bath sponge. She shut her eyes and let him do it.

It felt very good, and then he leant over and did the other arm, and her shoulders and neck. When he took her foot, she bent her leg and he soaped her feet, then her calves and knees, and the part of her thigh not in the water. She had thought it would tickle when he'd first

241

put the soapy sponge under her toes, but it didn't. It was delicious.

'Kneel up, Lotte,' he said, his voice a fraction deeper than usual. 'Away from me. I want to soap your back.'

Lotte opened her eyes and looked at him. He was perfectly still, easy and unruffled. No hand flying to his forehead. No stammer. How interesting, she thought, remembering that first awkward kiss in the library. Must be the champagne.

She did as she was told. He put his hands on each side of her waist, and held them there for a second or two. She could feel the first stirrings of desire, and she relaxed into it. Good, she thought, it's happening. I'm not going to have to pretend.

At first he used the sponge on her shoulders and neck as he had on her arms and legs. But then he soaped a rough loofah and rubbed her shoulders and back firmly. It felt scratchy but wonderful, as though her skin was waking up, strip by strip. Soon she could feel the warmth radiating off her. She knew she must be bright pink.

His breathing was quick and deep. She imagined that he would turn her round, soap her belly and breasts, maybe tell her how beautiful she was. But suddenly he was standing up, holding out a towel, saying, 'If you put the pizza in the oven, I'll jump in your fancy-smelling bath, and be down in ten minutes.'

She couldn't believe it. She was tempted to reject the towel and force him to make love to her then and there. But he wrapped the towel round her, lifted her bodily out of the bath and put her down without letting go of her. He said, breathing into her hair, 'If I soaped your front, or kissed you properly, this would all be over in ten minutes. And we've got all night, haven't we?' She could hear the desire in his voice, slower and darker than usual. He released her, and smiled.

'Besides,' he said, 'my glasses get steamed up in here.'

They ate the pizza and then the damsons with ice-cream in their usual companionable way, with no feeling of tension or expectation. Lotte, washing up the plates while Peter stoked up the sitting-room fire, wondered if she'd dreamt the scene in the bathroom. They were hardly dressed for romance: she was wearing Peter's dressing-gown, an old-fashioned one of the kind prep-school boys might wear, with a twisted cord of maroon and brown. He'd changed into corduroy trousers and a clean but crumpled warm shirt. They both wore Peter's socks and no shoes.

But then, after they'd watched the news side by side on the sofa, Peter returned from the kitchen with a small glass jug containing half an inch of oil. He said, 'I suppose peanut oil will do?' Lotte looked up, puzzled. 'It says you have to dilute this stuff with a base oil. Can't get much baser than Tesco's. How many drops do you think?'

He was squinting at the print on the little bottle of rosemary oil. 'Right, this is guaranteed to revitalize, invigorate, stimulate and energize.'

He put the jug down on the coffee table and shook the rosemary oil over it. As soon as she smelt the sharp, clean perfume, Lotte knew it would be all right. Even good, even wonderful. But Peter suddenly knelt in front of the sofa and grasped both her hands in his. 'Oh Lotte, I love you so deeply, so completely. If this doesn't work, will I lose you?' He looked into her face, then said, 'It's OK, you don't have to answer. You don't have to love me like I love you. All you have to do, the only thing you have to do, is be here.' His voice caught and broke, and he stood up abruptly.

Lotte had been right. It was fine. More than fine. Peter spread a bath-towel on the carpet in front of the fire, and rubbed and massaged and caressed every inch of her. And when she couldn't bear it any longer, they pulled his clothes off and made love, missionary style. It was perfect. Just as it should be: loving, and sexy, and deeply satisfying. Peter pulled a couple of cushions off the sofa and Lotte tucked her head into his shoulder, mumbling contentedly.

'What did you say?' Peter asked, stroking her shoulder.

Lotte lifted her head to look at him. 'I said, it's not the rosemary oil. It's you.'

18. Winter

She loves him she loves him not, she is confused:
She picks a fist of soaking grass and fingers it:
She loves him not.
The message passing from head to heart
Has in her stomach stopped,
She cannot quite believe the information is correct:
She loves him not.

Brian Patten (1946–), 'Forgetmeknot'

Annie was lying in wait for Jamie. She'd been surreptitiously watching him as he sprayed some evil-smelling
black stuff on to the trees in the orchard, dressed up like
a spaceman in a green plastic suit. She'd wanted to go and
talk to him, but he'd have had to take his mask off and
then she wouldn't know what to say and she'd make an
idiot of herself.

So she decided to ambush him in the coach-house.
She knew he knocked off at four and would come in
here to fetch his scooter. She'd planned the whole thing.
She would be lying under Peter's Harley Davidson, and
Jamie would ask her what she was doing and she'd say
something technical, dead casual, 'Oh, just fixing the
torque a bit.' And then she'd get into conversation

with him, and . . . well, she hadn't thought any further than that.

She got into position, lying on her back, her arms stretched above her head as if reaching for some part. That way her back arched and her belly showed between her jeans and her top. She looked her best on her back because her horrible fat stomach disappeared.

But it was freezing on the floor. She jumped up, telling herself she'd hear Jamie's boots scrunching on the gravel and have plenty of time to get back on the floor.

She wandered round the coach-house, examining its contents. Sad really, Mum's obsession with tidiness. Poor Jamie, it must be horrible doing work experience with her mother for his boss. You'd think world peace depended on things being in 'their proper place'.

The coach-house shelves were dead neat. The rows of paint were labelled with stickers facing front: Tennis court (RED); Tennis court (GREEN); Creosote (Dark Brown), etc., and the great bank of thick plastic mini-drawers were similarly labelled: Masonry Nails 3"; Brass Screws 2"; Tacks ½"; Vine eyes 3"; and so on. Her mother had a mania for labelling things. She'd once labelled the drawers in Annie's room: Knickers; Pyjamas; Tee-shirts, etc. in the hope that Annie would follow the instructions. Sad or what?

Annie looked out of the coach-house window across the walled garden: 'the productive garden' her mother called it, which got right up Annie's nose. Why couldn't she call it a veg patch like everyone else? In the summer every planted row had a label at the end of it. What for? Even she, Annie, could tell the difference between lettuce and corn on the cob. And what did it matter if the lettuce was Salad Bowl or Lamb's or Oakleaf. They were all horrible anyway.

She ought to see a shrink, Annie thought. It's a compulsive disorder, labelling things like she does. Every evening when she and Peter weren't poring over dusty plans or surreptitiously groping each other, Lotte was making olde-worlde labels on that machine. Which should be in a museum, not taking up half the sitting room.

Annie picked at the hem of her top. She wished she hadn't thought of Peter and her mother pawing each other. It was horrible. They thought they were so discreet, but even Christo had noticed what was going on. And what about Dad? I bet she hasn't told him she's having it off with Peter. Peter was OK of course, but they were both so *old*.

Suddenly Jamie was the other side of the window, his mop of straight blond hair and wide-mouthed smile filling her view. He'd come from the wrong direction, not over the gravel to the main door, but through the walled garden to the side. Annie felt herself go beetroot as Jamie grinned at her though the glass, then he was inside, lugging a backpack sprayer in one hand and a metal jerry-can in the other.

Caught off guard, Annie blurted, 'Why did you come that way? I thought you were in the orchard.'

And then she thought, oh God, what a stupid question, he'll tell me to bog off and mind my own business. But Jamie just put the sprayer on a shelf, neatly lined up with others just like it, and said, 'Yeah, but I had to change and have a shower. You sweat like a pig in that suit.' He turned and grinned his big blond grin at her. 'And even with it the tar-wash gets everywhere. It stinks something awful.'

Annie's throat was dry. Oh God, she thought, what do I say now? But then Jamie asked, 'Anyway, what are you doing here?'

'Nothing,' she replied, and then she realized what an idiot answer that was, and she said the first thing that entered her head, 'I'm just going down to the shop on Peter's bike.'

'Really?' Jamie, she was glad to see, looked impressed as well as surprised. 'Does he know?'

Annie's answer came out fast and indignant. 'Course he does. He lets me ride it whenever I like. If he's using his car, he leaves it in the coach-house for me.' This last bit was true, and Annie felt slightly calmer as she said it. She unhooked Peter's helmet from the seat and crammed it on her head without doing up the strap. Jamie didn't say anything, so Annie had no option but to go on. She turned the key and kicked the machine into life.

Then Jamie was saying something, but she couldn't hear with the din of the engine. She throttled back so she could hear.

'But you can't drive on the public roads, can you? That's a 1300 CC engine.' He walked over to her and put a hand on the handlebar. 'Your mother doesn't know, does she? She'll kill you, Annie.'

She couldn't bear it. The whole thing had gone wrong. Instead of her captivating Jamie, he was treating her like a child. She jammed the bike into gear and jerked her wrist down to full throttle, forcing Jamie to jump back as she swerved out of the coach-house doors. The bike skidded slightly as she hit the gravel.

Annie blasted down the drive. Peter's helmet didn't

have a visor, she hadn't put the goggles on, and tears ran in streaks from the corners of her eyes. It was starting to rain and she was freezing, the December wind drilling through her short fleece jacket. The rain and her tears made it difficult to see.

It was getting dark, and Annie didn't know how to turn the headlamp on, but she didn't want to stop. Jamie might catch her up on his scooter and that would be horrible. When she got to the big gates there was nothing coming either way and she crossed the road and turned right. She slowed a little, and concentrated on keeping steady and to the side. A car passed her from behind, flashing at her to turn on her lights.

Annie looked for the switch again, but peering over the handlebars made her wobble and she gave up, thinking she'd find the lights as soon as she stopped. She wished there was a turn-off before the village, so she could get off the main road and out of Jamie's route home. But there wasn't, not even a farm entrance.

At last the garage that heralded the village was in sight. And then, suddenly, a pantechnicon was behind her, the driver with his hand on the horn. The noise was terrifying, and she felt the shockwave as the great container roared past her. It was only inches away and she looked up in panic, her eyes on a level with its great wheels spraying mud and water over her.

The truck seemed to stay with her forever, threatening and close. She had to ride close to the kerb, at the point where the road sloped down to the gutter, and she was terrified she'd skid on the wet edge. Then suddenly the pantechnicon was past her, and she swayed in the turbulence of its wake. She slowed to a halt, gasping and close to tears.

She was at the edge of the garage forecourt, and she climbed off the bike and managed to wheel it a few yards in from the road. But the Fat Boy was huge and heavy, and the road sloped steeply down. She struggled to stop the machine either rolling away or falling over. She leant back, pulling on the handlebars, and managed to stop. With a desperate effort she kicked down the stand and yanked the bike back onto it.

It was stupid. She'd done this a million times before. Why couldn't she control the thing? She searched her jeans and jacket pockets in vain for a tissue, wiped her eyes and face on her sleeve, and ran towards the garage shop and the loo.

Her face in the little mirror over the basin looked childish and frightened under the helmet. Her bottom lip was quivering, and her eyes were wide and wet, with mascara smudges under them. She grabbed a handful of lavatory paper and blew her nose.

Annie sat on the loo seat, crying. She did not want to go out into the rain and dark, and drive home again.

Someone was banging on the door. A woman's voice, presumably belonging to the shop manager she'd seen as she came in, called, 'Hello. Are you Annie? Are you all right, love? There's a bloke here wants to see you.'

Oh God, it's the police, Annie thought, they'll tell my mum.

She crept round the edge of the door, head down, expecting grown-up retribution. Then she looked up to see Jamie standing there, his eyes anxious.

'Annie, you idiot . . .' he started, then she saw him clock her tear-streaked, blotchy face and stop in mid-sentence. He put his arm round her shoulders and shepherded her out of the shop, thanking the woman over his shoulder.

Annie felt like a lamb being led to slaughter. He'd insist on taking her home as though he was an uncle or something, and she'd have to endure him being patronizing and kind. But to her astonishment he said, 'What you need is a drink.'

She followed him meekly as he pushed the Harley out of the entrance to a parking place and locked it. Then he led her to his scooter and turned to do up her helmet strap as he might a baby's bonnet strings.

'Like I said, you're an idiot, Annie. What's the use of a helmet if it's going to fall off when you do?'

She sat behind him on the scooter with her arms round his waist. It felt OK. He'd looked so in charge when he'd done up her strap. And he was really cute-looking. She felt a little buzz of pride as they swept into the pub car park. It was like having a boyfriend: going out together. As if they were an item. It was great. She took her helmet off and tossed her head like the models do as they went in.

The pub was open, but empty except for a table of women drinking coffee. Jamie led her to a corner booth, with high wooden stalls. Annie hoped it was because he wanted to be alone with her, but she suspected he was probably ashamed to be seen with her.

To Annie's disappointment he put a lemonade down in front of her, but then he said, 'Couldn't buy you a drink since the geezer behind the bar says he knows you and you're under age. But if you drink some of that, I'll make you a shandy.'

Annie said, 'I hate lemonade.'

Jamie picked up her glass and poured the lemonade neatly into the pebbles surrounding a fake plant in a brass pot. Then he tipped half his pint into her glass.

Before it was half gone she could feel its effects: she became light-headed and giggly, and suddenly she didn't mind that Jamie was still behaving like a schoolteacher. Or maybe a big brother. She'd have liked to have a big brother.

'So what's up, young Annie?' he said, taking her hand. 'Why so unhappy?'

She found herself telling him how she still missed her London friends, how her mother drove her mad, and then, emboldened by the rest of the lager, she said, 'And I'm sick of all the boys at school. They're like so childish and stupid. I want to be taken seriously. Treated as a grown-up.' She looked up at him, her eyes on his. 'You don't think I'm a child, do you?'

Annie's gaze slid down to his movie-star mouth. He was so gorgeous it made her knees melt. As she waited, her eyes, apprehensive and pleading now, travelled up to his again. She was sorry she'd asked. He was going to say something patronizing and awful. She would not be able to stand it.

At last he spoke, quietly. 'You may be an idiot, Annie, but you are not a child.' And he leant forward slowly and kissed her lightly on the lips.

Annie had never been kissed before, though she'd thought and dreamt about it for at least three years. She didn't feel the rush of passion you were meant to feel. But she did feel a swelling pride, and a thrill of triumph. She could feel her lips start to smile under his, and she made an effort to keep them still.

He straightened up, reached for his helmet and said, 'C'mon, you've got to get home before your mum or that boyfriend of hers discover what you've been up to. I'll take you back to the garage, and then I'll follow you to Maddon. OK?'

OK? Of course it was OK. It was wonderful. Annie walked on air to the scooter, and climbed on behind him in a cloud of bliss. Then, as suddenly, it was terrible, doubt closing in on her as they weaved between the cars and on to the road. Would he kiss her again? Or had she put him off for good? What should she do if he did it again? Why had she just sat there like an idiot? Why hadn't she kissed him back?

She had to tell him she didn't know where the headlamp switch was, which was a bit humiliating, but the way he had a go at her for driving in the dark without it was really nice. He seemed to care what happened to her.

'You go in front. I'll be right behind you.' He grinned. 'And don't go fast. My scooter does forty max.'

Annie did as she was told, though it was tempting to show off a bit. She knew she rode well, and now Jamie was with her, the rain had stopped and she had lights, she'd have liked to roar past everything, leaning into the curves with the bike half over. Even Peter didn't know how good she'd got at it. Since she'd been allowed to ride the Maddon lanes on her own, she'd abandoned the 30 mph rule, though she was careful not to let anyone who'd tell on her see. Speeding had been a secret pleasure, mostly on the farm roads. She loved it: the deep-throated roar of the bike, the feeling of danger as she took the corners.

But she drove sedately, strictly within the speed limit. It took an amazingly short time to retrace the earlier nightmare journey on the main road. They were at the Maddon gates much too soon. She prayed as she slowed to let Jamie catch up, please let him come further with me, please don't let him go home.

Jamie took the corner without slowing, passed her and waved her on. She opened the throttle a bit and drew level with him. She couldn't see into his visor, but his wave had been cheerful and she smiled as they rode side by side up the long drive to the coach-house. The doors were still open and the light was on. Annie parked carefully, kicked down the side stand and got off.

She was still praying that Jamie wouldn't just give her a friendly wave and drive off. But he turned off his Vespa and removed his helmet.

Annie's heart leapt. If he was going to leave straight away, he'd just have raised his visor. He helped her haul the Harley on to the main stand, and waited while she took off her helmet and put it on the seat.

Now was her chance. She must get him to kiss her again now, or he'd think she was a little kid forever. She walked round to his side of the bike, and – not quite as confidently as she'd intended – put her arms round Jamie's neck.

For a moment she felt his shoulders stiffen, then she put her head back and reached up to kiss him. He was a lot taller than her, and she realized that if he didn't want to kiss her he only had to keep his chin up. That would be unbearable, so she said, 'Kiss me, Jamie.'

And he did. He put his hands on each side of her head, over her ears, and held her head still as he brought his mouth down on hers. This time it was less gentle, and Annie was aware of the tension in his hands, the urgency of his mouth, and she felt an answering lick of heat in her guts.

But then he was trying to get his tongue in her mouth, and she hated it. It was disgusting – like a hard little animal, an athletic snail, squeezing between her teeth. She shook her head and turned away. And immediately regretted it. If she wanted Jamie to love her, she'd have to do grown-up snogging. She turned her face back to his, her eyes wide.

This time he kissed her without his tongue, just holding his mouth there, making small kissing movements, breathing into her. He did it for what seemed like ages, and she was having trouble finding the space to breathe. But she didn't care. He was panting too, and when he dropped his arms to pull her waist into him, she knew this must be real love. The flash of warmth, like a geyser rushing up her legs and into her body, was frightening, but it was wonderful.

'Annie,' he groaned, 'Oh Annie,' as his hand fumbled and probed, searching for a way under her fleece. God, thought Annie, suddenly frightened, we are not going to do it, are we? Here? In the coach-house? She couldn't. She wanted to, but she couldn't.

She pulled away. And then he was standing apart from her, holding her shoulders at arm's length.

'Jesus, Annie. That was a bit sudden. Wow.' He pushed his hand up into his thick hair. 'You are dynamite, you are.'

Annie watched his blond hair part between his fingers and then fall back over his high, wide forehead. And his eyes . . . he was so good-looking.

She swallowed. 'I've got to go,' she said. 'It's really late and . . .'

'I know. You're right. I'm off.'

He turned the scooter, jammed his helmet over his head and swung round. His voice came muffled through the visor.

She thought he said, ''Bye, Annie, be good.'

She walked back across the walled garden, her life erupting, exploding, her whole body happy, happy, happy. She had a boyfriend. And what a boyfriend! Jamie wasn't some acne-covered sixteen-year-old. He was nineteen, at college. A grown-up man.

As Annie charged up the stairs Lotte called from the kitchen, 'Where have you been, darling? I was beginning to get worried.'

Annie shouted back, 'Don't be daft, Mum, I'm fine. Be down in a minute.'

She swigged mouthwash direct from her mother's bottle and gargled furiously. She didn't want anyone smelling the beer on her breath and starting an inquisition. She shoved the bottle back into the medicine chest. As she closed the mirrored door she looked at her image with surprise. Her skin was clear and pink, her eyes shiny, mouth wide and full. She looked fantastic.

19. Early Spring

Spring in the bloodstream, snow on the boots;
March with its toenails stirs up the roots.

Laurie Lee (1914–97), 'Spring'

Annie had hardly seen Jamie since he'd kissed her in the
coach-house just before Christmas, at least not to talk to,
or alone. And that was – she couldn't believe it – over
two months ago. The week after the kiss she was too shy
to go near him. He was always with Alex or her mother,
never alone. But she didn't mind. She hugged their secret
tight and was just so happy. He waved at her sometimes,
or shouted hi, and once he blew her a kiss behind her
mother's back. And the best was when he said goodbye
before going home to his folks for Christmas in North-
umberland; he put his arms right round her and hugged
her hard and kissed both her cheeks.

Then, for the first time ever, she and the other two
went to Dad and Frances for Christmas in London, and
had stayed until school started. Mum said this was because
they still complained about missing London. But the real
reason, Annie knew, was so she and Peter could snog in
peace. Not that she cared. At least her mum was off her
back these days.

She thought about Jamie every day and told her London friend Lynette all about him. And then, when they finally got home, Jamie was away on a month's course.

'But why?' Annie said, trying to keep her voice from betraying the pain she felt. 'I thought he was here for a year.'

'He's keen to learn some forest management and tree surgery, and we can't teach him that here,' Lotte said, 'and since we aren't very busy in the dead of winter and there's a space on the short course, it seemed a bit of luck. He gets what he wants and I don't have to pay his wages.'

The disappointment was acute. Annie'd wanted to e-mail Jamie or write to him, but if she'd asked for his address, her mother would have smelled a rat, right off. She tried snooping in the office, but the staff-files cupboard was locked, and she couldn't get into the computer. She'd tried all sorts of Mum-style passwords like Tradescant and CapabilityBrown, but no luck.

Once she fixed her mind on the date he'd return, however, she was high on happiness again. It was amazing. Everything seemed to be going right for once. She'd stopped stuffing her face, for a start, and had lost half a stone. And now that she had a boyfriend too, her once best friend, Rosie, was all over her again.

Jamie was back at work in the first week of March. One day, coming home from school, Annie heard banging as she approached the coach-house. She walked past the doors, super-casually, and looked in. Jamie and the old geezer, Andrew, were in there, fixing mowers it looked like. She dived quickly past and headed for home and the kitchen.

How could she accidentally-on-purpose run into him?

How long would he be in there? She'd have to get out of her school uniform, that was for sure. She opened the fridge and surveyed its contents. Then she remembered she was on a diet and shut it again. She turned to the kitchen window, still undecided, and saw Andrew walking across the walled garden. Her heart gave a lurch. That meant Jamie was alone in the coach-house.

Annie looked at her watch. Three-thirty. He'd be knocking off in half an hour. Please God, keep him in the coach-house until then.

She bounded upstairs, pulling at her school tie as she went. She wriggled out of her skirt and shirt and pulled on her favourite black trousers and the big sloppy jersey with the ragged neck. She stirred the pile of clothes on the floor and rumpled the bed in a hunt for her sneakers, but gave up and stuffed her feet back into her school shoes. She considered making up her eyes and mouth. She was pretty sure her mum wasn't home to object. But a sudden panic that Jamie would go home early, or leave the coach-house, made her swing out of her room, shutting the door on the mess inside.

She jumped down the first few steps to the landing, then had a quick look at herself in the long mirror. Pretty cool. She was sure her legs were thinner. The elastine trousers held her bottom and thighs firmly, but with no horrible bulges. And her hair looked great – untidy and spiky over her eyes. She'd have liked to have done her eyes, but then, Jamie was the type to like the natural look, she was pretty sure. As she plunged down the rest of the stairs and ran out of the house, she chewed her lips hard: at least they'd be red, if not glossy.

She slowed down in the walled garden and sauntered into the coach-house, swinging round the door-jamb, super-cool. Except her heart was racing.

'Hello, Annie,' said Jamie. He was crouching by a machine, holding a short piece of metal chain in his hand. He smiled at her, then returned to fixing the chain in place.

Annie felt a little stab of disappointment that he hadn't stood up and taken her in his arms like she'd imagined. But she dismissed it. He's probably shy too.

'What's that thing?' she said.

Jamie stood up and reached past her to grab a piece of blue paper from the dispenser. He wiped his hands on it, rubbing between his fingers and over the back of his hands.

'It's a flail mower. Brilliant machine. It can scythe through anything.'

Annie didn't want to talk about machines, but she asked, 'Yeah? So what do you use it for?'

Jamie manoeuvred the machine to the side of the coach-house, parking it beside the rotavator, all the while telling her about mowing Lower Maddon Meadows only once a year, when the grass was eighteen inches high, how they had to leave it until midsummer so the wild flowers could seed.

'That's why those fields have such brilliant flowers. We're imitating what would have happened when it was a hay meadow. In the old days the cows weren't let on to the meadows, which used to flood in the winter, until they'd dried out – and that meant the wild flowers had a chance to flower and seed before they got eaten. The flail mower does the cow's job.'

Annie thought how marvellous Jamie was to know this stuff. 'But it's winter, dummy. Hardly hay-making.'

She wanted him to stop working and concentrate on her, but he answered her almost idly while he picked up his tools and stacked them where they belonged, hanging the spanner neatly between a bigger and a smaller one, putting the little oil can on a shelf next to its big brother, fitting the monkey-wrench thing between two pegs beside the hammers.

'Yeah, but your mum is one hell of a boss, and every machine gets an overhaul in the winter.' Then he smiled, and his smile filled his face. 'Poor old Andrew doesn't know what's hit him.'

Annie smiled back, not sure if they were smiling about Andrew, or for each other. Each other, she hoped. And then suddenly Jamie was turning for the door: he was leaving. He wasn't going to say anything about the kiss, or anything loving at all. She took two steps after him and said, 'Where are you going?'

'To fill in the Maintenance Book in the office. We've all got to, every time we finish a machine.'

It was now or never. Annie was given courage by a small whorl of anger beginning to turn in her guts. He can't just walk away from me. He can't pretend nothing has happened. He can't pretend he didn't . . .

'Jamie, what about us? Don't you . . . don't you like me any more?' It sounded so pathetic she was instantly furious with herself.

Jamie turned round. 'Of course I like you, Annie. You're a great kid . . .'

Annie interrupted. 'Kid? You think I'm just some kid?

And that what we were doing was Ring o' Roses?' The more she talked, the hotter and more desperate she felt. 'I suppose it meant nothing to you, k-k-kissing me . . . and that.'

'Now, Annie . . .' Jamie took a step towards her, putting his arm out to her. But then he thought better of it and dropped it. 'Look, Annie . . . you are only fifteen . . .'

'So what?' Suddenly Annie knew she was going to cry. She could feel her lip wobble like Jo-Jo's. Oh God, I'm going to prove what a kid I am, she thought, struggling to stop the tears spouting. 'If it didn't mean anything to you . . . what we did . . .' A sob gathered in her throat and erupted. 'You shouldn't . . . Jamie. I thought . . . I thought . . .'

'Oh Annie, OK, OK. It's all my fault. I should never have kissed you. But you looked so sweet, and I just didn't think about you being a school kid . . . Or that you're my boss's daughter. I must have been mad.'

Annie was crying in earnest now. She turned her back on Jamie, wiping her eyes with her fists, and a disgusting sort of snort came out. And she was desperate for a tissue. Then she remembered the blue paper roll and lurched towards it, pulling off a yard of paper and burying her face in it. Her throat hurt with trying not to cry and she wanted to die.

She heard Jamie's anxious voice speaking to her back. 'It didn't mean anything, Annie. It was just a bit of fun. Nothing serious.'

Lotte pushed Annie's door open, shoving a tide of clothes before it. She put her head round the door and exploded. Annie was still in bed, under the duvet.

'Annie, for God's sake! Could you just for once do what you are told? I woke you twenty minutes ago. And this room is a tip. I've had just about enough . . .'

'But Mum . . .'

'Don't "But Mum" me. You are grounded until it's tidied. No clubbing at the weekend. No going to Rosie's this afternoon. You can come home and tidy this lot. OK?'

Annie pulled the covers closer round her and said, 'Christ, Mum, get off my back, can't you?'

Lotte marched across the room and whipped the duvet off the bed, flinging it on top of the sea of possessions. 'And don't swear, Annie. I won't have it. And no, I won't get off your back. If you can't get up for school on time, if you must behave like a spoilt brat, then you'll have to put up with me bullying you. So get up. Get dressed. And if your school clothes are under this mess, you had better look sharp because you are going to iron them, yourself, before you leave this house. Understood?'

Lotte went downstairs, seething. What was it with Annie? She'd been fine, even co-operative, lately. But for the last week she'd reverted to the old maddening Annie – morose, sulky, as unresponsive to kindness as to nagging.

Jo-Jo looked up from the breakfast table as Lotte came in, her eyes wide. 'Why are you being horrible to Annie?' she said.

'Yeah, what's up, Mum?' Christo joined in.

'Just eat your cereal, will you?' said Lotte, already feeling like the Gestapo. By the time she'd made the toast, she longed for a chance to hug her elder daughter and let her off the grounding. But she knew it wouldn't make any difference. Annie was just impossible.

At eight Annie had still not appeared, and Lotte decided to quit the battlefield. If Annie missed the school bus and had to take the village one, tough. She'd just have to be late for school and face the music.

Christo, of course, wanted to wait for his sister, but Lotte shooed him and Jo-Jo out. They went reluctantly, unused to the hostile atmosphere, not much comforted by Lotte's goodbye hugs.

Lotte stacked the dirty stuff in the dishwasher, but left the breakfast things on the table. Poor kid, she thought, if she's going to be late anyway, she might as well take two minutes to swallow some yogurt or cereal.

She walked fast across the park, shaking off domestic angst as she thought of the forthcoming monthly session with Brody. As always, she felt her pulse quicken, but she had her thoughts about Brody well in control now. It had just been lust, that was all, and now she had such a satisfactory love-life with Peter, she was in no danger of a repeat of the greenhouse episode. And Brody, once she'd made it so clear she was with Peter, had accepted it, and stopped wooing her. Even Jade was polite, if not friendly.

Lotte checked her watch as she kicked off her boots in the porch. Eight-fifteen. If they were through in half an hour, maybe she should show Brody the progress they were making on the walled garden. The pineapple house was up now, and so was the melon house. The apricots and plums for the walls were due this week, and the beds were ready for them.

Her heart lifted. If it wasn't for Annie playing up, I'd say life was pretty good, she thought.

The garden was, she felt, both a demanding master and a rewarding child. But with much more predictability than either. You fed things, they blossomed. You planted things, they grew. It was very satisfying. Month by month, even week by week, she could see the difference she was making.

One day soon, she thought, I'll be brave and tell Brody about the grotto and the Persian pool. She smiled, knowing that one reason why she hadn't done so was that she wanted to get further with it before she showed him. She wanted to hear him marvel at her commitment, exclaim at her willingness to work in her own time and for no money, wonder at her enterprise, her genius!

Lotte pulled herself up on this thought – Peter worked almost as hard as she did and was just as committed. Only, thought Lotte, his reasons are different. He's discovering history and pleasing me. I'm carrying on where Emma Fernley and Mr Ferguson and hosts of long-dead owners and gardeners went before. I'm tending, serving a garden.

As she rounded the corner to the front of the house, she saw the helicopter on the pad, with the pilot stowing Brody's briefcase and bags into it. Damn. No chance of a visit to the vegetable garden then.

Brody was not his usual relaxed and confident self. He was wearing a starched white shirt and plain blue tie, and his suit jacket was hanging on his chair-back. He looked distracted and barely listened to Lotte's monthly report, just saying, 'Good, good' at intervals. She stopped in the middle of an explanation about Jamie being off the books for a month while on the forestry course. Brody had stopped listening altogether.

'Is something wrong, Brody? Should I come back another – ?'

'No, no. Sorry.' He looked up at her and forced a grin. 'Go on.'

'I've finished, really. And anyway there's nothing important. Unless you've time to see how the pineapple and melon houses are doing. They are just about finished . . .'

But he opened his big hand in a no, and shook his head. 'Sorry, babe. I'd love to but I've got to be in the City this morning.' He stood up, shrugging his shoulders as if to dispel stiffness, and then put one arm over Lotte's shoulders.

She started to pull back, but Brody said, 'No, no, Lotte. Don't worry. I know when I'm beat. I wish it were different. I could do with some of your plain-speaking sense right now . . .'

Lotte looked at Brody's face. He looked exhausted. For the first time, she noticed the deep lines on each side of his mouth.

'Brody, you know I'll help you with anything. What's the matter? Is it Jade? . . .'

'No, nothing like that. Jade is in Paris. Or Milan. I forget. Anyhow, she's working. She's fine . . . It's just business stuff, boring banking problems.'

He walked her to the door, then suddenly laughed.

'Oh, the hell with it, Lotte. Let's go see the pineapple house. The rest can wait.'

20. Spring

For the willow tree will twist
And the willow tree will twine,
I wish I was in a young man's arms
That once had this heart of mine.

Anon

Brody pulled on his suit jacket, and with it his usual demeanour. The lines of anxiety on his face seemed to be smoothed out by an act of will. He waved at the pilot of the helicopter as he passed, calling to him that he'd be another twenty minutes.

His sudden energy and cheerfulness lifted Lotte. She gave him a fast précis of the state of the works: the builders were almost done, beds dug, plants ordered, wires in place for training the fruit trees.

They were standing by the pineapple house, Lotte regretting that heating the trenches with fresh horse manure, as they did at Heligan, wasn't feasible, when Brody's mobile phone rang.

'Keegan,' he said, his voice brisk. Then his face sobered and he looked at Lotte.

She presumed it was more business problems, but he held her gaze as he spoke. 'Where . . . ? Which direction . . . ?

Are you sure . . . ? Yes . . . Yes, you did right to tell me. Lotte's with me. Yes, I'll handle it, Jamie . . .'

'What is it, Brody?' said Lotte. 'Is he hurt? Or Andrew . . . ? Has there been an accident?'

'No, it's Annie. She's pinched Peter's bike and is on the A34.'

'What? No. No. She's at school . . .'

'Lott, Jamie just passed her on the Botley roundabout. She was going south. He recognized Peter's bike and helmet and thought it was him, but then realized it was Annie. She's wearing a purple leather jacket.'

Lotte pictured her daughter, hunched over the huge handlebars, face set and angry, capable of anything. Fear froze her mind. 'Oh God,' she said, 'Brody, what can we do?'

Brody was already through to the police. Lotte stood unmoving, her mind still not working as Brody briskly dealt with preliminary questions. Then he was saying, 'She's only fifteen. Yes, I'm with her mother. Three minutes ago she was seen heading south on the A34 at the Botley roundabout . . . big Harley Davidson. No, sorry. Just a moment . . .' Brody looked at Lotte. 'Do you know the bike's number? . . . Lotte? The number plate?'

Lotte shook her head. 'No, sorry . . .'

Again he looked at her. 'Do you know where she might be heading? . . . No, we don't know . . . Purple jacket. Helmet? Hold on.'

Lotte said, 'Black, black helmet,' and Brody nodded.

'Yes, black helmet,' he said. 'No, the bike isn't stolen. It belongs to a friend who . . . yes, that's it: taken without owner's consent . . . But surely you must stop her if she's under age and driving without a licence? . . . But can't you use a helicopter . . . ? But she's already been seen . . . OK, forget it.' He snapped the phone closed and pulled Lotte by the wrist.

'Come on, Lott. The police won't use a chopper until she's been sighted by a ground unit. But it will be all right, we'll use mine. The police will never catch her with a car.'

Lotte's mind had unjammed and was racing now as they ran back towards the house. Why had Annie done it? And where was she going? Not into Oxford if she'd taken the A34. Was she running away? Or just punishing her for the row this morning?

The helicopter engine was running, and Brody barked instructions as the pilot helped them aboard. Brody sat in the seat next to the pilot, with Lotte behind.

Lotte found she was praying. Please God, let her be OK. Just don't let her crash.

She looked out of the window at the land, some fields just showing the first green of winter wheat, and at the fine tracery of roads. She could make no sense of it. It looked nothing like a map, where the roads were colour-coded and labelled.

They flew low over the river, villages and country lanes, then over a couple of large roads. Brody turned round to her. Pointing, he shouted above the engine noise, 'That's the A34. We'll follow it. We'll soon catch her.'

She couldn't hear, and Brody reached across and handed her her ear-cans. She put them on and heard the pilot talking to someone about permission to enter airspace.

They followed the double carriage road, gradually

swallowing car after car, truck after truck. The vehicles loomed ahead, then disappeared out of sight under the helicopter, and then they were advancing on the next batch. Lotte had to lean forward or sideways to see the southbound carriageway, and she could not get a steady view. She wished she was in front.

After what seemed like hours they saw a motorbike in the distance and Lotte's heart leapt. But when they swooped down, they could see the bike was not at all like Peter's, and the driver was wearing a yellow helmet. The second and third bikes were not Annie's either, and Lotte began to wonder if she was still on the A34. Maybe she'd turned off. Maybe she'd crashed in a ditch and they'd missed her.

Brody turned so he could see her face and said, 'Lott, could she be heading for London, do you think?'

Lotte started to say, no, they always went to London on the M40, and then she thought: but would Annie realize that? She might just be following signs to London. Maybe she *was* going to London. To her friends. Or to Sam's. She nodded yes, yes, she could.

'We should ring my ex-husband,' she said. 'She might go there.' She pulled her mobile out of her back pocket, but the pilot said, without looking round, 'I'm afraid it's illegal to use mobile phones in the air . . .'

Brody said, 'Bugger that.'

But Sam's number was engaged, and Brody said, 'Leave it till we know where she's going, Lott.'

She nodded dumbly. And then a horrible thought struck her. Young girls went to London when they ran away from home, didn't they? And lived on Euston Station and on the streets, and charities who might help them never told their parents where they were if the children didn't want them to know.

The pilot said something she didn't catch, and Brody relayed the information. 'We have to go up above five hundred feet once we are over the motorway, but it will still be possible to see her, I'm sure.' He leant through the seats and patted her knee. Lotte shut her eyes, forcing herself to be calm.

In fact, they caught up with her just before the Newbury junction.

'There she is. That's her, isn't it?' said Brody. The pilot swung out to the side a little, parallel with the biker, so that Lotte could get a good view.

She said yes, but nothing came out and she said it again, 'Yes, that's Annie.'

'It's OK, Lotte, she's not going fast. She's driving sensibly. She'll be fine. Air Traffic Control will let the cops know and they'll send a car out to get her to pull up.'

The pilot was on the radio already. 'She's on the A34, just north of the M4 at junction 13. She's likely to take the M4 eastbound to London.'

Lotte's eyes were glued to the small dark shape, like a bobbin, that was her daughter. Annie seemed to be driving very straight, in the middle lane, overtaking slow-lane traffic without a swerve, but not moving to the left when she could. Lotte thought, oh God, she's too frightened to do anything but hold on.

Annie slowed down with the rest of the traffic as they neared the roundabout. On her left was a Waitrose container lorry and on her right a stream of cars. Lotte watched in horror as they entered the roundabout, with Annie still in the middle lane.

'Get to the left,' she shouted. 'Oh, she's going to get trapped.' Annie wobbled and swerved, obviously undecided, her sight blocked by the container truck on her left. She'd missed the exit for the M4. Then she suddenly accelerated, causing the car to her right to brake to a juddering stop, and the car behind it to swerve wildly. Lotte covered her eyes, then opened them to see Annie speeding up round the curve before swooping on towards Newbury, still on the A34.

For a moment Lotte was relieved Annie hadn't taken the motorway, but now what? How could they stop her?

'Oh God, where is she going?' she cried. 'Brody, what can we do?'

Brody's voice calmed her a little. He said that they could only keep track of her, and direct the police.

Then the pilot's voice said, 'Sir, if she goes into Newbury town we'll have trouble following her – we have to rise to fifteen hundred feet. We could lose her.'

'But we've got to stay with her, Brody. We can't lose her.' Lotte was fighting to keep calm. And then suddenly Annie swerved into a lay-by and stopped.

'Oh, thank God, thank God. Can we land, Brody? Can I get to her?'

Brody said something to the pilot and he circled round Annie, dropping lower. Annie suddenly looked up, and Lotte could see the oval of her face, cut in half by the goggles, staring up at the helicopter.

Then Annie jerked the bike into action, swung it back on to the road and headed on south. But now she kept looking up and Lotte watched in terror as she wobbled and swerved, trying to watch the helicopter and the road.

Brody spoke to the pilot, and they wheeled away a little. They watched Annie come into the next round-about, drive right round it and head north towards the motorway again.

Lotte put her face in her hands, trying not to look as Annie negotiated the big Newbury junction once more, this time successfully making it on to the London-bound M4.

The pilot took them up a lot higher, again explaining that only the police could fly low over motorways. 'Look,' he said, 'the cops are going to pick her up.' He was pointing at a police car sliding on to the motorway from a raised observation platform, like a crocodile into a pool, and then to another car coming up fast behind Annie. One passed her and tucked itself in front of her. The driver started to slow down, and Annie slowed with him.

Thank God, thought Lotte, she's going to stop. The second car drew level with Annie, driving close enough to signal to her to pull over. But Annie suddenly ripped between the two cars, leaning close over her handlebars and going fast into the outside lane. She ducked her head under her arm to see if she was being pursued and when she found she was, she started to swerve in and out of the traffic, overtaking on the right and left like something demented.

Lotte was gulping with terror now. She cried out, 'Brody, Brody, make them stop. They'll kill her. She'll crash. Oh Brody, please . . .'

Brody undid his seat-belt and clambered from the front seat into the back with her. He held her tight and she put her face into his jersey. He exuded strength, like strong whisky.

'Mr Keegan,' the pilot said, 'you must wear your seat-belt.'

'OK, John, you've done your duty and told me so. But you'll not mind if I take no notice.' He leant closer to Lotte, both arms round her. He watched the motorway over her head and said, 'It's OK, they've backed off. Don't worry, Lott, she's slowing down.'

But Annie was still driving way beyond the speed limit. Lotte could tell because she was passing fast-lane cars and everyone drove at eighty along the M4. Then, to Lotte's relief, after the traffic slowed at the Maidenhead turn-off, Annie resumed her original place in the middle lane.

They followed her all the way into London, the pilot getting clearance as they went, Lotte alternating between renewed panic and silent helplessness. When Annie got caught between an airline bus and a white panel van and then emerged miraculously unscathed, snaking her way to safety, Lotte thought she would be sick.

Annie seemed to have forgotten about the helicopter. She hadn't looked up since the police cars had tried to stop her. Lotte began to hope they'd be able to follow her all the way to wherever she was going. Oh, please let it be Sam's, she whispered.

Brody was incensed that he could not speak directly to the police but had to relay messages via Air Traffic Control. And once they were over London, they were no longer allowed to follow Annie but had to fly along the river to the Battersea heliport. Lotte was desperate to follow her street by street, but her pleading cut no ice.

Eventually a message came that an unmarked police motor-cyclist and a police car were ready to pick Annie up after the Hogarth Roundabout and before Hammersmith. That way they could track her if she went over Hammersmith Bridge to her father in Barnes or on into London. They were given a number to ring for information once on the ground.

But when they'd landed the police had lost her too. Or never found her. Lotte finally burst into tears, crying in Brody's arms, her face flayed with anguish.

'Lott, stop,' said Brody, wiping her tears with his thumbs. 'She probably came over Kew or Chiswick Bridge and into Barnes that way. And the police have put out another call for her.' He held her tight until she gulped herself back into a semblance of control. She'd have liked to stay in the dark of Brody's arms. But she pushed away.

'Sorry. Thanks, Brody. I'm OK now.'

Lotte rang Sam at work. She was still trying not to cry, and she wasn't making sense. Brody took the phone from her. 'Sam, this is Brody, Lotte's boss. There's a problem. Young Annie has nicked Peter's motor-bike and driven it all the way into London. And Lotte is hoping she's running away to you. If she is, she'll be at your house within half an hour. Could you meet Lotte there?'

There was a silence, then Brody said, 'Yes. That's right. No. I think she'll be fine. She rides a bike as well as anyone. But Lotte is in a hell of a state. No, we are in London – look, I'll bring her round. She'll explain . . . Fine. Thanks.'

They took a taxi to Sam's flat. It was in an Edwardian

block with an entry-phone security system. They rang the bell, but there was no answer.

Lotte said, 'Frances must be at work too. Thank God.' She could not bear Frances to see what a useless mother she was, to see her in this wreck of a state, to see Annie, if she came, so unhappy.

They stood in silence for a few minutes and then Lotte said, 'Brody, I'm so sorry. You must go. I'm really fine now. I can't thank you enough and . . .'

'I'll stay till Sam comes. I've kept the taxi.' He jerked his chin towards the waiting black cab. Lotte had not heard him tell the cabbie to wait, had not noticed the steady hum of the diesel engine at the kerb. Brody kept his arm around her shoulders while they waited, and she stood still, allowing his calm and confidence to seep into her.

Sam arrived, jumping out of another taxi. Brody shook his hand, gave Lotte a quick hug, and left. Lotte felt her throat contract. She didn't want Brody to go, to leave her alone with Sam.

Sam fitted his key into the lock, opened the front door and ushered her into the block of flats. She felt utterly wretched. A complete failure. In the lift she said, 'Oh Sam, what have I done?'

He put an arm round her. The first time in six years. He said, 'Don't give yourself grief. Teenage girls are hell.'

'But she's been so good lately. Why did she do it?'

Lotte looked into Sam's face and saw a reflection of her own fear. But he said, 'She'll ring within twenty-four hours, I bet.'

'Twenty-four hours? I can't survive twenty-four hours. What can we do?'

'I think the time-honoured thing is a cup of tea. Or a whisky.'

They found their daughter curled up against the flat door, her arms round her knees.

21. Spring

And frosts are slain and flowers begotten,
And in the green underwood and cover
Blossom by blossom the Spring begins.

Algernon Charles Swinburne (1837–1909),
'Atalanta in Calydon'

Peter had stepped into the aftermath of guilt and exhaustion that had enveloped Lotte after Annie's demonstration of teenage misery. He'd proposed an Easter holiday in Portugal, at a place that would be good for them all, he said.

Now he craned over Lotte's shoulder to look out of the plane window and point out the Barragem Santa Clara, the man-made lake in which, in perhaps three hours, they'd all be swimming.

Lotte looked down on the multi-coloured terrain of the Alentejo. She'd read about the spring flowers of Portugal, and guessed the purple swathes would be viper's bugloss, the orange ones wild poppies and the yellow, daisies. It looked little touched by man, except for the perfect circles of green where European money had paid for irrigation schemes. The hills were only sparsely dotted with trees and the endless dirt tracks meandered, empty. The lake looked like a huge, many-tailed, many-limbed and many-tongued dragon, its extremities licking round hills and snaking up valleys for mile on mile.

She hoped it would be all right. Perhaps they should have played safe and gone to the Algarve, somewhere where there would be other children, things for them to do.

She looked across at Annie, doubly isolated from the rest of them by ear-phones and sleep. Asleep, she had the unwritten face of a child. Lotte's heart contracted, remembering her face made ugly and desperate by adolescent pain that day at Sam's flat.

The memory still hurt. Annie had fallen into her father's arms and cried and cried. When Lotte had come up behind her to hug her too, Sam had enveloped Annie more tightly and swung her away, signalling to Lotte with a shake of his head over their daughter's shoulder that she was to stay out of it.

'Come on, darling. It's all right. It's all right. I'm here. You are safe now,' he said.

Lotte stumbled into the kitchen and tried not to mind. She made tea, forcing back tears, telling herself she must be grown-up, reasonable.

When she got back, they were sitting on the sofa, Sam holding his daughter's hands in his. Lotte put the tea on the coffee table and sat the other side of Annie, pulling her close, determined not to be rejected.

'How did you get in, darling? What have you done with the bike?' Lotte asked, choosing neutral questions to give them all recovery time.

Annie looked at her for the first time, her eyes flaring from misery to hostility. 'What does it matter, Mum? I parked round the back, got in the delivery door. Why? Are you worried Peter's precious bike will get stolen?'

Lotte met Sam's eyes but there was no sympathy there. She leant back on the sofa, removing her presence from her daughter's gaze.

Annie said, 'Dad, it was so horrible. I thought I didn't know the way. I thought I'd crash . . .'

'Shh, shh, darling,' Sam said. He looked across Annie's head at Lotte and asked, 'Tea?'

Lotte obediently poured three mugs and handed one to Annie, who drank it without meeting her mother's eyes.

In the end, Lotte went for a walk across the common and left them to it. She knew she should be offering thanks to the God she didn't believe in for returning her daughter to her, whole and safe. But instead she felt excluded and wounded. And inadequate. Why couldn't Annie confide in her? Shouldn't daughters turn to their mothers?

It was cold and overcast now, and she pulled her jacket tightly round her as she walked, head down, oblivious of the first bursts of willow leaf and chestnut buds. She wished Brody was with her. Brody had been so wonderful. She wanted that burly, stocky body to weep against.

Oh God, she thought, why am I not longing for Peter, solid, dependable Peter? And then she felt a wave of anger with herself. And a wash of guilt. She thought about the men in her life, and the garden, much too much. Between them, Peter, Brody and Maddon had occupied too much of her mind, too much of her time. She deserved Annie's defection.

She got back to find Sam and Annie eating tinned tomato soup and toast. No place laid for her.

'Mind if I join you?' she'd said, trying to make a joke of it.

After lunch, Annie went to sleep in Sam's bed. Sam and Frances's bed, thought Lotte. Then Sam told her about Jamie, and seemed to blame her for not noticing Annie's crush on him.

Now, of course, it was blindingly obvious. The picnic, before Christo got lost, when Annie'd been so happy. The few weeks of cheerful good humour. Of helping in the house. Of eating less. Why hadn't Lotte realized something was wrong when all that changed?

And then Sam said that Annie was angry and jealous because Lotte had Peter.

'That's ridiculous,' Lotte burst out. 'Is she jealous of you and Frances?'

'She used to be. Don't you remember? Only Christo was worse.' He frowned at his hands. 'I didn't know the Peter thing was serious. Is it serious?'

Lotte's hands flew up. 'Oh, how do I know, Sam? I don't know anything any more. Maybe.'

She wanted to say it was none of his business. But of course it was. Her future, because of the children, would always be his business.

She raked her hair with open fingers. 'Peter is good to me. And the children adore him. Not like you, of course – now you are absent, you've taken on hero status – he who can do no wrong.'

'Don't sound so bitter, Lotte.'

'It's true, though,' she exclaimed. 'I think the children

believe that if we'd never split up everything would be perfect.'

And he said, 'Which of course it wouldn't.'

They were circling over the outskirts of Faro, waiting to land. Lotte leant her head against the plane window, and felt a little spring of excitement. These two weeks might be really good. Time to mend. Time for the children to relax about her and Peter. Time for her to realize what was good for her. And for them.

She had changed her life, was changing it still. And it was better than the old life.

She thought, one thing is for certain. I am definitely over Sam. I may not be able to make my mind up about Peter, I'm drawn to Brody like a moth to a candle, but I do not want Sam back.

She no longer blamed him. Or Frances. She could admit now that her marriage to Sam would have unravelled sooner or later. He hadn't understood her unhappiness with her job, or her anger with him for leaving absolutely everything to her – from deciding on the children's schools to loading the dishwasher. But he wasn't all bad. He was a good father. He didn't spoil the children, or fight her over them.

As an ex-husband he was just fine.

The Quinta do Barranco da Estrada was perfect, its many terraces covered in plumbago, bougainvillea and grape vines. Twisting paths and huge rock steps took them down to the gin-clear lake, which stretched for a mile – flat, brilliant blue, still as a millpond – to the dam wall in the distance. A few small pine-covered islands spattered the surface. And there was a big raft, covered in artificial grass, floating like a billiard table within easy swimming distance of the shore.

On the upper terrace the guest bedrooms stood side by side, overlooking the lake. Peter and Lotte had one room, and Annie got to choose whether she wanted a room to herself or to share with Jo-Jo. To Lotte's surprise she opted for sharing, and Christo was jubilant.

On their third morning, Lotte was sunbathing on the moored raft, trailing her fingers in the water and watching Christo's attempts at water-skiing. She was vaguely anxious about his knee. True, it was nine months since he'd fallen through the grotto roof, but you could easily twist a knee on skis. Peter was in the water with him, steadying him by the shoulders and shouting 'Pull' to the hotelier's young son who was driving the boat, which also contained Annie and Jo-Jo. The boat would sway briefly as if gathering its strength, then plunge forward, prow up, planing away. Christo would manage to stand for a few seconds, then he'd straighten his legs or bend his arms and he'd crash into the water again.

'You're getting tired, Christo,' called Peter. 'One more go, and then Jo-Jo can have a turn. Just keep your arms straight and your knees bent, OK?'

Suddenly Christo was up and skiing round the bay, a little wobbly, but standing. They roared past Lotte's floating platform and she could see his eyes bright with triumph, his mouth wide and happy. And Annie and Jo-Jo were clapping and calling to him, as carefree as only children can be.

It was fine. All fine. Frank and Lulu McClintock, who owned and ran the Quinta, had an easy knack of making their guests feel at home, yet spoiled. Meals were eaten outside, usually at one big table. Counting the three young McClintocks, there were ten children. One of the girls was Annie's age, and after a day's circling round each other, they were inseparable, appearing only for meals. Lotte's children lived in the water, being taught to windsurf, water-ski and sail by the fourteen-year-old Archie. Or shrieking with terror and delight as he took them for three-sixty spins on the jet-ski, or clinging to him as he drove them out to see the turtles swimming under the drowned roots of trees, or to lift the crayfish pots. And when the sun went down they'd settle to endless games of Monopoly.

The children were easy about Peter and Lotte sharing a room. Before they'd left, Peter had sat them down and asked them if they'd mind. Peter constantly surprised – and pleased – Lotte. She could imagine him solemnly putting the question, with that little stammer that surfaced when he was anxious, his fingers smoothing imaginary tangles out of imaginary hair on his head. And solemnly listening to their answers. Weighing what they said with what they meant. And correctly concluding that it was OK.

The place was perfect, the dream setting for a family holiday. If there was a fly in the ointment, Lotte thought, it was nothing to do with the place or the company. It was what went on in her head.

She managed pretty well not to think of Brody, but she couldn't control her dreams. Mostly they were innocent enough, with Brody just there for some reason. But twice she'd dreamt they were making love, and she'd woken reluctantly – and then felt anguished and ashamed.

Maddon invaded her mind almost as insistently. Lying beside the sleeping Peter at night, she'd find her mind running over the spring jobs for the garden. She'd left day-by-day instructions for Andrew, but she doubted if he'd even read them. And the truth was she wanted to be there herself. She longed to telephone him about tying the sweet peas, sowing the melons and cucumbers in the melon house, scarifying and spiking the lawns, splitting the astilbe and hosta clumps, spraying the contorted willows with Bordeaux mixture before necrosis set in, and the apple and pear trees against scab. Even without the new glasshouses in the walled garden, even without her secret excavations in the Old Pond Yards, spring was the *worst* time to be away.

It was ridiculous. I'm only here for two weeks, she thought. What can go so wrong in two weeks?

But why couldn't she have waited until the summer? The weather would have been warmer – it was chilly here in the mountains once the sun had disappeared. And there would have been less to do in the garden.

But that's the point, she said to herself. She'd felt so guilty about Annie she'd wanted to make it up to her, to all of them somehow, with a holiday that proved she had her priorities right.

The sly thought that she was avoiding Brody would sometimes slide into her head, however. Brody had asked as much himself. When she'd requested the time off he'd said, 'But why now, Lott? I thought you said you were all working flat-out?'

'We are. I shouldn't ask, Brody. No decent gardener goes away in the spring. But I'm so worried about Annie. And the others. If I'm at Maddon I haven't the self-discipline to stop working at five. I need some time with them.'

Brody put his hands flat on the desk and pushed himself up. 'Of course you can have the time, Lott. Take whatever you need, whenever. You know that.' He came round to stand next to her and said, 'Are you sure you aren't making a mistake with Peter, Lott? Sure you're not running away from me?'

Her stomach did a flip and she took a quick step back. 'Of course I'm sure.'

'It's OK, Lott,' Brody said. 'I promised I'd leave you alone. I will.' He smiled, his eyes alive, teasing. 'I don't like it. But I'll keep my distance.'

And she believed him. She knew he'd never kiss her again. Not unless she kissed him, which she wouldn't. She would not let herself revisit those heady moments in the greenhouse, or that long-ago moment in Johnny Fox's when he'd been singing and it was as if he was singing to her, inside her. She'd felt his voice in her belly.

Lotte shut her eyes and refused to think of Brody. Of how good it had been to bury her head in his jacket on the helicopter. Of his hard arms round her.

She dived off the platform, gasping at the chilly water. She struck out towards the grassy terrace where Annie and Jo-Jo were sunbathing.

Two days before they were due to go home, Lotte and Peter left the children hauling up crayfish pots with the

McClintocks, and drove into Santa Clara to buy an evening picnic for two.

As they turned off the main road, they passed a group of old men sitting under the trees. Their eyes, old as time, followed Lotte and Peter without interest.

Peter parked outside the big blue and white church which dominated the little town with its paved square, crooked empty streets and mostly shuttered houses. They tried the church door but it was locked.

There was no one about, although the town's few shops had re-opened after the lunchtime siesta. They chose one with a battered ice-cream sign outside. The friendly smell of cheese and dried fruit, cooking oil and ham signalled that they'd made the right choice even before they'd stepped through the plastic-strip curtain and down a couple of steps into the gloom of the grocer's. A goat's bell, attached to the curtain, announced their arrival to the shopkeeper. She appeared, wiping her hands on her apron. They smiled at each other in mutual acknowledgement that they did not speak a word of one another's language.

Lotte picked out a bottle and peered at the label. 'Here,' she said, 'Cartaxo, 1998. Will this do?'

Peter took the wine bottle from her and wiped the dust of years off its shoulders. 'No idea. Must have been here for ever. It's either too horrible to drink or too expensive for the locals.'

'The latter, I'm sure. And I've yet to see another tourist.'

Lotte picked up a misshapen loaf and held it to her nose. She shut her eyes and breathed in. 'Smells like heaven,' she said, putting it in her basket with the wine.

They bought a good wedge of Queijo de Ovelha, runny in the middle, and a thick slice of quince marmalada.

They stepped out into the sun, blinking slightly. 'Are you sure it's OK to leave the children?' Peter asked, returning his ancient cricket hat to his head.

'Yes, I'm sure. They wouldn't be with us, anyway. They'd be playing ping-pong or Monopoly with the others. And anyway, it was the McClintocks' idea. Lulu said the ridge is where she and Frank go to get away from the likes of us. And we are only going to watch the sun set. How long can that take?'

As the heat was going out of the day, she and Peter climbed with their picnic basket (now also containing a couple of glasses, corkscrew, bread board and a knife borrowed from the kitchen) up a winding goat track to the top of the highest of the little hills that encircled the Quinta and overlooked the lake. It was a stiff climb, and by the time they sat down, they were both out of breath and hot.

Peter took his glasses off to wipe the sweat from his head and face, and said, 'If horses sweat, men perspire and ladies glow, you are a horse.'

Lotte laughed. She had tied her jacket over her jeans, and her face and neck above her bikini top were wet with sweat. When Peter leant over to kiss her she pushed him away.

'Yuk. I'm horrible. Go away,' she said, turning away from him to look down at the lake. 'Peter, isn't that wonderful?'

He ran his fingers down the hollow of her spine, between her bikini top and her jeans. 'You are not horrible. You are hot and sweaty and highly desirable.'

Lotte ignored his fingers. It was pleasant, but her attention was elsewhere. She took a long pull from her water bottle, thinking: and that is why you are the best offer I'll ever get. You will find me desirable when I'm at my ugliest. You haven't noticed that I've got a flabby forty-seven-year-old body with stretch marks on my thighs and tits. You will put up with my moods. You'll love me even though I'm half in love with Brody and completely obsessed by a garden. You'd love my children even if I stopped loving you. You are one hell of a good deal, Peter Childersley.

But she didn't say any of that. Instead, she pulled on her jacket and fished out the picnic things in a businesslike way, passing him the wine, corkscrew and glasses to deal with, cutting a slice each of cheese and marmalada and pressing them on to a chunk of bread. She passed this to him and did one for herself.

They hardly talked as the sun went down. She leant against his shoulder, beginning to feel the evening chill now. The lake looked like shiny steel. It stretched for miles without a ripple, perfectly welded to the curves and jags of the shore. Above the horizon the sky was streaked pink, orange and aquamarine. And the sun, ludicrously large like something from a pantomime, was slipping fast behind the distant hills, beaming a silver runway across the lake.

There was nothing moving anywhere. From where they sat, the Quinta was hidden below them, and on the surrounding hills not a house, not a goat, not a chicken was visible. But all around them the swells and folds of the Alentejo glowed ochre in the setting sun, and great swathes of wild white cistus covered the hills like drifts of snow.

It was so beautiful that it made Lotte want to cry. And then they heard, close overhead, a sudden whirring sound. They looked up to see a cloud of tiny birds swirling in tight formation, heading low over the ground down towards the lake.

'Those are the house sparrows that roost at the Quinta,' said Peter. 'Frank says they come in exactly twenty minutes before dark. You can set your watch by them.'

Lotte stood up. 'Oh Peter, I am glad we are not in some beach hotel on the Algarve. Thank you. What would I do without you?'

Peter smiled his wry, shy smile. 'You'd be fine,' he said. 'But I'd be dead.'

22. Spring

So I turn'd to the Garden of Love,
That so many sweet flowers bore.

And I saw it was filled with graves,
And tomb-stones where flowers should be:
And Priests in black gowns, were walking their rounds,
And binding with briars, my joys and desires.

William Blake (1757–1827), 'The Garden of Love'

It was late afternoon when they drew up outside Gardener's Cottage. The children clambered out of the car first, and while they were getting their stuff out of the boot, Lotte leant over and kissed Peter.

'Peter, how about you sleep at your place tonight? I've got a heap of stuff I want to sort out. Do you mind?' She put up her hand and caught his, already worrying his hairline. 'It's OK,' she teased, 'this is not rejection. It's "poizon'l space", baby.'

'Yes, sure. I could do with a sort-out and some clean clothes myself. Though since I met you, my darling, personal space has lost its charm.' He held on to her arm for a second. 'It was a wonderful holiday, Lotte.'

'Yes,' she said, 'it was.'

The answer-machine was bleeping. Lotte dumped her bags on the floor and pressed playback, and almost immediately Brody's voice, so familiar with its hint of Irish, filled the room.

'Hi, Lott. Hope the holiday was good. Can you come and see me at Maddon first thing tomorrow, before you start work? Early as you like. Eight a.m.? It's important.'

Lotte reached for the kettle, aware of her heart slowing after the leap at Brody's voice. How odd, she thought, he usually saw her at nine or ten. Must have some new madcap idea that can't wait.

There was a similar message on her office machine, from Brody's office. 'Mr Keegan has asked me to let you know that he'd like to see you at Maddon at eight a.m. tomorrow. He'll be in his study.' Must be really important. I wonder why he doesn't just ring me? He knows we get home today. She shrugged slightly and called to the children, 'Tea? Anyone hungry?'

But, full of airline food and tired from the journey, no one felt like anything.

'OK,' said Lotte, 'we'll have cornflakes or toast or something later if we feel like it. I'm going to walk round the garden. Anyone want to come?'

But of course they didn't, preferring to mooch round the familiar rooms, make phone-calls to their friends and flop out in front of the telly.

Lotte was guiltily glad of this as she slipped out alone and set off across the park. She breathed in great draughts of English spring air, as if she'd been deprived of it for years, not just two weeks.

It was not yet dusk, but the day was dull and the colours

of flowers, leaves and grass had the depth and vibrancy only achieved out of the sun. As she walked, she felt caressed by the smells of spring: soft earth, blossom, trees budding or bursting, the drifts of narcissus. She marvelled at the shrillness of green and the tenderness of texture. Oh, she thought, how can all this have happened in two weeks? How could I have gone away?

Thousands of daffodils lined the drive and swept in great informal swathes and clumps over the park. As she neared the house she felt like a child in a sweetshop, unable to decide which way to go, every bed and corner beckoning. The raised terraces were overflowing with primroses, alyssum and aubrieta: common things that had been there for years, but they tumbled over the steps and terraces like carelessly thrown carpets. And among them were more special things she'd put in last year – furry pulsatillas, alpine dicentras, both pink and white, dripping tiny hearts all along their stems, miniature pink and green tulips, and the rich Madonna-blue gentians.

She walked towards the lake, her pleasure momentarily spoiled by the fact that the lawn had not been mowed. Perhaps it had been too wet, she thought. She walked slowly down the path to the side of the great 'Powerscourt' green terraces, delighted by the thickness and condition of the young grass. Beside the path, rich blue grape hyacinths had taken over from the snowdrops, and the cherry, apple and almond trees above her head were on the point of explosion, every twig bearing fat buds.

To her surprise, one ornamental apple tree, which once had been near-strangled by a Russian vine, was already blooming, three weeks earlier, she reckoned, than the other *Malus*. She'd pruned it last year and the shape was now a perfect umbrella. She stood under it, looking up, drowning in blossom. She wished she had a camera. The blossoms ranged from buds of deep rose to near-white open flowers. The leaves, fine as gossamer, were tiny, tender and pinkish-brown. I wonder what variety it is, she thought. She reached up and broke off a sprig. I'll send it to Wisley, maybe they'll be able to identify it.

She hadn't time to check the lake. She'd leave that for tomorrow. It was colder down there, and the plants were generally a week behind their sheltered garden cousins. But even from here, she could see the clouds of amelanchier and the banks of kingcups blazing away at the water's edge.

Her gaze was held by the little jetty where she and Brody had stood the day she got the job. God, she thought, I was lucky. Unbelievably lucky.

She looked at her watch. She should go back, unpack, see if the children wanted any supper. But there was just light enough to check on the walled garden before she went in.

She was irritated to see that the gardeners had failed to sow anything in the vegetable plots. She'd left a list: salads, late-summer caulis, main-crop carrots, purple sprouting broccoli. She looked round, trying to see if Andrew had done anything at all. Everything was as it had been, with only the potatoes, early peas and summer spinach which she had planted before she left in neat labelled rows. She looked across at the nursery bed and could see at once that the summer cabbages and several varieties of salad greens under cloches were more than ready for planting out. And the rest of the vegetable garden, dug over before the frosts, had yet to be broken up and raked to a decent tilth.

But it was only when she entered the greenhouse that she realized something was seriously wrong. 'Oh my God,' she said aloud. Nothing had been watered: seedlings lay prostrate in their trays, dead or dying. The compost in pots was pale and dry, soil rock-hard in the larger ones. The sweet-pea plants, which she'd sown in October and nurtured all winter, and which she'd last seen healthy, strong and ready for planting out, were withered corpses, hanging dry and brittle on their canes. Some of the larger pot-plants, like the cineraria and *Primula kewensis*, had a little green life left in them, but their flowers were dead and their leaves lay draped to the ground, withered at the edges.

Her first reaction was one of horror. And the next was fury. She swung towards the door, opening her mouth to yell for Andrew: that lazy, incompetent, bloody Andrew who could not have been in here once since she'd been away. And then she remembered he would have left hours ago. And so would the others.

She could not believe it. It was the first rule in the garden: check the greenhouses. Something must have happened to the irrigation. And then a worse thought struck her. If no one had checked the irrigation in here, what about the glasshouses where there was no irrigation?

She sprinted across the garden to the melon house. One glance told her that Andrew had planted neither melons nor cucumbers. That was a relief. What wasn't planted could not die.

Any hopes of the pineapple experiment working this year were dashed as soon as Lotte entered the pineapple house. The sliced pine-tops were still neatly sitting on their pots of compost, but one look at the grey curled leaves and you knew that, far from rooting, they were dying. Lotte picked one up. It was too dry even to rot.

That left only the orchard house and the vinery. Lotte crossed the central path, her mind numb. Neither house had been tended. The new leaves, just appearing when she left, were curled and withered on the stalk. It was the same story in the orchard house. The fig, peach, nectarine and plum trees were all leafless, or near leafless.

None of them would die. But hope for fruit this year was thin.

Lotte fetched the hose and watered the vines and fruit trees. She didn't bother with the propagation greenhouse. There was little left to save, and what there was she'd repot tomorrow.

She didn't telephone Andrew, or either of the students. Or tell the children. She fed them toast and boiled eggs, and they were too silent or self-absorbed to notice any cloud on her. She unpacked her holiday clothes, chucking most of them into the laundry bin. As her gaily striped bikini landed on top of her sarong, she looked at them as though they came from another planet. Portugal seemed eons away.

She tried not to think what she'd say to Brody in the morning. What could she say? Except that she'd gone away at the busiest time of the year and allowed everything that could die in two weeks to do so.

*

The following day, when she entered Brody's study, she saw at once that something was wrong. Brody looked as if he hadn't slept, and his usually energized face was drawn. He looked older too. He said at once, 'Lotte, you are not going to like this. And I'll understand if you hand in your notice right away, but I have laid off all your gardeners: both students, Andrew, and the lad that does the estate fences and so on.'

Lotte's face went blank with incomprehension. She didn't speak. Or move. She just tried to absorb the information.

'I know it's a hell of a shock. I'm sorry,' Brody said. 'But I've got to haul my belt in, I'm afraid. I won't bore you with the details, but I've got a real cash-flow problem. And raising money at the moment is . . . well, blood out of a stone would be easy.'

Lotte found her voice. 'And you've sacked all my staff?'

'Yes. Had to, I'm afraid. I'm sorry.'

'You've sacked Andrew without consulting me? And the students? How could you do such a thing?' Lotte's face flushed deep pink. 'For God's sake, Brody, why didn't you say anything? If there was laying-off to be done, I should have –'

'There was no point, Lott. You wanted time off. I didn't know for sure until a fortnight ago. No point in haemorrhaging money for any longer than necessary.'

Lotte started to protest, but Brody mowed her down. 'Anyway, it's all done. That college the lads come from, they've already found them alternative placements. And I did try to get Andrew to work out his notice so he'd be around until you got back but he's so fed up he called in sick.'

Lotte shook her head in disbelief. Brody went on, 'You always said he wasn't much good . . . Anyway, he doesn't deserve it, but he can keep his cottage for the time being, and I've doubled his redundancy entitlement. He's no right to whinge.'

'That's not the point,' snapped Lotte. Her mind was swirling about. 'Are you sacking me too?'

Brody reached across the desk as if to touch her, then sank back. He smiled, but his voice was bleak. 'No, Lott, not if you want to stay . . . We need to discuss –'

But Lotte interrupted again. 'Are you going to sell Maddon?'

'Hope not. But might have to, I suppose. For the moment I'm trying to stem the outgoings rather than actually raise money. I've got to keep *find-on-line* going for a month or two. It's a good business, but even good dot.coms are going belly up right now.'

He sat back in his chair and pushed the fingers of both hands through his thick hair, shutting his eyes briefly, as though summoning strength. 'I'll have to sell some stuff to settle immediate debts and then tramp round the City looking for equity investment. And those vultures will try to screw me out of the company for nothing.' He shrugged, but Lotte thought his casualness was forced. 'Of course, if I can't do a deal, then everything goes.'

She shook her head in disbelief. 'But you are so rich! The Rodin! Jade's new Lamborghini.'

'Yeah, well, the Rodin and the Lamborghini will have to go too. We'll have a resin copy made of the statue. They can make them look incredibly good, you know.' He twiddled his gold fountain pen round and round in his fingers and went on, 'But Jade isn't happy. Even less so about the car. You can't make a resin copy of that.'

Brody's eyes met hers. His were expressionless, bleak. He gave the tiniest shake of his head, a sad, defeated shake. Lotte felt sympathy engulf her: she wanted to put her hand over the pen-twirling fingers the way she stilled Peter's forehead-tapping hand.

'Oh, poor Brody,' she said. 'I am so, so sorry. Just when you and Jade could really enjoy the place. I was walking round last night, and the garden is at last looking –'

'I know, Lotte. I've walked round it a lot while you've been away, cudgelling my brains about *find-on-line*. And then I'd find I was just looking at some bit of the garden, and thinking how good it looked.' His face seemed to lighten a bit, resuming some of its old animation. He went on, 'And wishing you were around to say so to. You've done such a great job, Lotte. You really have.'

This reminded Lotte of the death and destruction in the propagation greenhouse. But next to Brody's problems, a season's worth of seedlings hardly counted. Feeling suddenly drained, she said, 'What do you want me to do?' As she spoke, she dreaded the answer: he'd want her to organize a handover to a contractor, some impersonal company who'd send in unskilled men to stamp through her borders, prune things with a hedge-trimmer, scalp the lawns with a tractor-mower instead of the rotary. And when she'd found the contractor and done the deal, she'd be out of a job too. It would be like organizing her own funeral. She couldn't bear it.

But he said, 'What I want you to do is mothball everything.'

'Mothball it? Brody, it's not a ship!'

He smiled. 'I know, I mean just keep it ticking over. Do the essential minimum.' Lotte stared at him, speechless. 'But I know I hired you to develop Maddon,' he went on. 'If you want to quit, it's understandable.'

Lotte put her head in her hands. For a full minute her mind swept over the garden. And at every point there were her plans, now in ruins.

How could he give up on the lake? They were to build the Chinese boat-house this summer . . . And what was she to do with Bill Pye's cascades? Turn them off and let the moss grow?

Her mind swung up past the mount, which would be wonderful in a year, to her embryo plan to plant Brody's maze to the right of the house, below the west terraces.

And then to the rose garden which was to have a fifty-foot tunnel of 'Sander's White' and the clematis 'Perle d'Azur' leading into the existing round garden, encircled with pillars. She was planning great thick ropes looping between them, on which the old ramblers would hang in festoons. She'd already ordered the metalwork and booked the blacksmith.

And the topiary garden on the left of the drive. Peter had found letters describing a 'garden of beasts fashioned from box and yew', and she'd just cut back the overgrown yew and box and started to reshape them.

And what about Brody's pot garden? Ever since he'd seen pictures of Prince Charles's collection of giant terracotta pots from all over the world, of every shape and size, grouped in clumps under trees, Brody had had a dealer buying up pots wholesale.

Above all there were her old Pond Yards, not yet uncovered. And the grotto, which Brody had no idea they'd started on, and the Persian pool which he didn't know existed. Now maybe he never would.

As she toured Maddon in her mind, sadness seemed to pile on sadness. How can I bear it? How can Brody bear it? she thought.

Brody was talking. 'If you stay, you'll have to sit down and think of everything we need not do at all, and everything that we absolutely have to do, and the cheapest way to do it.'

He looked at her for a reaction, but Lotte felt her mind sluggishly following him, unable to keep up or leap ahead. He went on, 'I presume we don't have to do anything in the vegetable garden, for example. But it would be false economy not to repair broken panes, etcetera. And we have to mow the lawns but we don't need any new plants . . . What are you smiling at?'

Lotte was indeed smiling – a sad, ironical smile. She said, 'As none of the greenhouses have been watered for a fortnight, there aren't any new plants, and nothing to plant in the vegetable garden anyway. I found them last night, and I was ready to slaughter Andrew for neglecting everything. I was going to ask your permission to sack the poor guy this morning.'

She walked out of Brody's office feeling not quite real. It was as though all this was happening to someone else. In the end she'd agreed to come up with an economy plan, and to let him know how much she thought she could manage on her own.

Lotte walked home slowly, her mind gradually shifting

from the garden to the people. Poor Andrew, she thought. He'd been so unco-operative at first, and then reluctantly amenable, and finally capable of an occasional hello or smile. She'd got almost fond of the monosyllabic Scot. And she'd miss Jamie. He'd been happy here, and he was fascinated by the Old Pond Yards. He had the makings of a good gardener.

As she walked back across the garden, Lotte looked at the same bursting cherry trees, the same iridescent green lawns, the same jiggling drifts of daffodils, and thought what a horrible difference twenty-four hours could make.

Four days later, Lotte e-mailed Brody two plans. One was what he'd asked for, and it amounted to the fact that she'd do almost nothing but feeding, weeding, and cutting back. There would be no development, and she'd sow the vegetable garden with rough grass and top it once a year. Mowing, mower maintenance, tree surgery, clearing ditches and mending fences would be contracted out.

But her other plan was the one she'd set her heart on. They should turn the gardens into a 'living museum' along the lines of Audley End or Heligan. They would start a gardening school for amateurs, using the guest-rooms over the stables to offer working gardening holidays for City dwellers. They'd be given gardening lectures or visit famous gardens in the mornings and work on the estate in the afternoons, learning as they toiled. They would learn organic vegetable production as well as working in the pleasure gardens. And in the evenings they would take turns to cook a communal dinner in the old brewhouse, with a trained cookery teacher or vegetarian chef to guide them.

Lotte also proposed opening the gardens and the house (just the ground floor and the basement cellars, pool and gym) from Monday to Thursday, when the Keegans were not often at home. The gate might not take much, but it would help spread the word, and encourage volunteers. Gradually, they would build up a band of volunteers to continue the restoration of the garden: they could tackle the folly in the woods, maybe even the Old Pond Yards.

Lotte's Option One was a single sheet, but Option Two – her gardening school idea – was a fully worked-up business plan, with Aims and Objectives, Profit and Loss and Cash-flow projections, Return on Investment, the lot. She'd worked the whole weekend on it, and though she knew a lot of her assumptions would need testing, she wasn't ready for Brody's reaction.

He rang her up about an hour after she'd sent the documents. He sounded amused.

'Well, Lott. You have been working hard.'

She didn't like his patronizing tone, and her reply was stiff. 'Well?'

'Option One, I'm afraid.'

'But Brody . . . can't we discuss . . .'

Brody laughed out loud. 'Lott, my darling. Don't be daft. You are the best gardener in the world, but I'm not having Joe Public tramping all over Maddon, thank you very much. If I can't get myself out of the hole I'm in, I'll just sell up. No sweat. It's only a house.'

23. Summer

O Rose thou art sick,
The invisible worm
That flies in the night
In the howling storm:

Has found out thy bed
Of crimson joy:
And his dark secret love
Does thy life destroy.

William Blake (1757–1827),
'The Sick Rose'

Lotte inspected the old-fashioned roses that erupted in voluptuous fountains either side of the rose walk and thought she might abandon her new policy of minimum intervention. Every bush was crawling with greenfly, and some of them, notably the great bushes of 'Fantin Latour', eight feet high and as many across, had leaves as ugly with blackspot as the flowers were beautiful.

She was so overstretched these days that she'd not had time, even if she'd wanted to, to spray the roses. They had been doing well, and she'd decided to give up spraying altogether. It would save her time, it was better for the environment, and once the garden was pesticide-free there would be more ladybirds to keep the bad bugs in check.

That was the theory. But this was too much. The moss roses' furry buds were almost invisible under a slowly stirring mass of aphids, and her favourite rose, 'Madame Hardy', with its tiny green eye in the middle of a flat, quartered, white face, had stems encrusted and sticky with her unwanted guests. Even the *Rosa mundi*'s candy-striped blooms were struggling out of infested buds.

She walked fast round the side of the house to Brody's square bed of orange roses. She had failed to persuade him that 'Tequila Sunrise' was too strident and coarse for the garden, but she was fairly sure he now accepted – without admitting it of course – that the middle of the front lawn was the wrong place for them.

But she had to admit the solid square of shimmering orange was quite a sight. It hurt the eyes, but it made her want to laugh too. The roses were so bright, with slightly darker edges, like a drag queen's lipstick. She turned one of the blooms over, and there, sure enough, were hundreds of greenfly.

Right, that was it. She might be able to bear the unpleasant side of nature, but Brody had no time for her green leanings. She could hear his voice: 'Zap the bloody things, Lott. Don't be such a wimp!'

She filled the backpack sprayer with Malathion, carefully measuring the exact amount for the twenty litres of water in the tank. She was about to set off when her mobile rang. It was Jade.

'Lotte. It's me. Look, I've got some friends coming for Saturday night and I need some flowers for the house. I won't be home much before they arrive, and since I don't have a bloody housekeeper any more, will you do them?'

Her tone, as always, irritated Lotte and she replied, 'Jade, I'm a gardener, not a florist. And I'm a bit short-handed myself, as you know . . .'

'Christ, Lotte, I'm only asking you to pick some of those sodding flowers you and Brody spend so much loving care on, and put them in the house. What are they for, for God's sake? The garden is stuffed with them.'

Lotte backed off. 'OK, Jade. I'll have a go. But it's not going to be exactly Moyses Stevens.'

Jade laughed. Victory always made her sweet, Lotte thought. Jade said, 'Oh, never mind. You'll manage.' Then she giggled. 'Talking of Moyses Stevens, their toffee-nosed bird rang last week to ask why I'd withdrawn my custom! I told her I was buying from Lavender's Blue. Wasn't going to tell her we were skint.'

Lotte gritted her teeth. I really do not like this woman, she thought. But she said, 'What about vases?'

'No idea. But that big glass bucket affair in the drawing room would look pretty stylish full of those orange things from Brody's precious rose-bed. They'll go with the peach curtains. And he won't know we've nicked them – he's in America trying to find a white knight to save the business. And you can do what you like in the dining room and bedrooms.'

Thank you very much, m'lady, thought Lotte. So kind.

Jade also wanted her to organize some extra help in the house. Could she get the cleaner in to do some extra hours bed-making and laying the table and washing up and so on? They'd need the three main guest-rooms. And would

Lotte ask around for anyone who could cook the dinner. Just a couple of roast chickens or something. She'd bring down some sushi for the first course. But could Lotte pick some strawberries? Jade said, 'People like all that home-grown, fresh-out-of-the-garden stuff. Enough for seven or eight of us. OK?'

Thoroughly put out, Lotte left her sprayer and went round to her office, thinking crossly that Brody's financial difficulties had hardly cramped his wife's style at all. Jade entertained, with or without Brody (more without these days – he was so often in the States), and she still did absolutely nothing herself. But at least the spoilt cow usually got London caterers in, and brought down her Eaton Square housekeeper to fix the rooms. But this time, it seemed, the guests didn't warrant showing off for. Probably not famous enough, Lotte muttered as she picked up the phone.

It took an hour to arrange things. The cleaner was fine – she'd even stay to help serve and wash up the dinner things, but she wanted time-and-a-half. Fair enough, Lotte thought. The publican's wife, who did a bit of catering on the side, said she'd be too busy in the pub on Saturday night to be there, but she agreed to make a chicken casserole, some parsley mash and a big salad, and deliver them.

Lotte very nearly offered to do the salad and veg herself. It went against the grain that the mistress of the house would be eating Waitrose stuff when the productive garden sported three different lettuces, spring onions, rocket, and every herb you could think of. Since they'd laid off all the staff, Lotte had given up on vegetables, but Peter had planted salads and a few rows of veg for themselves. And since it was late June, everything needed eating.

But she kept her mouth shut. Saturday was her day for the children and Peter, not playing housekeeper. Bad enough that her Friday afternoon would be wasted arranging flowers.

Still, she thought, it will be nice to use the cutting garden as it's meant to be used. Next year that, like the vegetable garden, would be nothing but rough grass.

But first the greenfly, she thought. If 'Tequila Sunrise' was to grace the drawing room on Friday, she'd have to spray today to give the things time to die and fall off.

'I don't believe it!' she wailed aloud, as she stepped outside the office and saw the waving trees and darkening sky. It was raining. Spraying was out of the question. She sprinted through the rain to the coach-house. With fast, irritated movements she locked the backpack sprayer in the poisons cupboard, and returned her gloves and mask to the drawer.

It was still drizzling when she went home for a lunch-time sandwich, and the sun did not come out until four o'clock. The leaves were still too wet to spray. Damn it, she thought, it will have to wait until tomorrow.

But by suppertime it was a lovely, still, warm evening, and Lotte's mood had completely lifted. Peter and Christo barbecued chicken and sausages, which they ate with new peas, podded by Jo-Jo, and potatoes dug up an hour before.

Annie, her mouth full of sausage, said, 'Peter, this is so delicious. You'd think we were, like, veggies the way Mum stuffs peas and beans and salad, salad, salad, down us. I even had, like, salad sandwiches for school today. Urgh.'

Lotte was tempted to tick off her daughter for using that awful teenage word 'like', but what did it matter? Why disturb the mood produced by good food, a couple of glasses of wine, balmy evening air and happy children? Instead she laughed. 'Right, young lady. Tomorrow you can make your own. And those sandwiches were tomato and basil. London foodies would pay good money for those.'

They carried the supper dishes indoors and, to Lotte's surprise, Peter's ruling that it was Annie's turn to wash up met no opposition. He said, 'Shall we have a last glass outside, Lotte?'

'Sorry, Peter, but I can't. I'm off to spray the roses. The weather is perfect and I've just rung the Weatherline and it's going to rain again tomorrow.'

Peter looked at her in dismay. 'But darling Lotte, it's nearly eight o'clock! You cannot go on doing twelve-hour days! How many times this week have you put in two hours before everyone else is up? And you knock off closer to seven than four, day after day. It's crazy.'

'I know. But I can't help it.' She pulled on her denim jacket and leant over to kiss his cheek. But he turned away.

'Goodbye,' she said, walking out and calling to the children, 'I'll be back about ten, before it gets dark.'

'And I'll babysit, shall I?' called Peter, his voice bitter.

Lotte, stung, rapped back, 'Do what you like! They are perfectly safe for a couple of hours in broad daylight.'

She closed the door with a little jerk. Not a slam, but nearly.

She was still angry when she pulled the sprayer out of the poisons cupboard. It was very heavy, so she set it on the workbench to get her arms into the straps more easily. She hoisted it off the bench and pulled on her gloves and mask. She was meant to wear the safety suit but she couldn't bear it, and who was there to see anyway? She'd been rigorous about regulation when she had been responsible for staff. But now she just wanted to get the job done as fast as possible, and the suit slowed things up. It got so hot you had to keep stopping to take the hood off.

By the time she'd been spraying for half an hour, she was beginning to feel guilty about her sharp exchange with Peter. He'd never before opposed her or shown the slightest resentment. And he was right: she was working too hard.

She took particular care to do a thorough job on the old-fashioned shrub roses: they mostly bloomed for only three glorious weeks – and late June was their big moment. The *Alba* mountains of 'Great Maiden's Blush' and 'Queen of Denmark'; the sprawling 'Rambling Rector'; huge arching fountains of 'Nevada' – she sprayed them all, sticking the nozzle into the bush and spraying upwards and sideways to catch every lurking bug.

But each time, before she attacked a variety with the smell of pesticide, she pulled up her mask and buried her face in a flower, marvelling that the Bourbons, *Gallicas*, moss roses, *Albas*, *Centifolias* could all smell so different, and yet all smell like roses. Most were just bursting from bud to bloom, and their scent was at evening double-strength.

The only hybrid teas in the main garden were Brody's 'Tequila Sunrise' and they did not take long. They were lowish bushes, and she could get at them easily. She had sprayed every rose on the estate by nine-thirty, except the cutting-garden hybrid teas, which she'd do last, the Scotch briars and *Rugosas* behind the tennis court which were showing no signs of infestation, and the 'Kiftsgate Filipes' which was so vigorous no amount of greenfly would worry it. Not that she could reach it anyway: it had engulfed two apple trees and a forty-foot wild pear in the West Wood, and any day now would smother them all under a snow-drift of blossom.

The tank was almost empty now. But it lasted long enough to do the cutting garden and the row of lupins, not yet in bloom and also thick with aphids. She hated to spray so close to the vegetables, but she was tired now, and all she wanted was to finish the job, rid the place of greenfly.

God, she was exhausted. She rinsed the tank and nozzle and stored the sprayer on its shelf.

When she'd showered off the memory of Malathion, Lotte slipped into bed and kissed Peter. He held on to her and said, 'Sorry about being so snarky. I should have come and helped you spray, rather than groan about you doing it.'

She kissed his high bald crown. 'Don't be daft. You were quite right. I can't go on like this forever, but I'm too tired to think about how to make it better. And I don't want to quit.'

She flopped back on the bed and said, 'Peter, whoever

planted that rose walk was a genius. It's the most wonderful collection, and I can't name half of them. Some, most perhaps, are older than I am, but they are in their prime.'

'They must be tough as old boots.' He smiled at her, pretending to cringe under the duvet. 'Just proves they could have survived without you killing yourself to spray them.'

Lotte, grinning, pounded his head with the pillow. 'Ah, but one of the reasons they are so good this year is all the TLC I gave them last year. They've had all the old wood chopped out of them, they've had tons and tons of horse manure, and foliar feed, and fish, blood and bone –'

'OK, OK, I give in, I give in. Spare me the gory details.'

Lotte pushed herself up on to her elbow to look at him. 'You've got to see them. And could you take some pics for me? There's one, "Great Maiden's Blush", which is the most exquisite thing you ever saw. In bud, half open, fully open, it's always perfection. And it smells like distilled paradise.'

'"Great Maiden's Blush"! What a wonderful name!'

Lotte laughed. 'In French it's called "Cuisses de Nymphe". Thighs of the Nymph. Or "Cuisses de Nymph Emue". Thighs of an Aroused Nymph. I guess that was too strong for the English and they toned it down a bit.'

Peter put his hand under the duvet and stroked Lotte's thigh, murmuring, 'As thighs of the nymph go . . .'

But she was too tired. He didn't press her.

Lotte woke at first light, feeling troubled. She lay in the semi-dark, watching the strip of light under the curtain brighten to a neon-like shine. Her mind was still full of visions of enormous bushes, smothered under trusses of white, pink and deep red roses, but they gave her no pleasure.

And then she saw what it was that was making her anxious. It was the image of her backpack sprayer, the empty one she'd rinsed last night and put on its shelf.

There had been only two empty sprayers next to it but there should have been three. Four altogether. She could see the labels on the shelf edge:

Pesticides
Fungicides
Broad-leaf herbicide
All-purpose herbicide

There was only one other place the missing sprayer could be: in the poisons cupboard. And it would only be in there if it had something in it. She was punctilious about washing out the sprayers before putting them back on the shelf — just in case someone took the wrong backpack. And she was as punctilious about locking them in the cupboard if they weren't empty.

She sat up with a jerk. Peter stirred; and murmured something, but she ignored him. Think. Think. No, it could not be. She had measured the Malathion so carefully. Exactly fifty millilitres to ten litres. She remembered that as clear as a bell.

But she knew the worst had happened.

She stared at the strip of light under the window as the memory of everything she'd done came back, with the inevitability and mercilessness of a nightmare. She remembered now that the smell had been wrong. Malathion had an overpowering, choking smell. But she'd been able to smell the roses, even if she'd just sprayed the neighbouring bush.

She had sprayed the roses with weedkiller, not Malathion.

She held her breath, praying that it wasn't true. But now she could see herself stowing the full sprayer in the poisons cupboard when the rain started. And she saw herself taking it out again after supper.

Except that she'd put it in the cupboard on the left of the shelf, and taken it out on the right.

And then she remembered the last piece of the jigsaw. Andrew had been spraying the gravel drives, tennis court and stable yard with their spring dose of Supertox which would keep them weed-free for the summer. She hadn't had any weedkiller out since then.

Lotte knew that if she checked the Poisons Book, she'd find that on the last day before she went on holiday, he'd have started the job – but not finished it before he left.

It was only five-fifteen. She'd wake Peter if she dressed, so she crept downstairs, naked, and pulled on his Burberry, belting it tightly. The thermometer in the hall said seventy degrees, but she was shivering. She stepped into her Wellies and hurried across the park.

It was exactly as she knew it would be. The poisons cupboard contained one full backpack sprayer. Feeling sick, she turned the tag that hung from the harness and read, '*Pesticide*'.

The label on the empty sprayer on the shelf read, '*All-purpose herbicide*'.

Lotte shut and locked the cupboard, and locked the coach-house as she left it. She walked slowly, aware of the soft light of the morning, the beauty of the shrubbery, the blaze of the herbaceous borders, but she gazed at the gardens as a condemned man must gaze at the world.

Long before she got to it, she could see the foaming, blowsy, exuberant beauty of the rose walk, with its massed pinks and whites, and reds as dark as blood. When she got close, every flower seemed to be straining to open its face to the rising sun, every one pumping its fragrance into the morning air. She thought she'd never seen anything lovelier. Every flower displaying its beauty as eagerly as the leaves had sucked up the poison.

It takes five days for a systemic weed-killer to do its work. And once it's started, it cannot be stopped.

A month later there was not a single leaf or petal on any of the roses. The massed clumps of dead bushes were visible, it seemed to Lotte, from everywhere in the garden.

Lotte was in a bad way. She longed to rip out the dead bushes and replant, but there was no labour and no money to do it. And she was too busy anyway.

The whole future of Maddon seemed uncertain. Brody had been in the States when she'd killed the roses and had not returned yet, and Jade's last visit had been that weekend, immediately after she'd done it.

Jade hadn't noticed the dying roses when Lotte went to see her on the Sunday morning. Perhaps she and her guests had not walked in the garden, or maybe they were just unobservant. She greeted Lotte civilly. 'Hi, Lotte, what are you doing here on a Sunday?'

'I need to talk to you, Jade. I'm sorry, but it's serious.'

'Yeah, well,' said Jade, walking ahead and talking over her shoulder, 'if it's to do with me ordering you about over the flowers and supper and stuff, I'm sorry. And I am grateful. You did a great job.'

Lotte followed Jade into the drawing room, still littered with the debris of last night's dinner party. Jade flung herself on to the sofa and waved at the vase of white delphiniums. 'And those things are stunning. Better than orange roses.'

Lotte sat on the chair opposite. 'It's not about your dinner party.'

Jade raised an elegant eyebrow and said, 'OK. So what is it about? It's obviously bad news. Are you quitting or something?'

'That's up to you. Or Brody.' Lotte took a steadying breath and said, 'I would sack me if I was you. The fact is I've poisoned all the roses. Every bush in the rose garden and Brody's bed of orange ones you asked for, and all the roses in the cutting garden.'

Jade, frowning with incomprehension, asked, 'Why?'

Tears were threatening Lotte's eyes. But she answered evenly, 'I made a mistake. I thought I was spraying them for greenfly. I picked up the wrong sprayer. It's unforgivable. Totally unprofessional.'

Jade sat silent, looking bemused. Lotte had expected her to crow a bit, or take the opportunity to sack her in Brody's absence. But in the end she said, quite gently, 'Poor Lotte. I suppose Brody will mind. A bit anyway. But you are more obsessive about the garden than he is. You'll mind more.'

Lotte was touched by this unexpected sympathy and she felt her eyes prick again. Jade continued, 'But surely it's not the end of the world? You can plant new ones. How many were there, anyway?'

'Over three hundred. And many were old roses I can't even identify. They were in their prime. It would take ten years . . .'

'Wow,' said Jade, 'three hundred. You sure do things properly when you do them.' But Lotte's flinch made her recant. 'Sorry. I shouldn't have said that. But the truth is, if Brody saves his business he will relish replanning and replanting the rose garden – probably make it twice the size or something. And if he doesn't, then we are all stuffed anyway.'

That phrase of Jade's, 'we are all stuffed anyway', haunted Lotte. She had not heard from Brody, though she'd written to him about the roses, and e-mailed her usual monthly report. She had not offered to resign again. She knew he could not hire anyone better than her, in spite of the devastation she'd caused. She was still working twelve-hour days, trying to do everything.

But she felt increasingly desperate. She wasn't on top of anything, and her relationship with Peter was suffering.

One evening, when she wasn't home in time for supper, Peter put the pasta in the bottom of the Aga and dialled her mobile. When she answered, she was obviously running, her breath coming in quick pants.

'Oh Peter,' she said, 'thank God it's you. Can you meet me at the lake? Bring the children. The cattle have got in. They're wrecking everything.'

He started to protest that it wasn't her problem, but he knew it was useless.

The park was dry and firm enough to drive across. They turned down the gravel path that bordered the green terraces and bumped down to the lake edge, the children excited at the prospect of playing cowboys.

Lotte had already rung Tim Elders, the tenant at Home Farm, and between them all they drove the thirty Herefords back across the park and into the west field. It took a lot of running to outflank and head off the beasts as they ran in any direction other than back to their field.

The children enjoyed it, but once the excitement was over, they wanted home and supper. Lotte insisted on inspecting the damage, however.

'Darling,' said Peter, 'whatever damage they have done will be there in the morning. Leave it.'

Lotte turned an anguished face to him. 'I can't. I have to see. At least half of them were in the new border planting. They'll have –'

Peter interrupted, his voice lifeless. 'OK, Lotte. Have it your own way. But it's eight o'clock. And we are going home.'

'Yeah, Mum, I'm starving,' said Annie. Jo-Jo grabbed Lotte's sleeve and pulled. 'C'mon, Mum.'

Only Christo hesitated, saying, 'Mum, do you want me to come with you?'

Lotte said no, and they all got in the car again and went home.

Lotte watched Peter slam the car door in exasperation and drive fast back up the path, and she started to cry.

He was right. She should have gone with them.

She could not stop crying. She inspected the trampled

Lysimachia punctata, its little golden stars squashed in the mud. The *Artemisia gisa* whose white fronds and bronze upright foliage had swayed in rhythmic waves yesterday was now twisted and mangled in all directions. The hostas' great leaves were torn and trampled. The rodgersia and ligularia were unrecognizable, broken and covered in mud. The whole enormous bed was covered with foot-deep hoofprints, filled with muddy water.

Lotte sat on the great oak log she'd had carved to make a rustic seat, and blubbed like a child. She could not bear it. She and Jamie had spent hours last autumn rotavating compost and grit into this bed, and planting hundreds and hundreds of plants in elegant sweeping drifts. It had been a triumph, and until a few hours ago was looking its absolute best.

Eventually she wiped her face first with her palms and then with the back of her hands, and stood up. I'm losing it, she thought. Every one of these plants is as tough as old boots. Next year, even if I do nothing about it, they will all be up and blooming as if not a single heifer had been in here. What's the matter with me?

In fact, she knew her distress was mostly due to tiredness and the conviction that she wasn't coping. This week she'd wasted precious hours on the telephone getting the irrigation fixed; the lawn contractor had failed to show and, instead of leaving it, she'd lost two days mowing the main terraces herself. The weeds, in spite of her heavy spring mulches, were winning the war. And every day, many times a day, she looked at the dead roses.

The following day she rang Tim Elders. 'You owe me one, Tim.'

He sounded genuinely contrite. 'I am sorry, Lotte. That's young heifers for you. I swear they could break out of a jail. What can I do for you?'

'You can bring your digger round and pull out some bushes I need to get rid of. It would take me months with a spade. But you could do it in a day.'

He protested that he was in the middle of combining, and that he could not spare anyone. But Lotte said, 'Tim, it's going to rain all day tomorrow. You can't harvest in the rain. But you can dig up my dead roses.'

24. Late Summer

I compared you,
to the burning sun,
as it set tonight.

I remembered your smile,
And thought of how
happiness rises.

Evelyn John Holtzhausen (1950–),
'Happiness Rises'

Brody felt a small thrill of excitement. Or satisfaction. He was going to have lunch with Lotte.

The last few months had been both hellish, and exciting. He liked the guys in Silicon Valley. A lot of them were in the same boat as he was, struggling to save their Internet companies and themselves from ruin, and a lot more had already lost their businesses, or their jobs, and were starting the climb from the bottom again. That was what he liked about Americans. There was no stigma to going bust. You just dusted yourself down and started all over again.

Today was a good day. He'd come in on the red-eye, come straight to the hotel for breakfast and a shower, done his rounds to City investors (two successful, one not – not a bad strike rate). And now a date with Lotte.

Apart from anything else, and there was plenty of else, it would be nice to lunch with a woman who had an appetite. Jade's constant dieting used to both irritate him and worry him. It was the thing that had triggered their split.

They'd been in New York, dining in Brasserie Les Halles, and she had picked at her black sea bass crusted with salt and then left two-thirds of it. He'd said, 'For God's sake, Jade. It's delicious. Why you come out to dinner with me I don't know. Is it just to be ogled by the glitterati?'

She leant back in her seat and gave him a cold stare. 'I don't know why I come either. It's not for the company, that's for sure. You talk nothing but business.' She flicked back her hair and said, 'And anyway, we hardly ever go out. I have more fun when I'm working.'

Brody thought, but didn't say, that he had more fun when she was working, too. What he said was, 'The "till death us do part bit" isn't going to happen, is it?'

She wouldn't look at him, and he felt curiously sorry for her. She wasn't getting what she'd bought into. Then there had been endless parties, holidays, presents, fancy cars, fancy friends.

Looking at her ruined sea bass, she said, 'Anyway, there's someone else. I'm sleeping with someone else.'

She'd moved in with her photographer boyfriend the following weekend. And now her lawyer was demanding half of everything. Poor Jade, thought Brody, she should have divorced me a year ago. Half of everything wasn't much right now.

He looked at himself in the lift mirror as he went downstairs. He was wearing dot.com formal wear – chinos and open-necked shirt. Back in the office they mostly wore baggy shorts and tee-shirts but he thought that might be too much for the Brits. He'd lost weight, and he was horribly pale under the freckles. First time I've ever worked through the summer, he thought. Once upon a time it was holidays in Antigua or St-Tropez. Now time off meant a quick lunch with his gardener.

He smiled at the thought of her. Her letter about poisoning the roses had been so touching. You'd think she'd murdered his children, she was so remorseful. He should have replied to her, but he kept thinking he'd be back in England and would see her, and then it had been too late.

Brody's e-mail had said:

I'll be in London for twenty-four hours on Tuesday August 8. No time to come to Maddon. Can you meet me at the City Hotel, Fenchurch Street at 1 p.m.? I'll buy you lunch. Brody.

Lotte knew it was a business summons, not a social invitation, and she told herself a dozen times that she wasn't interested in Brody, that she was in love with Peter. But she could not stop herself making a hair appointment with her old London hairdresser for the morning and changing from a new summer dress to trousers and jacket, and finally to a skirt and top.

As she dusted off her old briefcase and put a folder of her monthly reports and the spreadsheets of her accounts into it, she wished she was putting in her plans, drawings for future developments, ideas and dreams.

Lotte was nervous as she walked into the City Hotel's lofty steel-and-glass atrium. She used to take places like this in her stride. Indeed, she used to design them. But now she felt a country hick. And she couldn't see Brody.

Then suddenly his hand was on her shoulder and as she turned he held her by the shoulders and said, 'That can't be an English tan. Have you been skiving off to the Med?' Those curious greenish-hazel eyes danced at her.

'If you were out all day, wind or rain, you'd get a tan too.'

She thought he looked slighter, leaner than before, even a bit older. And he'd lost that rich man's quality, as if expensive sun, or sun-lamps, favoured the wealthy. She'd forgotten his chipped tooth.

They went straight into the restaurant and Brody declared they'd eat fish and chips. His assumption that he'd choose her food reminded her of the Irish pub and how he'd ordered lobster followed by cobbler for all of them, and no arguing.

'Why are you smiling?' he said.

'Because you always assume that if you like something, everyone will.'

He looked puzzled. 'But you like fish and chips, don't you? Everyone does.'

She agreed to the fish and chips but not to beer.

'OK,' he said, 'just to prove I'm not a bully or an Irish peasant, we'll have a bottle of Montrachet. How's that?'

She smiled. 'I thought you were broke.'

'Not that broke,' he retorted.

He didn't want to see her reports or accounts. He wanted to talk to her about Maddon.

'I know you love the place, Lott. Probably more than I do, which is plenty. But I'm going to be pretty well stuck in the States for the next couple of years . . .'

Her stomach dived. 'You're going to sell?' She couldn't bear it.

'I hope not. But I might have to. Jade's gone off with a jet-set fashion photographer. We are getting a divorce and she wants half of everything.'

'Oh Brody, I'm so sorry.' She was too. But she was also thinking, oh God, he can't sell Maddon. He can't. What will I do? Instead, she said, 'Being walked out on is hell, isn't it?'

But Brody put his hand over hers and said, 'It's been on the cards for months. The only good thing is that half of my shares in the business are not worth a lot, and I've got some loot stashed in Jersey that Jade and her lawyers can't get their hands on. It was to be my life-line if the business went belly up. I just hope it will be enough to keep her lawyers quiet without my losing Maddon or any more of the company than I've already lost to the Yanks.'

'But you'll be broke?' Lotte's eyes were dark with sympathy.

'Well, not as skint as when I was a baker's boy.'

He looked happy, Lotte thought, as she watched him turn to reach the wine in the ice bucket behind him. How could he be happy? The wine waiter appeared, eager to do the pouring for him, but Brody brought the wet bottle across the table and tipped what remained into their glasses. He handed the dripping bottle to the waiter, who took it with a resigned flourish and jammed it upside down in the ice bucket.

Oblivious to the waiter's little burst of petulance, Brody said, 'I know I'll come back, Lott. Financially I mean. I still own thirty per cent of *find-on-line* and forty per cent of *going-going-gone*, and my American masters give me a pretty free hand. Within a year or two one of the big fish will be on the prowl again, and we have what they'll want – the software and a growing corner of the market. They'll buy me out and I'll come back with the loot and start something else.' He took a gulp of wine and grinned. 'Well, that's the plan.'

She thought how wonderful it must be to have such a bounce-back personality. To see adversity as a challenge, as fun almost.

'You're enjoying it, aren't you?' she said.

'Too right. I like a fight. And it's more fun in Silicon Valley than it is in England. Those guys never sleep.'

They talked about Lotte's children, and Brody's interest in them was warm and real. Then they moved on to Maddon and she told him about the cattle getting into the lake, and how she'd blackmailed Tim to dig up the dead roses.

She felt none of her usual desperation, none of her anxiety about too much work and losing the game. It was partly the wine, of course, but it was just so good to talk to someone who loved the place as she did. And when he said it was she who had taught him to notice that the colour green contained a myriad shades from yellow to blue, and that the shape of plants mattered as much as the colour, she felt wonderful.

They were half-way through their panna cotta and Lotte was about to tell him — she couldn't resist — about the grotto and the Persian pool, when he leant forward and interrupted her. 'Lott, I have to make love to you.'

His eyes drilled into her. 'Now,' he said. 'Right now.'

Lotte felt her breath disappear and her insides melt. She could not pull her eyes away from his.

'Brody,' she said, 'no . . .'

'Yes,' he said, standing up and waving to the waiter for the bill. The waiter started to fuss, wanting to know if there was anything wrong with the pudding.

Brody, suddenly agitated, said too forcefully, 'No, it's fine, we just don't want it.' And he leant across to take Lotte's spoon out of her hand. 'Do we?'

Lotte did not say a word. While he was signing the bill, she thought, I must stand up, right now, and walk out of this room. Just go. But she knew already that she wouldn't.

Brody seemed to think she might bolt too, because he held her wrist in his, like a policeman walking with a prisoner in handcuffs. He marched her to the lift.

Lotte watched the lift numbers light up as they rose. Between floors four and five she said, 'Brody, I . . .'

But he shushed her by putting his hand over her mouth. And then Lotte knew she would do whatever he asked. His hand was warm and smelled faintly of soap and more of Brody. It made her breath disappear and her knees give way. She leant against the lift wall and closed her eyes.

As soon as they were in Brody's room, he kicked the door shut and shucked out of his jacket.

'Lotte Warren,' he said, 'I've wanted to make love to you since the first day I clapped eyes on you.' Lotte knew it wasn't true, but it didn't matter. His voice was what did it to her, like that night in Johnny Fox's when he was singing.

She just wanted him to keep talking to her. To caress her with that dark voice tinged with Irish.

He kept her very close to him as he undressed her, as if air between them might cool their ardour. He talked to her all the time and she felt weak under the drenching of his words. He cupped her jaw in his hand, making her look into his eyes as he told her how lovely she was. He slid his thumb into her mouth, caressed her lips with his fingers, and breathed a kiss deep, deep into her. She could hardly hear what he said, he seemed to be murmuring to himself as much as to her. He said that he loved her warm breath, the smell of her neck, the cool smoothness of her breasts.

Somehow, very quickly, she was almost naked, her skirt, blouse and bra on the floor at their feet. She had stood passive but with her body on fire as Brody undressed her, and now she came to life, undressing him with less skill but more urgency.

Then Brody pushed her back on the bed. He lay on top of her and held her eyes with his. His voice was shaky as he said, 'Now?'

'Now.'

Lotte could not believe what she had done. It was exactly what Sam had done to her, and it was unforgivable.

Making love to Brody had been so overpowering and liberating – so glorious – that any moral sense had vanished like water on a hotplate. She thought if Frances and

Sam had that effect on each other she could understand Sam's defection. But she knew that for them it was more than torrid attraction: they were going to make a happy old couple.

And Lotte was fearful about any long-term future with Brody. Even with Jade gone it was impossible. Brody and she were chalk and cheese. He'd hardly read a book in his life and his idea of music was Eighties pop or Irish folk songs. She tried to tell herself that his charisma, energy and charm were enough. But she knew that without the sex, there'd not be much. Certainly not the depth of friendship she had with Peter. And anyway, Brody was younger than she was. How long would it be before he found another Jade?

For a week Lotte veered between guilt and longing for Brody. She would catch herself wallowing in memory or fantasy like a teenager. She half hoped, but also feared, that Brody would write to her, or ring her up. But she heard nothing.

And then, two weeks later, she recognized his writing on an envelope. She felt her heart batter her chest, and she folded the envelope quickly and shoved it into her pocket. Thank God she was alone. She was behaving like a schoolgirl, her face flushed with guilt.

She walked quickly out of the house into the walled garden, past Peter's little vegetable patch to the swing-seat he had bought them. She looked up at the windows of the house, but there was no one visible. Peter had gone to his own house, and the children weren't up yet.

The swing-seat faced away from the house, and she lay curled up in it so she would be invisible. The envelope contained a slip of paper with just the scribbled words *I miss you, B.* on it. The slip was attached to an open return ticket to San Francisco, first class.

Lotte's mind swirled about. The demonstration of love – if it was love – was intoxicating. But her overwhelming thought was that it was so typical of Brody: impulsive and extravagant – he was supposed to be scrimping and saving. And thoughtless: how could she go gallivanting off to the States and leave the children? And Peter? And Maddon?

But she didn't send the ticket back. She put it into the back pocket of her briefcase and shoved it back on top of the filling cabinet.

Sam and Frances were taking the children to Cornwall for the last two weeks of August, and Peter suggested they go away too, just the two of them. But Lotte said, 'Peter, I can't. You know I can't. I'm working.'

His voice patient, Peter said, 'Lotte, you already work twice as hard as you are paid for, and by my calculations you have only taken two weeks off – ten working days – since last summer. You are owed at least –'

'Peter, that's not the point. There is no one else to look after –'

He interrupted. 'I thought you told me August was the one time in the garden when there wasn't anything to do.'

'There is less to do. But I'm on my own . . .'

Peter reached out and took her by the wrist. 'Don't you want to go away with me? Is that it?'

'Of course I do . . . Yes . . . But . . . No. No, I don't. I can't.'

He let her go and turned away. Lotte lifted her hand to

stop him, then dropped it. What was the point? She could not give in.

That evening she made a Salade Niçoise with tinned tuna and vegetables from the garden – beans, potatoes, red onions and tomatoes. She was peeling hardboiled eggs when Peter came in. He kissed her cheek and said, 'What's this? Guilty conscience?'

It was, and Lotte's smile was rueful. 'Yes,' she said. 'And it's to soften you up because I'm going out again tonight – to take rose cuttings. I thought you might come. It's a lovely evening and . . .'

Peter said quite gently, 'Lotte, you have got to stop. This is madness . . . Maddon is not your garden. And you cannot save it on your own.'

She shook her head, pleading. 'No, no. You don't understand. This is a jaunt. It will be fun. I've persuaded the head gardener at Baxendale House to let me take cuttings of all his ramblers and shrub roses. Please, Peter. It's one of the great gardens of England, and they have the best collection of old roses for miles around. Well, they do now, since I took us out of the running.'

Of course Peter agreed, and they put the Salade Niçoise in a plastic box with two forks and Lotte stuck a bottle of wine and a couple of glasses in a cooler. They would find somewhere for an evening picnic.

For the first hour, the Baxendale gardener helped Lotte take the cuttings, which she was grateful for. It wasn't straightforward – some bushes had no unflowered stems at all, and some, especially the ramblers, had shoots that were too small, too tender or too long. Lotte knew she'd have more success grafting buds on to briar rootstocks, but she hadn't the time. As long as half of her cuttings took, it would be worth it.

She worked without gloves, and after an hour her hands were scratched and red from many tiny thorn pricks. They gently pulled nine- to twelve-inch non-flowered branches from the main stem, taking care to get a good heel on every base, and pulling off all the leaves except a few at the top. Peter wrote the roses' names on freezer bags, slipped them in and tied the tops.

They took three cuttings from each old shrub variety and from all the ramblers and climbers. Lotte said the low strike rate for cuttings from hybrid teas made including them a waste of time.

'The truth is,' Peter teased, 'you are such a snob you think hybrid teas are common and vulgar.'

Lotte was indignant. 'No I don't. They are wonderful for cutting, and some of them are beautiful anywhere.' She grinned. 'But I do hate "Tequila Sunrise". Happily, they wouldn't dream of having any at Baxendale.'

It was a wonderful garden, and when they'd finished taking the cuttings they sat in a hornbeam arbour, looking out over the formal green parterres of clipped box in elaborate patterns on well-watered lawns, and beyond them to pasture and fields.

It should have been heaven on earth, sitting there, eating Salade Niçoise and watching the steady progress of a distant combine-harvester changing the colour of a field, strip by strip, from golden to beige. But Lotte was restless. When she looked at her watch for the second time, Peter said, 'Relax. No bathtime for Jo-Jo. No homework. No cooking. We could go for a drink in a pub.'

Lotte said, 'It's not that. It's . . .'

'You want to get back and plant the cuttings, don't you?'

'Yes,' she said. 'The sooner we get them in the more chance of them taking.'

'I thought you said they'd last overnight in the fridge, in their bags?'

Lotte looked cornered as she said, 'Yes, well, they would. But it's better . . .'

Peter took her hand. 'Lotte, for God's sake be reasonable. Leave it till tomorrow. Give yourself, give me, a night off.'

Lotte pulled away and said, 'Tomorrow I've got too much to do anyway. And it's going to be hot. It's better to do this in the cool . . .'

'Lotte, I'm sure there is a horticultural argument to support every hour of the seventy hours a week you are doing. But there sure as hell isn't a social one. You just should not be doing all this. Why are we taking rose cuttings anyway? I thought you are only meant to keep Maddon tidy.'

'Peter, you know why. I killed all the roses on the estate. *I* did it. *Me*. It's the least I can do.'

Refusing to respond to Lotte's raised voice, Peter said quietly, 'Lotte, the house is uninhabited. Boarded up. Abandoned. If, which seems unlikely, Brody ever wants to live there again, I'm quite sure he'd authorize your buying the lot, fully grown and blooming. This nonsense is going to take years, isn't it?'

'Yes, it is. But I can at least plant them out next year. There will be something in the rose garden, even if they are only tiny. By the time Brody comes back . . .'

Peter held Lotte's hands again and said firmly and, for him, loudly and deliberately, 'Lotte, don't you see? You are obsessed with Maddon. To the detriment of us all.'

She flared up, yanking her hands out of his. 'Are you saying I neglect my children?'

Peter looked at her for a second, then said, 'Yes. No more than many parents who work too hard. But the difference is that you don't have to. You do it from choice.'

Lotte opened her mouth, then closed it. Peter was right. It was true. It was all true. But she couldn't help any of it. She stood up, feverishly gathering up the picnic things. 'Peter, just let me do what I have to do, will you? Don't lecture me, please.'

They hardly spoke in the car going home, and when they arrived, Peter said in a voice heavy with resignation, 'I'm afraid I'm not going to help you with those cuttings and I'm not going to wait up for you either. I'll go to my place. I'll see you tomorrow.'

'Fine,' said Lotte, unloading the car and avoiding his eyes.

She had already dug the long V-shaped trenches in the fine tilth of the vegetable garden and put an inch of horticultural sand at the bottom for drainage. She'd chosen the site carefully, where the cuttings would get some sun but be protected from the full blast of midday heat.

She was about to start planting the cuttings when she realized that once she took them out of their bags, she would not know one from the other. She had to make plant labels for them.

Deciding to do the labels first, she went back into the

cottage, leaving the cuttings in the shade of the wall. The heat had gone now, and they'd be fine.

She collected a pen and clipboard, and copied down the names on all the bags, then she went back into the cottage and carefully started making labels in alphabetical order from 'Albéric Barbier' to 'Zéphirine Drouhin'. They included ramblers, climbers, *Albas*, Provence roses, damasks, polyanthas, *Gallicas*, hybrid musks, hybrid perpetuals, sweetbriars, Portlands and Scotch briars. She had taken 310 cuttings in all.

Getting the bags into alphabetical order and writing out the white plastic markers took nearly as long as taking the cuttings, and it was nearly midnight before she was through. Her back ached and she knew she should go and fetch the roses, clear the fridge, put them all into it somehow, and start again in the morning. It was pitch dark outside anyway. And if she left them where they were, the morning sun would steam them in their bags.

She stood up and arched her back. The relief was terrific. What she needed now was a cup of coffee. She made one, and then, on an impulse, put a slug of whisky into it. It was wonderful.

It wouldn't take long to plant the cuttings, she thought. If she used the hurricane lamp she'd bought for Christo and his friend's camping adventure when they'd slept in a tiny tent in the walled garden, she'd be able to see all right.

Feeling less tired now, and adventurous – it was a relief that Peter had gone home and could not remonstrate with her – she found the lamp, filled it with kerosene and lit it. The wick burnt clean and clear.

She put the lamp down beside the first trench, and

started with 'Albéric Barbier'. First she put in the label, slightly to the side of the trench, then dipped each stem first into a jar of water, then into hormone rooting powder, before laying it in the trench. Then another label and another three cuttings. She laid the cuttings a few inches apart, all leaning against the same side of the trench. When she'd done a couple of dozen, she back-filled the trench, firming the ground gently.

By one-thirty she had filled both her long trenches. But she still had 100-odd cuttings to plant. For a second, she was tempted to take the rest inside with her and call it a day. But she knew that in the morning she had to pay the mowing-man, and the herbaceous borders looked like a jungle. She must just get on with this, and finish it.

She took the hurricane lamp with her to fetch the spade from the tool shed and started to dig another long trench. She hadn't dug three yards when the lamp sputtered and died. Damn, it was out of kerosene.

She went back inside and refilled the lamp. And then she put the kerosene container on the draining board while she screwed the top back on the lamp tank. The kerosene, unevenly balanced on an upturned plate, toppled forwards, arcing fuel as it fell.

Lotte dived. She failed to catch it but sent it on a second spin, spilling more fuel over the floor.

She looked in despair at the kerosene. Oh God, all I need now is a lighted match and the house will go up, she thought. She got some newspapers and laid them on the wet floor, then gathered them up. The kerosene stung her hands, already raw from the roses. She put them under the tap, dried them gingerly, and went back to the floor. It took another five minutes to mop it with detergent. But the kitchen still stank.

Utterly exhausted, Lotte could not think straight. For some reason, it had become vital that she finished the rose cuttings. She went back outside with the lamp and returned to digging the trench. And then she slammed the spade into her foot.

The pain shot from her toes to her thigh, and she dropped the spade and hopped about, crying out. She looked at her foot and saw blood seeping through the thin canvas of her old tennis shoes.

She sat down on the ground, whimpering with pain, and took off her shoe. It hurt like hell as she dragged it and the sock off. But her big toe wasn't broken. It was badly cut, and very, very sore. Lotte drew her knees up and lowered her head on to them, crying quietly.

After she did not know how long, she looked at her watch. It was 2.50 a.m. In another two hours it would be light. And she still hadn't finished the cuttings. This thought started her weeping again. But she could not dig with her foot hurting so. It was a good half hour more before she was back in the house, with the remaining cuttings in the fridge, and most of the food from the fridge on the kitchen table.

She was hobbling about, trying to find some disinfectant and a bandage, when she heard a car outside. For a second she felt pure panic: she was alone, it was 3.30 a.m., she was in no state for a fight. And then she realized it was Peter.

Relief flooded through her like a river of comfort. As

he hurried in, saying, 'Lotte, I've been so worried. I've been ringing you for hours,' she hobbled into his arms, crying.

'Oh Peter, I can't cope. I'm so tired, and I haven't done the cuttings, and I've bust my toe, and my hands hurt, and . . .'

Peter shushed her and gave them both a whisky. Kissing her hair, he said, 'And you smell like a petrol station.'

A week later Lotte wrote to Brody.

Beloved Brody (for you are, however much it should not be),

I would never have believed I could say this, but I'm quitting. I'm no good at just holding the fort. It seems I am an all or nothing woman. I've discussed everything with Terry Simons and he has asked Andrew to come back.

I've applied for a job with the Oxfordshire Council, teaching gangs of youths on Community Service how to rake leaves and mow churchyards. God knows how I will survive. But I know it's right. I need something less demanding of my heart than Maddon. Or you.

I should tell you too, that we are moving in with Peter at Swinford. Peter says, rightly, that Maddon is a dangerous obsession. It was. It is. Which is where I had better tell you that I have been working in secret on the Old Pond Yards (yes, I know, but it was in my own time). Almost the hardest thing is not being able to show the place to you. I think I worked that hard, just for that moment.

I've shown Andrew where they are, if you want to look. There is an early nineteenth-century Persian pool and English Heritage are in the process of listing the grotto, which has a roof studded

with shells and mirror pieces dating from 1740. The documents are
in my office, filed under Restoration Projects.

> *Oh Brody, Brody,*
> *Lott*

She enclosed the airline ticket.

25. Two Years Later:
Early Summer

I thought I could never let you know
How lovely all those roses were – some few
Had, bursting from their buds, commenced to blow,
Some had begun to blast, some were quite new . . .

Angelo Poliziano (1454–94), 'She Finds Herself in a
Garden', translated by John Hollander

Two years later, on her forty-ninth birthday, Lotte opened her eyes to see Jo-Jo kicking the door shut with her foot, and advancing with a breakfast tray. For a second Lotte had thought Jo-Jo was Annie, she was so tall and grown-up now.

'Happy birthday, Mum.'

Lotte sat up, pushing her hair back.

'Darling, this is very nice of you.' She leant over the tray to kiss her daughter. 'Why aren't you in your usual Sunday morning coma?'

'Dunno. But I forgot to buy you a birthday present. Sorry. So decided to do breakfast in bed for you.'

Peter came in from the bathroom and Lotte said, 'Peter, get back in bed. We've got breakfast for two for my birthday present.' She fumbled for her reading glasses, and picked up the little vase from the tray.

'Jo-Jo! How did you know those are my favourites?' She studied the single 'Madame Hardy' rose and the small spray of 'Great Maiden's Blush'.

'Peter told me. Last night when I was picking them. He wouldn't let me cut any more.'

Lotte put her nose against the pink rose and said to Peter, 'So you were in on this?'

'I was, and a good thing too, or she'd have cut every rose off our fledgling bushes.'

They ate the breakfast, Peter sitting on the edge of the bed, Lotte in it. Then he went off to shower, instructing her to do nothing. She said she'd lie in bed all morning and listen to *The Archers*.

But she didn't turn the radio on. She lay there thinking that she did not want to be fifty. Forty-nine was just about bearable, but in a year she'd be absolutely, unarguably middle-aged. Peter was in his fifties but he had always been middle-aged. Maybe archivists were born that way.

Lotte shook her head, very slightly, as she thought of her three children, all taller than her now. Jo-Jo was thirteen and, as always, no trouble. None of the teenage misery, puppy fat and sulks poor Annie had gone in for. Christo, sweet and studious as ever but now a spotty fifteen-year-old, had an equally studious and spotty girlfriend.

And Annie had been transformed from a duckling to a swan. She'd had very respectable GCSE results and was going into A-levels as a confident, slim, beautiful young woman. How did I do that, thought Lotte.

Then she answered her own question. Peter did it. Or rather, without Peter none of the children, or she, would have emerged from the Brody/Maddon years unscathed. Without Peter, she'd have started a real affair with Brody. And what a slippery slope that would have been. She'd never have kept him. She'd never have ended up mistress of Maddon, that was for sure. Brody was made to woo the Jades of this world – glamorous, demanding, famous.

Lotte smiled, imagining for a second how one could reconcile marrying a gardener with the idea of a trophy wife.

Suddenly she pushed the tray aside and got out of bed. This was nonsense. It was two years, almost to the day, since she'd left Maddon and she hadn't seen or heard from Brody since. She'd been divorced from Sam and married to Peter for a year. Happily married. She'd no right to think about Brody at all.

'He's gone, do you understand?' she muttered to herself. 'Gone. Bankrupt. Left the country. NOTHING TO DO WITH YOU.'

At 11 a.m., Lotte and Peter were sitting out on the little paved area at the back of the house, drinking coffee and surveying the garden.

'Looks good, doesn't it?' said Peter.

It did, for all the willow-leafed pear and the *Sorbus* 'Pink Pagoda' were spindly and small and the roses not yet three feet high. 'Madame Hardy' had only three stems, and 'Great Maiden's Blush' not many more.

But the borders had shape and colour, and the withy fence that separated them from the neighbours had a respectable covering of clematis and rambling roses. Lotte looked at cascading swathes of 'Sander's White' and the garlands of deep pink 'Excelsior' punctuated by the first few blooms of 'Perle D'Azur', and thought, well, I never managed my rose and clematis tunnel at Maddon, but at least I've got this.

Peter peered at her over his frameless glasses (she had eventually persuaded him to give up the horn-rims) and said, 'OK, birthday girl. What do you want to do?'

'Do you want the truth, or shall I be diplomatic?'

Peter laughed. 'I don't expect Jo-Jo will want to come. She says she's spent enough of her childhood in that wood.'

Christo was away on a school trip, and Annie was staying with a friend in Oxford, getting in maximum clubbing over the weekend. So there was only Jo-Jo to worry about.

'She'll be delighted to escape us and hang around Virgin Records with Melanie,' said Lotte. 'But what about you? Are you up for more squelching in the mud?'

'Sure I am.'

Lotte spent a lot of time in Maddon Woods, but she never went near the big house or garden. She could not bear to. From the edge of the wood she could see the terraces and the lake, and she sometimes saw the contractors topping the park or mowing the green terraces. Everything looked perfect from this distance. But she never went into the park or gardens proper. She knew that seeing the lake beds infested with bulrushes, the garden borders untended, the walled garden overgrown would upset her. She confined herself to the woods.

Soon after she'd resigned from her job at Maddon, Peter had gone to see Terry Simons, who was still Brody's land agent, and got permission for them to continue their excavations of the Old Pond Yards.

At first Lotte had been angry, saying she wanted a complete break from Maddon, that it was he, Peter, who had accused her of being obsessed with the place. Why was he pushing her back there?

But then she calmed down and began to worry that their work on the ponds would be obliterated by new layers of leaf-mould and moss. The garden could always be reclaimed, but the old Pond Yards, the folly, the grotto and the Merman's pool were all archaeological finds that mustn't be allowed to disappear again.

So she'd agreed, and it had been great. Therapy, almost. She could become so absorbed by the complications of the channels and ponds, she'd spend whole mornings without once thinking about the loss of Maddon – or of Brody.

Lotte found the first year in Peter's house, without Maddon, hard. She could not stop herself thinking about Brody. She longed for news of him, but when she read that he was locked in a divorce battle with Jade she'd felt her heart twist in anguish. How was he faring? Was he sad about Jade? Had his love of life been dulled? Had his business recovered? Would he ever return and reclaim Maddon? Did he ever think of her?

She'd been irrational too, sometimes jealous of the children's affection for Peter – the thing that had most pleased her before. Now she felt left out as they opted for Peter's company.

And Peter's solicitousness had stifled her. Sometimes she had to leave the house and walk along the river by herself. Once she snapped, 'For God's sake, Peter, I'm fine. I'm not tired. I'm not stressed, I'm not in need of anything other than a whisky. I *like* my gang of young louts. Anyone would think I spent the day governing Parkhurst the way you go on.'

And then she'd seen a look of sympathy pass between Peter and the children. They were humouring her.

Gradually, though, she had become less fraught, and Maddon and its owner had ceased to dominate her mind to such an extent. She had relaxed, and so had Peter. He never irritated her now.

Working so closely, and so much, in the Old Pond Yards had brought them really close. They worked well together, mostly in silence, but sometimes chatting companionably. Within six months, labouring only at weekends, they had managed to establish where all the main channels and ponds used to be. The largest pond, about thirty feet across, must have been fed by a channel from the river at a higher point. A second channel took the overflow from the first to the second pond, and then, they surmised, back to the river via the grotto and its pool. To one side of the second pond were a short stone wall and a short arched underwater tunnel to the smallest pond to the side.

Peter believed the big ponds would have been stewponds for carp and bream and other large fish, with the smaller side pond for eel and for trapping fish more easily when they were needed for the table. On the small-pond side of the tunnel were deep vertical grooves cut into the stone on each side. Peter was convinced they would have taken some kind of wooden gate that could be dropped into place once the fish had been chased into the pond.

Clearing the undergrowth, draining the ponds and digging out the silt and leaf-mould of ages to get down to firm clay would be a massive job. Lotte had been back to see Brody's agent.

'The thing is, Terry,' she said, 'we want to use volunteers from the local history group to help us dig them out, to see if we can get the water channels going again.'

Terry leant back in his chair and studied her. 'Lotte, I've always admired your energy. But couldn't it be put to better use than working for the Council and grubbing around derelict ponds? I could get you any number of estate manager or head gardener jobs . . .'

'I've already got a job. And I don't want to be an estate manager or head gardener ever again.'

'Well, I can understand that after Brody's financial troubles and the disaster with the roses . . .'

Lotte's head shot up. 'How did you know about that?'

He didn't answer, and Lotte subsided in her chair. Of course he knew. Brody would have told him. He was his agent after all. But still, she didn't like it.

He said, 'But Lotte, that sort of experience makes you a better, not a worse gardener.' She frowned at him, not understanding, and he smiled back. 'You are probably one of the few gardeners in the country that I would wager my life would never muddle up herbicide and insecticide in the future.'

He was right, of course. She forced a smile. 'Nevertheless,' she said, 'I like my present job. It's nine to four, leaves me time for our own garden and the old Pond Yards. And Peter likes the excavation too. We both do.'

'So why do you need volunteers?'

'So we can go faster. And also I think I could persuade the Probation Service that this would be more interesting and educational for some of the youngsters I currently supervise than sweeping up leaves and clearing litter.'

'Hardly community service, though, is it? And aren't these young men vandals and villains? I don't think Brody –'

Lotte interrupted him, 'No. The real villains go to jail. These are just aimless youngsters, most of them bored stiff, who could do with a chance to achieve something. They'd be no trouble.'

Simons looked sceptical and started to speak, but Lotte was in full flight. 'And as to the community – why not let the public into the woods? Not at once, of course. We'd have to hack some paths through, and fence it off from the park. We could do that if we got some sponsorship for posts and rails. But they are the most beautiful woods, and it's such a waste.'

In the end, Simons agreed to ask Brody about the community service youths and the volunteer group. But he didn't hold out any hope of public access.

Driving home, Lotte admitted to herself that Terry was probably right. Brody wouldn't mind free labour, would approve of hooligans doing some honest hard graft. But Joe Public picnicking in his woods, even if he never visited them, would go against the grain.

26. Summer

. . . Let my beloved come into his garden, and eat his pleasant fruits.

Song of Solomon 4: 16

A month later, and almost two years after he and Lotte had made love in London, Brody returned to Maddon. He was now a wealthier man than when he'd first bought the place.

He leant back in the soft leather of his big Mercedes and thought about his time in California. It had been incredibly hard work, but exhilarating. He'd driven himself and everyone else mercilessly until *find-on-line* and *going-going-gone* had hundreds of global customers and thousands of smaller ones. Both companies had taken off – just as he'd promised Lotte they would.

Of course they had. They saved their customers a shed-load of money, and both were market leaders in their fields. Selling his stake had been a breeze. There had been enough interest to drive the price up and he'd made a killing. So here he was, rich again. Seriously loaded in fact, and he was fancy-free. He'd take off a couple of months, maybe a year. Go where the wind blows. Maybe invest in a few little start-ups. Maybe buy another business. Who knows?

Today he'd have a look at Maddon. See what little Lotte was up to.

A wave of uneasiness tightened his chest. Maybe Lotte wouldn't see him. Maybe she'd married that archivist she moved in with and had forgotten all about him.

The slate-blue Mercedes came softly to a stop outside the main entrance and the driver got out. Brody watched him ring the bell, inspect the lock, push and pull the immovable iron gates and ring the bell again.

Impatient, Brody climbed out himself, saying, 'They used to work on a remote. God knows where that is. Probably still in my old Jag.' He tapped the entry system. 'Anyway, this used to ring in the house, not the Gardener's Cottage – which is where the security office is now.'

'Not to worry, Mr Keegan,' the driver said. 'I'll ring the office and get your secretary to give them a bell. Or the agent.'

But Brody shook his head. 'No, don't bother, Frank. Drive me round to the Maddon Cottages entrance. Andrew, the gardener, lives there. That will be open. And if it's not, I'll get in somehow.'

At the cottages the bridle gate was unlocked, but the main-road gate had a chain and padlock on it. Frank said, 'Do you know which cottage this Andrew chap lives in, sir? He'll have a key.'

But Brody dismissed him, saying, 'I'll walk. Do me good. And Frank, I'll be a while, I expect, so you take the car and go off to the pub or something. I'll telephone you when I'm through.'

Brody wanted his eager driver gone. Nor did he want an escort in the form of old Andrew or his agent. He watched his Merc's stately progress down the lane. It was nice to have a decent car again, that was for sure.

It was a good three miles through the farm, but Brody enjoyed the walk. It was warm, with patchy cloud. Not exactly dressed for the country, he thought, as he slung his Savile Row jacket over his shoulder and redirected his steps to the grass verge – his expensive shoes were not designed for lumpy farm tracks.

Home Farm looked just as before. Being tenanted, it was unaffected by Brody's troubles, but he knew farmers were having a rough time. Terry Simons is a good agent, he thought: won't let the tenants get away with old bedsprings for gates or with fields of thistles.

Of course the garden will be a wreck. Old Andrew on his own is hardly Lotte plus four assistants. Brody found his heart speeding up as he neared the house. Exertion or excitement? Or the thought of Lotte?

He knew she was still working, the madwoman, on her crazy ponds at the weekends. But today was Wednesday. He was glad there was no danger of seeing her. He wanted to plan their meeting, not surprise her in the shrubbery like in a novel.

Brody approached the house through the park, and from a distance it looked as lovely as that day when Lotte and he had stood on the jetty and she'd given him a lecture on the mellowness of Cotswold stone. There was the same soft light on the walls now, and the windows glinted in the sun. He was standing to the west of the lake, and he walked round the edge to the fountains. They weren't turned on of course, and the sculpted stone steps of the cascades had dried moss on their surfaces and weeds in the cracks. Should have had the fibre-glass version, he thought. Hell of a sight cheaper and I bet moss doesn't grow on fibre-glass.

But all in all, the lake and waterworks looked fine.

Best of all, his wonderful 'Powerscourt' terraces looked as if they could withstand decades of neglect, never mind a couple of years. The grass was too long, and full of weeds, but the shape was there. It was still a triumph.

Cheered, Brody walked fast along the path through the park. He skirted the ha-ha, crossed the main lawn and stopped in front of his rose bed. Bloody Andrew, he thought. He could at least have pulled up the corpses and grassed over the graveyard.

The grass of the lawn had encroached into the big square bed, but it was more weeds than grass. Cow-parsley and nettles looked strong and healthy, coming up between the dead roses, which were now leafless brown sticks, still standing in formal rows.

Brody smiled. Poor Lotte. She always hated this bed, but what a way to get her heart's desire! Brody bent down, parting the grass to reach the elaborate brass label, now dull and barely legible. The ground was dry and he had to yank hard to extract it. '*Tequila Sunrise*'. Brody gave a rueful shake of his head. As always, Lotte had been right: she'd said brass was a bad idea – it needed polishing. And that the rose bed was a mistake. He'd have to tell her he'd shed no tears at all.

The rose walk had gone, with only brambles and lumpy ground to mark its place and the walled garden was as sad a sight. But so what? It wasn't as if the house had burnt down. Brody looked about him, anticipation giving his face energy and life. It won't take long to get the place right again, he thought. Apart from a few broken panes, the glasshouses seemed in pretty good nick. He stopped at an overgrown bed by the wall, noticing a couple of labels lying on the ground. He picked one up. R. *Centifolia Christata* he read, and R. *Blairi No. 2*. They were stout, white-painted batons, with neat black lettering. Lotte's writing. He looked along the wall and saw, among the weeds, hundreds of labels, mostly still standing. He pulled a few out at random and read them: R. *Cécile Brunner*; R. *Cardinal de Richelieu*; R. *Koenigin von Dänemarck*; R. *Fantinh Latour*. Whatever it was she'd planted here with such care had not survived.

He smiled at the memory of her labelling. She insisted on using that antique machine for anything in the gardens proper, and home-made ones like this in the walled garden. She wouldn't tie labels on to plants, she thought it spoilt them. On the stone terraces and rockeries she wrote names on smooth pebbles, varnished to an earthy brown. She said that labels (except in the walled garden) should be clear for people who wanted to read them and unobtrusive for people who didn't.

Poor Lotte, he thought, dropping the labels. But we can do it all again.

Brody had now walked a good four miles, and he was thirsty. He set off towards Lotte's old cottage, thinking he'd get a glass of water from the security men, and maybe some help with breaking and entering his own house. The security people must be a useless bunch, he thought. If they were any good, I'd have been brought to the ground by a bloody great wolfhound by now.

There was only one security guard, and he was watching cricket in what used to be Lotte's sitting room. He came to the door with a can of Budweiser in his hand, a German Shepherd at his heels. He jerked his chin at Brody. It meant: and what do you want then?

Brody's 'Good afternoon' got another upward tip of the chin. Nettled, he said, 'I'm Brody Keegan. And I pay your wages. So I suggest you say good afternoon, or hello, or can I help you, sir?'

The guard lost some of his composure at this and blustered, 'Well, how do I know who you are? You never said you was coming. You could be anyone.'

'Good thinking. I wouldn't want you letting anyone into my house.' Brody reached for his mobile and scrolled down for his agent's number.

'Hi, Terry. It's Brody. You're working late. Glad I got you. I'm at Maddon . . . Yeah, well I got in this morning . . . Decided to drive down and have a look-see for myself. Have you had estimates from the garden contractors and builders yet? . . . No? OK, I'll be down again next week. We'll walk round then.'

Brody walked in a tight circle, his phone to his ear, talking fast. 'Now, I'm in Lotte's old house and I need you to tell the security officer here that I'm the owner. And also see if you can persuade him to open up the house. I've got keys, but the place is boarded up . . . No. No. Thanks, but I'll probably drive straight back to London. But I'll be in touch, Terry.' He laughed. 'Yeah, it's good to be flush again all right. A lot nicer than being broke . . .'

He passed the telephone to the security man and went

in search of something to drink. Within seconds the man was in the kitchen, fussing around like an old woman, wanting to make him tea, explaining that he was only watching cricket for five minutes between his hourly rounds.

My fat foot, thought Brody, I've been on this estate for at least an hour, but he said, 'Look, lad. Forget all that. Just get the front-door boards off, OK? And you needn't worry to put them back when I'm gone.'

'It's no trouble, Mr Keegan. I'd be glad to . . .'

Brody cut him short. 'That door is solid oak and it's got three locks on it. I've got keys, and when I've finished my walk, I'll let myself in. And out again when I'm done. I'll call you when I'm going, and leave a message on this phone. What's the number?'

It was Lotte's old number, of course, and Brody didn't need to write it down.

He looked across the park to the edge of the woods, to where, must be three years ago, they'd brought Christo out. He didn't think he'd remember the way back to the grotto. He'd have to ask Andrew next time he came. Or Lotte, if she'd talk to him. But you never knew, he might be lucky. Anyway, it was a lovely evening and he could walk back to the house via the woods.

In fact, he found a well-trodden track almost at once. He didn't know if it was the same one but he turned into it and saw a red Clio parked deep in the shade. His heart jumped. But Lotte didn't drive a Renault. She drove a Subaru, didn't she? Perhaps it was Peter's, or one of Lotte's Friends of Maddon Park? But on a Wednesday? Maybe it was just a trespasser.

His heart calmer, he squeezed past the little car, peering into it for clues to ownership. There was a sun-hat on the back seat, but he didn't recognize it. He followed the track through the laurels, thick and dark as he remembered. It was cool in here, and rather than carry his jacket, he put it on. After he had walked down a gentle slope for ten minutes the laurels thinned and were replaced by bushes and brambles interspersed with trees. The ground sloped more sharply here and soon it was damp underfoot, and then positively soggy. He tried to keep his shoes out of the mud, but it was hopeless.

Suddenly he came into a clearing. At first it looked like some kind of building site, with mounds of freshly dug earth all over the place. But when he came up close, he saw that they'd been digging three round ponds, all with a murky puddle of water in the bottom. They were unimpressive to look at – he'd imagined square ponds lined with stone or brick, like swimming pools. There was only one bit of what he'd call evidence of historic human activity, and that was a kind of stone tunnel between one large and one small pond.

There was no one about. He walked round all the ponds, marvelling at Lotte's madness. He found a second track leading uphill. It wasn't as wide as the one he'd followed to get here but it was obviously well used and he took it now. It led him back into some thicker undergrowth and he had to watch his step over rough roots.

And then he turned a corner and heard a woman's frightened voice, half gasp, half scream. It took a second to realize it was Lotte, and then he had his arms round her, saying, 'It's all right, Lott. It's OK. It's me. Brody.'

She pulled away, panting. He wanted to keep her in his arms. He wanted her face to register joy at seeing him.

'Oh my God,' she said, 'it's you. You gave me such a fright.'

'I didn't mean to, Lott. I'm sorry.'

She didn't look pleased. She looked bewildered. And upset. She said, 'What are you doing here?'

Brody, calm now, took the bag of tools and the cool-box from her, saying, 'I was going to say the same to you. It's Wednesday. I thought you worked for Oxford Council?'

'I thought you were in the States.'

'Come,' he said. 'Were you heading home? I've a long tale to tell you, but I'd like to see the famous grotto and Persian pool first.'

They looked at each other. Lotte was smiling now, a little tentatively, and Brody felt his stomach tighten. She was exactly as he'd thought of her for two years. A touch thinner maybe, but otherwise unchanged.

'How did you know about the Persian pool?' she said.

'You wrote to me.'

She looked confused then, ashamed and embarrassed, and she turned away. 'So I did, I'd forgotten.'

He knew she hadn't forgotten, yet he didn't contradict her. He wanted to say so much, but he wanted everything to be told at once. He wished Lotte could somehow just know everything, without him having to do any explaining. But how could she? She hadn't had one word from him in two years. He'd not even told her he didn't give a stuff about the roses. She probably still thought . . .

'How long have you got?'

He thought she'd say she had to go. Or that she'd need

to ring Peter, or the children needed collecting. But she looked directly at him and said, 'As long as you like.'

'Then let's see the grotto and the pool, and then we'll talk.'

Later, as they walked back to Lotte's little car, Brody thought how alive with pride and pleasure Lotte's face was. Quite right too – she'd made miracles happen in that wood.

The grotto's roof had been repaired with a grant from English Heritage. And the inside, with its shell garlands and glittery quartz, was amazing. The Persian pool was empty and clean, the blue and rust mosaics bright as flowers. Lotte's eyes had been shining like a child's when she explained that the grotto was exactly as it had been in some seventeen-something drawings. Brody, more aware of the colour of her eyes and the flush of her cheeks than of what she was saying, had lost the thread a bit. Something about an older pool replaced by the Persian tiled job. Whatever it was, it was quite something to come across in a wood.

They drove straight across the park, the grass cropped short by the farmer's sheep, and across the weedy gravel to the front door. Several lengths of timber and the sheet of MDF that had boarded up the door were propped up in the porch against the study window. There was also a large torch with a note: 'Electricity is off.' Maybe, thought Brody, that security man wasn't so bad after all.

He felt vaguely anxious about the conversation to come. It wasn't meant to be like this. Coming across Lotte had not been part of his plan.

'I could do with a drink. How about you?' he said as they entered the gloom of the hall.

'But surely there won't be any?'

Brody laughed. 'Yes there will. All the best stuff is still in the cellar. There's enough booze down there to supply the *Titanic*.'

Lotte didn't follow him into the cellar, as he'd thought she might. She said she'd wait in the drawing room. Maybe she was rehearsing her righteous rejection, he thought. No, she wouldn't do that. That letter of resignation had been as near to a declaration – without actually saying, 'I love you' – as you could get. He might show it to her – she wouldn't believe he'd kept it in his wallet for two years.

Brody hurried down the stairs to the cellars, the torch in one hand, his keys in the other. He didn't go into the pool room and gym – too many memories of Jade – but turned left into the wine cellar. He had trouble with the locks and feared that they had been changed, but then the key turned and the studded oak door opened.

Inside, the air was cool and slightly musty, smelling faintly of wine. The floor was damp between the flagstones. The torch illuminated rack upon rack of dusty bottles in old brick bins, all labelled. Brody walked the length of the cellar, past the ports with tags hung round their necks to compensate for the now unreadable labels, past the Riojas, the New World reds, old Burgundies, younger Burgundies. He stopped at the Bordeaux section, hesitating. God knows why I bought all this stuff, he thought. I knew nothing about wine. Still don't. Playing the country squire, I guess.

He pulled out a bottle of Cos D'Estournel 1985, walked to the champagne bins and reached for a Veuve Clicquot La Grande Dame 1998. He relocked the cellar door and took a deep breath. Now for it, he thought. And don't cock it up.

The furniture in the drawing room was covered in dust-sheets, and Lotte was standing in the shuttered gloom. She'd taken off her muddy boots, and the sight of her bare feet, brown and child-like, stirred him. He said, 'Fizz or claret?'

'Oh, fizz, don't you think?'

Brody put the bottles on the floor next to the sideboard, and knelt down to lift the dust-sheet and crawl under it. Lotte laughed.

'What are you doing? You look like the back of a pantomime horse.'

He retreated, triumphant, holding four glasses: two champagne flutes and two enormous goblets. He opened the champagne, thinking how surprisingly unflustered she seemed. Relaxed and happy. He poured her a glass.

'You look happy. Are you?' he asked.

She smiled at him, a broad, easy smile. 'Yes, of course.' Then she hesitated for a moment and looked away. 'Yes, I am. Although I miss this place.' She looked as if she wanted to go on, say more, maybe tell him what a wonderful fellow Peter was . . .

But Brody suddenly didn't want that conversation. And he didn't want to tell her anything yet either: not about the gradual recovery of *find-on-line* and *going-going-gone*, their eventual domination of the trade sourcing market. How the value of the combined companies had steadily risen until he could sell his shares for £200 million. It was all too complicated and boring. And he didn't want to go into the gory details of his and Jade's protracted divorce proceedings and final settlement.

He just wanted to sit here and look at her. And ask her if she loved him.

She reached for the glass but he shook his head slightly and put both bottle and glass down on the shrouded coffee table. He took her hands and slowly drew her to him. She stood very straight, not resisting. He brought his hands up, one on each side of her head, and held her while he lowered his face to hers. He didn't kiss her at once, just held his mouth close to hers, under her spell, remembering the smell of her. The warmth of her breath seemed enough to last forever. But then he felt her tip her head, ever so slightly, and the touch of her bottom lip against his sent a fast hot shock through his body.

Yes, he thought, oh yes.

27. Late Summer

This close-companioned inarticulate hour
When twofold silence was the song of love.

Dante Gabriel Rossetti (1828–82),
'Silent Moon'

Lotte felt almost detached, as in a dream. Peter and the children seemed very far away.

The closeness of Brody's face sent gossamer flutters up and down her cheeks. His concentrated desire lifted her out of reality. His arms were round her waist, pulling her to him while he kissed her deeply and completely. She let her arms hang limp at her sides like a rag doll's.

He ran his hands slowly over her back, her breasts, her bum. Almost reverently, she thought, as though I were a goddess. He was murmuring between kisses, 'Lott, oh Lott, I've wanted you every, every day . . .'

She stood unmoving as he undressed her, but her breath quickened. Joy and excitement were blooming in her, filling every inch of her.

And lust. Oh God, she thought, how had she denied this for two whole years?

He pushed her jeans and knickers down together, and she stepped out of them, shaking with longing, but still being led by Brody. It wasn't until he touched her nipples, and she felt them harden and rise — electric sensation spreading like slow explosions over her body — that she spoke.

'Brody,' she said, over and over again.

Lotte thought 'IN LOVE' must be branded across her forehead.

She felt benevolent to all the world. More fond, if anything, of Peter, delighted with Jo-Jo and Christo, close to Annie who had never seemed easier. She had the energy of a horse, working with the community service youths, cooking proper suppers for the family, even tackling the mountain of junk in Peter's garage.

It was such a cliché, but she felt both exhilarated and beautiful, 'happy in her skin'. She'd even had the courage to tell Brody she was forty-nine, and one day when they had made love in the woods under July's heavy green, with a few bright coins of sunlight spattering their bodies, he'd examined every inch of her, and kissed her stretch marks and her flabby inner thigh, and teased her about her grey hairs. And declared her perfect.

The dust-sheeted house became their private island. Lotte finished work at four and perhaps three times a week, she'd find a reason for being late home. She marvelled at her lack of conscience. How could she, once so appalled at Sam's desecration of her trust, once so sure of her moral core, be doing what she was doing? And yet she was not contrite. She was ecstatic.

She thought Brody might represent all her future happiness. Sometimes she was sure of it: happiness = Brody.

But when she was with Peter, and the children, she was happy too, her only cloud one of guilt. And to her astonishment it was a small cloud, nothing like as big as it should have been.

Lotte told Peter that Brody wanted to move back into Maddon and had offered her a job as a sort of consultant, to oversee a small army putting the garden to rights in a hurry. He jumped up from his chair and put his arms around her. 'Lotte darling, that's wonderful! Oh sweetheart, I am so happy for you.' And he was. His whole face showed it.

Lotte looked at herself in the mirror over his shoulder, thinking, you criminal cow, how can you be doing this?

Peter released her, saying, 'And this time you'll have proper help. That's such good news. Will you leave the community job?'

'I thought I'd ask them if I can go half-time. Just do the practical stuff with the lads, and be let off the office work.'

'Good idea,' Peter said, rooting under the stairs for a bottle of champagne. 'This was going to be for Annie's birthday. Seventeen deserves a toast. But then so does this.'

They clinked glasses to Lotte's new future and the future of Maddon, and she felt hollow and sick. She'd forgotten Annie's birthday.

Peter said, 'And we should drink to Brody. Let's hope his business horrors and divorce nightmare are truly behind him, poor fellow.'

Two weeks later, on the sofa in the still-shrouded drawing room, Brody said, 'Lott, remember your scheme for gardening holidays?'

'Mm?' Lotte was half asleep, post-coital lassitude like an all-over balm.

'I think we should do it.'

She snuggled against him. 'Why? You thought it was a terrible idea, and you don't need the money now.'

Brody shifted on the sofa so he could look at her. 'That was before I saw the pleasure your Friends of Maddon get from scraping mud out of ancient holes in the ground.' He bent over and kissed her nose. 'Before my epiphany.'

Lotte burst out laughing. 'Epiphany? That's a big word for an Oirish boy!'

'It is and all. And it's an Irishman that taught it me. James Joyce called the moment of realization that you'd got it all wrong an epiphany.' He rubbed her hair as he might a puppy's. 'I know, I know, you didn't think I read books. You're right. But I remember that from school.'

She loved Brody's honesty. He could have claimed to have read Joyce. Just to surprise her. She said, 'So, explain your epiphany then.'

'OK. Though it's more a series of mini-epiphanies. Last week when I met your volunteers at the ponds and realized that giving people the chance to enjoy Maddon might be more fun than keeping them out. And yesterday, lying here with you, half asleep, when I realized that this room, shuttered and all covered up, has seen more real happiness in it in the last two weeks than in all its previous Keegan existence. For all it was filled with orchids and champagne and London's glitterati.'

They both looked round the room, grey in the half-light. 'It's heaven here,' Lotte said. 'Like being at sea. Or on an island. I'd almost like it to stay this way.'

Brody fiddled with the fingers of her hand, pulling them gently, and said, 'But you know my most important epiphany.'

She knew of course, but she wanted him to say it.

'What's that?'

He cupped her face in his hands and kissed her. 'When I realized that a forty-something mum and gardener would make me happy and a glamorous super-model didn't.'

'Just as well you mostly see me in this gloom. I look good in gloom.' Lotte laughed. 'And don't say, "And even better in the dark"!'

'You would look good in a morgue,' he said.

Lotte met Brody whenever she could, under the guise of advising him about the future of Maddon. She'd told him of her ideas for a rose arbour, for the mount with his maze at the bottom of it, and for the topiary garden. They spent happy hours designing Brody's sculpture trail through the woods, now to include the Old Pond Yards, Persian pool and grotto, and a final climb up to the folly.

Brody had become so excited about the project that Lotte felt some of her old misgivings about him taking over. Only now she got her way with less of a battle.

'Brody, by all means let's get some engineers to find where the water was channelled out of the river and where the underground streams are. But let's leave the volunteers to do the work.'

'Nonsense, darling,' said Brody, 'that will take for ever. A team of pros will have it done before the summer is out.'

'And where will that get us?' She took him by the jacket lapels and shook him. 'It's like eating all your dinner in two minutes flat. Brody, ninety per cent of the pleasure of gardening, and of garden restoration, is the slow doing of it, the gradual revelation, the achievement of having done it yourself. Don't spoil it for the Friends. Or for me and Peter. Or for you.'

'Lotte Warren, you can do anything you like. As long as you leave Peter and marry me.'

Lotte had laughed when he'd said that, shaking off the idea. She was too happy to dwell on complications.

The cloudless contentment, the sense of being blessed, saved, special, lasted all through the summer and autumn. She was careful to give Peter no cause for alarm, but that was easy. Peter was as sure of her as he was of himself. But occasionally, when he made some remark about how well she looked or how much energy she had, or said something like, 'You know, Brody is really a much nicer man than we ever gave him credit for when Jade was around,' Lotte would feel a stab of guilt.

Mostly she just didn't think about the future. The present was perfect. And it was enough.

Only Brody was putting on the pressure. 'Lott, I know you don't love Peter the way you love me. And it's not as if he's the father of your children.'

'You'd never know it to see him with them. He adores them,' said Lotte. 'He's wonderful.'

'And I wouldn't be?'

Lotte hated it when Brody's brow knitted into lines of frustration or worry.

'Oh Brody, don't be silly.' She stroked his cheek. 'They've only just accepted Peter . . .'

Brody paced around in circles. He looked, Lotte thought, as if he might kick the furniture like Jo-Jo did when she couldn't get her way.

Lotte did long to leave Peter and marry Brody. Not because Peter wasn't everything he'd promised to be. But because she wasn't in love with him. And she was dizzyingly and all-consumingly in love with Brody.

How could she have been so weak as to agree to marriage? It might have been easier if they weren't married. She knew she meant everything to Peter. And he had never let her down. Never would.

But to be mistress of Maddon! To be by Brody's side as of right. To give the children the chances that that kind of money can make happen. To have Brody's zest for new business ventures, new holidays, new madcap schemes for the estate. How could she turn that down to stay an academic's wife in a little cottage, with the choice between a Subaru and a Renault Clio being the highlight of her year?

As the days got shorter and colder, conducting an illicit affair became more difficult. The electricity and heating were not yet on in the house, and the shortening days limited the time Lotte could claim to be discussing the garden or supervising her young men in the Old Pond Yards. Also, she had to be in the office, and working in and around Oxford, for some of the week.

'Brody,' she said one lunchtime, when he'd driven into Oxford to meet her in Browns, 'when we are through with all these builders and stuff, why don't you give me my old job back? I long to get on with the garden, and it needs a full-time head gardener. If we are going to replant the rose walk, now's the time.'

She'd spoken lightly and was surprised at the intensity of his eyes and voice as he answered, 'Because, Lott, I've got a better job for you. Wife.' He stilled her protest with an impatient shake of his head. 'Listen, woman. You are driving me mad. I cannot move back into Maddon without you. The whole place is Jade's doing. All that designer chic and stuff. I don't want it any more. I want you to come and live there with the children and turn it into a home, for God's sake. With ponies in the paddock and dog hairs all over the sofas and roast lamb and rhubarb crumble on the table.'

His voice had been rising as he spoke, and when he finished, most of the other customers were watching, riveted.

'Brody, sshhh.' Lotte ducked her head and muttered into the tabletop, 'Keep your voice down, for God's sake.'

'And I will not,' said Brody, lifting his head and glaring at a neighbouring table of students. 'I don't care a fuck who hears,' he said, his accent reverting to Irish. 'I love you, you stupid bloody woman, and you are going to marry me, do you hear?'

Lotte had been so embarrassed that she'd been on the point of dashing for the door. But suddenly the students were clapping and laughing and calling, 'Good on yer, mate' and 'Go for it'.

Suddenly the boldness and recklessness of Brody's declaration were irresistible. It was as if she was in a play, with her lines written for her.

She found she didn't care about the people round her. She burst out laughing. 'OK, OK, you old bully. Let's do it.'

28. Late Autumn

A love lives by slowly moving towards its end and is sharpened by the snakebite of farewell in it.

Laurie Lee (1914–97)

Four months later, Lotte still had not told Peter, and Brody was getting impatient.

'For Christ's sake, Lott, first you wanted time to think. Then Peter had flu, then Jo-Jo was having a bad time at school, now it's to be after Christmas!'

Lotte put her arms round him from the back, resting her head between his naked shoulders. 'Darling, I know. I know. I will tell them. I will. And we will move in here.' She slipped under his arm to face him. 'I wouldn't have been doing all the changes here if I didn't mean it, would I?'

Jade's steel four-poster, buried under white lace cushions and surrounded by billowing French muslin, had been replaced with a big divan with a blue and green patchwork quilt. The wire designer chairs had gone, and a plain blue sofa stood in their place, and the white silk curtains now had blue and green striped borders.

Brody captured her hands in his and pulled her against him. 'OK. But make it soon, Lott. I want a wife. A real Lott-type wife who comes complete with kids. I'm sick of waking up here alone. I'd have sold Maddon and stayed in the States if it wasn't for you.'

He pushed her away a little so he could look into her face. 'I want us to slop around on Sunday mornings in dressing-gowns. I want to buy Jo-Jo a pony, play tennis with Annie and Christo. I want the whole shebang, Lott, not just your body.' He kissed her, caressing the swell of her hips and the side of her breast with one hand. Lotte felt the familiar weakness in her legs, her whole bare body responding. But she pulled away.

'No, Brody, not again. I'm late. I have to collect Jo-Jo from choir practice.'

She could feel his unvoiced resentment as she pulled on her clothes and kissed him goodbye. He didn't come downstairs with her as he usually did. He stayed in bed, flicking the television into life before she'd reached the stairs.

She drove into Oxford on autopilot. As ever these days, her mind was on Brody and Maddon.

The past months, spent fixing the rooms at Maddon, had been wonderful. Like playing at houses. Brody had expected her to throw out everything that Jade's London designers had done: furniture, decoration, the lot. But apart from the main bedroom, Lotte's changes had been small. She'd replaced the little Chinese rug on the oak floor of the drawing room with a big warm Persian carpet. She'd got rid of the stainless-steel chef's 'pass' unit in the middle of the kitchen and replaced it with a large pine table for family breakfasts. And she'd sold some of the more pompous features like the oversized Venetian chandeliers, antique portraits of long-dead strangers, and false leather book-backs in the library. But Maddon was a grand house, and she'd left most of Jade's costly furnishings.

What she'd most enjoyed was converting the brewhouse and the stable-yard guest-rooms into accommodation for the gardening guests. She'd stripped the brewhouse back to stone walls, stone floor and roof timbers, and furnished it with simple refectory tables and benches, with a modern kitchen – including the expensive professional chef's unit from the house – at one end.

Jade had decorated the rooms in what she called 'English Country Style': expensive antiques; padded chintz curtains held back with braided silk loops and topped with swagged pelmets; ruched blinds like frilly knickers; cushions everywhere.

Lotte smiled, thinking of Brody's first sight of her transformations. His open-mouthed astonishment and admiration had been wonderful.

She'd not let him in until the last picture was on the wall, and he'd loved everything: the simple stained furniture, blue and white patterned duvets, plain cotton-rep curtains and bright Moroccan rugs. Lotte had stood at his side, proud and pleased. The rooms did look lovely – fresh and sunny and comfortable.

'And here's me thinking you have to call in designers for this stuff!' he said.

He asked how much it had cost and Lotte laughed. 'Nothing. This is one make-over that's made a profit.' He looked confused, as if she'd made some joke he didn't get.

'I paid for everything out of the sale of the antiques,' she explained. 'The cheval mirrors, dressing-tables, chests of drawers, armoires. Lovely things mostly, but no good for short lets to gardeners. They'd have been covered in coffee rings and cigarette burns in no time.'

Lotte was driving well below the speed limit. Drooling along, Brody would call it. She was indulging in what still seemed a fantasy – the idea of being Brody's wife. She'd be good at it, she knew. Good at the family bit, and good at the garden. She'd restrain his instincts to show off with grand projects and instead channel his wealth to better ones. Already they'd hired three good horticultural graduates, and found a new man for the estate work. And the dour Andrew had been mollified by a summer-only job for which he could keep his cottage. Lotte, whose cuttings had not survived two years of neglect in the walled garden, had ordered 230 replacement roses from Peter Beales, and read gardening books and suppliers' catalogues in bed.

The thought of anyone else now making the smallest decision about Maddon was unbearable. If she married Brody, she'd go on tending and developing the garden until the day she died. And she'd be free to go on digging in record offices and libraries for more of its history.

She made new plans daily. She could teach the students to make withy wigwams for the runner beans and sweet peas. They could create a laburnum walk to the old brewhouse; a bog garden at the lake edge. They might even get the pineapple house to work on the old stable-muck principle.

They had already registered with an agency that sold upmarket activity holidays and Lotte was starting to plan what the students would do: who would teach them (she'd got two of her old Wroxton College teachers, now retired, signed up already); what gardens they would visit; what books she'd expect them to read.

And what a chance for the children! To have the run of Maddon, and Brody's influence and money behind them. Their chances in life would be hugely bettered with Brody as a step-father. He wanted them to have a New York apartment so she could be with him sometimes when he was there to check up on the companies he'd invested in. Lotte's mind flitted ahead to the thought of Christo or Annie at Harvard.

Then she frowned, ashamed of herself. But it was silly not to admit it: even if she and Brody eventually broke up, she'd be set up for a comfortable retirement. And the children would have been mixing with other rich children, making contacts, building networks.

She shook off this line of thinking. What are you, she muttered, another gold-digging Jade? Anyway, they weren't going to break up. They loved each other. And the age gap no longer seemed to matter. When Jade had been around, so young and flawless, Lotte had felt middle-aged next to her and Brody. But, damn it, she thought, I'm only five years older than him, and if he doesn't have a problem with that, why should I?

As she headed down the Botley Road, Lotte at last confronted the thought of Peter. Her jaw tightened and she could feel the tension in her neck. I'm not going to think about fairness, she thought, or how wonderful he's been. Or how much the children love him. How much I love him.

I am just going to tell him straight. He'll understand.

But almost at once, she knew that he wouldn't. How

could he? For twenty years he had shied from the risk of loving again. How could she deal him a second, worse, blow?

His utter trust of her made telling him impossible. Even when she'd resigned from the Council altogether and started working full-time for Brody again – this time with a brief to get the house as well as the garden in order – Peter had just been delighted for her. He would, she knew, deny under torture that his wife was making love to her boss.

Lotte put her head on the steering-wheel, her throat tight. The depth charge of Brody's love, she thought, has shattered my willingness to tell right from wrong. I know there is no way of not hurting Peter – except to give up Brody. And I can't do that: those hours of love are what I live for.

Her mind, which she'd tried to steer towards Peter, would return to Brody, and thinking of him drove the anguish underground. Oh, how could she bear the veering winds of inner weather?

When Lotte finally got the electricity on, Brody had moved into Maddon, and they had gradually, it seemed, made love in every room in the house. Sometimes on the bare floorboards, sometimes on carpets, on sofas, on dust-sheets. Once against the wine racks of the cellar, slipping slowly down to the damp cold flagstones, going at each other with voracity and abandon. Once on the new kitchen table with a man polishing the marble in the hall just through the door, the risk of him turning off the polisher and opening the door stoking their excitement. Lotte had to bite her lip not to cry out.

Oh God, she thought, I can't live without Brody. I'd wither and fade like a leaf in winter.

She pulled up outside the choir school and looked in the rear-view mirror. You've got to do it, she told herself. If you don't, you will lose Brody. And Maddon. And die a disappointed old woman.

In late November Lotte found Christo and his school-books occupying most of the sitting-room floor. She kicked his schoolbag out of her way, protesting, 'Darling, why are you working in here? You're supposed to do your homework in the kitchen, remember?'

Christo barely looked up. 'Yeah, I know. Sorry, Mum. But Jo-Jo chundered all over the kitchen and it stinks.'

Peter came in and said, 'It's OK, Lotte. She hasn't got a fever. And she's stopped vomiting at last. She's had three goes at it, poor thing. She's asleep now, in our bed.'

Lotte bolted upstairs, and sure enough Jo-Jo was asleep, her face unusually pale, a large empty bucket on the floor by the bed. Next to it lay a still warm hot-water bottle, and there was a mug of water on the bedside table.

Puzzling over what Jo-Jo might have eaten, Lotte came downstairs and went into the kitchen, which smelt heavily, not of sick as she'd expected, but of bleach.

Annie was easing the ring-pull off a Diet Coke. Lotte kissed her and said, 'Hi, darling. Thanks for cleaning up after poor Jo-Jo.'

'I didn't,' said Annie. 'Peter did.'

Lotte swung towards her daughter. 'Oh darling, you shouldn't have . . .'

'He insisted. Thank God he did, Mum, it was *disgusting*. I'd have puked myself if I'd had to do it.'

Lotte took an opened bottle of white wine out of the fridge, picked up two glasses and went in search of Peter. She found him in his little study, looking at the surveyor's report on the Maddon underground water channels.

For once, Lotte did not want to discuss the ponds. She sat on the chair opposite him and put the glasses and wine on the desk.

'Darling Peter. You should have made Christo or Annie clean up Jo-Jo's vomit. It's too bad they let you do it . . .'

'Oh Lotte. Don't be silly. Besides, they'd have done a hopeless job, and I'd have had to do it again anyway.'

Lotte poured them each a glass and handed one to Peter. 'Here,' she said. 'You deserve it.'

'Poor Jo-Jo. The doc says he'll come in the morning if she's still chucking up. He says she must drink lots of water.'

'Did he prescribe the hot-water bottle too, and our bed?'

She was amused to see his hand hover nervously over his forehead. He hardly did that any more.

'Shouldn't I have? I just thought . . .'

Lotte laughed. 'Of course it's not wrong! Did she demand the big bed?'

'No, poor kid, she wasn't talking at all. I just carried her up and put her in there. My mum used to let us have their bed if we were sick. And a hot-water bottle. It was sort of comforting. Made you feel Mummy's darling.'

Jo-Jo was sick twice more before they went to bed, and each time it was Peter who heard the creak of floorboards or hurried steps upstairs. Lotte went up and held Jo-Jo's hair out of her face, and bathed her face with a cool flannel and kissed her back into bed.

When they went up themselves, Peter said, 'I haven't the heart to move her. I'll sleep in her bed.'

'This bed's so wide we could all sleep in it,' said Lotte.

Peter considered this for a second, then said, 'No. Better not. She's thirteen, and might be embarrassed to think she'd been babied by her stepfather. Mums are different.'

He pulled his pyjamas from under his pillow. 'And Social Services would definitely not approve. Bad enough that I pulled her trainers and jeans off.'

When he'd gone, Lotte washed and moisturized her face, cleaned her teeth slowly, and finally climbed in beside Jo-Jo. She was conscious of the faint smell of Peter on this side of the bed. It was warm and pleasant. She leant over and kissed Jo-Jo, who snuggled up beside her just as she had as a little girl. She looked better now, her colour back, breathing evenly.

Lotte lay on her back. This always happened. When she was with Brody, she wanted only Brody. When she was with Peter, leaving him was unthinkable.

The room was pitch dark, but Lotte had her eyes open. She could not think with them closed.

She had no grounds for leaving Peter. She loved him. She enjoyed his company. She liked working with him. He did not even mildly irritate her. And the truly puzzling thing — she still slept with him.

Not often these days. And not at her instigation. But when Peter put his book down and rolled towards her, or wrapped his arms round her when she came out of the shower, she couldn't hurt him with a trite excuse. Rejection would have his anxious fingers stroking his brow, would make him cringe, snail-like, out of the sunshine he'd only so recently gained.

She couldn't do that. And anyway, she didn't want to. She wanted Peter – darling, solid Peter – to be happy. She found that although all she felt at first was affection, allowing him to make love to her soon led to comfortable, predictable and satisfying pleasure. It was only afterwards that she'd feel uneasy, marvelling that she could sleep with both men. And enjoy it.

And then she and Peter had a proper family life. Peter loved the children for themselves, in a way she knew Brody never could. Peter was interested in every aspect of their lives: Christo's astronomy project, Annie's love-life, the succession of Jo-Jo's animals: tortoises, rabbits, bush-babies. And what other man in the wide world would have cleaned up Jo-Jo's vomit?

Of course Brody would be wonderful to the children, but they would be sort of trophy children in the way Jade had been a trophy wife. To be showered with ponies and motorbikes, to be sent to smart schools and taken on skiing holidays.

Her thoughts went back to Sam's desertion of her for Frances, and even now the remembered misery of it sent a squall of anxiety through her. How can I do that to Peter, she thought, who was my saviour then, and who is my anchor, helpmeet and best friend now?

29. Winter

Out of danger from the wind,
Out of danger from the wave,
Out of danger from the heart,
Falling, falling out of love.

James Fenton (1949–),
'Out of Danger' 1993

As Lotte and Peter sat waiting in the drab hall of the New Bodleian Library for Bill Moxton to collect them, Lotte said, 'I can't stand the suspense, Peter. Tell me.'

Peter looked definitely triumphant. And agitated. His fingers were doing a jig on his hairline.

'Guess,' he said.

'I know it's to do with Maddon. It has to be.'

Peter smiled, neither confirming nor denying. Lotte said, 'It's a Mary Delany paper proving the grotto is hers?'

'Nope, 'fraid not.'

'The missing Ferguson diaries?'

He shook his head, and Lotte stood up, impatient. 'Peter, for God's sake just tell me. I hate being teased.'

'I know you do, darling, but I want you to see it as I did – with no prior knowledge of what it was.'

Pacing about, Lotte said, 'I wish this Moxton would

appear.' She stopped. 'It's a manuscript telling us who Henry the Eighth stole Maddon from?'

Before Peter could answer, Bill Moxton was there, telling the porters not to worry that Lotte had no Reader's Ticket — he would vouch for her. He said hello to Peter and shook Lotte's hand.

'And you must be Mrs Childersley. I'm delighted to meet you.' He smiled at her like a benevolent uncle. 'I'd have bet my pension that old Peter here would die a bachelor. So much for certainties.'

He shepherded them past the desk and along a corridor hung with enormous portraits of long-dead English kings.

Lotte was amused by him, but she wasn't concentrating as he prattled on up the stairs and down the corridor. She was thinking about Maddon. Was she about to discover if it had been a nunnery, a priory, or a just a tract of land belonging to a Catholic family?

Moxton led them into a large room with huge, high windows. It was filled with giant tables, the height of work-benches. Several had one or two people standing round them, peering at documents.

Moxton stopped at an empty table. It was almost covered by an old vellum map, protected in a clear plastic folder. 'There,' he said, pleased as punch.

Lotte knew at once that it was a map of Maddon Park. She exclaimed, 'Oh my God. Where did you get it?'

'We've had it since 1867, when the Bodleian bought a private library for its rare Chinese books. And within the collection were all sorts of extraneous documents.' His small eyes were alight with satisfaction. 'The Sinologists passed the map to us. It's rare to have such a big one.

Look, it's actually two skins, stitched together and trimmed square. Large maps were often made on smaller pieces of vellum or paper, and you had to piece them together.' He looked up at Lotte, delighted with himself.

But Lotte was scarcely listening. She was deep in the map. Almost every feature was recognizable: the house and stables, the vegetable garden and lake, the mount in the park. The detail was extraordinary, with deer in the park, cows beyond the park perimeter on the farm, rows of cabbages and what looked like artichokes in the vegetable garden all drawn in ink with a fine quill. It was quaint and charming, with the park coloured green, the lanes ochre and the vegetable garden pink. But it was also professionally, painstakingly, accurate. It was, Lotte thought, a working estate document.

The Road to Oxford was marked in large letters along the road passing the main gates, and in the right-hand corner was an elaborate compass rose with a needle pointing north, and in the opposite corner a pair of decorative dividers formed a pointed arch in which was written the scale: *Forty Chains to One Inch*. Each parcel of land or field was labelled with a letter of the alphabet and then listed in an *Abstract of the Survey* giving its name and acreage:

A. *West Deere Parke, 28 acres, 1 rood, 10 perches*
B. *Mayddon Meadow, 12 acres, 2 roods, 3 perches*, etc.

Lotte said nothing for minutes. When she did speak, her voice was hushed.

'Look, Peter, we were right. Those old oaks *are* the relics of an avenue leading to the ponds! *Oake Avenue.*'

'I know,' said Peter, 'and that means those three trees are two hundred and fifty years old.'

Lotte frowned, her eyes scanning the bottom perimeter of the map. 'But how do you know? This has no date on it.'

'But it does,' Moxton said. He bustled round to the end of the table and lifted the end of the map in its plastic. 'Come and look,' he said. 'If you rolled the map up correctly you'd see this – like the title of a book on the binding.'

Faded but clearly visible on the back of the map was an ornamental cartouche bearing the words:

Mapp and Survey of the Domaine and Landes of Lord Augustus Fernley, Seventh Earl of Axtrim, knowne as Maydon Park, lying in the Parish of Osley in the County of Oxfordshire. Survey'd by my Lord's most humble and Obedient Servant, Thomas Hely of Bladon, in the Seventeen Hundred and Forty Seventh Year of our Lord.

'Fernley! Peter, that must be our Emma Fernley's father! It's only seven years after her drawing of the grotto and pool.' Lotte looked at both men, her face lit by excitement. 'How long can I stay?' she asked. 'I need hours.'

'We could get it photographed for you,' Moxton said. 'You would have to fill in an application of course. But you can stay while I talk to Peter about St Aldwyn's lending us a map for an exhibition.' He positively twinkled at her. 'All the Colleges are notoriously unco-operative about lending maps, but since I've done your Peter a favour he can hardly refuse me now, can he?'

Lotte caught Peter's smile behind Moxton's shoulder. Peter said, 'We'll be in Bill's office if you want us. If you get lost, ask for Head of Maps. Otherwise we'll collect you for lunch.'

But Lotte was too absorbed to go with them for lunch. She stayed behind, making notes.

The stables had lost some grace and grandeur over the years. What had happened to these pilasters? And was the pediment with its oval window still there with the second storey built over it? Could it be in the hayloft above? She would have to get up there and look.

The main drive had been a double avenue but she could not tell what the trees were. The two rows looked different, one wider and shorter, one taller and narrower. Oaks and elms perhaps? But they could be anything.

Now she was into the detail, the differences came thick and fast. The map showed an unwalled vegetable garden, which surprised her – she'd known the walls with the stoves and flues for keeping the frost off the espaliered fruit trees were Victorian, but she'd thought they might replace older walls.

And, as she'd suspected, the main lawn in front of the house had been entirely filled by an elaborate formal parterre, and in the park beyond what was now the ha-ha was a rectangular orchard. Both orchard and parterre were overlooked by the mount at the south-west corner.

The boundary of park and garden used to be entirely dry-stone walling – today it was mostly fencing. The main entrance's grand stone pillars (still there) were once topped by plain round balls. The shrubberies and rose gardens were now in completely different parts of the garden. The differences were as great as the similarities. They were fascinating.

The detail of the woods was amazing. Lotte saw at once that she'd got the water channels wrong: the source of the water was not the Isis, but Diana's spring, which she did not know existed. Maybe it had dried up? And the Hermit's dwelling looked like her folly at the top of the hill in the woods – except that in 1747 the hill had been bare of trees, a large clearing in the wood which would have been visible from the house.

Most exciting of all, there was a Diana's temple still to be found. And Bill Moxton had said that there were other papers and documents from the same library collection. Maybe whoever inherited or obtained the map had other Maddon stuff? Maybe even the missing Ferguson diaries?

Going home with Peter in the car, she said, 'Darling, this has been a perfect day.'

'Darling?' he said. 'You never call me darling.'

Lotte fetched a ladder and climbed up to the trap-door in the covered entrance to the stable kitchen. The door was stuck with the dirt of decades and she had to tap it all round with a hammer before she could shove it open. It fell back on its hinges with a bang, lifting clouds of dust. Coughing, but excited, Lotte climbed into the loft.

It was freezing up here, and she pulled her woolly cap over her ears. She had a torch clipped to her belt, and she examined the floor first – she'd never been up here before and didn't want to go crashing through rotten boards. But it was dry and sound and she crossed to the outside wall.

The outline of the old pediment was easy to see: the

builders had simply built on to it, using it as the start of the raised front wall of the now double-storey stable-block. They had used brick, not stone, and had painted the wall without plastering it. Lotte looked at the triangle of smooth plastered pediment, surrounded by gloss-painted brick. I knew it, she thought, delighted. Now for the window.

At first she couldn't find any evidence of it at all: it had been bricked up and plastered, but when she fetched the big searchlight, she found an oval crack running right round what must have been the window, dead centre in the pediment.

Pleased with herself, and anxious to ring Peter and tell him what she'd found, she hurried to the trap-door. She was about to go down the ladder again when she heard footsteps, and peered down. The new student gardener, Melissa, was wheeling a barrow of empty flowerpots on her way to wash them in the big sink. She stopped at the step into the kitchen, apparently oblivious of the open trap-door above her or the ladder to it. Lotte was about to call to her when she heard Brody's voice as he stepped into view. It was not just that he was doing his stage Irish: there was something about the tone of it, intimate and with a hint of laughter, that made her hesitate.

'Those t'ings will kill yer, yer mad woman,' he said.

Lotte could not see his face, but he reached out a hand and took the cigarette from Melissa's mouth. 'And smokin' wit'out hands! 'Tis not a good sight, that it's not. An' you so pretty an' all an' all.'

Melissa was blushing, but pleased. She looked at Brody with wide, captivated eyes.

Lotte pulled herself together and started to climb down. Brody looked up at the noise, and his face opened in pleasure at seeing her.

He has no idea he flirts, Lotte thought. But he does it all the time.

That night, unusually for December, it snowed silently, thickly, for hours. But by the morning it had stopped and the sun blazed out of a high blue sky.

As she stepped from her car, Lotte narrowed her eyes at the blast of white light. The garden looked like a stage set – every twig carrying its exact allocation of snow, the hedges roofed in icing, each conifer branch with a white coverlet. The beauty of it took your breath away.

The white expanse of park was criss-crossed with the delicate tracks of deer and foxes. Lotte was thrilled by them – the straight lines of tiny footprints were a reminder of just how busy and purposeful nature was at night.

Lotte stepped reluctantly on to the creaky snow. Human footprints were so ugly, she thought, so scuffling, wavering, clumsy.

Brody had no such scruples. He bounced out of the house, kicking the snow like a schoolboy as he wheeled in a circle. 'Let's make a snowman,' he said.

Lotte laughed. 'You big baby!' Then her face straightened as she remembered why she was here. 'Let's go for a walk, Brody. I have to talk to you.'

She was glad he was wearing one of those puffy jackets because when he hugged her she felt insulated from him. She knew that if she could feel his body her courage would drain away.

They hadn't walked fifty paces towards the rose garden when she stopped and turned to him. 'Brody, I'm not going to marry you.' She held her hands out to prevent him touching her or saying anything. 'Please, darling, please just listen. Just hear me out. OK?'

He said nothing, and she risked a glance at his face. He looked blank. Uncomprehending.

'I love you, Brody. But it would never last, I know it –'

Brody interrupted. 'That's balls, Lott . . .'

'No it isn't. You want me so badly because I'm not yours. You like winning. You'd lose interest if you thought you owned me. You like to own things: nice cars, Maddon, my children. Me.'

Brody shook his head. 'Lott, that is complete rubbish. I love you. You love me. I've got heaps of money and you've got none. It's a marriage made in heaven.'

Lotte, bleak but determined, said, 'Please, Brody, hear me out. I need to explain.'

'There's nothing to explain.' Brody stood over her, his voice harder now. 'Either you love me or you don't. Which is it?'

'I do love you. But not enough to ruin my life for you.'

Brody looked at her with disbelief. 'Ruin your life? What the fuck are you talking about, Lott?'

She looked at the trampled snow underfoot, then at him, her face set. 'Brody, I'm in love with you. You make me ache with longing. You make me feel the whole world is wonderful. But you won't *do*, Brody.' She paused, her face earnest, her eyes full of tears. 'Plus I love Peter too. The children love him.' She looked away and said, 'I'd rather be married to Peter.'

Brody did not answer. His face registered both disbelief and anger. 'I don't believe you,' he said. 'If you were in love with Peter, do you think you could do what you do with me every other day? . . . You can't get enough . . .'

Lotte shook her head violently. 'I didn't say I was in love with Peter. And I didn't say I was in lust with him either. I said I love him.' Her eyes were in danger of overflowing and she looked unblinking and unseeing at the distant line of bare trees that bordered the drive. 'And he's a better long-term bet as a husband. He doesn't deserve to be deserted. I can't leave him, Brody.'

Brody did not touch her and his voice was harsh. 'But cheating on him is OK, is it?'

Lotte took a deep breath and said, 'No, it's not OK. But I can't help it.'

Tears started to run down her face and her voice kept breaking. But she seemed unaware of this and was pleading in earnest. 'I've thought so much about this, Brody, and I've got to just tell you what I want.'

'I'm listening.'

Lotte wanted to reach for his hands, tell him not to be cold, not to be angry, to try to understand. But his whole demeanour was so unsympathetic she didn't dare. She forced back her tears and kept her voice as steady as she could.

'Darling, it's for your sake too. You love me now. But I'm older than you, and one day you'll fall for someone else, I know it. You are irresistible to women. Someone younger and more exciting, who will want your children . . .'

Brody put his arms on her shoulders then, and his voice had recovered some of its warmth. 'Oh Lott, that is nonsense. I want your children, and you . . . You're just having cold feet about making the break from Peter.'

She shook her head, thinking, oh God, why am I doing this?

'Lott,' he said, 'don't you understand how you've changed me? I am not the same man. You made me see what's important – real people, family. Nature, the seasons. And a sense of place. All that.'

Again she shook her head. 'No, the truth is you are in love with an idea – the idea of a ready-made family to occupy Maddon.'

He held her eyes for a second, then dropped his hands from her shoulders. 'I don't believe you really think that.'

They walked in silence until they got to the rose arbour, the new young ramblers leafless now. Brody brushed the snow off the seat with a gloved hand, and they sat down. He said, his voice grim, 'What's really changed your mind, Lotte?'

'I don't know. Not one thing. Nothing's changed. I love you and want you as much – more – than ever. But every time I'm with Peter I know I can't leave him. And every time I'm with you, I'm seduced again. But Brody, if you will just not interrupt, please let me make my prepared speech.'

Brody reached for her, saying, 'I don't want to hear it, Lott, if it's –'

Lotte jumped up, out of reach. 'Just shut up and listen, Brody. And don't touch me. I can't think if you touch me.'

'Shoot,' he said.

Lotte sat down again. She paused for a moment, getting her thoughts straight.

'The other day, outside the stable kitchen, I watched you with Melissa. The way you took her cigarette out of her mouth was a caress. I couldn't see your face, but I knew from hers that you were looking at her as you looked at me, years ago, outside Jade's sauna. It's what made me start to fall in love with you.' She raised her hand to stop him protesting. 'I know, I know. I'm not saying you were intentionally flirting with her. But Brody, I've seen it so many times. You are the kind of man that women fall for. And one day, on a plane, in New York, in London, you will meet someone else.'

Lotte watched a cock pheasant stalking arrogantly yet delicately across the snow. 'And then there will be the misery of divorce again, and more horrors for the children. I couldn't bear that.'

She paused, but again held up her hand to prevent Brody speaking. She was determined to say it all. 'But even if I didn't believe that, even if I had a guarantee that we'd grow old together, I would not leave Peter for you. Peter and I have the same interests: history, music, books. You and I have nothing in common except sex, and a love of this place.'

'Jesus, Lotte,' Brody burst out, 'that's balls. It's love, and you know it.'

'How do I know? Every time I'm near you I'm in thrall to you. If there was no sex, would I still feel like that? Can you imagine a life with me without sex? You can't. And that's what we'd get to. Passion fades, Brody. It just does.' Lotte had taken off one glove and was twisting it round and round in her hands.

Brody put his hands over hers. His eyes were dark and

desperate. 'And Maddon? Don't you think Maddon would keep us together?'

Lotte had to turn away but her voice was under control again as she said, 'We might not always have Maddon. You might buy a business in Japan. You might go broke again. Or move to California. Anything could happen.'

Brody pulled his hands away. 'Good God, Lotte. What are you, a calculating machine? Of course I could go bust again. It's unlikely because I've stashed a heap away. But I could. And, yes, we might live in the States.'

'But don't you see? You could be happy anywhere. You could fall in love with a Californian vineyard or a Tuscan hillside or a Spanish hacienda. I have to be here.'

They were both silent for a while. Lotte looked across the snow-covered garden, the rolling park with its perfectly placed groups of snow-etched trees, past the mount like a white jelly turned out of a spiral mould, down to the flat frozen lake, the woods beyond.

She thought, though she did not say, that her work was her anchor. That without the seasons, without the plants, without the gradual uncovering of the past and the slow progress to the future garden, she would be unhappy. How could she explain to Brody why being part of a long line of English gardeners, Maddon's gardeners, was so important to her?

Instead she said, 'Brody, the children are happy and settled now. But they are still children. Jo-Jo is not yet fourteen. And they are more important to me than anything. Even you, Brody.'

Brody looked into her face and then down at his hands, his face solemn. The sight of those strong dark hands, so familiar and beloved, made her want to bury her face in them. Her determination faltered for a second. But she rallied.

'I'm sorry, Brody. But I'm quite sure now. The fact is, I'm as obsessed with Maddon as I am with you. I asked myself a question the other night, and the answer shook me. If there was no Maddon, and no intoxicating sex, would I be in love with you? The answer is no.'

They were both silent for a moment, holding each other's gaze, and then Lotte finished her speech.

'Brody. I want to be your lover and your gardener. But not your wife.'

Epilogue

... let all things go free that have survived.
Let smells of mint go heady and defenceless
Like inmates liberated in that yard ...

Seamus Heaney (1939–), 'Mint'

Seven years later, Maddon still belonged to Brody Keegan, and Lotte was its mistress. Not as he had wanted her to be, sleeping in his bed, her children in the house, their ponies in the stables. But she did rule the roost.

When Brody moved permanently to the States, Lotte had persuaded him not to sell Maddon, but to let the public in. Typically, Brody had gone one further, turning it into a profitable business.

The Maddon estate, in its new guise as a visitor attraction, was no longer a formal tribute to a rich man's importance. It had become a public place, a playground with children running down the mount or shouting in the maze, with families rowing the boats to the island and picnicking on the great green terraces.

Elderly couples gazed at the planted knot gardens and formal parterres now taking up most of the main lawn, peered at the plant labels or enjoyed cream teas on the terrace. Later, they would queue for the loos in the stable yard, then visit the Victorian walled garden and exclaim that the scythes in the tool shed were just like the ones their grandfathers once used. Or they would read the explanation of the workings of the pineapple pits or the forcing-room to each other. And they would come away with pots of Maddon lemon cheese or greengage catsup with gingham tops, bought from the shop housed in the old Gardener's Cottage.

Hardier visitors tramped the modern sculpture trail, baffled but pleased by the strange and sometimes beautiful shapes that nestled in trees or stood in clearings. They marvelled at the intricacy of the Persian pool and the shell-studded grotto. They looked into the Old Ponds, now inhabited by multi-coloured Koi carp, and climbed up to the Hermit's folly and then strolled down to Diana's spring. You could still stoop to drink the water in the shell-shaped overflowing basin. But the natural spring had long since dried up and now water was pumped from the lake and chemically purified in a chamber behind the spout. On the winding way down, walkers rested in Diana's temple (10 per cent original, 90 per cent reconstruction), then followed the woodland trail round the lake.

Keen gardeners came several times a year – to see the explosion of bulbs and blossom in the spring, the June rose fest of blowsy trusses smothering the old shrub roses, the autumn colour on the lake with its bold planting of Michaelmas daisies, hues merging from red to rust, to orange, then pink, then purple. They discussed organic vegetable growing with the horticultural students in the walled garden, and sometimes sneaked an illegal cutting from a rare shrub or herbaceous perennial.

Lotte liked the visitors. They were a spur to constant improvement and a justification for new projects. But her satisfaction went deeper than that. She liked the symbiotic relationship of garden and visitors: they were there to admire Maddon, like pilgrims paying tribute, and the garden was there to give them brief pleasure, or peace, or knowledge.

Brody was more excited by the transformation of Home Farm. It was the real money-spinner. Acres of garden centre, rare breeds' enclosures, a pets' corner and restaurants had replaced the unprofitable business of farming. The garden centre sold everything Lotte most detested: water features, decking, sentimental sculpture, plastic patio chairs, Japanese wind chimes, even 'Tequila Sunrise' roses. It made a fortune.

Lotte knew she was in the dying days of a great love affair. It had lasted longer than she ever thought it would, but she and Brody spent more time discussing the business than making love now. Maybe they would never make love again.

She didn't mind. Her ardour had cooled, too. But she would always be grateful for these years. She had had a love affair in middle age that had stirred her whole being and unbalanced her good sense, one that had made her feel beautiful and powerful and loved. For years, she and Brody had stolen brief hours at Maddon, and sometimes a day and a night in London. Those times, drenched in sex and satisfaction, had been the illicit counterpoint to what she knew was her real life – of children, a loving husband and work.

She marvelled now at how drivingly selfish she had been. She'd traded on Peter's unquestioning trust, on the children's teenage self-absorption, on her own wit and guile to have it all.

She shuddered at the risk she'd run. But she knew that she had had no choice. She could not have given up Brody then any more than she could have given up Maddon.

And she had got away with it. She didn't deserve it, but she had got away with it.

Poetry Acknowledgements

Thanks are due to the following for permission to include the following copyright material in this book:

Hoagy Carmichael: Extract from 'Skylark' by Hoagy Carmichael © and John H. Mercer (A), reprinted by permission of International Music Publications.

Steve Ellis: Extract from *Gardeners' Question Time*, reprinted by permission of the author.

James Fenton: Extract from 'Out of Danger', published by Penguin, reprinted by permission of PFD on behalf of James Fenton.

Robert Frost: Extract from 'Birches' from *The Poetry of Robert Frost*, edited by Edward Connery Lathem and published by Jonathan Cape, reprinted by permission of the Estate of Robert Frost and The Random House Group Limited. Extract from 'Birches' from *The Poetry of Robert Frost*, edited by Edward Connery Lathem, Copyright © 1969 Henry Holt and Company, Copyright © 1944 Robert Frost, reprinted by permission of Henry Holt and Company, LLC.

Thom Gunn: Extract from 'The Garden of the Gods', reprinted by permission of the author.

Seamus Heaney: Extract from 'Mint' from *Opened Ground* by Seamus Heaney, reprinted by permission of Faber and Faber throughout UK and Commonwealth. Excerpt from 'Mint' from *Opened Ground: Selected Poems 1966–1996* by Seamus Heaney, Copyright © 1998 Seamus Heaney, reprinted by permission of Farrar, Straus and Giroux, LLC for USA.

Evelyn John Holtzhausen: Extract from 'Happiness Rises' from *In the Palm of My Soul*, published by Snailpress Poetry, reprinted by permission of the author.

Ted Hughes: Extract from 'New Year Song', reprinted by permission of Mrs Carol Hughes.

Laurie Lee: Extract from *Laurie Lee, The Well-Loved Stranger*, reprinted by permission of PFD on behalf of The Estate of Laurie Lee. Extract from 'Spring', reprinted by permission of PFD on behalf of The Estate of Laurie Lee.

Edna St Vincent Millay: Extract from 'The Hardy Garden' from *Collected Poems of Edna St Vincent Millay*, published by HarperCollins, Copyright © 1928, 1955 Edna St Vincent Millay and Norma Millay Ellis. All rights reserved. Reprinted by permission of Elizabeth Barnett, Literary Executor.

Brian Patten: Extract from 'Forgetmeknot', published by Flamingo Books, London.

Angelo Poliziano: Extract from 'She Finds Herself in a Garden', translated by John Hollander, published by Everyman's Library. Reprinted by permission of the translator.

Craig Raine: Extract from 'Karma', reprinted by permission of the author.

Anne Ridler: Extract from 'Snakes-head Fritillaries' from *Collected Poems of Anne Ridler*, reprinted by permission of Carcanet Press Limited 1994.

Theodore Roethke: Extract from 'Transplanting' by Theodore Roethke, reprinted by permission of Faber and Faber Ltd as the publishers. Extract from 'Transplanting', Copyright © 1948 Theodore Roethke, from *Collected Poems of Theodore Roethke*, reprinted by permission of Doubleday, a division of Random House, Inc.

Vita Sackville-West: Extract from 'The Rose', reprinted by permission of Nigel Nicolson, Literary Executive.